P9-DFK-567

Also by George P. Pelecanos

Hell to Pay

The Sweet Forever

Shame the Devil

King Suckerman

The Big Blowdown

Down By the River Where the Dead Men Go

Shoedog

Nick's Trip

A Firing Offense

GEORGE P. PELECANOS

RIGHT
AS
RAIN

WARNER BOOKS

An AOL Time Warner Company

WARNER BOOKS EDITION

Copyright © 2001 by George P. Pelecanos
All rights reserved. No part of this book may be reproduced in any form or by any electronic or mechanical means, including information storage and retrieval systems, without permission in writing from the publisher, except by a reviewer who may quote brief passages in a review.

Cover design by Mario Pulice and Diane Luger
Cover art by Tony Greco

Warner Books, Inc.
1271 Avenue of the Americas
New York, NY 10020

Visit our Web site at
www.twbookmark.com.

 An AOL Time Warner Company

Printed in the United States of America

Originally published in hardcover by Little, Brown and Company.
First International Paperback Printing: September 2001
First U.S. Paperback Printing: February 2002

10 9 8 7 6 5 4 3 2 1

RIGHT AS
RAIN

chapter 1

WHAT Derek Strange was worried about, looking at Jimmy Simmons sitting there, spilling over a chair on the other side of his desk, was that Simmons was going to pick some of Strange's personal shit up off the desktop in front of him and start winging it across the room. Either that or get to bawling like a damn baby. Strange didn't know which thing he wanted to happen less. He had some items on that desk that meant a lot to him: gifts women had given him over the years, tokens of gratitude from clients, and a couple of Redskins souvenirs from back in the 1960s. But watching a man cry, that was one thing he could not take.

"Tell me again, Derek." Simmons's lip was trembling, and pools of tears were threatening to break from the corners of his bloodshot eyes. "Tell me again what that motherfucker looked like, man."

"It's all in the report," said Strange.

"I'm gonna kill him, see? And right after that, I'm gonna kill his ass again."

"You're talkin' no sense, Jimmy."

"Fifteen years of marriage and my woman's just now

decided to go and start taking some other man's dick? You're gonna tell me now about sense? God *damn!*"

Jimmy Simmons struck his fist to the desktop, next to a plaster football player with a spring-mounted head. The player, a white dude originally whose face Janine's son, Lionel, had turned dark brown with paint, wore the old gold trousers and burgundy jersey from back in the day, and he carried a football cradled in one arm. The head jiggled, and the Redskins toy tilted on its base. Strange reached over, grabbed the player, and righted it before it could tip over.

"Take it easy. You break that, I can't even charge you for it, 'cause it's priceless, hear?"

"I'm sorry, Derek." A tear sprang loose from Simmons's right eye and ran down one of his plump cheeks. "Shit."

"Here you go, man." Strange ripped a Kleenex from the box atop his desk and handed it to Simmons, who dabbed tenderly at his cheek. It was a delicate gesture for a man whose last day under three hundred pounds was a faded memory.

"I need to know what the man looked like," said Simmons. "I need to know his name."

"It's all in the report," Strange repeated, pushing a manila envelope across the desk. "But you don't want to be doing nothin' about it, hear?"

Simmons opened the envelope and inched out its contents slowly and warily, the way a child approaches an open casket for the first time. Strange watched Simmons's eyes as they moved across the photographs and the written report.

It hadn't taken Strange all that long to get the goods on

Denice Simmons. It was a tail-and-surveillance job, straight up, the simplest, dullest, and most common type of work he did. He had followed Denice to her boyfriend's place over in Springfield, Virginia, on two occasions and waited on the street until she came out and drove back into D.C. The third time Strange had tailed her, on a Sunday night when Jimmy Simmons was up in Atlantic City at an electronics show, he had waited the same way, but Denice did not emerge from the man's apartment. The lights went out in the third-story window where the man lived, and this was all Strange needed. He filled out the paperwork in the morning, picked up the photographs he had taken to a one-hour shop, and called Jimmy Simmons to his office the same day.

"How long?" said Simmons, not looking up from the documents.

"Three months, I'd say."

"How you know that?"

"Denice got no other kind of business being over in Virginia, does she?"

"She works in the District. She's got no friends over in Virginia —"

"Your own credit card bills, the ones you supplied? Denice has been charging gas at a station over there by the Franconia exit for three, three and a half months. The station's just a mile down the road from our boy's apartment."

"You think she'd be smarter than that." Simmons nearly grinned with affection. "She never does like to pay for her own gas. Always puts it on the card so I'll have to pay, come bill time. She's tight with her money, see. Funny for a woman to be that way. And though she knows

I'll be stroking the checks, she always has to stop for the cheapest gas, even if it means driving out of her way. I bet if you checked, you'd see they were selling gas at that station dirt cheap."

"Dollar and a penny for regular," said Strange.

Simmons rose from his chair, his belly and face quivering as if his flesh were being blown by a sudden gust of wind. "Well, I'll see you, Derek. I'll take care of your services, soon as I see a bill."

"Janine will get it out to you straightaway."

"Right. And thanks for the good work."

"Always hate it when it turns out like this, Jimmy."

Simmons placed a big hat with a red feather in its band on his big head. "You're just doing your job."

Strange sat in his office, waiting to hear Simmons go out the door. It would take a few minutes, as long as it took Simmons to flirt with Janine and for Janine to get rid of him. Strange heard the door close. He got out from behind his desk and put himself into a midlength black leather jacket lined with quilt and a thin layer of down. He took a PayDay bar, which Janine had bought for him, off the desk and slipped it into a pocket of the jacket.

Out in the reception area of the office, Strange stopped at Janine Baker's desk. Behind her, a computer terminal showed one of the Internet's many sites that specialized in personal searches. Janine's brightly colored outfit was set off against her dark, rich skin. Her red lipstick picked up the red of the dress. She was a pretty, middle-aged woman, liquid eyed, firm breasted, wide of hip, and lean legged.

"That was quick," he said.

"He wasn't his usual playful self. He said I was looking lovely today —"

"You are."

Janine blushed. "But he didn't go beyond that. Didn't seem like his heart was all that in it."

"I just gave him the bad news about his wife. She was getting a little somethin'-somethin' on the side with this young auto parts clerk, sells batteries over at the Pep Boys in northern Virginia."

"How'd they meet? He see her stalled out on the side of the road or something?"

"Yeah, he's one of those good Samaritans you hear about."

"Pulled over to give her a jump, huh."

"Now, Janine."

"This the same guy she was shackin' up with two years ago?"

"Different guy. Different still than the guy she was running with three years before that."

"What's he gonna do?"

"He went through the motions with me, telling me what he was going to do to that guy. But all's he'll do is, he'll make Denice suffer a little bit. Not with his hands, nothin' like that. Jimmy wouldn't touch Denice in that way. No, they'll be doing some kind of I'm Sorry ceremony for the next few days, and then he'll forgive her, until the next one comes along."

"Why's he stay with her?"

"He loves her. And I think she loves him, too. So I guess there's no chance for you and Big Jimmy. I don't think he'll be leaving any time soon."

"Oh, I can wait."

Strange grinned. "Give him a chance to fill out a little bit, huh?"

"He fills out any more, we'll have to put one of those garage doors on the front of this place just to let him in."

"He fills out any more, Fat Albert, Roseanne, Liz Taylor, *and* Sinbad gonna get together and start telling Jimmy Simmons weight jokes."

"He fills out any more —"

"Hold up, Janine. You know what we're doing right here?"

"What?"

"It's called 'doing the dozens.'"

"That so."

"Uh-huh. White man on NPR yesterday, was talking about this book he wrote about African American culture? Said that doing the dozens was this thing we been doin' for generations. Called it the *precursor* of rap music."

"They got a name for it, for real? And here I thought we were just cracking on Jimmy."

"I'm not lying." Strange buttoned his coat. "Get that bill out to Simmons, will you?"

"I handed it to him as he was going out the door."

"You're always on it. I don't know why I feel the need to remind you." Strange nodded to one of two empty desks on either side of the room. "Where's Ron at?"

"Trying to locate that debtor, the hustler took that woman off for two thousand dollars."

"Old lady lives down off Princeton?"

"Uh-huh. Where you headed?"

"Off to see Chris Wilson's mom."

Strange walked toward the front door, his broad, muscled shoulders moving beneath the black leather, gray salted into his hair and closely cropped beard.

He turned as his hand touched the doorknob. "You

want something else?" He had felt Janine's eyes on his back.

"No . . . why?"

"You need me, or if Ron needs me, I'll be wearin' my beeper."

Strange stepped out onto 9th Street, a short commercial strip between Upshur and Kansas, one spit away from Georgia Avenue. He smiled, thinking of Janine. He had met her the first time at a club ten years earlier, and he had started hitting it then because both of them wanted him to, and because it was there for him to take.

Janine had a son, Lionel, from a previous marriage, and this scared him. Hell, everything about commitment scared him, but being a father to a young man in this world, it scared him more than anything else. Despite his fears, their time together had seemed good for both Strange and Janine, and he had stayed with it, knowing that when it's good it's rare, and unless there's a strong and immediate reason, you should never give it up. The affair went on steadily for several months.

When he lost his office manager, he naturally thought of Janine, as she was out of work, bright, and a born organizer. They agreed that they would break off the relationship when she started working for him, and soon thereafter she went and got serious with another man. This was fine with him, a relief, as it had let him out the back door quietly, the way he always liked to go. That man exited Janine's life shortly thereafter.

Strange and Janine had recently started things up once again. Their relationship wasn't exclusive, at least not for Strange. And the fact that he was her boss didn't bother either of them, in the ethical sense. Their lovemaking simply filled a need, and Strange had grown attached to the boy as well. Friends warned him about shitting on the dining room table, but he was genuinely fond of the woman, and she did make his nature rise after all the years. He liked to play with her, too, let her know that *he* knew that she was still interested. It kept things lively in the deadening routine of their day-to-day.

Strange stood out on the sidewalk for a moment and glanced up at the yellow sign over the door: "Strange Investigations," the letters in half of both words enlarged inside the magnifying-glass illustration drawn across the lightbox. He loved that logo. It always made him feel something close to good when he looked up at that sign and saw his name.

He had built this business by himself and done something positive in the place where he'd come up. The kids in the neighborhood, they saw a black man turn the key on the front door every morning, and maybe it registered, put something in the back of their minds whether they realized it or not. He'd kept the business going for twenty-five years now, and the bumps in the road had been just that. The business was who he was. All of him, and all his.

Strange sat low behind the wheel of his white-over-black '89 Caprice, listening to a Blackbyrds tape coming from the box as he cruised south on Georgia Avenue. Next to him on the bench was a mini Maglite, a Rand McNally street atlas, and a Leatherman tool-in-one in a sheath that he often wore looped through his belt on the side of his hip. He wore a Buck knife the same way, all the time when he was on a job. A set of 10×50 binoculars, a cell phone, a voice-activated tape recorder, and extra batteries for his flashlights and camera were in the glove box, secured with a double lock. In the trunk of the car was a file carton containing data on his live cases. Also in the trunk was a steel Craftsman toolbox housing a heavy Maglite, a Canon AE-1 with a 500-millimeter lens, a pair of Russian-made NVD goggles, a 100-foot steel Craftsman tape measure, a roll of duct tape, and various Craftsman tools useful for engine and tire repair. When he could, Strange always bought Craftsman — the tools were guaranteed for life, and he tended to be hard on his equipment.

He drove through Petworth. In the Park View neighborhood he cut east on Irving, took Michigan Avenue past Children's Hospital and into Northeast, past Catholic U and down into Brookland.

Strange parked in front of Leona Wilson's modest brick home at 12th and Lawrence. He kept the motor running, waiting for the flute solo on "Walking in Rhythm" to end, though he could listen to it anytime. He'd come here because he'd promised Leona Wilson that he would, but he wasn't in any hurry to make this call.

Strange saw the curtain move in the bay window of Leona's house. He cut the engine, got out of his car, locked it down, and walked up the concrete path to Leona's front door. The door was already opening as he approached.

"Mrs. Wilson," he said, extending his hand.

"Mr. Strange."

chapter **2**

W<small>ILL</small> you help me?"

They sat beside each other in the living room on a slip-covered sofa, a soft, crackling sound coming from the fireplace. Strange drank coffee from a mug; Leona Wilson sipped tea with honey and lemon.

She was younger than he was by a few years but looked older by ten. He remembered seeing her in church before the death of her son, and her appearance since had changed radically. She carried too little weight on her tall, large-boned frame, and a bag of light brown flesh hung pendulous beneath her chin. Leona wore a maroon shirt-and-slacks arrangement and scuffed, low-heeled pumps on her feet. The outfit's presentation was rushed and sloppy. Her shirt's top button had been lost, and a brooch held it together across a flat chest terraced with bones. Her hair had gone gray, and she wore it carelessly uncombed. Grief had stolen her vanity.

Strange placed his mug on the low glass table before him. "I don't know that I can help you, ma'am. The police investigation was as thorough as they come. After all, this was a high-profile case."

"Christopher was good." Leona Wilson spoke slowly, deliberately. She pronounced her *r*'s as *ah*-rahs. She had been an elementary teacher in the District public school system for thirty years. Strange knew that she had taught grammar and pronunciation the way she had learned it, the way he had learned it, too, growing up in D.C.

"I'm sure he was," said Strange.

"The papers said he had a history of brutality. They implied that he was holding a gun on that white man for no good reason when the other police officers came upon them. But I don't believe it. Christopher was strong when he had to be, but he was never brutal."

"I have an old friend in the department, Mrs. Wilson. He tells me that Chris was a solid cop and a fine young man."

"Do you know that memorial downtown, in Northwest? The National Law Enforcement Officers Memorial?"

"I know it, yes."

"There are almost fifteen thousand names etched on that wall, the police officers in this country who have been killed in the line of duty since they've been keeping records. And do you know that the department has denied my request to have Chris's name put on that wall? Do you know that, Mr. Strange?"

"I'm aware of it, yes."

"The only thing I have now is my son's memory. I want other people to remember him for the way he was, too. The way he really was. Because I know my son. And Christopher was *good*."

"I have no reason to doubt what you say."

"So you'll help me." She learned forward. He could smell her breath, and it was foul.

"It's not what I do. I do background checks. I uncover

insurance fraud. I confirm or disprove infidelity. I interview witnesses in civil cases for attorneys, and I get paid to be a witness in court. I locate debtors, and I have a younger operative who occasionally skip-traces. Once in a while I'll locate a missing child, or find the biological parent of an adopted child. What I don't do is solve murder cases or disprove cases that have already been made by the police. I'm not in that business. Except for the police, nobody's in that business, you want to know the plain truth."

"The white policeman who killed my son. Did anyone think to bring up his record the way they brought up my son's record?"

"Well, if I recall . . . I mean, if you remember, there was quite a bit written about that police officer. How he hadn't qualified on the shooting range for over two years, despite the fact that they require those cops to qualify every six months. How he was brought onto the force during that hiring binge in the late eighties, with all those other unqualified applicants. How he had a brutality-complaint sheet of his own. No disrespect intended, but I think they left few stones unturned with regard to that young man's past."

"In the end they blamed it on his gun."

"They did talk about the negatives of that particular weapon, yes — the Glock has a light trigger pull and no external safety."

"I want you to go deeper. Find out more about the policeman who shot my son. I'm convinced that he is the key."

"Mrs. Wilson —"

"Christopher was proud to be a police officer; he would have died without question . . . he did die, *without question,* in the line of duty. But the papers made it out to seem as if he was somehow at fault. That he was holding his gun on an innocent man, that he failed to identify himself as a police officer when that white policeman came up on him. They mentioned the alcohol in his blood. . . . Christopher was *not* a drunk, Mr. Strange."

Nor an angel, thought Strange. He'd never known any cop, any man in fact, to be as pure as she was making him out to be.

"Yes, ma'am," said Strange.

He watched Leona Wilson's hand shake with the first stages of Parkinson's as she raised her teacup to her lips. He thought of his mother in the home, and he rose from the couch.

Strange walked to the fireplace, where a slowly strobing light shone behind plastic logs, the phony fire cracking rhythmically. An electric cord ran from beneath the logs to an outlet in the wall.

He looked at the photographs framed on the mantel. He saw Leona as a young woman and the boy Christopher standing under her touch, and another photograph of Leona and her husband, whom Strange knew to be deceased. There were a few more photographs of Christopher, in a cap and gown, and in uniform, and kneeling on a football field with his teammates, the Gonzaga scoreboard in the background, Christopher's gaze hard, his eyes unsmiling and staring directly into the camera's lens. A high school boy already wearing the face of a cop.

There was one photo of a girl in her early teens, its color paled out from age. Strange knew that Chris Wilson had had a sister. He had seen her on the TV news, a pretty, bone-skinny, light-skinned girl with an unhealthy, splotched complexion. He remembered thinking it odd that she had made a show of wiping tears from dry eyes. Maybe, after days of grieving, it had become her habit to take her sleeve to her eyes. Maybe she had wanted to keep crying but by then was all cried out.

Strange thought it over, his back to Leona. It would be an easy job, reinterviewing the players, retracing steps. He had a business to maintain. He wasn't in any position to be turning down jobs.

"My rates," said Strange.

"Sir?"

He turned to face her. "You haven't asked me about my rates."

"I'm sure they're reasonable."

"I get thirty dollars an hour, plus expenses. Something like this will take time —"

"I have money. There was a settlement, as you know. And Christopher's insurance, his death benefits, I mean, and his pension. I'm certain he would have liked me to use the money for this."

Strange went back to the couch. Leona Wilson stood and rubbed the palm of one hand over the bent fingers of the other. She was eye to eye with him, nearly his height.

"I'll need access to some of his things," said Strange.

"You can have a look in his room."

"He lived here?"

"Yes."

"What about your daughter?"

"My daughter doesn't live here anymore."

"How can I reach her?"

"I haven't seen Sondra or talked with her since the day I buried my son."

Strange's beeper, clipped to his belt, sounded. He unfastened the device and checked the readout. "Do you mind if I use your phone?"

"It's right over there."

Strange made the call and replaced the receiver. He placed his business card beside the phone. "I've got to run."

Leona Wilson straightened her posture and brushed a strand of gray hair behind her ear. "Will you be in church this Sunday?"

"I'm gonna try real hard."

"I'll say a prayer for you, Mr. Strange."

"Thank you." He picked his leather up off the back of a chair. "I'd surely appreciate it if you would."

Strange drove down South Dakota to Rhode Island Avenue and hooked a left. His up mood was gone, and he popped out the Blackbyrds tape and punched the tuner in to 1450 on the AM dial. Joe "the Black Eagle" Madison was on all-talk WOL, taking calls. Strange's relationship with OL went back to the mid-sixties, when the station's format had first gone over to what the newspapers called "rhythm and blues." Back when they'd had those DJs Bobby "the Mighty Burner" Bennett and "Sunny Jim" Kelsey, called themselves the Soul Brothers. He'd been a WOL listener for, damn, what was it, thirty-five years now. He wondered, as he often did when thinking back, where those years had gone.

He made a left turn down 20th Street, Northeast.

Leona Wilson's posture had changed when he'd told her he'd take the job. It wasn't his imagination, either — the years had seemed to drop off her before his eyes. Like the idea of hope had given her a quick shot of youth.

"You all right, Derek," he said, as if saying it aloud would make it so.

He'd been straight up with Leona Wilson back at her

house, as much as anyone could be with a woman that determined. Her temporary hope was a fair trade-off for the permanent crash of disappointment that would surely follow later on. He told himself that this was true.

Anyway, he needed the money. The Chris Wilson case was a potential thousand-, two-thousand-dollar job.

Down along Langdon Park, Strange saw Ron Lattimer's Acura curbed and running, white exhaust coming from its pipes. Strange parked the Caprice behind it, grabbed his binoculars and his Leatherman, climbed out of his car, and got into the passenger side of the red coupe.

Lattimer was at the finish line of his twenties, tall and lean with an athlete's build. He wore a designer suit, a tailored shirt, and a hand-painted tie. He held a lidded cup of Starbucks in one hand, and his other hand tapped out a beat on the steering wheel. The heater fan was blowing full on, and jazzy hip-hop came from the custom stereo system in the dash.

"You warm enough, Ron?"

"I'm comfortable, yeah."

"You doin' a surveillance in the winter, how many times I told you, you got to leave the motor shut down 'cause the *ex*haust smoke, it shows. Bad enough you're driving a red car, says, Look at me, everybody. Notice *me*."

"Too cold to leave the heat off," said Lattimer.

"Put that overcoat on you got there in the backseat, you wouldn't be so cold."

"That's a *cashmere,* Derek; I'm not gonna wear it in my car. Get it all wrinkled up and shit, start looking like I picked it up at the Burlington Coat Factory, some bullshit like that."

Strange took a breath and let it out slow. "And what I tell you about drinking coffee? What you need to be doing, you keep a bottle of water in the car and you sip it, a little at a time, when you get good and thirsty. Coffee runs right through you, man, *you* know that. What's gonna happen when you got to pee so bad you can't stand it, you get out the car lookin' for some privacy, tryin' to find a tree to get behind, while the subject of your tail is sneaking out the back door of his house? Huh? What you gonna do then?"

"The day I lose a tail, Derek, because I been drinkin' an Americano —"

"Oh, it's an *Americano,* now. And here I was, old and out of touch like I am, thinking you were just having a cup of coffee."

Lattimer had to chuckle. "Always tryin' to school me."

"That's right. You got the potential to be something in this profession. I get you away from focusing on your *lifestyle* and get you focused on the business at hand, you're gonna make it." Strange nodded toward the face-plate of the stereo. "Turn that shit off, man, I can't think."

"Tribe Called Quest *represents.*"

"Turn it off anyway, and tell me what we got."

Lattimer switched off the music. "Leon's over there in that house, second from the last on the right, on Mills?"

Strange looked through the glasses. "Okay. How'd you find him?"

"The address he gave the old lady, the one he took off? He hadn't lived there for a year or so. One of the neighbors I interviewed knew his family, though — both of them had come up in the same area. This neighbor told me that Leon's mother and father had both passed, years ago. Got the death certificate of his mother down at that records office on H, in Chinatown. From the date on that certificate, I found her obituary in the newspaper morgue, and the obit listed the heirs. Of the family, only the grandmother was still alive. Leon didn't have any brothers or sisters, which makes him the only heir to g-mom. I figured Leon, hustler that he is, is counting on the grandmother to leave him everything she's got, so Leon's got to be paying regular visits to stay in her grace."

"That the grandmother's house we're looking at?"

"Uh-huh. I been staking it out all this week. Leon finally showed up today. That's his hooptie over there, that yellow Pontiac Astra with the rust marks, parked in front of the house. Ugly-ass car, too."

"Sister to the Chevy Vega."

"People paid extra for that thing 'cause it had the Pontiac name on it?"

"Some did. Nice work."

"Thanks, boss. How you want to handle it?"

Strange gave it some thought. "I think we need to brace him in front of his grandmother."

"I was thinking the same way."

"Come on."

They got out of the Acura, Lattimer retrieving his overcoat first and shaking himself into it as they walked alongside Langdon Park toward Mills Avenue. A couple of young boys, school age, were sitting on a bench wearing oversize parkas, looking hard at Strange and Lattimer, not looking away as Strange glanced in their direction.

"Hold on for a second, Derek," said Lattimer, putting a little skip in his walk and side-glancing Strange. "I got to find me a tree. . . ."

"Funny," said Strange.

They were past the park and onto Mills. Lattimer said. "You want me to take the alley?"

"Yeah, take it. I don't feel like running today if I

don't have to. My knees and this cold aren't the best of friends."

"I don't feel like running, either. You know how I perspire quick, soon as I start to buck, even in this weather."

"I don't suspect he'll be going anywhere, but you never know. Speaking of which . . ."

Lattimer saw Strange pull the Leatherman tool from his pocket and flick open its knife as they neared Leon's yellow Astra. Still walking, Strange drew change from his pocket and dropped it on the street beside the door of the car. He got down on one knee to pick it up, and while he was down there, punctured the driver's-side tire with the knife. He retrieved his change, closing the tool and replacing it in his pocket as he rose.

"See you in a few," said Strange.

He took the steps up to the porch of the row house as Lattimer cut into the alley. He waited half a minute for Lattimer to get behind the house, and then he knocked on the door.

Strange saw a miniature face peer around a lace curtain and heard a couple of locks being turned. The door opened, and a very small woman with prunish skin and a cotton-top of gray hair stood in the frame. The woman gave Strange a thorough examination with her eyes.

She looked back over her shoulder toward a nicely appointed living room that spread out off the foyer. Then she raised her voice: "Leon! There's a police officer here to see you."

"Thank you, ma'am," said Strange. "And tell him not to run, will you? My partner's out back in the alley, and he'll be awful mad if he gets to perspiring. The sweat, it stains his pretty clothes."

* * *

Strange took Leon Jeffries out the kitchen door to a small screened-in porch. The porch gave to a view of a gnarled patch of backyard and the alley. After Strange got Leon out to the porch, he waved Lattimer in from there. Leon confessed to bilking the old woman from Petworth with a pyramid investment scheme shortly thereafter.

"What y'all gonna do to me now?" asked Leon. He was a small, feral, middle-aged man with pale yellow eyeballs. He wore a pinstriped suit jacket with unmatching black slacks and a lavender, open-collar shirt.

"You need to give our client back her money, Leon," said Strange. "Then everything'll be chilly."

"I *planned* on gettin' her money back to her, with interest. Takes a little time, though. See, the way I worked it, I used the next person's investment to pay the, uh, previous person's investment, in installments. Sort of how some folks stay ahead of the game with multiple credit cards."

"That's a *legal* kind of scam, Leon. What we're talking about here is, you were taking off old ladies that trusted you. How you think that's gonna look to a jury?"

"A jury trial for a small-claims thing?"

"You got a sheet, Leon?" asked Lattimer.

"I ain't never been incarcerated."

"So you got a sheet," said Lattimer. "And this goes before a judge, forget about a jury, you get a judge on a bad day he ate the wrong brand of half-smokes for breakfast, some shit like that, they gonna put your thin ass *away*."

"We need the money for our client now," said Strange. "That's all she wants. She's a good woman, which you probably saw as a weakness, but we're gonna forget about that, too, if you come up with the two thousand you took from her straightaway"

"I'd have to get me a job," said Leon. "'Cause currently, see, I don't have those kind of resources."

"You gonna wear that outfit to the job interview?" said Lattimer.

Leon, wounded, looked up at Lattimer and touched the lapel of his lavender shirt. "This right here is a designer shirt. An Yves Saint Laur*ent*."

"From the Singapore factory, maybe. Man your age ought to be wearin' some cotton by now, too, instead of that sixty-forty blend you got on right there."

Strange said, "How we going to work this out with the money, Leon?"

"I ain't got no got-damn money, man; I told you!"

Some spittle flew from Leon's mouth and a bit of it landed on the chest area of Lattimer's overcoat. Lattimer grabbed Leon by the lapels of his jacket and pulled Leon toward him.

"You spit on my cashmere, man!"

"All right, Ron," said Strange. Lattimer released Leon.

"Everything all right over there?" said an elderly man from the backyard of the house to the left. An evergreen tree grew beside the porch, blocking their view of the man behind the voice.

"Everything's fine," said Strange, speaking loudly in the direction of the man. "We're officers of the law."

"*No,* they ain't!" yelled Leon.

"Go on inside now," said Strange. "We got this under control."

Strange squared his body so that he was standing close to Leon. Leon backed up a step and scratched at the bridge of his dented nose.

"Well," said Leon haughtily.

"Well *water,*" said Lattimer.

"Look here," said Strange. "What me and my partner are going to do now, we're going to go back inside and talk to your grandmother. Explain to her about this misunderstanding you got yourself into. I think your grandmother will see that she has to give us what we need. I'm sure this house is paid for, and from the looks of things around here, it won't be too great a burden for her to write the check. I know she doesn't want to see you go to jail. Shame she has to settle up the debt for your mistakes, but there it is."

"Won't be the first time, I bet," said Lattimer.

"What ya'll are doin', it's a shakedown. It's not even legal!" Leon looked from Strange to Lattimer and drew his small frame straight. "Not only that. First you go and insult my vines. And now you're fixin' to shame me to my granmoms!"

"Sooner or later," said Strange, " everybody's got to pay."

Strange split up with Lattimer, drove down to the MLK Jr. library on 9th Street, and went up to the Washingtoniana Room on the third floor. He retrieved a couple of microfiche spools from a steel drawer where the newspaper morgue material was chronologically arranged. He threaded the film and scanned newspaper articles on a lighted screen, occasionally dropping change into a slot to make photostatic copies when he found what he thought he might need. After an hour and a half he turned off the machine, as his eyes had begun to burn, and when he left the library the city had turned to night.

Outside MLK, Strange phoned Janine's voice mail and

left a message: He needed a current address on a man. He gave her the subject's name.

"Hey, what's goin' on, Strange?" said a guy who was walking by the bank of phones.

"Hey, how you *doin'*?"

"Ain't seen you around much lately."

"I been here," said Strange.

Strange headed uptown and stopped at the Raven, a neighborhood bar on Mount Pleasant Street, for a beer. Afterward he walked up to Sportsman's Liquors on the same street and bought a six-pack, then drove to his Buchanan Street row house off Georgia.

He drank another beer and got his second wind. He phoned a woman he knew, but she wasn't home.

Strange went up to his office, a converted bedroom next to his own bedroom on the second floor, and read the newspaper material, a series in the *Washington Post* and a *Washington City Paper* story, that he had copied from the library. As he looked them over, his dog, a tan boxer named Greco, slept with his snout resting on the toe of Strange's boot.

When he was done, he logged on to his computer and checked his stock portfolio to see how he had done for the day. The case for *Ennio Morricone: A Fistful of Film Music* was sitting on his desk. He removed disc one from the case and loaded it into the CPU of his computer. The first few strains of *"Per Qualche Dollaro in Piu"* drifted through the room. He turned the volume up just a hair on his Yamaha speakers, sat back in his reclining chair with his hands folded across his middle, closed his eyes, and smiled.

Strange loved westerns. He'd loved them since he was a kid.

chapter **3**

HE locked the front door of the shop and checked it, then walked up Bonifant Street toward Georgia Avenue, turning up the collar of his black leather to shield his neck from the chill. He passed the gun shop, where black kids from over the District line and suburban white kids who wanted to be street hung out on Saturday afternoons, feeling the weight of the automatics in their hands and checking the action on guns they could buy on the black market later that night. Integras and Accords tricked out with aftermarket spoilers and alloy wheels parked outside the gun shop during the day, but it was night now and the street had quieted and there were few cars of any kind parked along its curb. He passed an African and a Thai restaurant, and Vinyl Ink, the music store that still sold records, and a jewelry and watch-repair shop that catered to Spanish, and one each of many braid-and-nail and dry-cleaning storefronts that low-rised the downtown business district of Silver Spring.

He crossed the street before reaching the Quarry House, one of two or three neighborhood bars he frequented. About now he could taste his first beer, his mouth nearly salivating at the thought of it, and he wondered if this was what it felt like to have a problem with drink. He'd attended a seminar once when he had still worn the uniform, and there he'd learned that clock-watchers and drink counters were drunks or potential drunks, but he was comfortable with his own reasons for looking forward to that first one and he could not bring himself to become alarmed. He liked bars and the companionship to be found in them; it was no more complicated or sinister than that. And anyway, he'd never allow alcoholism to happen to him; he had far too many issues to contend with as it stood.

He cut through the bank parking lot, passing the new Irish bar on the second floor of the corner building at Thayer and Georgia, and he did not slow his pace. He neared a black man coming in the opposite direction, and though either one of them could have stepped aside, neither of them did, and they bumped each other's shoulder and kept walking without an apology or a threatening word.

On the east side of Georgia he passed Rosita's, where the young woman named Juana worked, and he was careful to hurry along and not look through the plate glass colored with Christmas lights and sexy neon signs advertising Tecate and other brands of beer, because he did not want to stop yet, he wanted to walk. Then he was passing a pawnshop and another Thai restaurant and a *pollo* house and the art supply store and the flower shop . . . then crossing Silver Spring Avenue, passing the firehouse and the World Building and the old Gifford's ice-cream parlor, now a day-care center, and across Sligo Avenue up to Selim, where the car repair garages and aikido studios fronted the railroad tracks.

He dropped thirty-five cents into the slot of a pay phone mounted between the Vietnamese *pho* house and the NAPA auto parts store. He dialed Rosita's, and his friend Raphael, who owned the restaurant, answered.

"Hey, amigo, it's —"

"I know who it is. Not too many gringos call this time of night, and you have that voice of yours that people recognize very easily. And I know who you want."

"Is she working?"

"Yes."

"Is there a *c* next to her name on the schedule?"

"Yes, she is closing tonight. So you have time. Are you outside? I can hear the cars."

"I am. I'm taking a walk."

"Go for your walk and I'll put one on ice for you, my friend."

"I'll see you in a little bit."

He hung the receiver in its cradle and crossed the street to the pedestrian bridge that spanned Georgia Avenue. He went to the middle of the bridge and looked down at the cars emerging northbound from the tunnel and the southbound cars disappearing into the same tunnel. He focused on the broken yellow lines painted on the street and the cars moving in rows between the lines. He looked north on Georgia at the street lamps haloed in the cold and watched his breath blow out into the night. He had grown up in this city, it was his, and to him it was beautiful.

Sometime later he crossed the remainder of the bridge and went to the chain-link fence that had been erected in the past year. The fence prevented pedestrians from walking into the area of the train station via the bridge. He glanced around idly and climbed the fence, dropping down over its other side. Then he was in near the small commuter train station, a squat brick structure with boarded windows housing bench seats and a ticket office, and he went down a dark set of stairs beside the station. He entered a fluorescent-lit foot tunnel that ran beneath the Metro and B & O railroad tracks. The tunnel smelled of nicotine, urine, and beer puke, but there was no one in it now, and he went through to the other side, going up another set of concrete steps and finding himself on a walkway on the west side of the tracks.

He walked along the fence bordering the old Canada Dry bottling plant, turned, stood with his hands buried in his jeans, and watched as a Red Line train approached from the city. His long sight was beginning to go on him, and the lights along Georgia Avenue were blurred, white stars broken by the odd red and green.

He looked across the tracks at the ticket office as the passing train raised wind and dust. He closed his eyes.

He thought of his favorite western movie, *Once Upon a Time in the West*. Three gunmen are waiting on the platform of an empty train station as the opening credits roll. It's a long sequence, made more excruciating by the real-time approach of a train and a sound design nearly comic in its exaggeration. Eventually the train arrives. A character named Harmonica steps off of it and stands before the men who have come to kill him. Their shadows are elongated by the dropping sun. Harmonica and the men have a brief and pointed conversation. The ensuing violent act is swift and final.

Standing there at night, on the platform of the train station in Silver Spring, he often felt like he was waiting for that train. In many ways, he felt he'd been waiting all his life.

After a while he went back the way he had come and headed for Rosita's. He was ready for a beer, and also to talk to Juana. He had been curious about her for some time.

Juana Burkett was standing at the service end of the bar, waiting on a marg-rocks-no-salt from Enrique, the tender, when the white man in the black leather jacket came through the door. She watched him walk across the dining room, navigating the tables, a man of medium height with a flat stomach and wavy brown hair nearly touching his shoulders. His face was clean shaven, with only a shadow of beard, and there was a natural swagger to his walk.

He seated himself at the short, straight bar and did not look at her at first, though she knew that she was the reason he was here. She had met him briefly at his place of employment, a used book and vinyl store on Bonifant, where she had been looking for a copy of *Home Is the Sailor,* and Raphael had told her that he had been asking for her since and that he would be stopping by. On the day that she'd met him she felt she'd seen him before, and the feeling passed through her again. Now he looked around the restaurant, trying to appear casually interested in the decor, and finally his eyes lit on her, where they had been headed all the time, and he lifted his chin and gave her an easy and pleasant smile.

Enrique placed the margarita on her drink tray, and she dressed it with a lime wheel and a swizzle stick and walked it to her four-top by the front window. She served the marg and the dark beers on her tray and took the food orders from the two couples seated at the table, glancing over toward the bar one time as she wrote. Raphael was standing beside the man in the black leather jacket and the two of them were shaking hands.

Juana went back to the area of the service bar and placed the ticket faceup on the ledge of a reach-through, where the hand of the kitchen's expeditor took the ticket and impaled it on a wheel. She heard Raphael call her name and she walked around the bar to where he stood and the man sat, his ringless hand touching a cold bottle of Dos Equis beer.

"You remember this guy?" said Raphael.

"Sure," she said, and then Raphael moved away, just left her there like that, went to a deuce along the wall to greet its two occupants. She'd have to remind Raphael of his manners the next time she got him alone.

"So," the man said in a slow, gravelly way. "Did you find your Jorge Amado?"

"I did find it. Thank you, yes."

"We got *Tereza Batista* in last week. It's in that paper series Avon put out a few years back —"

"I've read it," she said, too abruptly. She was nervous, and showing it; it wasn't like her to react this way in front of a man. She looked over her shoulder. She had only the one table left for the evening, and her diners seemed satisfied, nursing their drinks. She cleared her throat and said, "Listen —"

"It's okay," he said, swiveling on his stool to face her. He had a wide mouth parenthesized by lines going down to a strong chin. His eyes were green and they were direct and damaged, and somehow needy, and the eyes completed it for her, and scared her a little bit, too.

"*What*'s okay?" she said.

"You don't have to stand here if you don't want to. You can go back to work if you'd like."

"No, that's all right. I mean, I'm fine. It's just that —"

"Juana, right?" He leaned forward and cocked his head.

He was moving very quickly, and it crossed her mind that what she had taken for confidence in his walk might have been conceit.

"I don't remember telling you my name the day we met."

"Raphael told me."

"And now you're going to tell me you like the way it sounds. That my name sings, right?"

"It *does* sing. But that's not what I was going to say."

"What, then?"

"I was going to ask if you like oysters."

"Yes. I like them."

"Would you like to have some with me down at Crisfield's, after you get off?"

"Just like that? I don't even know —"

"Look here." He put his right hand up, palm out. "I've been thinking about you on and off since that day you walked into the bookstore. I've been thinking about you *all* day today. Now, I believe in being to the point, so let me ask you again: Would . . . you . . . like . . . to step *out* with me, after your shift, and have a bite to eat?"

"Juana!" said the expeditor, his head in the reach-through. "Is up!"

"Excuse me," she said.

She went to the ledge of the reach-through and retrieved a small bowl of chili *con queso,* filled a red plastic basket with chips, and served the four-top its appetizer. As she was placing the *queso* and chips on the table, she looked back at the bar, instantly sorry that she had. The man was smiling at her full on. She tossed her long hair off her shoulder self-consciously and was sorry she had done that, too. She walked quickly back to the bar.

"You're sure of yourself, eh?" she said when she reached him, surprised to feel her arms folded across her chest.

"I'm confident, if that's what you mean."

"Overconfident, maybe."

He shrugged. "You like what you see, otherwise you wouldn't have stood here as long as you did. And you sure wouldn't have come back. I like what *I* see. That's what I'm *doing* here. And listen, Raphael can vouch for me. It's not like we're going to walk out of here and I'm gonna grow fangs. So why don't we try it out?"

"You must be drunk," she said, nodding at the beer bottle in his hand.

"On wine and love." He saw her perplexed face and said, "It's a line from a western."

"Okay."

He shot a look at her crossed arms. "You're gonna wrinkle your uniform, you keep hugging it like that."

She unfolded her arms slowly and dropped them to her side. She began to smile, tried to stop it, and felt a twitch at the edge of her lip.

"It's not a uniform," she said, her voice softening, losing its edge. "It's just an old cotton shirt."

They studied each other for a while, not speaking, as the recorded mariachi music danced through the dining room and bar.

"What I was trying to tell you," she said, "before you interrupted me . . . is that I don't even know your name."

"It's Terry Quinn," he said.

"Tuh-ree Quinn," she said, trying it out.

"Irish Catholic," he said, "if you're keeping score."

And Juana said, "It sings."

chapter **4**

"WHERE'S your car?" asked Juana.

"You better drive tonight," said Quinn.

"I'm in the lot. We should cut through here."

They went through the break in the buildings between Rosita's and the pawnshop. They neared Fred Folsom's sculpted bronze bust of Norman Lane, "the Mayor of Silver Spring," mounted in the center of the breezeway. Quinn patted the top of Lane's capped head without thought as they walked by.

"You always do that?" said Juana.

"Yeah," said Quinn, "for luck. Some of the guys in the garages back here, they sort of adopted him, looked out for him when he was still alive. See?" He pointed to a sign mounted over a bay door in the alley, a caricature drawing of Lane with the saying "Don't Worry About It" written on a button pinned to his chest, as they entered an alley. "They call this Mayor's Lane now."

"You knew him?"

"I knew who he was. I bought him a drink once over at Captain White's. Another place that isn't around anymore. He was just a drunk. But I guess what they're trying to say with all this back here, with everything he was, he was still a man."

"God, it's cold." Juana held the lapels of her coat together and close to her chest and looked over at Quinn. "I've seen you before, you know? And not at the bookstore, either. Before that, but I know we never met."

"I was in the news last year. On the television and in the papers, too."

"Maybe that's it."

"It probably is."

"There's my car."

"That old Beetle?"

"What, it's not good enough for you?"

"No, I like it."

"What do you drive?"

"I'm between cars right now."

"Is that like being between jobs?"

"Just like it."

"You asked me out and you don't have a car?"

"So it's your nickel for the gas." Quinn zipped his jacket. "I'll get the oysters and the beers."

They were at the bar of Crisfield's, the old Crisfield's on the dip at Georgia, not the designer Crisfield's on Colesville, and they were eating oysters and sides of coleslaw and washing it all down with Heineken beer. Quinn had juiced the cocktail sauce with horseradish and he noticed that Juana had added Tabasco to the mix.

"Mmm," said Juana, swallowing a mouthful, reaching into the cracker bowl for a chaser.

"A dozen raw and a plate of slaw," said Quinn. "Nothin' better. These are good, right?"

"They're good."

All the stools at the U-shaped bar were occupied, and the dining room to the right was filled. The atmosphere was no atmosphere: white tile walls with photographs of local celebrities framed and mounted above the tiles, wood tables topped with paper place mats, grocery store–bought salad dressing displayed on a bracketed shelf . . . and still the place was packed nearly every night, despite the fact that management was giving nothing away. Crisfield's was a D.C. landmark, where generations of Washingtonians had met and shared food and conversation for years.

"Make any money tonight?" said Quinn.

"By the time I tipped out the bartender . . . not real money, no. I walked with forty-five."

"You keep having forty-five-dollar nights, you're not going to be able to make it through school."

"My student loans are putting me through school. I wait tables just to live. Raphael tell you I was going to law school?"

"He told me everything he knew about you. Don't worry, it wasn't much. Pass me that Tabasco, will you?"

He touched her hand as she handed him the bottle. Her hand was warm, and he liked the way her fingers were tapered, feminine and strong.

"Thanks."

A couple of black guys seated on the opposite end of the U, early thirties, if Quinn had to guess, were staring freely at him and Juana. Plenty of heads had turned when they'd entered the restaurant, some he figured just to get a look at Juana. Most of the people had only looked over briefly, but these two couldn't give it up. Well, fuck it, he thought. If this was going to keep working in any kind of way — and he was getting the feeling already that he wanted it to — then he'd just have to shake off those kinds of stares. Still, he didn't like it, how these two were so bold.

"That's not fair," said Juana.

"*What* isn't?"

"You been asking about me and you know some things, and I don't know a damn thing about you."

You *been*. He liked the way she said that.

"That accent of yours," he said.

"What accent?"

"Your voice falls and rises, like music. What is that, Brooklyn?"

"The Bronx." She shook an oyster off her fork and let it sit in the cocktail sauce. "What's yours? The Carolinas, something like that?"

"Maryland, D.C."

"You sound plenty Southern to me. With that drawl and everything."

"This *is* the South. It's south of the Mason-Dixon Line, anyway."

He turned to face her. Her hair was black, curly, and very long, and it broke on thin shoulders and rose again at the upcurve of her smallish breasts. She had a nice ass on her, too; he had checked it out back at the restaurant when she'd bent over to serve her drinks. It was round and high, the way he liked it, and the sight of it had taken his breath short, which had not happened to him in a long while. Her eyes were near black, many shades deeper than her brown skin, and her lips were full and painted in a dark color with an even darker outline. There was a mole on her cheek, above and to the right of her upper lip.

He was staring at her now and she was staring at him, and then her lips turned up on one side, a kind of half smile that she attempted to hold down. It was the same thing she had done back at Rosita's with her mouth, and Quinn chuckled under his breath.

"What?"

"Ah, nothin'. It's just, that thing you got going on, your *almost* smile. I just like it, is all."

Juana retrieved her oyster from the cocktail sauce, chewed and swallowed it, and had a swig of cold beer.

"How do you know Raphael?" she said.

"He came in the shop one day, looking for Stanley Clarke's *School Days* on vinyl. Raphael likes that jazz-funk sound, the semi-orchestral stuff from the seventies. Dexter Wansel, George Duke, like that. Lonnie Liston Smith. I knew zilch about it, and he was happy to give me an education. I call him when we buy those old records from time to time."

"You always worked in a bookstore?"

"No, not always. What you want to know is, am I educated, and if so, why haven't I done anything with it. I went to the University of Maryland and got my criminology degree. Then I was a cop in D.C. for eight years or so. After I left the force, I thought I was ready for something quiet. I like books, a certain kind, anyway. . . ."

"Westerns."

"Yeah, and there's nothing quieter than a used book and record store. So here I am."

She studied his face. "I know where I've seen you now."

"Right. I'm the cop that killed the other cop last year."

"It's the hair that's changed."

"Uh-huh. I grew it out."

Quinn waited, but the usual follow-up questions didn't come. He watched Juana use her elbow to push the platter of oyster shells away from her. While he watched her, he drank off an inch of his beer.

"How about me?" asked Juana. "Anything else you want to know?"

"Not really. What I know so far I like."

"Not a thing, huh?"

"Can't think of anything off the top of my head right now."

"Let me go ahead and get it out of the way, then, all right? My mother was Puerto Rican and my father was black. I'm comfortable in a few different worlds and sometimes I'm not comfortable in any of them."

"I didn't ask you that."

"You didn't ask me that *yet*."

"What I mean is, I don't care."

"You don't care tonight. Tonight there's only attraction and do we connect. But this world we got out here and the people in it, right now, they're not gonna let us *not care*. Like those two guys over there, been staring at us all night."

"How about we deal with it as we go along?" Quinn signaled the barrel-chested man with the gray mustache behind the bar. "Sir? You wanna shuck us a dozen more?"

"Thanks, Tuh-ree," said Juana.

Tuh-ree. He liked the way she said that, too.

On their way out the door, Juana noticed Quinn glance over his shoulder at the two men who had been staring at them all night and give them both a short but meaningful look.

Out on the street Juana put her arm through his as they walked to her black Beetle, parked in the lot of a tire store. She was cold and it warmed her to be close to him, and it felt natural to touch him, like they had moved past something and were onto something else. He was easy to talk to and he listened, didn't seem to be the type of man who was always thinking of what he'd say next. He didn't boast, either, didn't talk about his big plans, hadn't tried too hard to impress her in any way, in fact, which had made an impression in itself.

"Where do you live?" she asked.

"I got a place down off Sligo Avenue. What about you?"

"I'm over on Tenth Street in Northeast. Near Catholic U?"

"You mind dropping me off before you head back?"

"What're you, kiddin'?"

"'Cause I could walk."

"Yeah, I heard you like to walk at night."

"Raphael told you, huh?"

"And that you like westerns. He said you were reading one the first time he went into your shop and every time since."

"So what was all that 'It's not fair, I don't know a damn thing about you' stuff?" Quinn laughed. "You're a liar!"

"All right, I lied," said Juana. "But I promise you, I'll never lie to you again."

She stopped the Volkswagen out front of his place, a

small brick apartment building, and let it idle. A convenience store and beer market sat closed and dark across the street, and boys in parkas were standing around outside its locked front door. The apartment units were dark as well.

"Here we are," he said.

"Thanks for everything. It was nice."

"My pleasure. I'll see you around, okay?"

"Okay."

He squeezed her hand and it felt like a kiss. Then he was out of the car and crossing the unlit street, his jacket black and flat against the night.

She drove home listening to a Cassandra Wilson tape, thinking of him all the way.

Quinn washed and got under the covers of his bed. He tried to read a Max Evans that was sitting on his nightstand but found it hard to concentrate on the plot. He turned off the light, thinking of Juana, trying not to expect too much, hoping it could work.

Just before dawn he dreamed that he had gotten into a violent argument with a black man in a club. Punches were thrown and a gun was drawn. Then there were screams, blood, and death.

When he woke he was neither startled nor disturbed. He'd been having dreams like this for some time.

chapter **5**

R AY Boone's jaw was tight from the thick line of crank he'd done. He unglued his tongue from the roof of his mouth and licked his dry lips. Ray went behind the long mahogany bar he and his daddy had built themselves, looking to fix himself a drink.

"Daddy, where's that Jack at?" he hollered.

Ray couldn't hear his own voice above the old Randy Travis number that was coming from the Wurlitzer jukebox he'd bought at an auction of the furnishings from a bankrupt restaurant. Edna had turned up the volume way high.

Earl Boone was sitting in front of a video screen playing electronic poker. He took a sip from a can of Busch beer and dragged on his cigarette. He tapped ash off the cigarette into a tray without taking his eyes off the screen. "Wherever the hell you left it, Critter, last time you took a drink."

"I see it," said Ray. The Jack was on a low shelf beside the steel sink, in front of a Colt automatic his daddy had hung on a couple of nails he'd driven into the wood behind the bar. Ray grabbed the black-labeled bottle and a tumbler, filled the glass with ice from a chest beside the sink, and free-poured sour mash whiskey halfway to the lip. He filled the rest of the glass with Coke and stirred the cocktail with a dirty finger.

"Ain't you gonna fix me one, baby?" asked Edna Loomis, sitting at a card table covered in green felt. Edna was speed wired, her usual condition this time of the afternoon. She was stacking and restacking a pile of white chips with one hand and playing with her feather-cut shag with the other.

"Don't want you gettin' wasted too early, now," said Ray, talking to her as he would a child.

"I won't. Just want a little somethin' to sip while I'm back at the house watching my shows."

Ray mixed a weak one and walked it over to Edna, who stood to take it from his hand. She reached for the glass, running her long fingers over the backs of his, and clumsily licked her lips. He felt a stirring in his jeans.

"We got time?" she said, looking over his shoulder briefly at the old man.

"Uh-uh," said Ray. "Me and Daddy are about to make a run into D.C."

"When you get back, then," she said, tossing a head of damaged orange-blond hair off her shoulder, winking as she took a sip of her drink. She moved her hips awkwardly to the Travis tune as she drank, keeping her eyes on him over the glass, and sang as the chorus returned to the song, " 'Forever and ever, ay-men.' "

Ray looked her over. Boy, she thought she was so sexy. He wondered what she saw when she looked in the mirror. She was getting up around thirty, and it was showing in the lines around her mouth. Dimples had begun to pucker below her ass, too, and she'd never had young eyes. She did have a nice set, though, the kind that stood at attention, with sharp pink button-nips. She ever let those bad boys go to seed like the rest of her was doin', Ray'd have to think about trading her in for a new model.

"Huh?" she said. "I asked you a question, *Critter*. We gonna make like bunny rabbits and do the deed when you get back, or what?"

Her mouth, that was the other thing. Proud titties or no, she didn't learn to shut her mouth some, he might trade her in sooner than she knew.

"Don't call me Critter," said Ray. "Only Daddy can call me that."

"Well, are we?"

"Maybe," he said. But she'd be sloppy as hell by the time he came back from the city, cooked on crank and drunk as a sailor on shore leave, too. He couldn't stand to fuck her when she got like that.

"Ray?"

"Huh?"

"You're gonna be gone a few hours, right?"

"Uh-huh."

"Whyn't you leave me some of that ice?"

"You know you're likin' that stuff too much."

"Please, baby?"

"A little bit, then. All right." He looked past her and said, "You about ready, Daddy?"

Earl Boone said, "Yep," and flicked ash into the tray.

Ray went to a large door at the back of the barn. The door was steel fortified and it was set in a fortified, fire-proofed wall. He took the set of keys he hung from a loop of his jeans and opened the door, which he kept locked at all times. He went in, closed the door behind him, and threw the slide bolt.

On one side of the room sat a weight bench and barbells and plates, with mirrors angled toward the weight bench and hung on the walls. A workbench ran along the opposite wall, with shelves above it and a Peg Board with hooks holding tools. A couple of safes sat beneath the workbench, and in the safes were money, heroin, and guns. Beside the workbench stood a footlocker next to a stand-up case made of varnished oak and glass in which four shotguns were racked.

On the third wall was a single-unit kitchenette with a two-burner electric stove, sink, and refrigerator stocked with bottled water and beer. Ray used the stove to make his private stash of methamphetamine, both the powder and the crystal, which he cooked on the stove in a small saucepan. On the steel countertop of the kitchenette were bottles of Sudafed and carburetor cleaner, and the other chemicals he used to make the crank.

Ray and his father had plumbed in some pipes and put a bathroom in the room, too. It was big and private, with a solid oak door. Ray could sit on the crapper and look at his stroke books back in there, and if he had a mind to, when he was done wiping himself clean, he could just turn around and pump a load off into the bowl and flush the whole dirty mess.

Beneath the carpet remnant that lay beside the weight bench was a trapdoor. Under that trapdoor was a tunnel that he and his father had dug out the summer before last. The tunnel was their means of escape, in the event that one was needed, and it went back about fifty, sixty yards or so, into the woods behind the barn and the house.

Ray Boone loved this room. Only he and his daddy were allowed back here, that was the rule. Nobody, none of Daddy's friends or his own friends or Edna, would think of coming back here, even if they had access to the key. Edna knew that the drugs she loved so much were in this room. Dumb as she was, though, and she was dumber than a goddamn rock, she was plenty smart enough to know not to try.

Ray picked up a set of barbells and stood before one of the mirrors. He did a set of twenty alternating curls. He dropped the barbells and checked himself out. His prison tats showed just below the sleeves of his white T-shirt. A dagger with blood dripping from it on one arm, a cobra wrapped around the staff of a Confederate flag on the other: standard-issue stuff. The good tattoos, a swastika between two lightning bolts and a colored guy swinging from a tree, he kept covered up on his shoulder and back.

Ray made a couple of serious faces in the mirror, raised his eyebrows, first one, then the other. He wasn't too good-looking so anyone would mistake him for a pretty boy, and he wasn't all that ugly, either. He had acne scars on his face, but they'd never scared any girls off, not that he'd noticed, anyway. And some women liked the way his eyes were set real deep under his hard, protruding brow. A couple of times when he was growing up, some boys called him cross-eyed, and he just had to go ahead and pop those boys hard, square in the face. If he was cross-eyed, he didn't see it himself. Edna said he looked like that guy on the *Profiler* TV series, always played a drug dealer in the movies. Ray liked that guy. There wasn't nothin' pretty about him.

When Ray was done admiring himself he grabbed a vial holding a couple of meth crystals and slipped it into a pocket of his jeans. He took off his sneakers and put on a pair of Dingo boots with four-inch custom heels, opened the safe, and removed a day pack holding plastic packets of heroin the size of bricks that he had scaled out earlier in the day. He found his nine-millimeter Beretta, checked the load, and holstered the automatic in the waistband of his jeans. From the footlocker he withdrew a heavy flannel shirt and jacket, and put them both on, the tail of the shirt worn out to cover the gun. He slung the day pack over his shoulder, left the room, and locked the door behind him.

Edna was waiting for him out in the bar. She gave him a wet kiss as he palmed the vial over to her, then left the barn with her drink in her hand.

"Ready, Daddy?"

"Sure thing."

Earl hated the city. There was only one thing good about it, far as he was concerned. It was down in the warehouse they called the Junkyard. For him, it was worth the trip.

Earl Boone stabbed his cigarette out in the ashtray. He killed his beer and crushed the can in his hand, dropping the empty in a wastebasket beside the electronic poker game. He slipped a deck of Marlboro reds into his shirt pocket and watched his son take his own pack of 'Boros off the bar and do the same.

Earl stood as his son crossed the room. Earl was a weathered version of the boy, the plow lines on his cheeks somewhat masking the acne scars, and deep-set, flat eyes. He was taller than Ray by six inches and wider across the shoulders and back. Unlike the boy, he'd never lifted a weight when he wasn't paid to do so, and he didn't understand those who did. A hitch in the Marine Corps and hard work had given him his build.

"Let's do it," said Ray.

Earl smiled a little, looking at those high-heeled boots on his boy's feet. Ray sure did have a thing about his lack of height.

"Somethin' funny?" said Ray.

"Nothin'," said Earl.

Earl picked up a cooler that held a six-pack and looked around the bar and gaming area before he shut down the lights. He was real proud of what they'd done here, him and his boy. The way they had it fixed up, it looked like one of those old-time saloons. The kind they used to have in those towns out west.

Edna Loomis filled the bowl of a bong with pot and dropped a crystal of methamphetamine on top of the load. She stood at the window of the bedroom where she and Ray slept in the house and watched Ray and Earl leave the barn and head for their car, a hopped-up Ford parked between an F-150 pickup and Ray's Shovelhead Harley.

Edna flicked the wheel of a Bic lighter and got fire. She held the flame over the bowl and drew in a hit of ice over grass. Holding in the high, she watched Ray dismantle the top of the car's bumper, then take the heroin out of the day pack and stuff the packets into the space between the bumper and the trunk of the car.

She coughed out the hit, a mushroom of smoke exploding against the glass of the bedroom window.

Ray put a strip of rubber or something over the heroin and replaced the top of the bumper, pounding it into place with the heel of his hand. Earl was facing the wide gravel path that led in from the state road, keeping an eye out for any visitors. The both of them, thought Edna, they were just paranoid as all hell. No one ever came down that road. There was a locked wooden gate at the head of it, anyhow.

Edna was still coughing, thinking of Ray and Earl and their business, and her head started to pound, and for a moment she got a little bit scared. But she knew the pounding was just the rush of the ice hitting her brain, and then she stopped coughing and felt good. Then she felt better than good, suddenly straightened out right. She lit a Virginia Slim from a pack she kept in a leather case, picked up her drink, and sipped at it, trying to make it last.

She went to the TV set on the bureau and turned up the volume. Some white chick with orange hair was up on a stage, sitting next to a big black dude. The white chick was fat and asshole ugly, not surprising, and now some bubble-assed black chick was walking out on the stage and, boy, did she look meaner than a motherfucker, too. Looked like she was about to put a hurtin' on the white chick for sleeping with her old man. And damn if she wasn't throwing a punch at the white chick now. . . . Edna had seen this one, or it could have been that she was just imagining that she had.

She went back to the window and looked down at the yard. Earl and Ray were three-point turning, heading down the gravel and into the trees.

She checked the level of her drink. It was going down real good today. Nothing like a little Jack and some nicotine behind a hit of speed. Course, Ray wouldn't like it if he came home and found her drunk, but she didn't have to worry about that yet.

She had a sip from the glass and then, what the hell, drank it all down in one gulp. Maybe she'd go down to the barn and fix one more weak one, mostly Coke with just a little mash in it to change its color. Ray wouldn't be home for another few hours anyway, and besides, he'd be all stoked and occupied for the rest of the night. Ray liked to count the cash money he brought back after he made his runs.

Ray and Earl's property was set back off Route 28, between Dickerson and Comus, not too far south of Frederick, at the east-central edge of Montgomery County. There was still forest and open country out here, but not for long. Over the years the Boones had seen the development stretch farther and farther north from D.C., white-flighters, mostly, who claimed they wanted "more land" and "more house for the buck." What they really wanted, Ray knew, was to get away from the niggers and the crime. None of them could stand the prospect of seeing their daughters walking down the street holding the hand of Willie Horton. That was the white man's biggest night-mare, and they ran from it like a herd of frightened animals, all the way out here. Ray could understand it, but still, he wished those builders would go and put their new houses someplace else.

Ray moved the car to the on-ramp of 270 and drove south.

"Here," said Ray, handing his pistol butt-out to his father. Earl took the gun, opened the glove box, hit a button, and waited for a false back to drop. He placed the Beretta in the space behind the glove box wall.

Ray had bought this particular vehicle from a trap-car shop up in the Bronx. It was your basic Taurus, outfitted with more horses than was legal, more juice than Ford used to put in its high-horse street model, the SHO. The bumper was a false bumper, which meant it could withstand a medium-velocity impact and could also accommodate relatively large volumes of heroin between its outer shell and the trunk of the car. Hidden compartments behind the glove box, to the left of the steering column, and in other spots throughout the interior concealed Ray's guns and his personal stash of drugs.

Ray lit a cigarette off the dash lighter, passed the lighter to his daddy so he could light his.

"You'd know we was the bad guys," said Ray, "if this here was a movie."

"Why's that?"

"'Cause you and me smoke."

"Huh," said Earl.

"Down county, I hear they want to outlaw smoking in bars."

"That so."

"They can have mine," said Ray, beaming at his cleverness, "when they pry 'em from my cold, dead fingers. Right?"

Earl didn't answer. He didn't talk much to begin with, and he talked even less with his son. Ray had been absent the day God passed out brains, and when he did say something, it tended to be about how tough he was or how smart he was. Earl had twenty years on Ray, and Earl could take Ray on his weakest day. Ray knew it, too. Earl figured this was just another thing that had kept the chip on his boy's shoulder his entire life.

Earl popped the top on a can of Busch.

Ray dragged on his cigarette. It bothered him that his father barely gave him the time of day. It was him, Ray, who had set up this business they had going on right here. It was him, Ray, who had made all the right decisions. If he had left business matters up to his father, who had never even been able to hold a longtime job on his own, they'd have nothing now, nothing at all.

Course, it took a stretch in Hagerstown, where Ray had done a ten-year jolt on a manslaughter beef, for him to find the opportunity to connect to this gig he had here. Ray had been paid to kill some K-head who'd ripped off the stash of a dealer out in Frederick County. Ray had killed a couple of guys for money since high school, and he'd gotten a rep among certain types as the go-to man in that part of the state. He'd never intended to become a hired murderer — not that he ever lost any sleep over it or anything like that — but these were people who deserved to die, after all. After his first kill, who begged and didn't go quick, it had been easy.

This particular job, Ray's idea had been to do it in the bathroom of a bar where the K-head hung out, then climb out the window and make his escape. After he gutted the thief with a Ka-Bar knife, though, the bar's bouncer came in to take a leak and disarmed Ray, holding him until the pigs could get to the scene. Ray should've killed the bouncer, too, he had replayed it in his head many times, but the bouncer was one of those cro-mags, he broke Ray's wrist real quick, and then there wasn't all that much Ray could do.

What he did do, he claimed the dust bunny had attacked *him,* and lucky for Ray, a piece-of-shit .22 was found in the jacket pocket of the corpse. So the hard rap couldn't stick, and Ray drew manslaughter and Hagerstown.

Prison life was okay if you could avoid getting punked. The way to avoid it some was strong attitude, but mostly alliances and gangs. The whites hooked up with Christian Identity and the like. The blacks hung together and so did the Spanish, but the whites and Spanish hated the blacks more than they hated each other, so once in a while Ray made talk with a brown or two.

One of them was Roberto Mantilla. Roberto had a cousin in the Orlando area, Nestor Rodriguez, who worked for the Vargas cartel operating out of the Cauca Valley in northern Colombia. Nestor and his brother Lizardo made the East Coast run, selling powder to dealers in D.C., Baltimore, Wilmington, Philly, and New York. Purer heroin at a lower cost had expanded their market, crushed their foreign competition, and fueled the growth of their business. Roberto said that his cousins could no longer handle the logistics of the transactions themselves and would be willing to sell to a middleman who could make the back-and-forth into D.C. and satisfy the demands of the dealers more readily than they. For this, said Roberto, the middleman would receive a ten-thousand-dollar bounce per transaction.

Ray said, "All right, soon as I get out, I'd like to give that a try." A year later, after a parole board hearing at which he convinced the attendees that the good behavior he had exhibited during his term was not an aberration, he was out of Hagerstown. And two years after that, when he had completed his outside time and said good-bye to his PO, he was free to go to work.

Ray supposed he had Roberto Mantilla to thank for his success. But this was impossible, as Roberto had been raped and bludgeoned to death by a cock-diesel with a lead pipe shortly after Ray's release.

"This load we got, it's eighty-five-percent pure, Daddy," said Ray, thinking of the heroin sealed in the bumper compartment at the rear of the car.

"Lizardo tell you that?" asked Earl, needling his son, knowing Ray hated the Rodriguez brother who never showed Ray an ounce of respect.

"*Nestor* told me. Down in Florida, they got brown heroin, it's ninety-five-percent pure when it hits the street."

"So? What's that do?"

"For the Colombians, it kills the competition. I'm talkin' about the Asians, who were putting out seven-, ten-percent product, and the Mexicans, too. The Colombians upped the purity and lowered the price, and now they're gonna own most of the U.S. market. And what this pure shit does, it creates a whole new class of customers: college kids, the boy next door, like that. It's not just for coloreds anymore, Daddy. 'Cause you don't have to pop it, see, to get a rush. You can smoke it or snort it, you want to."

"That's nice."

"You're not interested in what we're doin'?"

"Not really, no. Get in, sell it, get out; that's all I'm interested in. Wasn't for the money, I'd just as soon never set eyes on that city again. Let them all kill themselves over this shit for all I care."

"You wouldn't want that," said Ray, smiling at his father across the bench. "Wouldn't have no customers, they all up and died."

"Critter?"

"What."

"Someday, you and me, we're gonna wake up and figure out we got enough money. You ever think about that?"

"I'm startin' to," said Ray, goosing the Ford into the passing lane.

Truth be told, Ray had been thinkin' on it for quite some time. Only piece missing was a way to get out. That's all he and his daddy needed: some kind of plan.

chapter **6**

Bʏ the time Earl had killed another beer, Ray had gotten off the Beltway and was on New Hampshire Avenue, heading south into D.C. Later, on North Capitol, down near Florida Avenue, he made a call on his cell phone and told Cherokee Coleman's boys that he and his father were on their way in.

He turned left onto Florida when things were really starting to look rough, and went along a kind of complex of old warehouses and truck bays that had once been an industrial hub of sorts in a largely nonindustrial town but were now mainly abandoned. The entire area had been going steadily downhill since the riots of '68.

Ray passed by Cherokee Coleman's place of business, one of several small brick row houses in the complex, indistinguishable from the rest. Coleman's place was across the street from what folks in the area called the Junkyard, a crumbling warehouse where crack fiends, blow addicts, and heroin users had been squatting for the past year or so. They had come to be near Coleman's supply.

Ray drove slowly down the block. Coleman's army —

steerers, pitchers, money handlers, lookouts, and managers — was spread out on the sidewalk and on several corners of the street. An M3 BMW, an Acura Legend, a spoilered Lexus, and a two-seater Mercedes with chromed-out wheel wells, along with several SUVs, were curbed along the block.

A cop car approached from the other direction. Ray did not look at its uniformed driver but rather at the large numbers printed on the side of the cruiser, a Crown Vic, as it passed.

"Ray," said Earl.

"It's all right," said Ray, matching the numbers on the car to the numbers he had memorized.

In the rearview, Ray saw the MPD cruiser make a right at the next corner, circling the block. Ray punched the gas and made it quickly to a bay door at a garage on the end of the block. He honked his horn, two shorts and a long. The bay door rose and Ray drove through, into a garage where several young men and a couple of very young men waited.

The door closed behind them. Ray got his gun out of the glove box trap and pushed his hips forward so that he could holster the .9 beneath the waistband of his jeans. He knew his father had slipped his .38 into his jacket pocket, back in the barn. He didn't care if the young men in the garage saw the guns. He *wanted* them to see. Ray and Earl got out of the car.

There was no greeting from Coleman's men, no nod of recognition. Ray knew from his prison days not to smile, or show any other gesture of humanity, because it would be seen as a weakness, an opening, a place to stick the knife. As for Earl, he saw hard black faces, one no different from the other. That was all he needed to know.

"Money, clothes, cars," rapped a dead, even voice from a small stereo set up on a shelf. "Clockin' Gs, gettin' skeezed . . ."

"It's behind the bumper," said Ray to the oldest of the bunch, whom he'd seen on the last run.

"Then get it, chief," said the young man, the manager, with a slow tilt of his head.

"You get it," said Ray.

Now you're gonna look at each other for a while, thought Earl, like you can't decide whether to mix it up or fall in love.

That's what they did. Ray stared them down and they stared him down, and a couple of the older ones laughed, and Ray laughed some, and then there were more hard stares.

And then the manager said, "Get it," to one of the younger ones, who nodded to the guy next to him. Those two dismantled the bumper and got the heroin packs out of the space.

Coleman's employees scaled the heroin out quickly on an electronic unit that sat on a bench along a wall while Ray and Earl smoked cigarettes. They did not taste it or test it, not because they trusted these two but because Coleman had instructed them to leave it alone. Coleman knew that Ray and Earl would never try and take him off. What they had with him, it was just too tight.

"The weight's good," said the manager.

"I know it's good. Call Cherokee and tell him I'm coming in. We'll be back for our car."

The group began chuckling as the Boones walked from the garage, after one young man started singing banjo notes. Ray didn't care; all of them would be croaked or in the joint soon anyway. It felt good walking out of there, not even looking over his shoulder, like he didn't give a good fuck if they laughed themselves silly or took another breath. He felt strong and he felt tall. He was glad he'd worn his boots.

Ray and Earl stepped quickly down the block. The cold wind blew newspaper pages across the street. Ray met eyes with a young man talking on a cell, knowing that the young man was speaking to one of Cherokee Coleman's lieutenants. They kept walking toward Coleman's place, and when they neared it a door opened and they stepped inside.

They were in an outer office then, and four young men were waiting for them there. One of them frisked Ray and Earl and took the guns that he found. Ray allowed it because there was no danger here; if something was to have gone down it would have gone down back in the garage. Coleman didn't keep drugs, handle large amounts of money, or have people killed anywhere near his office. He had come up like everyone else, but he was smart and he was past that now.

The one who had frisked them nodded, and they went into Coleman's office.

Cherokee Coleman was seated in a leather recliner behind a desk. The desk held a blotter, a gold pen-and-pencil set, and one of those lamps with a green shade, the kind they used to have in banks. A cell phone sat neatly next to the lamp. Ray figured this kind of setup made Coleman feel smart, like a grown-up businessman, like he worked in a bank or something, too. Ray and his father often joked that the pen-and-pencil set had never been used.

Coleman wore a three-button black suit with a charcoal turtleneck beneath the jacket. His skin was smooth and reddish brown against the black of the suit, and his features were small and angular. He wasn't a big man, but the backs of his thick-wristed hands were heavily veined, indicating to Earl that Coleman had strength.

Behind Coleman, leaning against the frame of a small barred window, was a tall, fat, bald man wearing shades with gold stems. He was Coleman's top lieutenant, Angelo Lincoln, a man everyone down here called Big-Ass Angelo.

"Fellas," said Coleman, lazily moving one of his manicured hands to indicate they take a seat before his desk.

Ray and Earl sat in chairs set lower than Coleman's.

"How's it goin', Ray? Earl?"

"How do," said Earl.

"How do what?"

Angelo's shoulders jiggled, and a *sh-sh-sh* sound came from his mouth.

"Looks like everything checked out all right," said Coleman.

"No doubt," said Ray. "The weight's there, and this load is honest-to-God high-test. Eight-five per."

"I heard."

Coleman didn't feel the need to tell Ray this puritypercentage stuff was straight-up bullshit. If the shit was eighty-five, ninety percent pure for real, you'd have junkies fallin' out dead all over the city, 'cause shit that pure was do-it-on-the-head-of-a-matchstick stuff only.

Got so even the dealers were startin' to believe the press releases comin' out of the DEA.

"You hear it from the Rodriguez brothers?"

"Yeah. They called me to discuss some other business."

"This business involve my father and me?"

"It could." Coleman turned to his lieutenant. "Looks like we got a killer batch on our hands, Angelo. What we gonna call it?"

Coleman liked to label the little wax packets of heroin he sold with brand names. Said it was free advertising, letting his "clients" know that they were getting Cherokee's best, that there was something new and potent out on the street. He liked to think of the brand names as his signature, like the special dishes cooks came up with in those fancy restaurants.

Ray watched Angelo, staring down at the floor, his mouth open as he thought up names, a frown on his blubbery face. Angelo looked up, nodding his head, proud of what he'd come up with.

"Kill and Kill Again," said Angelo with a wide grin.

"I don't like that. Sounds like one of those Chuck Norris movies, Angie, and you know what I think of him."

"Death Wish Too?" said Angelo.

"Naw, black, we used that before."

"How about Scalphunter, then?" Angelo knew that his boss liked those kinds of names. Coleman thought himself kin to the Indian nation.

Coleman pursed his lips. "Scalphunter sound good."

Earl shifted in his chair. The room was warm and smelled of oils or perfume, some shit like that. Colored guys with their paper evergreen trees hanging from the rearview mirrors and their scented crowns and their fancy fucking smells.

"About the Rodriguez brothers," said Ray.

"Nestor," said Coleman, "now he's gone and added cocaine to that sales bag of his. Had to explain to him, I'm getting out of that business. Blow fiends and pipeheads, their money's green, too, don't get me wrong. But all the cash is in brown powder right now, and that's where I see the money of the future, too. And the cocaine I do buy, I buy from the Crips out of L.A. Thing I'm tryin' to say is, I don't want to be beholdin' to just one supplier. Gives 'em too much power with regards to the price structure and negotiations side of things, you know what I'm sayin'?"

Beholdin' to, with regards to, price structure and negotiations side of things . . . Christ, thought Earl, who the fuck does this nigger think he is?

"What'd Nestor say to that?" said Ray.

"He implied that it might imperil our business relationship, I don't buy all my inventory from him. And I don't like those kinds of words. Almost sounds like a threat, you understand what I'm talkin' about?"

"I'm hip," said Ray. "I'm with you."

Oh, you hipper than a motherfucker, thought Coleman. And of course you're *with* me. Where the fuck else *would* you be, it wasn't for me? Out in the fields somewhere with a yoke around your neck, a piece of straw hangin' out your mouth, you Mr. Green Jeans–lookin' motherfucker. . . .

"We done?" said Earl.

"You in a hurry?" said Coleman with a smile. "Got a lady waitin'?"

"What if I do?" said Earl.

Coleman's smile turned down. His voice was soft, almost tender. "Now, you gonna flex on me, old man? That's what you fixin' to do?"

"C'mon, Cherokee," said Ray. "My daddy was only kiddin' around."

Coleman didn't look at Ray. He kept his eyes on Earl. And then he smiled and clapped his hands together. "Aw, shit, Earl, that little redbone don't mean nothin' to me anymore. I done had that pussy when it was fresh. You go on and sweet-talk your little junkie all you want, hear?"

"I guess that'll do 'er," said Ray. He stood and looked at his father, who was still seated in the chair, one eyebrow cocked, his gaze on Coleman.

"Go ahead, Earl," said Coleman. "She's waitin' on you, man. Got that stall of hers all reserved. Guess she heard you was comin' into the big city today."

Earl stood.

"Now, Ray," said Coleman. "Think about what I said about that Rodriguez thing. No disrespect to my brown brothers, but maybe you ought to talk to them next time they drop off the goods, tell them straight up the way I feel."

"I hear you," said Ray.

"Good. Your money will be waiting for you back in the garage. You can pick up your guns on the way out."

"See you next time," said Ray, and he turned for the door.

"Hey, Ray," said Coleman, and when Ray looked back Coleman was standing, looking over the desk at Ray's feet. "Lizardo Rodriguez, he asked me to check and see if you was wearing those fly boots of yours today."

"Oh, yeah?"

"I see you are."

Ray's expression was confusion. He said, "Later," and he and his father walked out of the room, closing the door behind them.

Coleman and Big-Ass Angelo laughed. They laughed so hard that Coleman had to brace himself atop the desk. He had tears in his eyes and he and Angelo gave each other skin.

"Oh, shit," said Coleman. "Ray Boone, walkin' tall. Just like Buford T. Pusser, man."

"I am *hip*," said Angelo, and Coleman doubled over, stomping his foot on the floor.

A little later, Coleman said, "I got him to thinkin', though, anyway, about the Rodriguez boys, I mean."

"We lose the Rodriguez boys —"

"We'll find someone else to buy it from, black. Got a price and purity war goin' on in the business right now. It's one of those buyer's markets you hear about."

"That means we wouldn't be seein' Ray and Earl no more. Shame to lose all that entertainment. I mean, who we gonna laugh at then?"

"We'll find someone else for that, too." Coleman looked up at his lieutenant. "Angie?"

"What?"

"Crack that window, man. Smells like nicotine, beer, and 'Lectric Shave in this motherfucker."

"I heard that."

"Every time the Boones come in here, it reminds me: I just can't *stand* the way white boys smell."

Ray and Earl picked up their guns in the outer office, lit smokes outside of Coleman's building, and walked across the street. They went through a rip in the chain-link fence that surrounded the old warehouse. Yellow police tape was threaded through the links, and a piece of it blew like a kite tail in the wind.

They stepped carefully through debris, mindful of needles, and over a pile of bricks that had been the foundation of a wall but was now an opening, and then they were on the main floor of the warehouse, puddled with water leaked from pipes and rainwater, fresh from a recent storm, which came freely through the walls. There were holes in all four walls, some the product of decay, others sledge-hammered out for easy access and escape. Pigeons flew through the space, and the cement floor was littered with their droppings.

A rat scurried into a dim side room, and Ray saw a withered black face recede into the darkness. The face belonged to a junkie named Tonio Morris. He was one of the many bottom-of-the-food-chain junkies, near death and too weak to cut out a space of their own on the second floor; later, when the packets were delivered to those with cash, they'd trade anything they had, anything they'd stolen that day, or any orifice in their bodies for some rock or powder.

Ray and Earl walked past a man, one of Coleman's, who held a pistol at his side, a beeper and cell attached to his waist. The man did not look at them, and they did not acknowledge him in any way. They went up an exposed set of stairs.

At the top of the stairs they walked onto the landing of the second floor, where another armed man, as unemotional as the first, stood. Arched windows, all broken out, ran along the walls of this floor. They went through a hall;

passing candlelit rooms housing vague human shapes sprawled atop mattresses. Then they were in a kind of bathroom without walls that Ray guessed had once been men's and women's rest rooms but was now one large room of shit-stained urinals and stalls. Ray and Earl breathed through their mouths to avoid the stench of the excrement and vomit that overflowed the backed-up toilets and lay pooled on the floor.

In the doorless stalls were people smelling of perspiration and urine and wearing filthy, ill-fitting clothes. These people smiled at the Boones and greeted them, some caustically, some sarcastically, and some with genuine fondness and relief. Ray and Earl passed stalls where magazine photos of Jesus, Malcolm X, and Muhammad Ali, and Globe concert posters were taped up and smudged with blood and waste. They kept walking and at the last stall they stopped.

"Gimme some privacy, Critter," said Earl. "I'll meet you back at the stairs."

Ray nodded and watched his father enter the stall. Ray turned and walked back the way he'd come.

"Hello, young lady," said Earl, stepping into the stall and admiring the damaged, pretty thing before him.

"Hello, Earl." She was a tall girl with splotched light skin and straightened black hair that curled at its ends. Her eyes were tinted green, their lashes lined, the lids shadowed. She smiled at Earl; her teeth carried a grayish film. She wore a dirty white blouse, halfway opened to expose a lacy bra, frayed in several spots and loose across her bony chest.

Votive candles were lit in the stall, and a model's photograph, ripped from a *Vanity Fair* magazine, was taped above the commode. The bowl of the commode was filled with toilet paper, dissolved turds, and matchsticks, and brown water reached its rim.

"Got somethin' for me, Earl?" Her voice was that of a talking doll, wound down.

Earl looked her over. Goddamn if she wasn't a beautiful piece, underneath all that grime. No thing like this one had ever showed him any kind of attention, not even when he was a strapping young man.

"You know I do, honey pie." Earl produced a small wax packet of brown heroin that he had cut from the supply. She snatched the packet from his hand, making sure to smile playfully as she did.

"Thank you, lover," she said, tearing at the top of the packet and dumping its contents onto a glass paperweight she kept balanced atop a rusted toilet-roll dispenser. She tracked it out with a razor blade and did a thick line at once. And almost at once her head dropped slightly and her lids fluttered and stayed halfway raised.

"Careful not to take too much, now," said Earl. But she was already cutting another line.

When she was done, Earl gently pushed down on her shoulders, and she dropped to her knees on the wet tiles. He unzipped his fly because she was slow to do it and wrapped his fingers through the hair on the back of her head.

When he felt the wetness of her mouth and tongue, he put one hand on the steel of the stall and closed his eyes.

"Baby doll," said Earl. And then he said, "God."

Ray checked his wristwatch. Fifteen minutes had passed and still his old man had not showed. Ray was ready to leave this place, the Junkyard and the city and the trash who lived in it. He flicked the ass end of a 'Boro against the cinder-block wall and watched embers flare and die.

It disgusted him, thinking of what his daddy was doing back there with that high-yellow girl. She did have white features, but she was mud like the rest of them, you could believe that. His father and him, they disagreed on a few things, but none more than this. What was Earl thinkin', anyway? Didn't he know how that girl got to keep that stall on the end of the row? Didn't he know what a prime piece of real estate that was, what you had to do to keep it? Ray knew. If you were a man you had to fight for it, and if you were a woman . . . Girl was probably on her back or on her belly or swallowing sword ten times a day just for the right to squat in that shit hole. Didn't his father think of that?

But Ray was tired of pressin' it. Once he had made the mistake of calling that girl common nigger trash, and his father had risen up, told him to call her by her name. Hell, he could barely *remember* her name. It was Sandy Williams, somethin' like that.

Ray Boone flipped open the top of his box and shook another smoke from the deck.

Sondra *Wilson*. That's what it was.

chapter 7

TERRY Quinn was behind a display case, sitting beside the register reading a book, when he heard a car door slam. Quinn looked through the plate glass window of the store and out to the street. A middle-aged black guy was locking the door of his white Chevy. Then he was crossing Bonifant on foot and heading toward the shop.

The car looked exactly like a police vehicle, and the gray-haired, gray-bearded black guy looked like a plainclothes cop. He wore a black turtleneck under a black leather, with loose-fitting blue jeans and black oilskin work boots. It wasn't his clothes that yelled "cop," but rather the way he walked: head up, shoulders squared, alert and aware of the activity on the street. The guy had called, said he was working in a private capacity for Chris Wilson's mother, asked if Quinn would mind giving him an hour or so of his time. Quinn had appreciated the direct way he had asked the question, and he'd liked the seasoning in the man's voice. Quinn said sure, come on by.

The chime sounded over the door as the guy entered the shop. Just under six foot, one ninety, guessed Quinn. Maybe one ninety-five. All that black he was wearing, it could take off a quick five pounds to the eye. If this was the guy who had phoned, his name was Derek Strange.

"Derek Strange."

Quinn got out of his chair and took the man's outstretched hand.

"Terry Quinn."

Strange was looking down slightly on the young white man with the longish brown hair. Five nine, five nine and a half, one hundred sixty-five pounds. Medium build, green eyes, a spray of pale freckles across the bridge of his thick nose.

"Thanks for agreeing to see me." Strange drew his wallet, flipped it open, and showed Quinn his license.

"No problem."

Quinn didn't glance at the license as a gesture of trust. Also, he wanted to let Strange know that he was calm and had nothing to hide. Strange replaced his wallet in the back right pocket of his jeans.

"How'd you find me here?"

"Your place of residence is listed in the phone book. From there I talked to your landlord. The credit check on your apartment application has your place of employment."

"My landlord supposed to be giving that out?"

"Twenty-dollar bill involved, *supposed to* got nothin' to do with it."

"You know," said Quinn, "you get your hands on the transcripts of my testimony, you'll be saving yourself a whole lot of time. And maybe a few twenties, too."

"I'm gonna do that. And I've already read everything that's been written about the case in the press. But it never hurts to go over it again."

"You said you were working for Chris Wilson's mother."

"Right. Leona Wilson is retaining my services."

"You think you're gonna find something the review board overlooked?"

"This isn't about finding you guilty of anything you've already been cleared on. I'm satisfied, reading over the material, that this was just one of those accidents, bound to happen. You got two men bearing firearms, mix it up with alcohol on one side, emotion and circumstance, preconceptions on the other —"

"Preconceptions?" You mean racism, thought Quinn. Why don't you just say what you mean?

"Yeah, you know, preconceptions. You mix all those things together, you got a recipe for disaster. Gonna happen from time to time."

Quinn nodded slowly, his eyes narrowing slightly as he studied Strange.

Strange cleared his throat. "So it's more about exonerating Wilson than anything else. Wiping out the shadow that got thrown across his name, what with everything got written and broadcast about the case."

"I didn't have anything to do with that. I never talked to the press."

"I know it."

"Even his own mother should be able to see that."

Quinn spoke quietly, in a slow, gravelly way, stretching his vowels all the way out. Out-of-towners would guess that Quinn was from somewhere south of Virginia; Washingtonians like Strange knew the accent to be all D.C.

"Have you spoken with his mother?" asked Strange.

"I tried."

"She's single-minded. Probably didn't make it too easy on you."

"No. But I can understand it."

"Course you can."

"Because I'm the guy who killed her son."

"That's a fact. And she's having a little trouble getting beyond that."

"The finer points don't matter to her. All those theories you read about, whether or not I was doing my job, or if I made a bad split-second decision, or if it was the lack of training, or the Glock . . . none of that matters to her, and I can understand it. She looks at me, the only thing she sees is the guy who killed her son."

"Maybe we can just clear things up a little," said Strange. "Okay?"

"There's nothing I'd like more."

Quinn put the paperback he had been reading down on the glass top of the display case. Strange glanced at its cover. Beneath it, in the locked case, lying on a piece of red velvet, he saw several old paperbacks: a Harlan Ellison with juvenile-delinquent cover art, a Chester Himes, an *Ironside* novelization by Jim Thompson, and something called *The Burglar* by a cat named David Goodis.

Strange said, "The owner of the shop, he into crime books?"

"*She*'s into selling first editions. Paperback originals. It's not my thing. The collecting part, and also those types of books. Me, I like to read westerns."

"I can see that." Strange nodded to Quinn's book. "That one any good?"

"*Valdez Is Coming*. I'd say it's just about the best."

"I saw the movie, if I recall. It was a little disappointing. But it had Burt Lancaster in it, so I watched it through. That was a man, right there. Not known especially for his westerns, but he was in some good ones. *Vera Cruz, The Professionals* —"

"*Ulzana's Raid.*"

"Damn, you remember that one? Burt was a scout, riding with some wet-behind-the-ears cavalry officer, played by that boy was in that rat movie . . . yeah, *Ulzana's Raid,* that was a good one."

"You like westerns, huh?"

"I don't read the books, if that's what you mean. But I like the movies, yeah. And the music. The music they put in those is real nice." Strange shifted his weight. For a moment, he'd forgotten why he'd come. "Anyway."

"Yeah, anyway. Where do you want to talk?"

Strange looked over Quinn's shoulder. There were three narrow aisles of wooden, ceiling-high shelves that stretched to the back of the shop. In the far right aisle, a thin man in a textured white shirt stood on a step stool and placed books high on a shelf.

"He work here?"

"That's Lewis," said Quinn.

"Lewis. I was thinking, you had the time, maybe *Lewis* could cover the shop and we could take a drive to the spot where it went down. It would help me to see it with you there."

Quinn thought it over. He turned around and said, "Hey, Lewis!"

Lewis stepped down off the stool and walked to the front of the store, pushing his black-framed glasses up on his nose. His eyes were hugely magnified behind the thick lenses of the glasses, and his hair was black, greasy, and knotted in several spots. There were yellow stains under the arms of his white shirt. Strange could smell the man's body odor as he arrived.

"Lewis," said Quinn. "Say hello to *Detective* Strange."

Strange ignored Quinn's sarcastic tone and said, "How you doin', Lewis?"

"Detective." Lewis did not look at Strange. At least Strange didn't think he did; Lewis's eyes were as big as boccie balls, unfocused, all over the shop. Lewis fidgeted with his hands and pushed his glasses back up on his nose. It made Strange nervous to be around him, and the man smelled like dog shit, too.

"Lewis, you don't mind, me and Detective Strange are gonna go out and take a ride. Syreeta calls, you tell her I clocked out for a while. That okay by you?"

"Sure."

"Nice meeting you, Lewis."

"You, too, Detective."

Quinn snagged his leather off a coat tree behind the counter. Strange and Quinn walked from the shop.

Crossing the street, Strange said, "He blind?"

"Legally, he is. I know he can't drive a car. He says he ruined his eyes reading under the covers with a flashlight when he was a boy. Had a father who thought Lewis was unmanly or something 'cause he read books."

"Imagine him thinking that."

"Lewis is all right."

"You're a friend to him, you *ought* to tell him about these new products they got on the market, called soap and shampoo. Got this new revolutionary thing called deodorant, too."

"I've told him. So has Syreeta. But he's a good clerk. She doesn't like to work too many hours and neither do I. He's the kind of guy, *his* hours might as well be painted on the front door. Hard to find help like that today."

"What, they got him in charge of the romance books or something? He looks like he might be an expert in that department."

Quinn looked over at Strange. "You'd be surprised."

"For real?"

"I'm not saying he's a player or anything like that. He's one of those one-woman men. Matter of fact, he's been faithful to a girl named Fistina for the last twenty years."

"They say that'll make you blind, too."

"I'm not blind."

"Neither am I. But you and me, we probably practice that kind of love in moderation. I bet Lewis in there, he just wears old Fistina out."

They got into Strange's Caprice. Strange turned the ignition, and the engine came to life. He looked through the windshield at the gun shop across the street.

"Real nice how they're running that place a half mile over the District line. Makes it real convenient for those kids downtown, don't have to drive too far to buy a piece."

"They don't buy them there. Too many restrictions, and who wants a registered handgun, anyway? They just kind of road-test the floor models."

"Just as bad, you ask me."

"You're thinking like a cop," said Quinn.

"That so."

"And you're driving a cop's cruiser. What's this, a ninety?"

"Eighty-nine. Three-fifty square block with a beefed-up suspension. Thicker sway bars and a heavy-duty alternator. Not as fast as those LTIs, you know, the ninety-six with the 'Vette engine. But it moves."

"Don't your tails get burned, driving this thing?"

"Sometimes. When I'm doing a close tail I take out a rental."

"I thought you *were* a cop when you pulled up out front of the place. Not just the car — the way you moved."

"Yeah, I got made as one by this old lady yesterday down in Langdon Park. Once you put on the badge, I guess you never lose the look."

"You tellin' me —"

"Yeah," said Strange. "I was a cop and then I wasn't. Just like you."

"How long ago was that?"

"Been about thirty years since I wore the uniform. Nineteen sixty-eight."

Strange pulled down on the tree and put the Chevy in gear.

They drove south on Georgia Avenue, music playing from the deck. Just past Kansas Avenue, Strange pointed out his shop, set back off the main drag in the middle of a narrow strip.

"That's me right there," said Strange. "That's my office."

"Nice logo."

"Yeah, I like it."

"You sell magnifying glasses, too?"

"Investigations, man. Little kid sees that symbol, he knows what it means. Hell, your boy Lewis sees it, he squints real good, *he* can tell —"

"I got you." Quinn looked across the street at a bar called the Foxy Playground. "What's that, your hangout over there?"

Strange didn't answer. He turned up the volume on the deck and sang under his breath. "We both know that it's wrong, but it's much too strong, to let it go now. . . ."

"I've heard this one," said Quinn. "Guy's hammering some married lady, right?"

"It's a little more subtle than that. Mr. Billy Paul, he justified an entire career with this single right here. Glad I recorded it before I lost my album collection. Had to throw them all out after the pipes busted in my house, couple years back."

"You can buy it on CD, I bet."

"I have a player. But I like records. Was listening to this Blackbyrds tape yesterday, *Flying Start*? Thinking about the liner notes on the inner sleeve of the original record. I sure wish I had that record today." Strange smiled a little, listening to the music. "This is kind of beautiful, isn't it?"

"If you were there, I guess."

"Don't you like music?"

"When it speaks to my world. How about you? You ever listen to anything current?"

"Not really. The slow jams got to be the end-all for me. Nothin' worth listening to, you get past seventy-six, seventy-seven."

"I was eight years old in seventy-seven."

"Explains why you don't have an appreciation for this song." Strange looked across the bench. "You're a D.C. boy, right?"

"Silver Spring."

"I heard it in your voice."

"Graduate of the old Blair High School. You?"

"Roosevelt High. Grew up in this neighborhood right here. Still live in it."

Quinn looked at the blur of beer markets, liquor stores, dollar shops, barbers, dry cleaners, and chicken and Chinese grease pits as they drove south.

"My grandparents lived down this way," said Quinn. "We'd come to see them every Sunday after mass. Thirteenth and Crittenden."

"That's around the block from where I live."

"I used to play out in their alley. It always seemed, I don't know, *dark* down there."

Because of all those dark *people,* thought Strange. He said, "That's because you were off your turf."

"Yeah. It made me a little bit afraid. Afraid and excited at the same time, you know what I mean?"

"Sure."

"One day these kids came up on me while I was playing by myself."

"Black kids, right?"

"Yeah. Why you ask that?"

"Just trying to get a picture in my mind."

"So these kids came along, and the littlest one of them picked a fight with me. He was shorter than I was and lighter, too."

"It's always the littlest one wants to fight, when he's in a group. Little dude got the most to prove. You fight him?"

"Yeah. I had walked away from a fight at my elementary school earlier that year, and I'd never forgiven myself for it. Matter of fact, I still can't bear to think of it today. Funny, huh?"

"Not really. This kid in the alley, you beat him?"

"I lost. I got in a punch or two, which surprised him. But he knew how to fight and I didn't, and he put me down. I got back inside the house, I was shaking but proud, too, 'cause I didn't back down. And I saw that kid a couple of years later, the day of my grandfather's wake. He was walking by their house and stopped to talk to me. Asked me if I wanted to play some football, down by the school playground."

"And you learned?"

"What breeds respect. Not to walk away from a fight. Take a beating if you have to, but a beating's never as bad as the feeling of shame you get when you back off."

"That's your youth talking right there," said Strange. "One day you're gonna learn, it's all right to walk away."

chapter 8

Down past Howard University, at the Florida Avenue intersection, Georgia Avenue became 7th Street. They stayed on 7th and then they were in Chinatown, passing nightclubs, sports bars, and the MCI Center, which anchored the new downtown D.C. Farther along there were more nightclubs and restaurants and the short strip of the arts and gallery district, and at Quinn's direction Strange hung a left onto D Street, two blocks north of Pennsylvania Avenue. He parked the Chevy in a no-parking zone, along a yellow-painted curb, and killed the engine. Then he reached into the glove box, withdrew his voice-activated tape recorder, and placed the recorder on the seat between himself and Quinn.

"This is it," said Strange. "You were right about here?"

"Except that we parked it in the middle of the street. We came in just like this, from Seventh. My partner was driving the cruiser."

"That would be Eugene Franklin."

"Gene Franklin, right."

"What made y'all pull over?"

"We were working. We had just come off a routine

traffic stop, guy in a Maxima had blown a red up at Mount Vernon Square. Up around Seventh and N, you want the exact location."

"So you were headed south on Seventh after that, and Franklin turned left onto D. He see something, or was that just some kind of pattern?"

"No, we hadn't seen anything yet until we made the turn. This stretch of D is unlit at night, and there's hardly any activity. Pedestrian traffic, none. Sun goes down, rats stroll across the street like they own the real estate."

"What about that night? You pulled onto D, what did you see?"

Quinn squinted. "We came up on a confrontation. A curbed red Jeep, a Wrangler, parked behind a shit-box Toyota. Next to the Toyota, on the street, a guy with his knee on another guy's chest, pinning him to the asphalt. In the aggressor's hand, a pistol. An automatic, and he had the muzzle smashed up against the pinned guy's face."

"Describe this aggressor."

"Black, mid-to-late twenties, medium build, street clothes."

"And the guy he had on the ground?"

"White . . ." Quinn looked over at Strange, then away. ". . . around thirty, street clothes, slight build."

"So you and your partner, you happen on the scene of this *confrontation*. What happens then?"

Quinn breathed out slowly. "Gene says, 'Look!' But I'm ahead of him, I already got the mic in my hand. I've got it keyed and I'm calling for backup while Gene flips on the overheads and gives the horn a blast. The aggressor looks up at the whoop of the siren, and Gene stops the cruiser in the middle of the street. But our presence doesn't change the aggressor's mind."

"You got a talent for reading minds?"

"I'll put it another way. The aggressor keeps the gun on the guy he's got pinned to the ground. He's made us as cops, but it hasn't changed his focus. From my perspective it hasn't changed his intent."

"His intent being, the intent of this black aggressor, I mean, to do harm to the white guy he's got pinned down on the street."

"I saw a man holding a gun on another man in the street."

"All right, Quinn. Keep going. Where are you now? You and your partner, I mean."

"We're about twenty-five yards back from them, I'd say."

"Okay," said Strange.

Quinn rubbed his thumb over his lower lip. "I'm out of the car right away, and I can hear Gene's door swing open as I draw my weapon. So I know he's behind the driver's-side door, and I know Gene's got his own weapon cleared from his holster as well."

"You do what next?"

"I've got my gun on the aggressor. I yell for him to drop his weapon and lie facedown on the street. He yells something back. I can't really hear what he's saying, 'cause Eugene's yelling over him, telling him what I'm telling him: to drop his weapon. The lights . . . the red and blue lights from the overheads are strobing the scene, and I can hear the crackle of our radio coming from the open doors of our cruiser behind us."

"Sounds like a lot of confusion."

"Yes. Gene and I are both yelling now, and there's the lights and the radio, and the aggressor, he's yelling back at us, not moving the gun from the guy's face."

"What's Wilson — what's the *aggressor* yelling now?"

"His name," said Quinn. "His name and a number. It didn't register . . . it didn't register until later on that the number he was yelling, it was his badge number. But he never moved his gun away from the guy's face. Not until he looked at us, I mean."

Strange stared through the windshield, trying to imagine the picture the young man was painting.

"What happened when he looked at you, Quinn?"

"It was only for a moment. He looked at me and then at Gene, and something bad crossed his face. I'll never forget it. He was angry at us, at me and Gene. He was more than angry; his face changed to the face of a killer. He swung his gun in our direction then —"

"He pointed his gun at you?"

"Not directly," said Quinn, his voice growing soft. "He was swinging it, like I say. The muzzle of it swept across me, and he had that look on his face. . . . There wasn't any doubt in my mind. . . . I knew. . . . I *knew* he was going to pull the trigger. Eugene screamed my name, and I fired my weapon."

"How many times?"

"I fired three rounds."

"From where you stood?"

"They say I walked forward as I fired. That I don't remember."

"According to the articles, the trajectory of the entrance wounds and the exit pattern of the shell casings for that particular weapon were consistent with your statement. But the three casings weren't found together in a group. Apparently you moved forward and fired the third round into him when he was down. The third casing was found about ten feet from the victim."

"I don't remember moving forward," said Quinn. "I know what they said, and I know about the casings, but I don't remember. And I don't believe I shot him when he was down. He might have been *going* down, still pointing his gun —"

"Weren't you concerned with hitting the other guy?"

"At that point I was concerned primarily with the safety of myself and my partner. I've already admitted as much." Quinn glared at Strange. "Anything else?"

"Okay, Quinn. Take a deep breath and settle down."

Strange's beeper sounded. He took it from his hip and checked the readout. He said, "Excuse me, man," reaching across Quinn to unlock the glove box and withdraw his cellular phone. He punched a number into the grid and spoke into the mouthpiece.

"What's up, Ron? . . . Uh-huh." Strange frowned. "Now, you gonna ask me to do this thing for you because you're down on K Street picking up a suit? . . . Yeah, I know you can't just pick it up, you got to try it on, too. . . . Uh-huh. . . . No, it's not 'cause I buy my shit off the rack that I don't understand. . . . I do understand. . . . Believe me, it's no thing. I got no problem with it, Ron. I sound like I do? Gimme the data, man."

Strange took the information, using a pen on a cord, writing on a pad affixed to the dash. He cut the line without another word and dropped the phone in the glove box, shutting the door a little too hard.

"I got something I got to do. Man jumped bail on a B&E beef, and there's this snitch we use, been hangin' in a bar this man supposed to frequent. Turns out the bail jumper just walked into the bar."

"Who was that on the phone?"

"My operative, young man by the name of Ron Lattimer, works for me."

"You do skip-tracing, too?"

"Ron handles that. I don't like to chase people down. But Ron's busy, see, picking up a suit. So this one goes to me. Shouldn't be too serious. I've seen the sheet on this guy, and he's all of one twenty if he's a pound. It's out of my way, but you want, I'll drop you off."

"I'll ride with you," said Quinn. "You can drop me when you're done."

"Suit yourself."

"Hold up a second." Quinn put his hand on Strange's arm. "Don't think I didn't notice what you were getting at with your questions there. All that black-aggressor, white-guy, black-this, white-that bullshit. What happened that night, you can try and paint it any way you want if it makes you feel any better. But it had nothing to do with race."

"Don't tell me," said Strange. "Don't tell me, 'cause I'm a *black* man, twenty-five years your senior, and I *know*. I'm just trying to get at the truth, and if I hurt your feelings or hit a nerve somewhere along the line, so be it. I didn't drop by to see you today 'cause I was looking for a friend, Quinn. I got plenty of friends, and I don't need another. I'm just doing my job."

Strange ignitioned the Caprice, engaged the trans, and swung a ∪ in the middle of D.

"One more thing," said Quinn. "Knock off that 'Quinn' shit from here on in. Call me by my given name. It's Terry, okay?"

Strange turned right on 7th and gave the Chevy gas. He reached for the sunglasses in his visor, chuckling under his breath.

"What's so funny?"

"You got a temper on you," said Strange.

Quinn looked out the window, letting his jaw relax. "People have told me that I do."

"That story about fighting in the alley. How you were shaking, afraid and excited at the same time. You liked the action your whole life, didn't you?"

"I guess I did."

"What you ended up becoming, that's not surprising. Guy like you, I bet you always wanted to be a cop."

"That's right," said Quinn. "And I was a good one, too."

chapter **9**

T HE bar was on the end of a strip of bars off M Street in Southeast, surrounded by fenced parking lots, auto repair and body shops, and patches of dead grass. Strange parked and nodded toward the corner business, a brick, two-story, windowless structure. The sign over the door read, "Toot Sweet: Live Girls."

"Sign says they got live girls in there," said Quinn.

"That's so the fellas who like dead ones don't get disappointed once they get inside," said Strange. "Should've known from the address Ron gave me it was gonna be a titty bar."

"They got the bathhouses down here, too, I remember right."

"They got everything down here for every kind. This particular place, guys come to look at women. Wait out here, you want to."

"I like to look at women."

"Suit yourself." Strange replaced his sunglasses atop the visor. "Let me do my job, though. And stay out of my way."

* * *

Strange got some papers out of the trunk. As he turned, Quinn noticed the Leatherman, the Buck knife, and the beeper, all affixed in some way to Strange's waist.

"You got purple tights," said Quinn, "to go with that utility belt?"

"Funny," said Strange.

At the door of the club, Strange paid the cover and asked for a receipt. The doorman, a black guy who looked to Quinn like he had some Hawaiian or maybe Samoan in him, said, "We don't have receipts."

"Go ahead and create one for me," said Strange.

"Create one?"

"You know, use your imagination. We'll be over by the bar. When you get it done, drop it by."

They walked through the crowd. At first Quinn pegged it as all black, but on closer inspection he saw that it was a mix of African Americans and other nonwhites: dark-skinned Arabs and Pakis, taxi-driving types. His partner, Gene, used to call them Punjabis, and sometimes "poon-cabbies," when they rode together as cops.

The dancers, black and mixed race as well, were up on several stages around the club and stroking the steel floor-to-ceiling poles that were their props. They weren't beautiful, but they were nude above the waist, and that was enough. Men stood around the stages, beers in one hand, dollar bills in the other, and there were men drinking at tables, talking and tipping the waitresses who would soon be dancing up onstage themselves, and there were other men with their heads down, sleeping, dead drunk.

Strange and Quinn stepped up to the unkempt bar,

damp and strewn with wet bev-naps and dirty ashtrays. Smoke rose off a live cherry in the ashtray before them, and Strange butted the dying cigarette out. The bar was unventilated and smelled of nicotine and spilled beer.

"Filthy," said Strange, taking a napkin off a stack and wiping his hands. "They got a kitchen in this joint, I expect, but damn if I'd ever eat the food." He glanced over his shoulder. He was searching for one face, Quinn could tell.

Some of the black men down along the bar were looking at the two of them, not bothering to look away when Quinn eye-shot them back. Quinn knew it was unusual, and suspect, to see a black and a white together in a place like this. To the men at the bar, they were either cops or friends, maybe even faggots, the kind of friends who "played for the other team." Any way those men looked at it, the two of them together wasn't natural, or right.

The bartender was approaching, and Strange said to Quinn, "You want a beer?"

"Too early for me," said Quinn.

"Give me a ginger ale," said Strange to the bartender, who sported a damp toothpick behind his ear. "From a bottle."

"I'll have a Coke the same way."

Quinn turned and put his back against the bar. He found a dancer he could look at. He was studying her breasts, the color of them and their shape, and wondering if Juana's would look the same. He'd made out with black women but had never had one in bed, not all the way. He was going to see Juana tonight, over at her place. That would give him time to cool down; God help her if he were to run into her right now. . . .

"Your soda's up," said Strange. "Gonna ruin your eyes like that, you stare too hard. Get like your boy Lewis, have to wear those glasses like he does. What kind of girl you gonna find to give you a second look then?"

Quinn turned back and faced the bar. He had a long swig from his glass. The sound system was pumping out a Prince tune from the eighties, and Quinn tapped his fingers on the glass.

"Remember this one?" said Quinn.

"Sure. Had that little Scottish freak in the video. That girl was delicious, man."

"You like Prince? Just curious, seeing as how it's not your era and all that."

"He's all right. But he's got a little too much bitch in him, you want to know the truth."

"Hate to break it to you, but I think the little guy gets a whole lot of play."

"Maybe so, but I listen to his music, I picture the way he's licking his fingers to smooth down his eyebrows, crawling across the floor, wearing that makeup and shit . . . Can't get past it, I guess."

"Racism's bad, but that kind of ism is all right."

"Just being honest with you. You get to know me better, you'll see; I tell it straight, whether you're gonna like what I'm saying or not. All I'm saying is, your generation, y'all can deal with that homosexuality thing better than mine can."

"It's black men in general who can't deal with that homosexuality thing, you ask me. If you were really honest, you'd admit it."

"Now you're gonna tell me, *in general,* what black men can and cannot deal with." Strange looked over his shoulder again, did a double take, and said, "There's my boy. Be back in a few."

Strange found his snitch back in the hall that led to the kitchen and bathrooms, and returned ten minutes later. He told Quinn that the subject of the skip, Sherman Coles, had gone upstairs an hour earlier.

"What's upstairs?"

"Private lap dances, shit like that."

"I'll come with you. Don't worry, I'm not going to get in your way."

"Look, I'm just checking out the situation. Might not be the right time and place to try and bring him in."

"Understood." Quinn picked a piece of paper up off the bar and handed it to Strange.

"What's that?"

"Your receipt."

Strange inspected it: a playing card showing a photograph of a bare-breasted woman on its back. Across her breasts was written, "In receipt of seven-dollar cover charge, for strip bar, Toot Sweet."

"Funny boy," said Strange.

"You told him to be creative."

"My accountant's gonna like it, anyway." Strange slipped the card into his jacket. "Come April, all those hours he puts in, he needs a little something to pick up his day."

They walked up a red-carpeted set of stairs. A guy was coming down, and he moved aside to let them pass, not looking them in the eye. There was an oval spot of wetness high on the front of the man's jeans, just below the crotch.

"You see that?" said Strange, as they hit the top of the stairs. "Man must have spilled something on his self."

"Yeah," said Quinn. "His seed."

"Bible says you're not supposed to do that."

"Probably on his way to confession right now."

"I was him, I wouldn't be wearing those blue jeans into church."

Up on the second floor, the lamps were conical and dimmed, and smoke hung in their light. Another bar ran along the wall, and there were tables spread around the bulk of the room, some in darkness, some barely lit. At the tables, a few guys were getting lap-danced by girls wearing G-strings, nothing else. The girls used their crotches, breasts, and backsides to rub one off for the customers, who were sitting low in chrome-armed chairs, languid smiles on their faces. The music up here was slow and funky, heavy on the wa-wa pedal, with a deep, silky male vocal in the mix.

Strange and Quinn had a seat at an empty deuce near the bar. Strange settled into his chair and patted the table in rhythm to the music.

"This here's more like it," said Strange. "*Joy,* by Isaac Hayes. I had the vinyl on this one, too. You could hear the champagne bubbles rising when you listened to the record on a nice box. But on the CD the sound quality just doesn't make it." He nodded to a light-skinned girl, on the thin side with a man's shirt worn open over panties, who was walking toward them with a drink tray balanced on her palm. "Speaking of champagne, check this out. She's fixin' to sell us some now."

"Can I get you gentlemen a drink?" asked the girl as she arrived.

"Waitin' on a third party to join us," said Strange, who was squinting, not looking directly at the girl, looking around the room. He pulled the Coles photograph from his jacket pocket, along with the Coles papers he had taken from the file box in the trunk. He studied the photograph until the girl spoke again.

"How about a private dance?"

"Maybe later, baby."

"We've got a special on champagne."

"Later, hear?"

She gave him a look, then gave Quinn one for good measure, and walked away.

Strange said, "They're selling some bullshit off-brand, two steps down from cold duck, for fifty dollars a bottle to these poor suckers in here. Guys making minimum wage, taking home one hundred and sixty a week, come in here on a Friday night and spend it all in an hour. Walk out of here after a hard week of work with nothin' to show for it but a headache and a big old stain on the front of their drawers."

"You some kind of expert?"

Strange looked over Quinn's shoulder. "Listen, you want to pay for a lady's time, I'll take you someplace you're gonna get your money's worth. This ain't nothing but a cheap hustle they got going on right here." He stood abruptly from his chair. "Excuse me for a minute while I do my job. Looks like I located Coles."

"Need some company?"

"Been doin' this for a long time. I think I'll just go ahead and handle it myself."

"Fine. I'll be back in the bathroom, taking a leak."

Quinn watched Strange cross the room, moving around

the tables, walking toward a four-top at the edge of the darkness, where a little man in a suit and open collar sat, a long cigarette in one hand, his other hand wrapped around a snifter of something brown.

The man wants to be left alone, thought Quinn, I'll leave him alone. He got up and moved toward a dark hall, where the head was always located in a place like this.

Strange was walking toward the table where Sherman Coles was sitting, and had gotten to within a few yards of it, when another man emerged from out of the shadows. He was a very big man, with wide shoulders and hard, chiseled features. The cut of his biceps showed beneath his shiny shirt.

Strange stopped walking just as the man flanked Coles. He could have averted his eyes, kept going past the table, but they had watched his approach all the way and would say something or stop him if he tried the dodge. He knew his shot at Coles was over for today. Any way he looked at it, he was burned. It made no sense for him to turn his back on them, though, or walk past them, or anything else. He had to stop and let it play out. And he was curious to know what Coles had to say.

"You lookin' for someone, man?"

"I was," said Strange, forcing a friendly smile. "From across the room there, I thought you were this fella I knew, from back in the neighborhood where I came up."

"Oh, yeah?" Coles's tone was high and theatrical. "You got to have twenty years on me, though. So how could we have come up together? Huh?"

Strange shook his head. "We *couldn't* have, you're

right. Now that I'm up close . . . The thing of it is, I can't see too good in this low light. And don't even get me started about my failing eyes."

Coles took a sip from the snifter before him and tapped ash off his cigarette. He glanced over his shoulder to the man behind him and said, "You hear that, Richard?"

A crescent scar semicircled Richard's left eye. "Man can't see too good in this light."

"Or maybe he thinks we can't see too good," said Coles. "'Cause we did see you, sittin' over there with your Caucasian partner, lookin' at whatever it is you put back in your pocket, tryin' to make me."

"Trying to make you as what?" Strange chuckled and spread his hands. "Brother, I told you, I just mistook you for someone else."

"Oh, you *mistook* all right." Coles smiled, then dragged on his cigarette.

"Whatever you're thinking," said Strange, his voice steady, "you are wrong."

"Tell you what," said Coles, looking past Strange. "I'll just go ahead and ask the white boy. Here he comes now."

Quinn had been turned away by a sign on the men's room door that told him it was closed for repair. He was coming back down the hall when he stopped briefly to look through the crack of a partially open door. In the candlelit room, a young man in a chair was being fellated by the waitress who'd been talking to them minutes earlier. Her head was between the guy's legs, her knees sunk into orange shag carpet, and there was a bottle of bad champagne and two glasses on a small table beside them, the hustle just as Strange had described. A sculpture candle of a black couple standing up, intertwined and making love, burned on the table next to the glasses. Quinn walked on.

He came out of the hall and along the bar and saw Strange in a dark corner of the room, standing in front of the table where Coles sat. A big man stood behind the table, cracking the knuckles of one hand with the palm of the other. Quinn walked toward them.

Quinn knew Strange had warned him to stay off, and he considered this while he continued on, and then he was standing next to Strange, thinking, I'm here, I can't change that now. He spread his stance close to the table, looked down on Sherman Coles, and affected his cop posture. It was the way he used to dominate, standing outside the driver's-side window of a car he'd stopped out on the street.

"Here go your backup," said Coles. "What you think, Richard? This salt-and-pepper team we got here, they cops?"

"Look more like the Orkin army," said Richard. "What's with those jackets, huh? Those y'all's uniforms?"

Strange realized for the first time that he and Quinn were both wearing black leather. Another thing for these jokers to crack on, but he didn't care. Now that Quinn had made the mistake of joining him, he was focusing on how the two of them were going to walk away. And then he began to think about Quinn's short fuse. And Strange thought, Maybe we ought to stay.

"I don't think they're cops," said Coles.

"White boy's too short to be a cop," offered Richard.

No, I'm not, thought Quinn.

"Look more like bounty hunters to me," said Richard.

His voice was soft in a dangerous kind of way, and it was difficult to hear him over the wa-wa and bass pumping through the house system.

"Kind of what I was thinking, too, Richard." Coles looked at Strange. "That what you are, old man? A bounty hunter?"

"Like I said," said Strange, keeping his voice on the amiable side. "I thought you were someone else. I made a mistake."

"Now, why you want to lie?" said Coles.

"'Cause he scared?" said Richard. "He does look a little scared. And *white* boy looks like he's about to dirty his drawers. How about it, white boy, that so?"

"How about what?" said Quinn.

"You gonna soil your laundry, or you gonna walk away right now before you do?"

"What'd you say?" said Quinn.

"Was I stutterin'?" said Richard, his eyes bright and hard.

"Let's go," said Strange.

"Don't you know," said Richard, smiling at Quinn, "white man just *afraid* of the black man."

"Not this white man," said Quinn.

"Oh, ho-ho," said Richard, "now Little Man Tate gonna give us some of that fire-in-the-belly stuff. That's what you gonna do now, *bitch?*"

Strange tugged on Quinn's sleeve. Quinn held his ground and stared at Richard. Richard laughed.

"We're leaving now," said Strange.

"What's a matter?" said Coles, holding his wrists out and together as if he were waiting for cuffs. "Ain't you gonna take me in?"

"Maybe next time," said Strange, his tone jocular. "See you fellas later, hear?"

Coles broke the imaginary chains on his wrists, raised the snifter in a mock toast. He drank and placed the glass back down on the table.

"When your bosses or whoever ask you why you came back empty-handed," said Coles, "tell 'em you ran into Sherman Coles and his kid brother. Tell him it was us who punked you out."

Strange nodded, the light draining from his eyes.

"We told you our names, white boy," said Richard, his gaze on Quinn. "Ain't you got one?"

Strange pulled harder on Quinn's jacket. "Come on, man, let's go."

This time Quinn complied. They walked toward the stairs, the Cole brothers' laughter on Quinn's back like the stab of a knife.

At the downstairs bar, Strange signaled the bartender for his unpaid tab and yelled out over the music for the tender to bring back a receipt. Strange turned to Quinn, who stood with his back against the bar, looking out into the crowd.

"Stupid, man. What'd I tell you about interfering with my shit?"

"I wasn't thinking," said Quinn. It was the first thing he'd said since their conversation with the Coles brothers on the second floor. "What do you do now? You ever gonna take him in?"

"Oh, I'll take him in. Didn't figure on Sammy Davis Jr. havin' a baby brother looked like Dexter Manley. Gonna be real calm about it, though, and wait for the moment.

It's just work, got nothin' to do with emotion. I had the situation under control until you stepped in, tried to get all Joe Kidd on their asses. You got to learn to eat a little humble pie now and again."

"Yeah," said Quinn, watching Richard Coles come down the stairs and sidle up next to a waitress. Richard was bending forward to whisper in the girl's ear. "I've got to work on that, I guess."

"Damn right you do," said Strange, glancing back to see the subject of Quinn's attention.

Strange saw Quinn watch Richard Coles as he headed off down the hall past the end of the bar.

"Here you go, man," said Strange, paying the bartender, taking his receipt.

"Appreciate it," said the bartender, and Quinn turned and read the man's name, Dante, which was printed on a tag he wore pinned to his white shirt.

"You ready?" said Strange to Quinn.

"Gotta take a leak."

"Another one? You just ran some water through it five minutes ago."

"The upstairs head was out of order. I'll see you out at the car."

Strange said, "Right," and walked from the bar. Quinn waited until he was gone and then headed down the hall.

On his way out, Strange told the doorman he'd be right back. He walked quickly to his car and pulled a set of handcuffs and a sap from the trunk, sliding the sap into the breast pocket of his jacket, then went back into the club. He took the steps up to the second floor two at a time and moved through the table area to the four-top where Sherman Coles still sat.

Coles's eyes widened, watching Strange moving in his direction, purpose in his step. Coles's neck jerked, bird-like, as he looked around the bar, searching frantically for a familiar face.

"Right here, Sherman," said Strange, and he kicked the table into Coles, sending him to the floor in a shower of drink and live ashes.

Strange got Coles up to his feet, turned him, and yanked his arms up, forcing Coles to his knees. Strange put his own knee to Coles's back while he cuffed him, and then he pulled Coles to his feet.

Strange drew his wallet, flipped it open, and showed his license to the room in general.

"Investigator!" shouted Strange. "Don't no one inter-fere and everything's gonna be all right!"

He did this in situations like this one, and nearly every time it worked. It wasn't a lie, and to most people, "inves-tigator" meant cop. The waitresses and patrons and the men who were being lap-danced all stopped what they were doing, but no one came near him and no one inter-fered.

Strange kept his wallet open, holding it out for all to see, as he pushed Coles along toward the stairs.

"Where my brother at, man?" said Coles.

"That white man I was with, he's talking to him, I expect."

"Richard'll kill him."

"Keep walkin', man."

On the stairs, Coles lost his footing. Strange pulled him back upright with a jerk to his arms.

Coles looked over his shoulder and said, "Bounty hunter, like I thought."

"They call us bail agents now, Sherman."

"Knew you'd be back," mumbled Coles. "You had that look in your eye."

"Yeah," said Strange. "But you didn't know I'd be back so soon."

Quinn walked down the hall, shakily singing along under his breath to another Prince tune that was playing now in the main portion of the club. There were small speakers hung in the hall, but their sound was trebly, not bass heavy like out near the stages, and this thin, shrill tone made his blood jump, as did the thought of what he was about to do.

"Gonna be a beautiful night, gonna be a beautiful night. . . ."

Quinn went straight back to the end of the hall, pushed on a swinging door, and went through the frame into a fluorescent-lit, dirty kitchen. The light came up bright off the steel prep tables that were spread about the room.

"Amigo," said Quinn to a small Salvadorian with a thin mustache, wearing a stained white apron, leaning against a prep table near the back of the kitchen and smoking a cigarette.

The man said nothing and his eyes said nothing. The kitchen radio blared in the room.

"Dante sent me back here," said Quinn, shouting so the man could hear. Quinn scanned the kitchen quickly and went to where a steel tenderizing mallet lay atop an industrial microwave oven. He picked up the mallet, measured its weight in his hand, waved it stupidly, and said, "Dante needs one of these out at the bar."

The man shrugged and dragged on his cigarette, dropping the butt on the Formica at his feet and crushing it under a worn black shoe.

"I'll bring it right back," said Quinn, but he knew the man didn't care. He was only talking now to hear his own voice and to keep the adrenaline going, and he was out of the kitchen just as quickly as he'd come in.

Now he was back in the hall and walking toward the men's room. Now he was pushing on the men's room door, walking through it and into the men's room, looking at Richard Coles taking a piss at one of the stand-up urinals against the wall.

Quinn kept moving. He said, "Hey, Richard," and when Richard Coles turned his head to the side, Quinn swung the mallet fast and hard and connected its ridged surface to the bridge of Richard's nose. Richard's nose shifted to the right, and blood sprayed off in the same direction. A stream of urine swung out and splashed at Quinn's feet. Richard's legs gave out from under him, and Quinn kicked him in the groin as he hit the tiles. He kicked him in the cheekbone, and blood splattered onto the porcelain face of the urinal. Quinn heard his own grunt as he kicked Richard in the side and was about to kick him again when he saw Richard's eyes roll up into his head.

Quinn's hands were shaking. He waited for the rise and fall of Richard's chest. He said, "Terry Quinn," and he dropped the mallet to the floor.

Out in the bar there was a buzz, a sense that something had gone down. The dancers were moving on the various stages, but the patrons were turned away from them, talking among themselves.

Men moved out of Quinn's path as he walked through the club. He felt the power, and it was a familiar feeling, though he hadn't felt it for a while. It was like he was wearing the uniform again, and he knew now that this was what he had been missing for a long time. He felt *good*.

Quinn got into the passenger side of Strange's car and looked over the lip of the bench. Sherman Coles was stretched out and cuffed, lying on the backseat.

Strange nodded at the blood on Quinn's boots. "You all right?"

"Yeah."

"Where my brother at?" said Sherman from the back-seat.

Neither Quinn nor Strange answered Coles.

"How'd you know I'd walk out of there?" said Quinn.

"I didn't know," said Strange. "What I did know, you'd give me enough time."

"Where's my brother!" yelled Sherman.

Quinn said to Strange, "You always go for the light work?"

"When I can." Strange ignitioned the Chevy. "I got to get little Sherman over to Fifth Street, process the paper-work. I know you don't want to stick around for that."

"Drop me at the first Metro station you see," said Quinn. "I need to get home. I'm seein' a lady tonight."

"Yeah," said Strange, thinking of his mother. "I'm seein' one, too."

Strange pulled off the curb and drove toward M Street. He looked over at Quinn, still intense, sitting straight up in his seat, his knuckles rapping at the window.

"Gonna split the agent's fee with you on this one, Terry. How's that sound?"

"How's this sound: You and me work together on that other thing."

"Together? You're the subject of my investigation, you forget about that?"

"I didn't forget."

"Look, you got nothin' to worry about. The review committee said you were right as rain on that shooting. I got no reason to doubt it."

"Right as rain. Yeah, I remember, that's exactly what they said."

"And you couldn't get with me on this, anyway. You don't have the license to be doing the kind of work I do."

"If you're going to stay on it, I want to be involved."

Strange goosed the gas, coming out of the turn.

"Don't worry," he said. "You and me, we're not through."

chapter **10**

DEREK Strange's mother, Alethea Strange, lived in the District Convalescent Home in Ward 3, the predominantly white and wealthy section of Northwest D.C. The home, a combination hospice and nursing facility, had been operating in the city since the nineteenth century.

Strange didn't like nursing homes, for the same simple reason he didn't care for hospitals or funeral parlors. After his mother had her stroke back in '96, he had brought her to his house and hired a round-the-clock nurse, but a clot sent her back to the hospital, where the surgeons took her right leg. She had gotten around before with a walker, but now she was permanently wheelchair-bound, paralyzed on her right side, and she had previously lost most of her speech and the ability to read and write. Alethea Strange managed to tell her only living child that she wanted to go somewhere else to live out her days, with people who were sick like her. He suspected she was only asking to go away so as not to be a burden on him. Still, he granted her wish and put her in the District Convalescent Home's long-term care facility, as they accepted patients on Medicaid and there was nothing else that he could see to do.

In the lobby of the home that night, they were having some sort of event, young folks with green shirts, a church group most likely, trying to lead the elderly residents in song. There was a dining facility and a library with an aquarium in it down here, too. Alethea Strange never attended these events or sat in these rooms, and she only came down to the first level when Derek brought her down. In the spring and early summer, she would allow her son to wheel her out to the nicely landscaped courtyard, where a black squirrel, a frequent visitor to the complex, drank water while standing on the lip of the fountain. She'd sit in a block of sun, and he'd sit on a stone bench beside her, rubbing her back and sometimes holding her hand. The sight of the squirrel seemed to bring something to her day.

Strange went to the edge of the hospice at the end of a long hall and took the elevator up to the third floor. He walked through another hall painted drab beige, and as he approached the long-term wing where his mother resided he smelled the mixture of bland food, sickness, and incontinence that he had come to dread.

His mother was in her wheelchair, seated at one of three round tables in a television room where the residents could also take their meals. Next to her was another stroke victim, an Armenian man whose name Strange could never remember, and next to him was a skeletal woman in a kind of reclining wheelchair who never spoke or smiled, just stared up at the ceiling with red-rimmed, hollowed-out eyes. At the table beside them a woman fed her bib-wearing husband, and next to them a man sat sleeping before an untouched tray of food, his chin down on his chest. No one seemed to be watching the basketball contest playing on the television set, or listening to the announcer who was loudly calling the game. Strange patted the Armenian's shoulder, pulled a chair from the other side of the room, and drew it to his mother's side.

"Momma," said Strange, kissing her on the cheek and taking her hand, light and fragile as paper.

She smiled crookedly at him and slowly blinked her eyes. There was a bead of applesauce hanging on the edge of her lip, and he wiped it clean with the napkin that had fallen into her lap.

"You want a little of this tea right here?"

She pointed with a shaking hand to two sugar packets. Strange ripped the packets open and poured sugar into the plastic cup that held the tea. He stirred it and put the cup in her hand.

"Hot," she said, the *t* soft as a whisper.

"Yes, ma'am. You want some more of that meat?"

He called it "that meat" because he wasn't exactly sure if it was fowl or beef, smothered as it was in a grayish, congealed gravy.

His mother shook her head.

Strange noticed that the table beside them wobbled whenever the wife leaned on it to give her husband another forkful of food. He got up and went to a small utility room, where he knew they kept paper towels, and he folded some towels in a square and wedged the square under the foot of the table that was not touching the floor. The wife thanked Strange.

"I fixed the table," said Strange to a big attendant as he passed her on the way back to his mother. She nodded and returned to her conversation with another employee.

He knew this attendant — he knew them all, immigrants

of color, by sight. This one was on the mean side, though she was always polite in his presence. His mother had told him that this one raised her voice to her and teased her in an unkind way when she had his mother alone. Most of the staff members were competent and many were kind, but there were two or three attendants here who mistreated his mother, he knew. One of them had even stolen a present he had given her, a small bottle of perfume, off the nightstand in her room.

He knew who these attendants were and he hated them for it, but what could he do? He had made the decision long ago not to report them. He couldn't be here all that often, and there was no telling what a vindictive attendant would do in his absence. What he tried to do was, he let them know he was onto them with his eyes. And he prayed to God that the looks he gave them would give them pause the next time they had the notion to disrespect his mother in this most cowardly of ways.

"Momma," said Strange, "I had a little excitement on the job today." He told her the story of Sherman Coles and his brother, and of the young ex–police officer who had come along. He made it sound funny and unthreatening because he knew his mother worried about him and what he did for a living. Or maybe she was done worrying, thought Strange. Maybe she didn't think of him out there, could no longer picture him, or her city and its inhabitants, at all.

When he was done his mother smiled in that crooked way she had of smiling now, her lips pulled over toothless gums. Strange smiled back, not looking at the splotchy flesh or the stick arms or the atrophied legs or the flattened breasts that ended near her waist, but looking at her eyes. Because the eyes had not changed. They were deep brown and loving and beautiful, as they had always been, as they had been when he was a child, when Alethea Strange had been young and vibrant and strong.

"Room," said his mother.

"Okay, Momma."

He wheeled her back to her room, which overlooked the parking lot of a post office. He found her comb in the nightstand and drew it through her sparse white hair. She was nearly bald, and he could see raised moles and other age marks on her scalp.

"You look nice," he said when he was done.

"Son." Those eyes of hers looked up at him, and she chuckled, her sharp shoulders moving up and down in amusement.

Alethea Strange pointed to her bedroom window. Strange went to the window and looked out to its ledge. His mother loved birds; she'd always loved to watch them build their nests.

"Ain't no birds out there building nests yet, Momma," said Strange. "You're gonna have to wait for the spring."

Walking from her room, Strange stopped beside the big attendant and gave her a carnivorous smile that felt like a grimace.

"You take good care of my mother now, hear?"

Strange went toward the elevators, unclenching his jaw and breathing out slow. He began to think, as he tended to do when he left this place, of who he might call tonight. Being here, it always made him want a woman. Old age, sickness, loss, and pain . . . all of the suffering that was inevitable, you could deny its existence, for a little while anyway, when you were making love. Yeah, when you were lying with a woman, coming deep inside that sucking warmth, you could even deny death.

"You want a little more?"

"Sure."

Terry Quinn reached across the table and poured wine into Juana Burkett's glass. Juana sipped at the Spanish red and sat back in her chair.

"It's really good."

"I got it at Morris Miller's. The label on the bottle said it was bold, earthy, and satisfying."

"Good thing you protected it on your little journey."

"I was cradling it like a baby on the Metro on the way over here."

"You really ought to get a car, Tuh-ree."

"Didn't need one, up until recently. My job is close to my house, and I can take the subway downtown, I need to. But I was thinking, maybe I should get one now."

"Why now?"

"Your house is kind of a far walk from the Catholic U station."

"You're pretty sure of yourself." Juana's eyes lit with amusement. "You think I'm gonna ask you back?"

"I don't know. You keep making dinners like this one, I'm not going to wait for an invitation. I'll be whining like a dog to come in, scratching on the door out on your front porch. 'Cause you are one good cook."

"I got lucky. This was the first time I made this dish. Baby artichokes and shrimp over linguini, it just looked so good when I saw the recipe in the *Post*."

"Well, it was." Quinn pushed his empty plate aside.

"Next time I take you to dinner. A little Italian place called Vicino's on Sligo Avenue, they got a red peppers and anchovies dish to make you cry."

"That's on your street."

"We can walk to it," said Quinn. "Stay in the neighborhood, until I get my car."

Juana went to get coffee and brandy from the kitchen. Quinn got up and walked to the fireplace, where a pressed-paper log burned, colored flames rolling in a perfect arc. He picked up a CD case from a stack of them sitting on top of an amp: Luscious Jackson. Chick music, like all the rock and soul with female vocals she had been playing that night.

Juana's group house was nicer than most. Her roommates were grad students, a young married couple named James and Linda. He had met them when he'd arrived, and they were good-looking and nice and, as they had disappeared upstairs almost immediately, considerate as hell. Juana told him that James and Linda had the entire top floor of the house, and she had the finished basement for a quarter of the rent. The furnishings were secondhand but clean. Postcard-sized print reproductions of Edward Hopper, Degas, Cézanne, and Picasso paintings were framed and hung throughout the house.

Juana came out of the kitchen carrying a tray balanced on one hand. She wore a white button-down shirt out over black bells, with black waffle-heeled stacks on her feet. Black eyeliner framed her night-black eyes. She placed the tray on a small table and went around the room closing the miniblinds that hung from the windows.

"Wanna sit on the couch?"

"Okay," said Quinn.

Quinn pulled the couch close to the fire. They drank black coffee and sipped Napoleon brandy.

"I downloaded all the stories they did on you last year off the Internet," said Juana.

"Yeah?"

"Uh-huh. I read everything today." Juana looked into the fire. "The police force, it sounds like it's a mess."

"It's pretty bad."

"All those charges of police brutality. And the cops, they discharge their weapons more times in this town, per capita, than in any city in the country."

"We got more violent criminals, *per capita,* than in any city in the country, too."

"And the lack of training. That large group of recruits from back in the late eighties, the papers said that many of those people were totally, just mentally unqualified to be police officers."

"A lot of them *were* unqualified. But not all of them. I was in that group. And I had a degree in criminology. They shouldn't have hired so many so quick, but they panicked. The Feds wanted some kind of response to the crack epidemic, and putting more officers on the street was the easiest solution. Never mind that the recruits were unqualified, or that the training was deficient. Never mind that our former, pipehead mayor had virtually dismantled the police force and systematically cut its funding during his *distinguished* administration."

"You don't want to go there, do you?"

"Not really."

"But what about the guns they issued the cops?" said Juana. "They say those automatics —"

"The weapons were fine. You can't put a five-shot

thirty-eight into the hands of a cop these days and tell him to go up against citizens carrying mini TEC-nines and modified full-autos. The Glock Seventeen is a good weapon. I was comfortable with that gun, and I was a good shot. I hadn't been on the range the official number of times, but I'd take that gun regularly out to the country. . . . Listen, believe me, I was fully qualified to use it. The weapon was fine."

"I'm sorry."

"It's okay."

"You're thinking, She doesn't know what she's talking about. Now she's going to tell me about cops and what's going on out in the street."

"I wasn't thinking that at all," lied Quinn. "Anyway, we've got a new chief. Things are going to get better on the cop side of things, wait and see. It's the criminal side that I've got my doubts about."

Juana brushed her hand over Quinn's. "I didn't mean to upset you."

"You didn't upset me."

"I've never been with someone who did what you did for a living. I guess I'm trying to, I don't know, tell myself it's all right to hang out with a guy like you. I guess I'm just trying to figure you out."

"That makes two of us," said Quinn.

She moved closer to him, her shoulder touching his chest. They didn't say anything for a little while.

And then Quinn said, "I met this man today. Old guy, private investigator. Black guy, used to be a cop, long time ago. I can say that he's black, right?"

"Oh, please. You're not one of those people claims he doesn't see color, are you?"

"Well, I'm not blind."

"Thank you. I was at a dinner party once, a white girl was describing someone, and her friend said, 'You mean that black guy?' and the white girl said, 'I don't know; I don't remember what color he was.' She was saying it for my benefit, see, trying to give me the message that she wasn't 'like that.' What she didn't realize was, black people laugh at people like her, and detest people like her, as much as they do flat-out racists. At least with a racist you know where you stand. I found out later, this girl, she lived in a place where you pay a nice premium just so you and your children don't have to see people of color walking down your street."

"I hear you," said Quinn. "I used to live in the basement of this guy's house in this neighborhood, about a mile or two from where I live now."

"You mean that nuclear-free bastion of liberal ideals?"

"That one.

"A lot of the people on the street I lived on, they had bumper stickers on their cars, 'Teach Peace,' 'Celebrate Diversity,' like that. I'd see their little girls walking around with black baby dolls in their toy strollers. But come birthday time, you didn't see any black *children* at those little white girls' parties. None of those children from 'down at the apartments' nearby. These people really believed, you put a bumper sticker on your Volvo so your neighbors can see it and a black doll in your white kid's hands, that's all you have to do."

"You're gonna work up a sweat, Tuh-ree."

"Sorry." Quinn rubbed at the edge of his lip. "So anyway, I met this old *black* PI today.

"Yeah? What'd he want?"

Quinn told her about his day. When he came to the Richard Coles part, he told her that he had kept Coles "occupied" in the men's room while Strange, the old investigator, made his bust.

"You were smiling just then," said Juana, "you know it? When you were telling that story, I mean."

"I was?"

"It made you feel right, didn't it, to be back in it."

Quinn thought of the swing of the hammer, and the blood. "I guess it did."

"You like the action," said Juana. "So why'd you leave the force?"

Quinn nodded. "You're right. I liked being a cop. And I wasn't wrong on that shooting. I'd give anything to have not shot Chris Wilson, to have not taken his life. But I was not wrong. They *cleared* me, Juana. Given all the publicity, though, and some of the internal racial stuff, the accusations, I mean, that came out of it . . . I felt like the only right thing to do at the time was to walk away."

"Enough of that," said Juana, watching the frown return to Quinn's face. "I didn't mean to —"

"It's all right."

Juana turned to him and placed the flat of her hand on his chest. Quinn slipped his hand around her side.

"I guess this is it," said Quinn.

Juana laughed, her eyes black and alive. "You're shaking a little bit, you know it?"

"It's just because you're so fucking beautiful."

"Thank you." Juana brushed Quinn's hair back behind his ear. "Well, what are you going to do now?"

"Keep working at the bookstore, I guess, until I figure things out."

"I mean *right* now."

"Kiss you on the mouth?"

"For an educated guy," said Juana, "you're a little slow to read the signs."

"Thought it would be polite to ask," said Quinn.

"Ask, hell," said Juana, moving her mouth toward his. "You nearly made me beg."

chapter **11**

ENTERING his row house, Derek Strange listened to a message from Janine, asking him over for a thrown-together dinner with her and her son, Lionel. She had made "a little too much" chicken, she said, and she didn't want "all that food to go to waste."

Strange phoned a woman named Shirley whom he dated from time to time, but Shirley was either not at home or not taking calls. Strange fed Greco and walked him around the block.

When Strange returned he checked his portfolio on the Net while listening to a reissue of Elmer Bernstein's sound track to *Return of the Magnificent Seven*. He took a shower and changed into a sport jacket over an open-collared shirt. He phoned another woman and was relieved to find her line busy, as this was not a woman he was anxious to see. His stomach grumbled, and he phoned Janine.

"Baker residence."

"Derek here."

"Hello."

"Got any of that chicken left?"

"I been keeping it warm for you, Derek."

"Can I bring Greco?" asked Strange.

Janine said, "I've got a little something for him, too."

They kissed for a long time, and then Quinn removed his shirt and Juana removed hers. She began to unfasten her black brassiere.

"Can I get that?" said Quinn.

"Sure."

He had some trouble with the clasp. "Bear with me."

She ran her fingers down his veined bicep. "I thought you meant *may* I get that."

"No, I can do it. Here we go, I got it, right here." He removed her bra. She let him look at her and touch her. He kissed her shoulder blade and one of her dark nipples, and he kissed the soft flesh of her breast and tasted the salt on her skin.

"That's nice," she said.

"Christ," said Quinn.

He got out of his jeans, and when he turned back to her he saw that she was naked now, too, and they embraced atop the blanket she had thrown on the couch. He kissed her mouth and rubbed himself between her thighs, and she moaned beneath him and laughed softly and with pleasure as his fingers found her swollen spot. Her skin was a very deep brown against his pale, lightly freckled body, and he intertwined his white fingers with her brown fingers and kissed her hand.

"You know what we're doing now?" whispered Quinn.

"Celebrating diversity?"

"I like it so far."

"We're all the same," said Juana, "deep down inside."

* * *

Strange owned a '91 Cadillac Brougham V-8, full power, black over black leather with the nice chromed-up grille, that he used when he wasn't working, only for short trips around town. He drove up Georgia Avenue, listening to *World Is a Ghetto* coming from the deck. Greco sat on his right on a red pillow Strange kept for him there, his nose pressed up against the passenger-side glass.

Janine and Lionel Baker lived in Brightwood, up on 7th and Quintana, in a modest red-shingled house. Strange parked out front, got Greco out by his leash and choke chain, and walked him to the front door.

Janine, Lionel, and Strange had dinner together in a small dining room where a portrait of the Last Supper hung on one wall. Janine had given Greco the bone from a chuck roast she had cooked the week before, and the boxer had taken it down to the basement to gnaw alone.

"Pass me those mashed potatoes, young man," said Strange.

Lionel was tall like his mother, and would be handsome soon but had not yet fully grown into his large features. He held the bowl out for Strange to take.

"Thank you," said Strange, who spooned a mound onto his plate and reached for the gravy bowl.

"Where you goin' tonight, Lionel?" asked his mother.

"Got a date with this girl."

"What's her name?"

"Girl I know named Sienna."

"How you gonna take a girl out on a date when you got no car?"

"Could I get yours?"

"Lionel."

"We're goin' out with Jimmy and his girl. Jimmy's got his uncle's Lex, gold style with some fresh rims."

"Where Jimmy's uncle get the money for a Lexus?" asked Janine, her eyes finding Strange's across the table.

"I don't know," said Lionel, "but that joint is *tight*." He gave Strange a sideways glance and said, "Course, it ain't tight like no Caddy, nothin' like that."

"You don't like my ride?" said Strange.

"I like it." And Lionel smiled and sang, "Best of all, it's a Cad-i-llac."

Janine and Lionel laughed. Strange laughed a little, too.

"He's got a nice voice," said Janine, "doesn't he, Derek?"

"It's all right," said Strange. "Too bad no one sings anymore on the records, otherwise he might have a career."

"I'm gonna be a big-time lawyer, anyway," said Lionel, reaching toward the platter of fried chicken and snagging a thigh.

"Not if you don't get your grades up," said Janine.

"You over at Coolidge, right?" said Strange.

"Uh-huh. Got another year to go."

"So what movie you going to see tonight?" asked Janine.

"That new Chow Yun-Fat joint, up at the AMC in City Place."

"Say you chewin' the fat?" said Strange.

"*That's* funny," said Lionel.

Strange looked at the Tupac T-shirt Lionel was wearing, the one with the image of Shakur smoking a blunt. "None of my business, but if I had a date with a young lady, I wouldn't be wearin' a shirt with a picture of another man on the front of it."

"Oh, I'll be changing into somethin' else, Mr. Derek. Bet it." Lionel looked at the watch on his gangly wrist. "Matter of fact, I gotta bounce. Jimmy'll be here any minute to pick me up."

Lionel dropped the thigh bone and took his plate and glass and carried them off to the kitchen.

"See what I put up with?" said Janine.

"He's a good boy."

"I do love him."

"I know you do."

Janine patted Strange's hand. "Thank you for coming over tonight, Derek."

"My pleasure," said Strange.

Ten minutes later a horn sounded from outside, and they heard Lionel's heavy footsteps coming down the stairs. Strange got up from the table. He walked into the foyer and met Lionel as he was heading for the front door.

"Later, Mr. Derek."

"Hold up a second, Lionel."

Lionel looked himself over. He wore pressed jeans and a Hilfiger shirt with Timberland boots. "What, you don't like my hookup?"

"You look fine."

"Got me some brand-new Timbs."

"Sears makes a better boot for half the price."

"Ain't got that little tree on 'em, though."

"Listen up, Lionel." Strange took a breath. He wasn't all that good at this, but he knew he had to try. "Don't be drivin' around smoking herb in a fancy ride, hear?"

"Herb?" Lionel said it in a mocking way, and Strange felt his face grow hot.

"All I'm telling you is, the police see a car with young

black men inside it, 'specially a gold Lexus with fancy wheels, looks like a drug car, they don't think they need a reason to pull you over. They find blunt or cheeva or whatever you're calling it these days inside the car, you got a mark on your record you can't shake. You might as well go ahead and forget about law school then. You understand what I'm saying?"

"I hear you, Mr. Derek."

"All right." Strange reached into his back pocket and pulled a twenty from the billfold. "Here you go. You don't want to be taking out a nice girl without a little extra money in your pocket. Take her over to that TGI Friday's they got up there after the show, buy her a sundae, something like that."

"Thank you." Lionel took the money and winked. "Maybe after that sundae, she might even give me some of that trim."

Strange frowned, put his face close to the boy's, and lowered his voice. "I don't want to hear you talking like that, Lionel. You have a nice young woman, you treat her with respect. The same way you'd want a man to treat your mother, you understand me?'

"Yessir."

Strange still had his wallet out, and he pulled a condom he kept for emergencies from underneath his business cards. He handed the condom to Lionel.

"In the event something *does* happen, though . . ."

"Thank you, Mr. Derek," said Lionel, smiling stupidly as he pocketed the rubber. The horn sounded again from out on the street. "I'm ghost."

"Have a nice time."

Lionel left, and Strange locked the door behind him.

Strange walked back to the living room, wondering just how bad he'd fucked that up.

Janine was waiting for him there. She had put *Songs in the Key of Life* on the stereo and had brought out a cold bottle of Heineken and two glasses and set them on the table before the couch. Janine was sitting on the couch with her stockinged feet up on the table. Strange joined her.

"You and Lionel have a little man-to-man?"

"Uh, yeah."

"There's so much I can't give him alone."

"I'm just a man, no smarter than any other."

"But you are a man. He needs a strong male figure to guide him now and again."

Strange smiled and flexed his bicep. "You think I'm strong?"

"Go ahead, Derek."

"I don't feel too strong tonight, I can tell you that."

"That Sherman Coles pickup do you in?"

"Good thing I had that young man with me."

Janine put a pillow behind Strange's head. "Tell me about your day."

They talked about work. He told her the Coles story, and she told him how she'd taken care of some loose ends at the office. When they were done talking and the beer bottle had been emptied, they went upstairs to Janine's room.

She had turned the sheets down, and he knew she had done it for him. Her clock radio, always set on HUR, had been turned on and was softly emitting some Quiet Storm. The room was strong with the smell of her perfume, and as he undressed her, taking his time, the room grew strong with her female smell, too.

He got out of his outer clothes and stripped himself of his underwear. They were naked and they kissed standing. He got his hand on her behind and caressed her firm, ample flesh.

"*Damn,* Janine."

"What?"

"You got some back on you, girl."

"You don't like it?"

"You *know* I do."

He pushed her large breasts together and kissed them, then kissed her mouth.

"Come on," she said, short of breath.

"You in some kind of hurry?" Strange chuckled and sucked a little on her cool lips.

"Sit your ass down," said Janine.

"Here?" asked Strange, pointing to the edge of the bed.

"You said you were tired," said Janine. "Let me do the work tonight."

"Who's this right here?" said Quinn.

"Lauryn Hill," said Juana. "You like it?"

"Yeah, it's pretty nice. But you have any music with a guy singer?"

"I got the Black Album. You know, Prince. Does that count?"

"Oh, shit," laughed Quinn.

"What's so funny?"

"I already had this conversation once today."

Quinn adjusted himself. He felt his erection returning, and he moved his hips against hers. He gave her a couple of short strokes to let her know he was still alive.

"You tryin' to stay in or get out?"

"Just testing the water," said Quinn.

"The water's warm."

"Deep, too."

"Cut it out." Juana smiled. "Some guys I know, they'd be tripping over themselves right about now, trying to get out the front door."

"I'd be trippin' over somethin', I tried to leave right now."

"Stop bragging."

"Anyway, I want to stay right here."

"You tellin' me you're not the type to hit it and split?"

"I've done it; I'm not gonna lie about that. But I don't want to do that with you."

They were still on the couch. Quinn pulled an afghan up over them. The fire had weakened, and a chill had come into the room. He looked at his white skin atop her brown.

"Think we can make this work?" asked Quinn.

"Do you want it to?"

"Yes."

Strange was under the covers, lying beside Janine, when Greco walked into the room. He dropped the chuck bone at the foot of the bed, then moved it between his paws as he got himself down on the carpet.

"He's tellin' me it's time to go home."

"I wish you didn't have to," said Janine. "It's nice and warm under this blanket."

"It wouldn't be proper to have Lionel come home and know that I was here."

"He already knows, Derek."

"It wouldn't be right, just the same."

Janine got up on one elbow and ran her fingers through the short hairs on Strange's chest.

"That lawyer I do business with from time to time," said Strange. "That Fifth Streeter with the cheap suit?"

"Markowitz?" said Janine.

"Him. He owes us money, doesn't he?"

"He's got an unpaid balance, I recall."

"Give him a call tomorrow, see if he can't get us the transcripts of the review board hearings on the Quinn case."

"You want to wipe out his debt?"

"See how much it is and settle it the way you see fit."

"What's your feeling on this Quinn?"

Strange had been thinking of Terry Quinn all night. Quinn was violent, fearless, sensitive, and disturbed . . . all of those things at once. A cocktail of troubles, a guy who could come in handy in situations like they'd had today, but not the kind of guy who needed to be wearing a uniform, representing the law.

"I don't know enough about him yet," said Strange. "Next thing I'm going to do, I'm going to read those transcripts. Then I'm gonna go out and try and talk to the other players."

"You think Quinn was wrong?"

"I think he's a white man who saw a black man holding a gun on another white man in the street. He reacted the way he's been programmed to react in this society, going back to birth."

"You saying he's that way?"

"He's like most white people. Don't you know, most of

'em will tell you they don't have a racist bone in their bodies."

"They're pure of mind and heart."

"Quinn doesn't *think* he's that way," said Strange. "But he is."

chapter **12**

NESTOR Rodriguez looked in the rearview mirror and spotted the green Ford, ten car lengths back. He punched a number into the cell phone cradled beside him, then snatched the phone up as it began to ring on the other end.

"Lizardo."

"Brother."

"We're almost there. I just now called Boone and told him to pick us up."

"We have to do this every time for the midget?"

"The jerkoff doesn't want us to know where he and his father live. He insists."

"Why can't we just make the trade in the parking lot?"

"Because the little one likes to scale out the *manteca* and test it at his house, in front of us. He's afraid of being ripped off."

"Shit," said Lizardo. It sounded like "chit."

The Rodriguez brothers did not have to worry about their conversation going out over the radio waves. Nestor had paid a young software engineer in Florida to alter his and his brother's electronic serial numbers and mobile identification numbers. Also, a Secure Cellular device called a Jammer Scrambler, attached to both of their phones, altered their voices.

Nestor was traveling north on 270 in a blue Ford Contour SVT. Lizardo Rodriguez followed in a green version of the same car. There were five kilograms of Colombian brown heroin in the trunk of Nestor's Ford and five in the trunk of Lizardo's.

The Contours looked liked family sedans, but at 200 horses were hardly that. The cars did 0 to 60 in 6.9 and could top out at over 140 miles per hour. The Fords' bland body styling was perfect for their runs, but the Rodriguez brothers preferred more flash driving on the streets of Orlando, their adopted city. Nestor in particular, who was the unmarried one of the two, was in love with pretty cars. He owned a new Mustang Cobra, also an SVT. His did 60 in 5.5. He was proud that he had not touched it cosmetically, as many Spanish were prone to do, but had left it stock. Well, not all the way stock. He had put two decals, silhouettes of naked girls with white-girl hair, on the back of the car, with "Ladies Invited" spelled out between the girls in neon letters. But that was the only extra thing he had done to the car.

"Who were you talking to a few minutes ago?" said Nestor.

"My woman," said Lizardo. "Her father doesn't want to change his crops. I tried to explain to him, the cartel will provide the fertilizer and the seeds, and a guarantee that what he reaps we will sell. The poppy will give him two crops a year, twice what he'll get from his single crop of coffee beans. And we'll pay his field-workers four times what they earn to harvest the crop."

"What is the problem?"

"He is a peasant," said Lizardo. "That is the problem. He sees the American helicopters, the black Bells with the door gunners, and he is afraid. He sees me, his own son-in-law, and he is afraid. He sees his own shadow, brother, and he is afraid."

"Farmers," said Nestor with contempt.

"Yes. I'm only trying to help him, to get my woman off my back. So that maybe then she can get on *her* back, for a change."

Nestor understood why Lizardo's woman did not care to sleep with him. Lizardo was often drunk, and when he was drunk he was not a gentleman in bed. When he was so drunk that he couldn't be a man, he hit her with his fists. Nestor believed that it was sometimes necessary to strike a woman, they expected it, even, but women lost their spirit if you struck them all the time.

"Bring him to stay with you in Florida," said Nestor. "You can afford it."

"He doesn't want to come. And I don't want the filthy bastard in my house. He showers, but still he smells like the country."

"Maybe your woman's brother can help, talk to your father-in-law for you."

"The priest? Ah! He has trouble helping himself."

"Is he struggling with his vow of celibacy?"

"He was never celibate. They have a saying in the old village: All the children call the priest father, except for his own children, who call him uncle!"

Nestor and Lizardo shared hearty laughter. Then Nestor hit his turn signal and got into the right lane, making sure his brother followed.

Nestor checked his face in the rearview. His black hair

was combed back and set in place with gel, and he wore a neat Vandyke beard. He had shaved the hair that had been between his eyebrows his entire life, so that now he had two separate eyebrows. He wore two gold earrings, one small hoop in each ear. His clothing was neat but not flashy. Nestor studied the pictures in the *Esquire* and *GQ* magazines so that he could see the latest styles and the proper way to dress. Then he bought clothing that looked like it did in those pictures but without the fancy labels for which you paid extra. He shopped at the Men's Wear-house and Today's Man.

A mile down the interstate stood a strip shopping center bordering a field where houses were being constructed. The parking lot was half filled. Nestor found a row of cars with two empty spaces. He pulled into a space and watched his brother pull into the other, situated at the very end of the row. Nestor reached beneath the seat and picked up his gun, a Sig Sauer .9 that held an eight-shot magazine. He slid the Sig into a leather holster inside his jacket.

"You talk to Coleman?" said Lizardo, still holding the phone.

"Not since the last time. I'll call him from Baltimore tonight."

"Will he take the cocaine on the next run?"

"He said that he buys his cocaine from a supplier in Los Angeles and he doesn't want to change. But I told him, if he wants our *manteca,* he will have to take the cocaine. I told him that we can no longer sell one without the other. We are selling the *manteca* to the Boones for a very good price. Even with the bounce the Boones put on it, Coleman knows he cannot buy the heroin any cheaper."

"What if he refuses?"

"We'll have the Boones sell the *manteca* to someone else."

Lizardo reached across the seat, dropped the glove box door, and removed his Davis .32. It was a small gun, good at close range, and it fit neatly in the pocket of his pleated black slacks. He dropped it there and for a moment considered the situation. Nestor never asked for his business advice, but sometimes Lizardo came up with good ideas. He thought he had one now.

"Listen," said Lizardo. "We'll go back to selling Coleman direct. It'll be cheaper for him, right? Maybe that will convince him to take the coke as well."

"You forget why we got the Boones involved to begin with?"

"We didn't. Our cousin Roberto did, when he and the little one were together in the joint."

"*We* asked Roberto to find a mule for us, remember?"

"Oh, yeah."

Nestor exhaled a long breath. He had to remember to be patient with his brother, whose brain worked very slowly.

"Lizardo. Do you want to go into that lousy city, deal with the niggers directly?"

"No."

"Then we need the Boones. For now, anyway. So leave little Ray alone, understand? You are always trying to get him excited."

"Fuck," said Lizardo. It sounded like "fawk."

Edna Loomis had the Ford pickup bouncing on the gravel road, doing a real good number on the shocks but not really thinking on it, as she was in a big hurry to get on back to the house. Travis Tritt sang loudly in the cab. She had turned up the volume on the dash radio to keep herself pumped.

The night before, she had made an impression of Ray's key in some special putty she'd picked up at the hardware store, on the advice of a girlfriend of hers who loved to smoke crystal, too. This girlfriend, a big-hair girl named Johanna, got her convinced that Ray would never miss a little here and there if she was to take it, and besides, all the good stuff Edna was giving away to Ray for free, it was owed her to get some of that stash on a regular basis. Edna was Ray's woman, after all, almost a wife, and why should a wife have to ask every time she wanted to get high? After a couple of Courage and Cokes, Edna began to see Johanna's point.

So, the night before, after Ray had gone to sleep, Edna'd slipped the key off that ring of his with the chain attached to it. He woke up in the morning, the key was right where it had been when he'd hung his jeans over the bedroom chair, and Ray was none the wiser. She had taken the putty to this dude Johanna knew, and he'd fixed her up. She had a shiny new key in her pocket now.

Edna pulled the F-150 into the yard between the Taurus and Ray's Shovelhead. Ray's legs were hanging out the open door of the Taurus, his steel toolbox on the ground at his feet. He was always fooling with that car, that or the Harley. He got to his feet and stood, brushing himself off, as Edna came down out of the truck's cab.

"Thought I told you to go out to a movie or somethin'," said Ray. "You know me and Daddy got business here today."

"Forgot my tape box," said Edna. "Can't be drivin' around all day without my music."

"Well, hurry up and get it, then get gone."

"Where's Earl?"

"In the house, why you ask that?"

"No reason, just wonderin' where he was. Look, don't worry about me, you just finish up whatever it is you're doin'."

Ray got back into the car and laid himself down between the bench seat and the gas and brake pedals, wondering why women talked so much about nothin'. He was putting the trapdoor by the steering column back together, having taken it apart and oiled the movable parts. The door had been dropping slow lately, and he couldn't have that. A little WD-40 to finish the job, then put everything back in place. After that, he and his father would be ready to meet the Rodriguez brothers, out by that mall.

Edna walked through the barn to the back of it real quick, running on adrenaline. She put her new key to the lock of the steel door and smiled as the key caught and turned. She went inside the drug room without even looking over her shoulder. Johanna had been right: If you had the guts, it was easy.

She didn't throw the slide bolt on the door because that would be worse, trying to explain to Ray why she was in here behind a locked door. The other way, he just walked in on her, she wouldn't look so guilty, and anyhow, she could always use that old excuse, female curiosity.

All right now, Edna, don't you go lingerin'.

She saw the stove where Ray cooked the meth straight

away. Above it was a shelf, and on the shelf were old prescription pill bottles, amber plastic with white plastic tops, and she opened one and found spansules, Ray's personal stash. This was not what she was looking for. She opened another and found it to be filled with rocks of ice. She dumped half the rocks out into her hand and dropped them in a film canister she carried in her pocket. What, was Ray going to count every piece of ice he had? Like Johanna liked to say, I don't *think* so.

Before she left the room she had a quick look around at Ray's tools and weights. Boys' toys. She'd never complain about his liftin' weights, though. Ray was on the short side, but he did make her damp down there when he took off his shirt at night. She liked that bulldog look.

Somewhere in here was the entrance to their little tunnel, too. She'd had a good laugh with Johanna over that one, after the two of them had had way too many drinks one time at this tavern, place that had the jukebox played Whitesnake and Warrant and those other groups Johanna liked, down near Poolesville. Ray liked to try and scare her, tell her about the snakes that lived down in the tunnel, but she didn't pay him much mind. She wasn't afraid of no snakes; snakes weren't nothin' but overgrown worms. And why would she want to go down in that dirty tunnel for, anyway?

She walked out of the room as confidently as she'd gone in. No one was in the saloon area of the bar that Ray and Earl had built and decorated themselves. No one had seen a thing.

She locked the door behind her, shaking hair off her shoulders. She'd done it, and she was proud of what she'd done.

* * *

Earl Boone sat on the edge of his bed, killing off a can of Busch beer. He crushed the can in his hand, dropped it in a wastebasket, where it clanged against other empties, and went to his bedroom window. He flipped open the lid on a box of Marlboros, shook out a smoke, and drew it from the box with his lips. He lit it with a Zippo that had a raised map of Vietnam on one side and the Marine Corps insignia on the other. Below the map were the words "Paid to Kill." Every time he looked at the lighter, he recalled with some bit of fondness that he was full of piss and vinegar when he was a kid.

Edna was coming out the barn like she was on fire, walking real fast and shaking that hair and ass of hers, heading for the truck. Girl was always going fast, 'cept in the morning, when she looked like somethin' that the cat wouldn't think of dragging indoors. Now she and Ray were talking or arguing over something, he couldn't never tell which. Earl didn't understand why Ray didn't just back-hand the girl when she got to sass-talking like she was prone to do. Around other men, Ray had a temper he couldn't control, but put him near anything with a fur piece between its legs and he was tamer than a broke-dick dog.

Some men were like that, but not Earl. Back when Earl was married to Ray's mother, Margo, God have mercy on her soul, he'd shown her the back of his hand and even a fist once or twice, when she got real brave and disrespectful behind that gin she liked to drink. The gin took her liver eventually. At the end, when she was on those machines with the tubes running out her nose, waiting on a transplant, he'd almost apologized for those times he'd raised his hand to her, but it was not in his nature to do so, and the moment had passed. Hell, he knew she'd never get a liver from the start. It would go to some rich person, even if that person was below her on the list. That was the way the world worked. He'd known it from the time he'd fallen out his cradle and begun to walk on two feet.

Now Edna was driving the truck out of the yard and down the gravel road.

Earl got into his winter jacket. He put his smokes and lighter in one pocket and his .38 in the other. He picked up his six-pack cooler and turned out the lamp in his room. Looked like Ray was done tamperin' with the car, and right about now he'd be looking to move out, nervous and ready to roll. Nervous in that way he got, when somethin' was about to happen.

chapter **13**

NESTOR Rodriguez saw the Taurus enter the parking lot and snake up and down the rows of cars. Ray Boone always looked for cops and DEA types in unmarked vehicles when he pulled into the lot. Nestor had already checked and was satisfied that there was no problem, as these kinds of cars were very easy to spot. But Ray was the kind of person who needed to know this for himself.

Into the phone Nestor said, "They're here," and, still watching the Taurus in his rear- and sideview mirrors, added, "Wait until I tell you, then lock your car down and walk on over to mine."

Ray Boone parked the Taurus next to Nestor's Contour. Nestor's eyes went past the old man, unshaven and looking like a two-day drunk as usual, and on to Ray, who was seated behind the wheel. Nestor nodded to Ray as he spoke into the phone: "All right, Lizardo, come on."

"How do our friends look today?" said Lizardo.

"Don't be funny," said Nestor, smiling slightly at Ray through the window as he spoke. "The little jerkoff doesn't like your humor. We just want to do our business and get on our way. And no Spanish, Lizardo; he doesn't like that, either."

"Okay," said Lizardo. "Here I come."

Nestor cradled the phone. He didn't like the playful sound in his brother's voice. Going back to when the two of them were kids, Lizardo was always with the jokes.

Lizardo exited his car, locked it, checked the locks, and walked along the row of cars, dropping his keys in his pocket. He wore his hair in the same fashion as his brother's but did not shave between his eyebrows, leaving one long brow like a furry black caterpillar stretched out across the base of his forehead. He had a small mustache but no hair on his chin, and dressed with less regard for style than his brother. He bought his clothing at Target and Montgomery Ward. He didn't like fabrics that wrinkled and wondered why fools paid extra for fabrics that did. At home, he often slept in his clothes when he'd had too much to drink.

Nestor got out of the Contour, locked it, and met Lizardo at the back of the car. He opened the trunk and flipped over the indoor / outdoor carpet piece that normally covered a well holding the spare but that now covered five identical gym bags with Adidas logos printed on their sides. He lifted two of the gym bags out, replaced the carpet, and locked the trunk. His movements were fluid, and both he and his brother were very calm.

Nestor and Lizardo split up, Nestor going to one side of the Taurus and Lizardo going to the other, and entered the backseat of the car.

"Hello, Ray," said Nestor. "Hello, Earl."

"Ho-la, amigos," said Ray.

"How do, Earl," said Lizardo, clapping Earl on the shoulder.

"How do," said Earl. He popped the ring on a can of Busch and took a long swig.

"Lie on down back there," said Ray. "It ain't far."

They didn't protest. This small thing seemed to put Ray at ease. Nestor and Lizardo arranged themselves the way they had many times before. Nestor let his legs dangle off the bench and put his face down on the seat, and Lizardo did the same in the opposite direction. Nestor's face was inches away from Lizardo's ass.

"Here we go," said Ray, backing out of his spot.

They had been on the interstate for a mile or so when Nestor heard a kind of sharp squeak. Then came an awful, wretched smell from the seat of Lizardo's pants.

"Lizardo," said Nestor. "Please."

"I can't help it, Nestor. The *huevos rancheros* I had this morning, at the Denny's on the interstate . . ."

"You *can* help it! You're forcing it out; I can hear the sound!"

"I'm sorry," said Lizardo.

But he wasn't sorry. And he couldn't help but giggle when he heard his brother gag.

Nestor felt the car slow down and then, after a sharp turn, the gravel beneath their tires as they drove onto the Boone property. The car kept going for a while, slowly, and finally came to a stop.

"Y'all can get up," said Ray, as he killed the engine.

All of them got out of the car. The yard was cluttered with tires and oil drums, old brake pads, cinder blocks, upended logs, a rusted-out backhoe. A Prussian helmet was hung by its chin strap on the sissy bar of an old

Harley, and a plastic buck's head was nailed over the barn door. The house beside the barn was badly in need of paint. A dead plant hung from the ceiling of the porch, and the porch listed to one side.

White trash, thought Nestor. You can give them money, but money will never buy them style.

"Let's go inside," said Ray, "warm up some while we work."

They walked toward the barn. Ray checked out Nestor, holding the gym bags loosely at his side. Nestor with his shiny suit, big pads under the shoulders, and those pointed spick shoes he liked, weaved on the sides like a basket. Colder than the tits on an old sow today, and here goes Nestor, wearing shoes with holes in 'em. Ray knew Nestor liked the ladies, and he bet that this brown boy thought he looked pretty attractive, dressed the way he was. He once told Ray that the girls called him Nestor the Molester down in Florida, and he was proud of it, too. Well, maybe they went for that look down there, but up in Maryland, out here in the country? He looked pretty god-damned stupid, you asked Ray.

"Hey, Nestor," said Ray, "how much you drop on that suit, a buck?"

"Buck and a half," said Nestor defensively.

"How about it, Daddy? Think I'd look good in a suit like that?"

"Huh," grunted Earl.

It was warm inside the barn. They had a couple drinks, Ray insisting on pouring them shots of tequila, the gold kind he had sitting up on the top shelf behind the bar, to go with their beers. Earl sat with them at one of those tables with green felt on it, the type cardplayers used, while Ray went into that secret room of his to scale out the brown, make sure it weighed out to two full keys. Ray claimed to have some chemical kind of test back there he ran it through, too, though Nestor had never actually seen the kit.

Earl didn't say much while Nestor and Lizardo sipped their tequilas and beers. He smoked a cigarette and then another, nodding when Nestor tried to include him in the conversation but not giving up more than the nod or a "yep" or "uh-huh" here and there.

"Take it easy with that," said Nestor, pointing to the Cuervo bottle that Lizardo was lifting off the table and bringing to his glass.

"Just a taste," said Lizardo, pouring three fingers and setting the bottle back down on the felt.

Nestor didn't like to be around Lizardo when he drank. Liquor made his brother more stupid, and much sillier, than he already was.

In the back room, Ray broke open a spansule of meth, poured the white speckled contents onto the crook of his thumb, and snorted it all into his nose at once. He paced around the room, hungry for a smoke, his heart beating rapidly. He did a set of preacher curls, then opened the door that led to the saloon area and stuck his head out into the room.

"Nestor, Lizardo! Come on back and get your money!"

Nestor looked at Lizardo and shrugged. They got up from the table and walked to the back room. Earl butted his smoke and followed. When all of them were in the room, Ray closed the door behind them.

Nestor had been curious about the back room. He had never been asked to come inside it, but now that he was here he felt somewhat disappointed. There was a tool bench, some shotguns in a case, a setup to cook drugs, a couple of safes, a weight bench, free weights strewn about, and a stack of porno magazines on a small table near the bathroom. It looked very much like the room Nestor kept in the basement of his house.

"Everything all right?" said Nestor.

"It all checked out fine," said Ray.

"Then we'll just take our money and get on our way."

"You got the rest of the run to make, right?"

"This is our first stop, Ray, same as always."

"Must be worried about the rest of your load, settin' back there in the trunks of those cars."

"If I'm worried," said Nestor, smiling cheerfully, "then it is *my* worry."

Lizardo laughed a little. Nestor could see from the familiar glassy sheen to Lizardo's eyes that his brother was feeling the tequilas and beers.

"Somethin' funny?" said Ray.

"It's the boots, *menino*," said Lizardo, his eyes traveling down to the custom Dingos on Ray's feet.

"What's that word, *me-nino?*" said Ray.

Nestor nearly winced. *Menino* meant "little man." It was something you would call a boy.

Nestor said, "It's another word for amigo, Ray. It's like calling you a friend."

"I *like* the boots," said Lizardo. "Honest, Ray. And the heels! Tell me, where could I get some like those?"

"What for?" asked Ray suspiciously.

Lizardo grinned. "I'd like to bring a pair back for my woman."

Ray took a step forward. Earl stifled a grin.

"He don't mean nothin', Critter," said Earl. "He's just havin' a little fun with you, is all. Go on and give these boys their money."

Ray went to the tool bench, picked up the gym bags the Rodriguez brothers had brought with them, and handed them to Nestor. Nestor unzipped one bag and looked inside.

"Count it," said Ray.

"I don't need to count it," said Nestor. "We are going to be in business together for a long time."

"Hey, Ray," said Lizardo, nodding to the weight bench. "You really pick up all that yourself?"

"Damn straight," said Ray. "Two hundred and fifty pounds. I'll bench that motherfucker all day."

"Let's go, brother," said Nestor.

"What," said Ray, "you don't think I can?"

"I don't know," said Lizardo, winking at Nestor. "You look pretty strong, but . . ."

"I'll show you," said Ray. "And not just one, either. I'm gonna do a set of ten, how about that?"

Lizardo made a spreading motion with his hands. "You want to show me, man, pfft, show me."

"Jerkoffs," said Nestor, stepping between Earl and the weight bench.

Ray stripped off his flannel, leaving on only his white T-shirt. He lay back on the bench, the pad of which had the word *Brutus* spelled across it. He got a grip on the bar, took a couple of deep breaths, and pushed the bar off the towers on which it rested. He bench-pressed the barbell once, twice, three times, counting aloud the reps, veins emerging on his forehead and neck. He benched it ten times and gently returned the bar to its place on the towers.

Ray sat up, checked his arms briefly, and smiled up at Lizardo. "Now you."

"You don't think I can?"

"Now you," said Ray.

"*Vamonos,* Lizardo," said Nestor.

"Y'all ain't gonna *vamonos* nowhere until he benches this bar," said Ray. "I did it; now he's gonna do it. C'mon, Li-zardo, can't you do it?"

"I can do it," said Lizardo. "But do I have to take off my shirt?" It sounded like "chirt."

Lizardo laughed shortly and lay down on the bench. He gripped, ungripped, and regripped the bar. He took a deep breath and held it in. Ray moved behind the towers and centered himself for the spot.

"One!" shouted Lizardo, as he raised the bar. Immediately he knew that he could only do but two or three. The weight was much heavier than he had imagined it would be.

"Two!" he said, his voice weak. He barely got the bar up to where his elbows locked. He brought it down slowly to his chest, breathed in, and pushed with everything he had.

He didn't count this time. It was difficult to get the bar up at all. His arms burned and shook, and he felt his face grow hot. The bar was only halfway up and it wouldn't, couldn't go any farther. He looked up pleadingly at Ray.

"I got it," said Ray. He reached over the towers and gripped the bar, pulling it up toward him.

"You got it?" said Lizardo.

"I got it," said Ray.

Lizardo let go of the bar and allowed his hands to fall to his sides. Ray drew the bar up to the height of the towers. He looked over at his father and smiled stupidly.

"Hey, Daddy," said Ray, as he released the bar.

Lizardo screamed, watching the barbell fall. The bar crushed his Adam's apple and windpipe, and broke his neck. For a moment, but only for a moment, Lizardo saw the spray of blood that he coughed up into the room.

Nestor dropped the gym bags. His hands shook wildly as he fumbled inside his jacket for the .9.

Earl drew his .38 and shot Nestor in the back of the head. Nestor's black hair crested, a wave of crimson arcing out above it, and as he pitched forward Earl shot him between the shoulder blades. When Nestor hit the ground, his legs kicking, Earl put his palm out above the hammer of the .38 and shot Nestor once more behind his ear.

Ray laughed nervously, squinting at his father through the cordite. There was only Ray's laughter for a while, and a ringing sound in their ears.

Earl slipped the .38 back into his jacket. He checked his clothing for blowback and saw that he was clean. He was glad he'd put his palm out as a shield. He washed his hands in the sink.

"Got a smoke, Daddy?"

"Yep."

Earl shook one out for himself and one for his son. He flipped open the Zippo, thumbed the wheel, and got flame.

Earl dragged and exhaled. "You plan that?"

"Kind of came to me," said Ray, "while we were out in the saloon, havin' our drinks."

"You were plannin' it, you shoulda told me."

"Seemed like an opportunity. Coleman was havin' a problem with those boys —"

"He asked you to talk to 'em, is all." Earl hit his smoke. "Guess you better get you a shovel, Critter."

"Ground's too hard for that. I got somethin' else in mind, least until this cold spell breaks. Meantime, I got to get over to that shopping center before it empties out. Clean those trunks out and get on back."

Earl nodded and smoked.

Ray smiled. "Well, Daddy, you said you wanted out."

"Uh-huh."

"Well, we are out now, aren't we? And we are going to be rich. Ain't nothin' we can't have."

"I could use some company," said Earl, thinking of that pretty little colored junkie, down in D.C.

"A woman, you mean?"

"You don't have someone to share it with," said Earl, "all this good fortune, it just don't mean a thing."

chapter **14**

STRANGE sat in his office, reading the transcripts of the Quinn hearings, Greco asleep at his feet. A red rubber ball with rubber spikes on it rested between Greco's paws.

Strange brought the boxer in to work with him once or twice a week, when the dog begged. Earlier that morning, when Strange had headed for the front door with the car keys in his hand, Greco had looked up at him with those big browns of his and whined something fierce. Strange couldn't bear to think of the dog standing in the foyer all morning, pacing back and forth, barking at every car that slowed down or parked on the street.

He picked up his phone and hit Janine's extension.

"Yes, Derek."

"Anything on Kane's address?"

"I've got it out here. He lives with his mother, apparently."

"What about his phone number?"

"I've got that, too. But it cost us twenty dollars. I put it on your credit card."

"Damn."

"You can get anything off the Internet, for a price."

"Ron out there?"

"Uh-huh."

"What's he doin'?"

"Looks like he's reading the newspaper to me."

"I pay him to read the paper?"

"You know I don't get into your business, Derek."

"Print out a copy of that page where you gave them my Visa. I need to show it on my expense sheet."

"I already did it."

"Good. And call Lydell Blue over at the Fourth District, see if he ran a sheet for me yet on Ricky Kane."

"I'll do it."

"I'll be out in a few."

Strange finished reading the transcripts. Much of the information had been duplicated in the newspaper and television reports. He carefully read Quinn's statement and the corroborating statement of his partner, Eugene Franklin. Then he read and reread the testimony of Ricky Kane.

On the night of the shooting, Kane, a restaurant and bar worker, was driving across town after his shift at the Purple Cactus, a trendy eatery on 14th and F, when he pulled over on D Street to urinate. Kane explained that he had downed "a beer" after work, had begun to feel the effects of a weak bladder, and saw that D Street was deserted as he drove east. Standing beside the open door of his Toyota, "I pulled out my penis and prepared to urinate," when a Jeep, "the military-looking kind," came from around the corner, its brights tapped on, and stopped behind his Toyota.

The lights from the Jeep were in his eyes and blinding as Kane "tucked myself back in" and zipped up his fly. A "large black man" came through the glare of the lights and was upon him at once, yelling in an extremely agitated manner for Kane to produce a license and registration.

"What did I do?" Kane asked the black man.

"You were pissin' in the street," said the black man. "And don't even think of lyin' about it, 'cause I saw you holdin' your little pecker plain as day."

The man was broad, "like a weight lifter," and taller than Kane by a head. Later, Kane would be told that the man's name was Chris Wilson and that he was an out-of-uniform cop.

Kane said here that he detected the strong smell of alcohol on Chris Wilson's breath.

When a man had been drinking, even one beer, thought Strange, it would be difficult to smell alcohol on another man's breath. Strange made a line through this statement with a yellow accent marker.

"Who are you?" asked Kane. "Why do you need to see my license?"

"I'm a cop," replied Wilson.

Kane was frightened, but "I knew my rights." He asked to see Wilson's badge or some other form of identification, and that's when Wilson "became enraged," grabbing Kane by the lapels of his shirt and throwing him up against the car. Kane suffered severe back pain immediately, he said.

"Aw, shit," said Strange under his breath. That was for the benefit of a future lawsuit, right there. Greco opened his eyes, lifted his head up, and looked up at Strange.

Kane claimed to have "a moment or two" of blackout then. He next recalled lying on his back in the street, with Wilson crouched down upon him, one knee on his chest.

There was a gun in Wilson's hand, "an automatic, I think," and he was holding it "point-blank" in Kane's face.

Kane said that he had never known that kind of fear. Spittle had formed on the edges of Wilson's mouth, his face was "all twisted up with anger," and he was repeating, "I'm gonna kill you, motherfucker," over and over again. Kane had no doubt that Wilson would. He was "embarrassed to say" that when Chris Wilson pressed the muzzle of the gun to his cheek and rolled it there, Kane "involuntarily voided" his bowels.

Strange read the police report from the scene. Going by the statement of one officer who reported that he detected a strong fecal smell coming off him, Strange concluded that indeed, Ricky Kane had dirtied his drawers that night.

Kane said that at the point when Wilson had him pinned to the ground, a marked police cruiser pulled onto the scene. Two police officers, one black and one white, got out of the cruiser and ordered Wilson to drop his weapon. Kane's description of the events that followed were roughly in keeping with the statements made by officers Quinn and Franklin.

Strange opened his newspaper clipping file. He went to a section he had marked, an interview with Chris Wilson's girlfriend, who had been with him earlier that night. The girlfriend confirmed that Wilson had been drinking on the night of the shooting and that "he seemed upset about something." She didn't know what it was that was making him upset, and he "didn't say." He made a mental note of the girlfriend's name.

Strange dialed a number, got the person he was trying to reach on the other end. After some give and take,

he managed to make an appointment for later that afternoon. He said, "Thank you," and hung the receiver in its
cradle.

"'Scuse me, old buddy," said Strange, pulling his feet
gently from beneath Greco's head. "I gotta get to work."

Strange got into his leather. The dog followed him out
of the room.

In the outer office, Strange stopped to talk to Janine while
Greco found a spot underneath her desk.

"You talk to Lydell Blue?"

Janine Baker handed him a pink message note, ripped
off her pad. "Lydell ran Kane's name through the local
and national crime networks. Kane has no convictions, no
arrests. Never got caught with a joint in his sock. Never
got caught doing something besides what he was supposed to be doing in a public rest room. No FIs, even,
from when he was a kid. No priors whatsoever."

"Okay. Remind me to give Lydell a call, thank him."

"He said he owed *you*. Somethin' about somethin' you
did for him when the two of you were rookie cops. Good
thing you still know a few guys on the force."

"The ones who aren't dead or retired. I know a few."

"Hey, boss," said Ron Lattimer from across the room.
Ron wore a spread-collar shirt today with a solid gold
tie and deep gray slacks. His split-toe Kenneth Coles
were up on his desk, and a newspaper was open in his
hands.

"What?"

"Says here that leather of yours is out. The zipper kind,
I mean. You need to be gettin' into one of those midlength

blazers, man, with a belt, maybe, you want to be looking up-to-the-minute out there on the street."

"You readin' that article about that book came out, on black men and style?"

"Uh-huh. Called *Men of Color,* somethin' like that."

"I read the article this morning, too. That lady they got writing about fashion, she's got a funny way of putting things. Says that black men have developed a dynamic sense of style, their 'tool against being invisible.'"

"Uh-huh. Says here that we black men 'use style like a sword and shield,'" said Lattimer, reading aloud.

"*All* of us do?"

"See, now, there you go again, Derek."

"'Cause I was wonderin', that old man, practically lives out on Upshur, with the pee stains on the front of his trousers? The one gets his dinner out the Dumpster? Think he's using style as a tool against being invisible? I seen this young brother gettin' off the Metrobus yesterday out on Georgia, had on some orange warm-up suit with green stripes up the side; I wouldn't even use it to cover up Greco's droppings. And look at me, I went and forgot to shine my work boots this morning. . . ."

"I get you, man."

"I just don't like anybody, and I don't care who it is, tellin' me what black men do and don't do. 'Cause that kind of thinking is just as dangerous as that other kind of thinking, if you know what I mean. And you know some white person's gonna read that article and think, Yeah, *they* spend a lot on clothes, and yeah, *they* spend a lot on cars, but do they save money for their retirement or their children's education, or do they do this or do they do that? You know what I'm sayin'?"

"I said I heard you."

"It's just another stereotype, man. Positive as it might look on the surface, it's just another thing we've got to live with and live down."

"Damn, Derek," said Lattimer, tossing the paper on his desk. "You just get all upset behind this shit, don't you? All the article's saying is we like to look good. Ain't nothin' more sinister behind it than that."

"Derek?" said Janine.

"What is it, Janine?"

"Where are you off to now?"

"Workin' on this Chris Wilson thing. I'll be wearing my beeper, you need me." Strange turned to Lattimer. "You busy?"

"I'm working a couple of contempt skips. Child-support beefs, that kind of thing."

"Right now?"

"I was planning on easing into my day, Derek."

"Want to ride with me this morning?"

"That Chris Wilson case isn't going to pay our bills. I do a couple pickups, it helps us all."

"Like to get your thoughts on this, you have the time."

"Okay. But I got to do some real work this afternoon."

"Give Terry Quinn a call," said Strange to Janine. "The name of the shop he works in is Silver Spring Books, on Bonifant Street. Tell him I'll be by in an hour, he wants to make arrangements to take some time off."

"You're gonna let the guy you're investigating ride with you?" said Lattimer.

"I'm getting to know him like that," said Strange. "Anyway, I told him I'd keep him in the loop."

Lattimer stood, shook himself into his cashmere, and placed a fedora, dented just right, atop his head.

"Don't feed Greco again," said Strange to Janine. "I gave him a full can this morning."

"Can I give him one of those rawhide bones I keep in my desk?"

"If you'd like."

On the way out of the office, Strange looked into Janine's eyes and smiled with his. That was just another thing he liked about Janine: She was kind to his dog.

Out on Upshur, Strange nodded at the fedora on Lattimer's head.

"Nice hat," he said.

"Thank you."

"That function as a sword or a shield?"

"Keeps my head warm," said Lattimer, "you want the plain truth."

chapter **15**

STRANGE drove the Caprice into Southeast. He popped *3 + 3*, in his opinion the finest record in the Isley Brothers catalog, into the deck. Ronald Isley was singing that pretty ballad "The Highways of My Life," and Strange had the urge to sing along. But he knew Lattimer would make some kind of comment on it if he did.

"This is beautiful right here," said Strange. "Don't tell me otherwise, 'cause it's something you can't deny."

"It is pretty nice. But I like somethin's got a little more flow."

"Song has some positive lyrics to it, too. None of that boasting about beatin' up women, and none of that phony death romance."

"You know I don't listen to that bullshit, Derek. The music I roll to is hip-hop but on the jazz tip. The Roots, Black Star, like that. That other stuff you're talkin' about, it doesn't speak to me. You ask me, it ain't nothin' but the white music industry exploiting our people all over again. I can see those white record executives now, encouraging those young rappers to put more violence into their music, more disrespect for our women, all because that's what's selling records. And you know I can't get with that."

"The soul music of the sixties and seventies," said Strange. "Won't be anything to come along and replace it, you ask me."

"Can't get with that, either, Derek. I wasn't even born till nineteen seventy."

"You missed, young man. You missed."

Strange turned down 8th Street and took it to M.

"Where we headed?" said Lattimer.

"Titty bar," said Strange.

"Thank you, boss. This one of those perks you talked about when you hired me?"

"You're staying in the car. This is the place I picked up Sherman Coles for you while you were admiring yourself in a three-way mirror. I just got to ask the doorman a question or two."

"About Quinn?"

"Uh-huh."

"I heard Janine say that the man Wilson pulled that gun on, he was clean."

"Maybe he was. One thing's certain, he made out. According to the papers, the department paid him eighty thousand dollars to make him happy. For the *emotional trauma* he went through and the back injury he sustained when Wilson threw him up against the car."

"What did Wilson's mother get?"

"A hundred grand, from what I can tell."

"Cost the police department a lot to make everyone go away on that one."

"The money was never going to be enough to satisfy his mother, though."

"You can dig it, right?"

Strange thought of his brother, now thirty years gone, and a woman he'd loved deep and for real back in the early seventies.

"When you lose a loved one to violence," said Strange, "ain't no amount of money in the world gonna set things right."

"How about revenge? Does that do it, you think?"

"No," said Strange, his mind still on his brother and that girl he'd loved. "You can never trade a bad life for a good."

Strange parked on the street, alongside one of the fenced-in lots fronting the strip-bar and bathhouse district. He said to Lattimer, "Wait here."

The doorman who'd been at Toot Sweet when Strange had picked up Coles was there again today. He'd gotten his hair cut in a kind of fade, and he wore a baggy sweat-suit, which didn't do a whole lot to hide his bulk. Boy looked liked some cross of African and Asian, but Strange figured the majority of it was African, as he'd never seen any kind of Chinaman that big.

"How you doin'," said Strange.

"It's still seven dollars to get in. We ain't gone and changed the cover since the other day."

"You remember me, huh?"

"You and your friend. White boy did some damage back in the bathroom."

Strange palmed a folded ten-dollar bill into the door-man's hand. "I'm not coming in today, so that's not for the cover. That's for you."

The doorman casually looked over his shoulder, then slipped the ten in the pocket of his sweatpants. "What you want to know?"

"I was wonderin' about what happened back there in the bathroom."

"What happened? Your partner fucked that big boy *up*. Went into the kitchen and got a tenderizing mallet, then went into the bathroom and broke big boy's nose real quick. Kicked him a couple of times while he was down, too. I had to clean up the blood myself. There was plenty *of* it, too."

"What you do with the big guy?"

"One of my coworkers drove him to D.C. General and dropped him off. They got a doctor over there, this Dr. Sanders, we've seen him put together guys got torn apart in this place real nice. So we figure we put him in good hands."

"Why didn't you phone the cops?"

"The big guy didn't want us to. Right away I'm thinkin' he's got warrants out on him, right? And the management, they don't want to see any cops within a mile of this place. Not to mention, you and your buddy, I know you're not cops, but whatever the fuck your game is, you probably know enough real policemen to make it rough on the owner to keep doing business here, know what I'm sayin'? I mean, we're not stupid."

"I didn't think you were."

"Next time you bring white boy around here, though —"

"I know. Put him on a leash."

The doorman smiled and patted his pocket. "You want another receipt?"

"It's tempting," said Strange. "But I'll pass."

On the way back to the car, Strange thought, Maybe I'm giving this Terry Quinn too much credit. Sure, it could have gone down the way he said it did with Wilson. But maybe it was just that some switch got thrown, like all of a sudden the "tilt" sign flashed on inside his head. A young man with that kind of violence in him, you couldn't tell.

Quinn was shaking the shoulder of a guy called himself Moonman, sleeping by the space heater in the room at the back of the shop. Moonman's clothes were courtesy of Shepherd's Table, and he showered and ate in the new Progress Place, a shelter off Georgia, behind the pool hall and pawnshops, back along the Metro tracks. Daytime he spent out on the street. Today was a cold one, and when it got bitter like this Quinn let Moonman sleep in the science fiction room in the back.

"Hey, Moon. Wake up, buddy, you gotta get going. Syreeta's coming in, and you know she doesn't like you sleeping back here."

"All right."

Moon got himself to his feet. He hadn't been using the showers at Progress Place all that often. That bad smell of street person that was body odor and cigarettes and alcohol and rot came off him, and Quinn backed up a step as Moon got his bearings. There were crumbs of some kind and egg yolk crusted in his beard. Quinn had given him the coat he was wearing, an old charcoal REI winter number with a blue lining. It was the warmest coat Quinn had ever owned.

"Take this," said Quinn, handing him a dollar bill, enough for a cup of coffee, not enough for a drink.

"A ducat," said Moon, examining the one. "Do you know, the term refers to an actual gold coin, a type of currency formerly used in Europe? The word was appropriated as slang by twentieth-century African Americans. Over the years it's become a standard term in the Ebonic vocabulary. . . ."

"That's nice," said Quinn, gently steering Moonman out of the room toward the front door.

"I'll spend it well."

As he walked behind him, Quinn saw the paperback wedged in a back pocket of Moonman's sorry trousers. "And bring that book back when you're done."

"*The Stars My Destination,* by Bester. It's not just a book, Terry. It is a mind-blowing journey, a literary achievement of Olympian proportions. . . ."

"Bring it back when you're done."

Quinn watched Moonman walk out the front door. People in the neighborhood liked to treat Moon as their pet intellectual, speculating on how such a "mentally gifted guy" could slip through society's cracks, but Quinn didn't have any interest in listening to Moonman's ramblings. He let Moonman sleep in the back because it was cold outside, and he gave him his coat because he didn't care to see him die.

Quinn stopped by the arts and entertainment room and looked inside the open door. A middle-aged guy with dyed hair and liver lips studied a photography book called *Kids Around the World.* He faced the wall and held the book close to his chest. He had the same look as the wet-eyed fat guy who hung back in the hobbies and sports room, and the young white man with the very short hair-cut, his face pale and acned, who lingered in the military history room and stared half smiling at the photos in the Nazi-atrocity books shelved there. Quinn recognized them all: the ineffectual losers and the creeps and the pedophiles, all the friendless fucks who didn't really want to hurt anyone but who always did. Syreeta said to leave them alone, that the books were a healthy kind of outlet for their unhealthy desires, the alternative was that they would be out there on the street.

Quinn knew that they *were* out there on the street. Syreeta was all right, a good woman with good intentions, but Quinn had seen things for real and she had not. Sick motherfuckers, all of them. He'd like to get them all in one room and —

"Hey, Terry." It was Lewis, standing before him, a box of hardbacks in his arms. Lewis's eyeglasses had slipped down to the tip of his nose. "I finished racking the new vinyl. Now I've got to get these fictions shelved. You want to watch the register for me?"

"Yeah, sure."

Quinn went up to the front of the shop. He phoned Juana to confirm their date for that evening. He'd had a long phone conversation with her the previous night. He'd gotten an erection just talking to her, listening to the sound of her voice. It was driving him crazy, thinking of her eyes, her hair, those dark nipples, that warm pussy, her fine hands. It had been that way with other girls who'd turned him on, but this was *different,* yeah, he wanted to hit it, but he wanted to just *be* with her, too. He left a message on her machine.

Quinn went behind the register counter and read some

of *Desperadoes,* a western by Ron Hansen. It was one of his favorites, a classic, and he was reading it for the second time, but he found it hard to concentrate, and he set the book down. He stood and flipped through the used albums in the bins beside the register area. Another Natalie Cole had come in, along with a Brothers Johnson, a Spooky Tooth, and a Haircut 100. He picked up a record that had a bunch of seventies-looking black guys on its cover, three different pictures of them jumping around out on a landing strip. He read the title on the album and smiled.

The bell over the door chimed as Syreeta Janes walked into the shop. Syreeta was at the tail end of her forties, on the heavy side, with a nice brown freckled face, high cheekbones, and deep chestnut eyes. Half of her time was spent in the shop, the other half at book conventions or in her home office, working on her Web site, where she bought and sold rare paperbacks. She wore her usual, a vest and shirt arrangement worn out over a flowing long skirt and clogs, with a brightly colored kufi atop dreads. Lewis, in one of his less serious moments, had described her look as "Harlem by way of Takoma Park."

"Terry."

"Syreeta."

"Taking off?"

"Soon as my ride comes. I might be asking for more time off, too."

"Long as Lewis covers, I don't mind." Syreeta put her canvas bag down on the glass counter. "Don't you need the money, though?"

"My pension's keeping me flush."

Quinn looked out the window as a white Caprice pulled to the curb. He rang the register, put money in the drawer, and cradled the record he had found in the bin as he grabbed his leather off the tree.

"That your ride?"

"Yeah."

"Looks like a cop car."

"It is."

"Terry?"

"Huh."

"Smells funky in here."

"Moonman. He borrowed a paperback, too. *The Stars My Destination,* you want to knock it off the inventory."

"That's a good one."

"Olympian," said Quinn.

"You're gonna let him sleep here," said Syreeta, "spray a little Lysol through the place before I get in."

Quinn didn't hear her. He was already out the door.

chapter **16**

A FTER I went through all that trouble," said Strange, "now you're gonna tell me you can't go?"

"I apologize," said Lattimer. "I know you went and got the tickets and all that, but Cheri said she doesn't want to go to some dark auditorium and watch two men beat the fuck out of each other all night."

"That girl of yours must be special, you gonna pass up tickets to a title bout. This is a Don King production, too, ain't no thing someone's puttin' on in their basement. You should have told me she was gonna act like that before I bought the tickets, man."

"I didn't know."

Strange watched Quinn cross the street, a record under his arm. "There he is."

"What's with white boys and flannel shirts?" said Lattimer. "A chain saw come with that outfit when he bought it?"

"Everybody's got their own thing."

"He don't look all that violent to me. And he doesn't look like a cop."

"He is on the short side," said Strange. "But, trust me, he can rise up."

Quinn opened the passenger-side door and got into the backseat.

"Terry. Meet Ron Lattimer, an investigator on my staff."

"Ron, how you doin'?"

"I'm makin' out."

Quinn reached his hand over the front bench, and Lattimer shook it.

"What you got there, Terry?" said Strange.

"It's for you."

Quinn passed the Blackbyrds' *Flying Start* up to Strange. Strange smiled as he examined the cover. He opened it and studied the inner sleeve, a photo of the group in an airplane hangar.

"Damn, boy. On the Fantasy label, too. I never thought I'd see one of these again."

"It just came in today."

Strange scanned the liner notes. "Just like I remember it. These boys were students at Howard when they cut this record. They were studying under Donald Byrd, see —"

"Derek," said Lattimer, "I got things to do this afternoon."

"Yeah, okay, right." Strange put the record on the seat beside him. "Y'all hungry?"

"There's a Vietnamese around the corner," said Quinn. "The soup there rocks."

"I'm into that," said Strange.

Strange engaged the trans and pulled off the curb. He went up to Georgia, turned left at Quinn's direction, and drove south. At the stoplight he opened the record again, chuckled to himself as he checked out the period threads and oversized lids on the members of the group.

"That was real nice of you, Terry."

"I know you're not looking for any friends," said Quinn, catching Strange's eyes in the rearview. "I just thought you'd like it, that's all."

Strange, Lattimer, and Quinn got a window table at My-Le, a former beer garden, now a *pho* house on Selim. Their view gave to the traffic on Georgia Avenue and the railroad tracks beyond.

"They're doing something over there," said Quinn, nodding to the station by the tracks. A blue tarp covered the roof, and plywood boards had replaced the windows.

"Looks like they're restoring it," said Lattimer.

"Either that or tearing it down. They're always tearing down things here now."

"Get rid of all these pawnshops —"

"Yeah, and the nail and braid parlors, and the barbershops, and the cobbler and the key maker, the speed shops and auto parts stores . . . the kinds of places working people use every day. So the yuppie homeowners can brag that they've got the music-and-book superstore, and the boutique grocery store, and the Starbucks, just like their counterparts across town."

"I take it," said Strange, "you're not all the way into the revitalization of Silver Spring."

"They're erasing all of my memories," said Quinn. "And to tell you the truth, I kind of like the decay."

The lone waiter, a genial guy named Daniel who painted

houses on the side, served them their soup and fresh lemonade.

Lattimer stared into his bowl and frowned. "There's none of that bible tripe or tendon or nothin' like that in there, is it?"

"Number fifteen," said Quinn. "Nothing but eye round."

The soup was a rich mixture of rice noodles, meat, and broth, with bean sprouts, hot green pepper, lime, and fresh mint served on the side. Strange and Quinn prepared theirs and added hot garlic sauce from a squeeze bottle. Lattimer slung his tie back over his shoulder, watched them, and followed suit.

"Were you a cop, too?" asked Quinn, the fragrant steam from the soup warming his face.

"Me?" said Lattimer. "Nah."

"He didn't like the way the uniforms were cut," said Strange.

"Go ahead, Derek. I always wanted to do the kind of investigative work I'm doing right now. Never wanted to do anything else. Besides, you don't mind my sayin' so, all the problems they got on the force, I feel lucky I *didn't* join up."

"There's a helluva lot more good cops on the force than there are mediocre ones," said Quinn. "And there's not many who are plain bad. The ones who weren't ready to be out on the street, that wasn't their fault. The situation you had back then, the fish stank from the head down."

"That explain all those shootings?" said Strange.

"Firing on unarmed suspects, firing at moving vehicles . . ." said Lattimer, picking up the ball from Strange.

"Who's gonna decide whether they're armed or unarmed in the heat of the moment, when some guy's reaching into his jacket, huh?" said Quinn. "In this climate we got now, out there on the street? With all the criminals having access to guns, the attitudes, the cold-blooded murder of cops . . . it's not much of a leap to make the assumption that if you're wearing a uniform, you're in harm's way. Look, man, what I'm trying to tell you is, a lot of us out there, we were scared. Can you understand that?"

Lattimer didn't answer, but he held Quinn's gaze.

Strange broke apart his chopsticks and used them to find some eye round in the bottom of his bowl. "Like I said, that doesn't explain everything."

"It's complicated," said Quinn. "*You* know that. You were out there, Derek. You *know*."

"All right, then," said Strange. "You had a couple of brutality complaints in your file, right?" He swallowed meat and noodles and wiped a napkin across his mouth.

"That's right," said Quinn. "So did Chris Wilson. So do a lot of cops. Legitimate or no, once a complaint gets made, it stays in your file."

"What were yours about?"

"Mine were about bullshit," said Quinn. "Guy hits his head on the lip of the cruiser's back door when you're putting him in, guy claims you slapped the cuffs on him too tight . . . like that. It never goes into the report what was said to you, how many times *you're* disrespected in the course of a night."

Strange nodded. He remembered all of that very well. He remembered, too, how cops got hardened after a while, until what they saw in certain parts of town were not the citizens they had sworn to protect but potential criminals, men and women and children alike. A white cop looking at a black face, that was something further still.

"Listen," said Quinn. "You guys remember a few years back, this black cop pulled over a drunken white woman, coming out of Georgetown or somewhere like it, late one night?"

"That's the girl that cop handcuffed to a stop sign," said Lattimer, "made her sit her ass down in the cold street. Some photographer happened to be there, caught a picture of the whole thing."

"Right," said Quinn. "Now, Derek, tell me what you thought about that incident, the first time you read it."

"I know what you're gettin' at," said Strange. "That the police officer, he didn't just do that to that girl for no reason. That she must have said something to him —"

"Like what?"

"I don't know. How about, 'Get your hands off me, you black bastard,' somethin' like that."

"Or maybe she even called him a nigger," said Quinn.

Lattimer looked up from his bowl. He didn't like to hear that word coming from a white man's mouth, no matter the context.

"Maybe she did," said Strange.

"The point is, whether it happened that way or not, those kinds of conversations go on in the street every night between cops and perps and straight civilians. And what's said, it never sees the light of day."

"You goin' somewhere with this?" said Strange.

"Yeah," said Lattimer, "I was kind of wondering the same thing."

"All right," said Quinn, leaning forward, his forearms resting on the four-top. "You want to know what happened that night? As far as my role in it, it's in the transcripts and the news reports. There's nothing been left out, no secret. A man pointed a gun at me, and as a police officer, I reacted in the manner I was trained to do. In retrospect, I made the wrong decision, and it cost an innocent man his life. But only in retrospect. I didn't know that Chris Wilson was a cop."

"Go on," said Strange.

"Why was Chris Wilson holding a gun on Ricky Kane? Why did Wilson have that look of naked anger that I saw that night on his face?"

"The official line was, it was a routine stop," said Strange. "Must have just degenerated into something else."

"An off-duty cop takes the time to pull over and hassle a guy for pissin' in the street?"

"Doesn't make much sense," said Strange. "I'll give you that. But let's suppose Wilson did just pull over and decide to do his job, whether he was wearin' his uniform or not."

"We don't know what happened between Wilson and Kane," said Quinn. "We don't know what was *said*."

"We'll never know. Wilson's dead, and all we've got is Kane's version of the event. Kane's got a clean sheet. *Kane* didn't shoot Wilson, so there wasn't any reason for the inquiry to be directed toward him."

"I'm not tellin' you guys how to do your jobs," said Quinn. "But if it was me got hired to make Wilson's memorial look better, I'd start by talking to Kane."

"I plan to," said Strange.

"But Kane's got no incentive to talk to anyone," said Quinn.

"It's gonna be difficult, I know."

"And he sure as hell's not gonna talk with me around," said Quinn.

"That's not why I picked you up today."

"Yeah? Who we goin' to see?"

"Eugene Franklin," said Strange. "Your old partner. We're meetin' him in a bar in an hour or so."

Quinn nodded, then placed his napkin on the table and went to the small bathroom next to the restaurant's karaoke machine.

Lattimer drank off the remaining broth from his bowl and sat back in his chair. "You gonna drop me off at the office on the way to that bar?"

"Sure," said Strange. "What do you think?"

"The man is troubled," said Lattimer. "But what he's saying, it makes sense."

They split the check and went to the car. Driving down Georgia Avenue, they passed the Fourth District Police Station, renamed the Brian T. Gibson Building in honor of the officer who was slain in his cruiser outside the Ibex nightclub, shot three times by a sociopath with a gun. Officer Gibson left a wife and baby daughter behind.

chapter **17**

DOWN on 2nd Street, blocks away from the District
Courthouse and the FOP bar, was a saloon called Upstairs
at Erika's, located on the second floor of a converted row
house, across from the Department of Labor. The joint
had become a hangout for cops, cop groupies, U.S. mar-
shals, and local and federal prosecutors. Next door was
another bar and eatery that catered to rugby players, college kids, government workers, and defense attorneys,
most of them white. There was business enough for both
establishments to exist side by side, as the clientele at
Upstairs at Erika's was almost entirely black.

Strange got a couple of beers from the bartender, a fine
young woman favored by the low lights, tipped her, and
asked for a receipt. When she returned with it he asked
her to put some Frankie Beverly and Maze on the house
box. He'd met a woman for drinks here one night, not too
long ago, and he knew they had it behind the bar. Maze
was a D.C. favorite; though recorded years ago, you still
heard their music all over town, at clubs, weddings, and at
family reunions and picnics in Rock Creek Park.

"Which one you want to hear?" asked the bartender.

"The one got 'Southern Girl' on it."

"You got it."

He carried the two bottles of beer back toward a table set against a brick wall, where he had left Quinn. Quinn was standing and giving a hug to a black man around his age, the both of them patting each other on the back. Strange had to guess that this was Eugene Franklin.

"How you doin'?" said Strange, arriving at the table. "Derek Strange."

"Eugene Franklin." Strange shook his hand, but Franklin's grip was deliberately weak, and the smile he had been sharing with Quinn began to fade.

Franklin was the size of Strange, freshly barbered and fit but with a face with features that did not quite seem to belong together. Strange thought it was the buck teeth, pronounced enough to be near comic, and Franklin's large, liquid eyes; they did not complete the hard shell he was trying to project.

"You want a beer, somethin'?"

"I don't drink," said Franklin.

They sat down and spent an uncomfortable moment of silence. A couple of guys with the unmistakable look of cops, a combination of guard and bravado, walked by the table. One of them said hello to Franklin and then looked at Quinn.

"Terry, how you doin', man?"

"Doin' okay."

"You look good, man. Long hair and everything."

"I'm tryin'."

"All right, then. Take it light, hear?"

Strange saw the other man give Quinn a hard once-over before he and his partner walked away. He figured that Quinn still had some friends and supporters on the force and that there were others who would no longer give him the time of day.

"You gonna be all right in here?" said Strange.

"I know most of these guys," said Quinn. "It's cool."

Strange glanced around the bar. By now word had gotten around that Terry Quinn was in the place, and he noticed some curious looks and a few unfriendly stares. Maybe Strange's imagination was running wild on him. It wasn't any of his business, and he wasn't going to worry about it either way.

"You called," said Franklin, "and I'm here. Not to rush you, but I'm due for a shift and I don't have all that much time."

"Right." Strange pushed a business card across the table. As Franklin read the card, Strange said, "I appreciate you hookin' up with us."

"You said you were working for Chris Wilson's mom."

"Uh-huh. She was concerned about her son's reputation. She thought it got tarnished in the wake of the shooting."

"The newspapers and the TV," said Franklin, with a bitter shrug. "You know how they do."

"I'm just trying to clear things up. If I can take away some of that shadow that got thrown on Wilson . . . that's all I'm trying to accomplish."

"It's all in the transcripts. You're a private investigator" — Strange caught the kernel of contempt in Franklin's voice — "you ought to have a way of getting your hands on the files."

"I already have. And Terry here has given me his version of the event. You don't mind, I'd like for you to do the same."

Franklin looked at Quinn. Quinn drank off some of his beer and gave Franklin a tight nod. Strange took his voice-activated recorder from his leather, turned on the power, and set the recorder on the table.

Franklin pointed a lazy finger at the unit. "Uh-uh. Turn that bullshit off, or I walk away."

Strange made a point of pressing down on the power button but did not press it hard enough to turn it off. He slipped the recorder back into his jacket.

"All right, man," said Franklin. "Where you want me to begin?"

Strange told him, then sat back in his chair.

Their beer bottles were empty by the time Franklin was done. Strange had to smile a little, watching Franklin watch *him,* waiting for some kind of reaction or reply. Because it was almost funny how identical Franklin's account was to Quinn's. And no two recollections of a single event could be that on-the-one, that tight.

"What?" said Franklin.

"Nothin', really," said Strange. "Not that it's significant or anything like that . . . What I was wondering is, if the danger was that imminent, that clear, why didn't you fire down on Wilson, too?"

"Because Terry fired first."

"You would have shot Wilson if Terry hadn't?"

"I can't say what I *would* have done."

"But you're sayin' he was right."

"He was *all* the way right. I saw where Wilson's gun was headed. I saw in his eyes what he planned to do. There's no doubt in my mind, if Terry hadn't shot Wilson, Wilson would have shot me. You understand what I'm sayin'? No doubt at all."

Strange ran his thumb along his jawline. "You're so sure . . . and that's what's botherin' me, Eugene. See, I was at MLK, pulling up all the newspaper stories, the ones they did at the time and the follow-ups, too, and there was this one thing I read that I just can't reconcile."

"Oh, yeah? What's that?"

"After your partner left the force, you joined that group of cops, called itself the Concerned Black Officers. Y'all had flyers put up tellin' the brothers in uniform to stage a protest. I believe you signed the petition your own self, too."

Franklin's eyes flickered past Quinn's. "I did."

"If Quinn was so right —"

"Look here," said Franklin. "Terry *was* right, in that particular case. But since ninety-five, we've had three off-duty African American police officers shot by white cops. It's bad enough, the danger I put myself in every day, without having to be a target for the guys on my own team. So yeah, I was concerned. And any way, Strange, that's internal police business, understand? It is not any business of yours. It's between me and my fellow cops, and my partner."

"Your ex-partner, you mean."

Something passed between Franklin and Quinn. Strange could see that their bond was strong. Maybe it even bordered on affection. But however strong it had been, it was tainted by the shooting, and what had been ruined was most likely beyond repair.

Franklin shook his head and looked down at the table. "You're somethin', Strange."

"Just doin' my job."

"Punch out your time card, then. 'Cause I am done talkin' for today."

"Yeah, I guess we covered it for now." Strange stood from his chair. "I'll leave the two of you alone for a few minutes. This beer goes through me quick."

As Strange went along the bar toward the head, Franklin watched his walk, the hint of swagger in it, the straight shoulders and back.

"Man walks like a cop," said Franklin.

"He was one," said Quinn, "a long time ago."

"Wasn't till I saw him move," said Franklin, "that it showed."

Strange stopped at the bar to talk to a cop he knew, now retired, named Al Smith. Smith had been partnered up for years with a guy named Larry Michaels. Smith had gone gray, and his paunch told Strange that this was where he spent his days.

"I buy you one?" said Smith.

"One's my limit in the daytime, Al, and I already had it."

"Next time. And if I don't see you here, I'll see you, hear?"

Strange chuckled. Al Smith had been using the same cornball expressions for the past thirty years.

Strange nodded to a big man with a high forehead and a flat-bridged, upturned nose, sitting at the bar and smoking a thick cigar, who looked at him dead-eyed as he passed. The man didn't nod back. He moved his gaze into his beer mug, raised it, and took a deep drink. Strange noticed that the MPD T-shirt fit tightly on the man's broad chest, his bulked-up arms stretching the fabric of the sleeves.

In the bathroom, he took a leak into a stand-up urinal, singing along to "Joy and Pain" as it came trebly through small wall-mounted speakers. He zipped up and turned around as the man in the MPD T-shirt entered, tall and looking like a bear on two feet, pushing the bathroom door so hard it hit the wall.

All right, you're drunk, thought Strange. Tell the world.

"Excuse me, brother," said Strange, in a friendly way, because the man was blocking his path. "Can I get by?"

But the man didn't move or react in any way. His expression was dull, and his face was shiny with sweat. Strange was going to ask him again but decided against it. He moved around the man, his back brushing the wall in the cramped space, and went out the door.

Strange had known plenty of uniforms like this one. Guy had a day off from all the bad shit out there, and instead of relaxing, he was in a bar, wearing his MPD shirt, getting meaner with every beer and looking to start a fight. One of those cops who was carrying serious insecurities, always trying to test himself. Well, if he was wantin' to try someone, he'd have to find someone else. Strange had left all that bullshit behind a long time ago.

"How you been makin' out?" said Franklin.

"I'm doin' okay," said Quinn. "Working in a used book store over the District line. It's real . . . *quiet.*"

"Gives you time to read those cowboys-and-Indians books you like."

"I do have time."

"Seein' anyone?"

"I have a girl. You'd like her. She's nice."

"She fine, too?"

"Uh-huh."

"Dog like you. Never known you to be with an ugly one."

"No one could say the same about you."

"Go ahead and crack on me. But it's one of the reasons I stopped drinkin'. Got tired of waking up next to those *fugly*-ass girls I was meetin' in the clubs."

"Wonder how many of them stopped drinkin' when they got a look at you."

"I guess I did send a few off to church."

Franklin and Quinn shared a laugh. Franklin's odd looks had always bothered him, along with his inability to make time with attractive women. Quinn had been one of the few who could broach the subject, and joke about it, with Eugene.

Quinn looked around Erika's. He recognized Al Smith, sitting on his usual stool, and a patrolman named Effers he'd played cards with once, and an ugly, friendless cop he knew by sight only, Adonis Delgado, who was pushing away from the bar.

"You miss it," said Franklin, "don't you?"

"I do."

"Listen, Terry . . ."

"What?"

"That thing Strange was talking about, the group I joined — Concerned Black Officers, I mean."

"I knew about it already."

"Didn't have anything to do with how I felt about you, or whether you were right or wrong on the Wilson thing. You understand that, don't you?"

"Sure."

"We'd been asking for radios for off-duty officers for

years, so that if you did get into a situation when you were in street clothes, you could call it in, let the dispatcher know that you were a cop and you were on the scene."

"I know it."

"If Chris Wilson had had that radio that night, and we had known who he was when we pulled up on him, he'd be alive today."

"Y'all got your radios now. I read about it, that the issue finally went through."

"It took that last shooting, and the threat of a protest, to get it done. And Chief Ramsey, he's toughened the firearms instruction requirements, instituted retraining. Got a whole lot of new initiatives drafted, with new hiring standards on the way, too."

"You tryin' to tell me it was a good thing that Wilson died? Don't go blowin' smoke up my ass, man, 'cause I've known you too long."

"I'm tellin' you that some good came *out* of it. Whatever I thought about what happened that night, it was on me to get involved, make sure that somethin' like that couldn't happen again."

"I bet it was good for your conscience, too."

"There was that."

"Don't worry, Gene. I don't blame you for anything. I would have liked to hear from you once in a while, but I don't blame you for a thing."

"I thought about calling you," said Franklin. "And then I thought, Outside of our shift, me and Terry never hung out, anyway. I don't recall us speaking on the phone more than once or twice when we were riding together, do you?"

"You're right. We never hung out."

"We got different things. Different kinds of lives, interests, different friends. You and me used to talk about it, remember? Ain't no kind of crime for people to want to hang with their own kind."

"It's a shame," said Quinn. "But it's no crime."

"Anyway," said Franklin, "I gotta bounce."

"Go ahead. Nice seeing you, Gene. Stay away from the fuglies, hear?"

Franklin blushed. "I'm gonna try."

They stood, hugged again, and broke apart awkwardly. Franklin did not meet Quinn's eyes before walking away. Franklin passed Strange on his way back from the head but did not acknowledge him at all.

"Friendly place they got here," said Strange as he arrived at the table. "Your boy Eugene is a card-carrying member of my fan club, and some Carl Eller–lookin' sucker back in the bathroom was wantin' to take my head off."

"You know cops," said Quinn. "They like to stick to their own kind."

"I've got a couple more stops today," said Strange. "I'd take you home, but it's not on my way."

"Drop me at the Union Station Metro," said Quinn. "I'll catch the Red Line uptown."

Strange pulled the Caprice away from the curb. "*Nevada Smith* is on TNT tonight. You know that one?"

"Uh-huh. That's a good one. McQueen was the real thing."

"That's the one ends with that old guy from *Streets of San Francisco*, with the nose —"

"Karl Malden."

"Yeah, him. McQueen shoots him a couple of times,

but he doesn't kill him. Gets off of that revenge trip he's been on right there, finds his humanity, and leaves Malden in the river. McQueen's riding away on his horse, and Malden's yellin' at him to finish him off, screaming, over and over, 'You're yella. . . . you haven't got the guts!' I get the chills thinkin' about it, man."

"You gonna watch it?"

"I'm takin' a woman to the fights."

"Your girlfriend?"

"More like a friend kind of thing, the woman who runs my office, Janine Baker. I been knowin' her for a long time. Nothin' all that serious."

"Friend kind of thing's the best kind, you ask me."

"Yeah, I believe you're right. What about you?"

"I got a date myself. Girl named Juana I been seeing."

Strange looked across the bench. "Y'all got specific plans?"

"We were just going to go out, figure it out then."

"Why don't the two of you come with me and Janine? I got extra tickets, man."

"I wouldn't mind. But I have to see if Juana's into it."

"Check it out with her and give me a call. My beeper number's on that card I gave you."

"I will."

Strange turned onto North Capitol. Quinn said, "Here's good," and opened the door as Strange slowed the car to a stop.

"Hey, Terry. Thanks again for the record, man."

"My pleasure," said Quinn.

They shook hands. Quinn walked toward Union Station. Strange drove north.

chapter 18

STRANGE stood in Chris Wilson's bedroom, examining the objects on his dresser. There was a cigar box holding cuff links, a crucifix on a chain, a Mason's ring with a black onyx stone, ticket stubs from the MCI Center and RFK, and a pickup stub from Safeway. There were shoehorns and pens in a ceramic police-union mug. A small color photograph of Wilson's sister, pretty and sharply dressed, had been slipped beneath the mug. A nail clipper, a long-lensed camera, a pearl-handled knife, a bottle of CK cologne, and a crystal bowl holding matches from various bars and restaurants sat atop the dresser, as did a well-used, autographed hardball, scuffed and stained by grass and mud.

Beside the dresser mirror, hung on the wall, was a framed photograph of Chris Wilson as a boy, standing under the arm of Larry Brown, with a message from Brown and his signature scrawled across the print. Team photographs of the Redskins going back fifteen years and posters, mounted and framed cheaply, of college and professional basketball players, local boxers, and other athletes and sporting events were hung on the walls as well. The room reflected an unsurprising blend of boy and man.

"I've left it exactly as it was," said Leona Wilson, standing behind Strange. "He was so proud of that picture we took with Larry Brown."

"I've got a signed photo of Larry myself," said Strange. "Proud to have mine, too."

"I remember one time I was straightening the picture, and Chris walked in and just got so upset, told me to leave it alone. Of course, he hardly ever raised his voice to me."

"Some things special to a man might seem trivial to others. I got this Redskins figure on my desk, got a spring for a neck —"

"Chris grew up in this room. He never lived anywhere else. I suppose if he had moved out and gotten his own place, his new room wouldn't have looked like this. He kept it much the same way as he did when he was a boy."

"Yes, ma'am."

"I never asked him to stay, Mr. Strange. After his father died, he took it upon himself to become the man of the house. He felt it was his role, to take care of me and his sister. I never asked him to do that. He took it upon himself."

Strange looked around the room. "Chris keep any kind of journals? He keep a diary, anything like that?"

"Not that I'm aware of."

"You don't mind, I'd like to take these matchbooks from this bowl here. I'll return them, and anything else I take."

Leona Wilson nodded and wrung her hands.

"Chris had a girlfriend at the time of his death, didn't he?" said Strange. "I'm talking about the one gave the statement to the newspapers."

"That's right."

"Think it would be possible to talk to her?"

"She's been wonderful. She has dinner with me once or twice a month. She and her little girl, a lovely child she had before she met Chris. I'll call her if you'd like."

"I would. Like to meet with her as soon as possible, matter of fact. And I'd like to speak to your daughter, too."

Leona lowered her eyes.

"Mrs. Wilson?"

"Yes."

"Do you know how I can get ahold of your daughter?"

"I don't." Leona shook her head. "We lost her to drugs, Mr. Strange."

"What happened?"

"How can anyone know? She was in college out at Bowie State and working as a hostess in a restaurant downtown. She was a beautiful girl. She was doing so well."

"She was living here then?"

"Sondra had gotten her own place, and that's when we began to lose touch. Chris and I saw her less and less frequently, and when we did see her . . . she had changed, physically, I mean, but also her attitude. I didn't recognize her, couldn't confide in her the way I always could before. It was Chris who finally sat me down and told me what was wrong. I didn't believe it at first. We were so watchful of her during her high school years, and she had gotten through them fine. After she got in trouble, it was as if she had forgotten everything she had learned, here at home and in church. I didn't understand. I still don't understand.

"The day of the funeral, she showed up at the cemetery. I hadn't seen her for a month or so. Her phone had been disconnected, and she had been fired from her job. She had dropped out of college, too."

"If you hadn't seen her, then how did you know all of those events had taken place?"

"Chris knew."

"He was in contact with her?"

"I don't know how he knew. He was close to her. . . . He was very upset, Mr. Strange. But in the end, even he had lost track of her. We didn't know if she had a roof over her head, if she was eating, where she lived, where she slept. We didn't know if she was living or dead."

"So she was at the funeral."

"She looked barely alive that day. Her eyes, even her steps were without life. I hadn't seen her for so long. I haven't seen her since."

"I'm sorry."

"If Chris were here, he'd find her." Tears broke and ran down Leona's sunken cheeks. "Excuse me, Mr. Strange."

She turned and walked quickly from the room.

Strange did not follow. After a while he heard her talking on the living room phone. He went to the dresser and emptied the crystal bowl of matchbooks, transferring them into the pockets of his leather. He slid the photograph of Sondra Wilson out from beneath the mug and placed it in his wallet. He paced the room. He sat on Chris Wilson's bed and looked out the window.

Strange could imagine Wilson as a boy, waking up in this room, hearing the songbirds, recognizing the bark of the same dogs every morning. Looking out that same window and dreaming about catching the winning pass, knocking one out of the ballpark with the bases full, a pretty girl he sat near in class. Smelling breakfast cooking, maybe hearing his mother humming a tune in the kitchen as she prepared it, waiting for her to poke her head through the door, tell him it was time to get up and off to school.

Strange heard Leona Wilson's sobs from out in the living room. Trying to stifle it, then crying full on.

"You all right, Derek," said Strange under his breath, feeling useless and angry at himself for having given the Wilson woman false hope.

He walked out to the living room and stood beside her where she sat on the couch, clutching a cloth handkerchief. Strange put a hand on her bony shoulder.

"It's so hard," she said, almost a whisper. "So hard."

"Yes, ma'am," said Strange.

She wiped her face and looked up at him with red-rimmed eyes. "Have you made any progress?"

"I'll have a report for you very soon."

Leona handed Strange a slip of paper off the coffee table. "Here's Renee's address. She's going to pick her daughter up at day care, but she'll be home soon. She'll see you if you'd like."

"Thank you," said Strange.

He patted her shoulder impotently again and walked away.

"Will I see you in church this Sunday, Mr. Strange?"

"I hope to be there," said Strange, keeping his pace.

He couldn't get through the door fast enough. Out on the sidewalk, he stood for a moment and breathed fresh air.

Renee Austin lived in a garden apartment complex set behind a shopping center in the Maryland suburbs, out Route 29 and off Cherry Hill Road. Strange waited in the parking lot, listening to an old Harold Melvin and the

Blue Notes, as Renee had not yet returned from picking up her daughter. Strange was singing along to "Pretty Flower," closing his eyes and trying to mimic Teddy's growl, when Renee's red Civic pulled into the lot.

They sat at her kitchen table, drinking instant coffee. Renee's daughter, a darling little three-year-old named Kia, sat on the linoleum floor. Kia had a dark-skinned doll in one hand and a freckly faced, cartoonish-looking white baby in the other, and she was pressing their faces together, loudly going, "Mmm, mmm, mmm."

"Honey," said Renee, "hush, please. We are trying to talk, and it's hard to hear ourselves with those sounds you're makin'."

"Rugrat kissing Groovy Girl, Momma!" said Kia.

"Yes, baby," said Renee. "I know."

Renee was a good-looking, dark-skinned young woman with long painted nails and a sculpted, lean face. Her hair had been chemically relaxed and she wore it in a shoulder-length, fashionable cut. She worked as an administrative assistant for an accounting firm on Connecticut and L, and she stayed there, she said, not for pay or opportunities but for the firm's flexible schedule, which allowed her more time with Kia.

She was a tired-looking twenty-one. Renee told Strange that she had planned to register for community college courses but that Kia's arrival and the father's subsequent departure had dimmed those plans. Strange noticed all the toys, televisions, and stereo equipment spread about the apartment, and Renee's Honda had looked brand-new. He wondered how far she was overextended, if she had dug a credit hole so deep that she couldn't even see the light from where she stood.

"Maybe when she gets into a full day of school," said Strange, "you can go after that college degree."

"Maybe," said Renee, her voice trailing off, both of them knowing that it would never happen that way.

Renee talked about Chris Wilson, how they had met, what kind of man he was. How he had been "a better father" to Kia than Kia's own blood had been.

"How about when he drank?" said Strange. "Was he good to her then?"

"Chris hardly drank more than one, maybe two beers at a time. When I first met him, he barely drank at all."

"What about the night he was killed?"

Renee nodded, looking into her coffee mug. "He had been drinking pretty heavy, here at the apartment, earlier that night. He had gone through, I don't know, maybe a six-pack over the course of the night."

"Unusual for him, right?"

"Yes. But the last few weeks before he died, he was drinking more and more."

"Any idea why?"

"He was upset."

"And he was upset the night he was killed, wasn't he?"

"Yes."

"Over what?"

"I don't know."

Renee bent forward from her seat and handed Kia a Barbie doll she had dropped. Then Renee sat up straight and sipped at her coffee.

"Renee?"

"Huh."

"What was Chris upset over? You told the news people you didn't know. But you *do* know, don't you?"

"What difference would it have made to talk about it? It didn't have nothin', *anything* to do with his death. It was family business, Mr. Strange."

"And here I am, only tryin' to help the family. Chris's mother hired me. Chris's mother sent me *over* here, Renee."

Renee looked away. She looked up at the clock on the wall and down at her daughter and around the room.

"Was it about his sister, Sondra?" said Strange.

She nodded hesitantly.

"Had he been in contact with her?"

"I don't know." Renee met his eyes. "I'm not lyin'; I do not know."

"Go on."

"After Sondra lost her job and her place, Chris got more and more distant. He was trying to find her, and do his job as a policeman, and make time for his mother, and me and Kia. . . . It got to be too much for him, I guess. And I learned not to ask too many questions about Sondra. It only upset him more when I did."

"Where was Sondra working when things started to fall apart on her?"

"Place called Sea D.C., at Fourteenth and K. She had been a hostess there for a short while."

"Her mother said she was basically a good girl, got in with the wrong crowd."

"Wasn't like she was wearing a halo or nothin' like that. Sondra always did like to party, from what Chris told me. And I had some friends who worked in restaurants and clubs downtown, and I'd hung with these people a few times after the chairs got put up on the tables. So I knew what time it was. In those places, at closing time?

Someone's always holding something. In that environment, it's easy to fall into that lifestyle, if you allow yourself to fall into it, Mr. Strange."

"Call me Derek."

"Sondra got into that heroin thing. Chris said she was always afraid of needles, so he figured she started by snorting it. Probably thought it was okay, doin' it like that, like she couldn't get a jones behind it in that way. Another mistake future junkies make. I know because I had an uncle who was deep into it. It's a slower way to go down is all it is. How you end up, it's all the same."

"The night Chris was killed. Describe what happened here before he went out."

Renee moved her coffee mug around the table. Her voice was even and unemotional. "He got a phone call on his cell. He took the call back in my bedroom. I didn't hear what was said and I didn't ask. But he was agitated when he came out of the bedroom, for real. He said he had to go out. He said he was going to a bar or something to grab a beer, that he needed to get out of the apartment and think. I didn't think it was a good idea, what with him already having been drinkin' and all, and I told him so. He told me not to worry. He kissed me and he kissed Kia on the top of the head, and then he left. Two hours later, I got a call from Chris's mother telling me he was dead."

Strange sat back in his chair. "Chris had some brutality complaints in his file. He ever talk about that?"

"Yes," said Renee. "He told me he had to get rough with suspects sometimes, but he said he never went off on someone didn't deserve it. And yes, he had been drinking heavily the night he was killed, just like they said. The newspapers and the TV and his own department, they can paint their pictures any way they want. None of that explains why he was murdered. Bottom line is, if that white cop hadn't come up on the scene, Chris would be alive today."

"That white cop didn't know Chris was a policeman," said Strange. "He saw a man with a gun —"

"He saw a *black* man with a gun," said Renee. "And you and I both know that's why Chris is dead."

Strange didn't reply. He wasn't certain that on some basic level she was wrong.

Strange leaned forward and touched Kia's cheek. "That your baby, pretty little girl?"

"*My* baby," said Kia.

"I hope I helped you," said Renee.

"You did," said Strange. "Thank you for your time."

Strange sat at the downstairs bar of the Purple Cactus, sipping a ginger ale, watching the crowd. It was mostly young white money in here, new money and livin'-off-the-interest kind of money as well. The waitresses and bar staff were pretty young women and pretty boys, working with a kind of rising intensity, serving the early, preshow dinner patrons who were just now beginning to flow through the doors. The dining room chairs were hard, and triangles and other geometric designs hung on the walls. Dim spot lamps brought an onstage focus to each table, so the patrons could be "seen" while eating the overpriced cuisine.

Upon its opening, the Cactus had been touted in the *Post*'s dining guide and in *Washingtonian,* and had become "the place" for that particular year. Strange had come here once when he was trying to impress a woman on a first date, always a mistake. He had dropped a hundred and twenty-five on three appetizers, portioned to leave a small dog hungry, and a couple of drinks. Then the waiter, another bright-eyed boy with bleached-blond hair, had the nerve to come out with a dessert tray and try to get them to sample a "decadent," twelve-dollars-a-slice chocolate cake that was, he said with a practiced smile, "architecturally brilliant." It had ruined Strange's night to feel that used. And to make things worse, the woman he was with, she hadn't even given him any play.

A waiter wearing a thin line of beard came up to the service end of the bar and said to the bartender, "Absolut and tonic with a lemon twist," then added, "Did you see that tourist with the *hair* at my four-top? Oh my God, what is she, on chemo or something?" The waitress standing next to him, also waiting on a drink and arranging her checks, said, "Charlie, keep your voice down, the customers will hear you."

"Oh, *fuck* the customers," said Charlie, dressing his vodka tonic with a swizzle stick as it arrived.

Strange wondered how a place like this could stay in business. But he knew: People came here because they were told to come here, knowing full well that it was a rip-off, too. Same reason they read the books their friends read, and went to movies about convicts hijacking airplanes and asteroids headed for earth. Didn't matter that none of it was any good. No one wanted to be left out of the conversation at the next cocktail party. Everyone was desperate to be a part of what was new, to not be left behind.

"You okay here?" asked the bartender, a clear-eyed blonde with nice skin.

"Fine," said Strange. "I do have a question, though. You remember a guy used to work here, name of Ricky Kane? Trying to locate him for a friend."

"I'm new," said the bartender.

"*I* remember Ricky," said Charlie the waiter, still standing by the service bar. Would be like old Charlie, thought Strange, to listen in on someone's conversation and make a comment about it when he wasn't being spoken to.

"He's not working here any longer, is he?" said Strange, forcing a friendly smile.

"He doesn't need to anymore," said Charlie. "Not after all that money he got from the settlement." Charlie sideglanced the brunette waitress beside him. "Course, he never did need to work here, did he?"

'Cause old Ricky had his income set up from dealin' drugs, it suddenly occurred to Strange.

"Charlie," admonished the waitress.

Charlie chuckled and hurried off with his drink tray. The bartender served the brunette waitress her drinks and said, "Here you go, Lenna."

After Lenna thanked her, the bartender came back to stand in front of Strange. "Another ginger ale?"

"Just the check," said Strange, "and a receipt."

Strange walked around the corner and four blocks up Vermont Avenue, then took the steps down to Stan's, a basement bar he frequented now and again. It was smoky and crowded with locals, a racial mix of middle-class D.C. residents, most of them in their middle age. Going past some loud tables, he heard a man call his name.

"Derek, how you doin'!"

"Ernest," said Strange. It was Ernest James from the neighborhood, wearing a suit and seated with a woman.

"Heard your business was doin' good, man."

"I'm doin' all right."

"You see anything of Donald Lindsay?" asked James.

"Heard Donald passed."

"Uh-uh, man, he's still out there."

"Well, I ain't seen him." Strange nodded and smiled at Johnson's lady. "Excuse me, y'all, let me get up on over to this bar and have myself a drink."

"All right, then, Derek."

"All right."

Strange ordered a Johnnie Walker Red and soda at the bar. At Stan's, they served the liquor to the lip of the glass, with the miniature mixer on the side, the way they used to at the old Royal Warrant and the Round Table on the other side of town. When Strange felt like having one real drink, and being around regular people, he came here.

Sipping his scotch, he felt himself notch down. He talked to a man beside him about the new Redskins quarterback, who had come over from the Vikings, and what the 'Skins needed to do to win. The man was near Strange's age, and he recalled seeing Bobby Mitchell play, and the talk drifted to other players and the old Jurgenson-led squad.

"Fight for old D.C.," said the man, with a wink.

"Fight for old *Dixie,* you mean."

"You remember that?" said the man.

"That and a lot of other things. Shame some of these young folks out here, talkin' about nigga this and nigga that, don't remember those things, too."

"Some of our people get all upset 'cause the word's in *Webster's* dictionary, but they hear it from the mouths of their own sons and daughters and grandkids, and they let it pass."

"Uh-huh. How are white people gonna know not to use that word when our own young people don't know it their *own* got-damn selves?"

"I heard that."

Strange's beeper sounded. He read the numbers, excused himself, went to the pay phones back by the bathrooms, and made a call. It was Quinn on the other end of the line.

"Lookin' forward to it," said Strange, when Quinn was done talking.

"Us too," said Quinn. "Where should we meet?"

Strange told him, racked the phone, and checked his wristwatch. He paid his tab, bought the man at the bar another round, and left Stan's.

At his row house, Strange dumped all the matchbooks and the photograph of Sondra Wilson onto his office desk, went through his mail, and changed into sweats. He went down to his basement, where a heavy bag hung from the steel beams of the ceiling, and listened to the sound track of *Guns for San Sebastian* on his boom box while he worked the bag. He fed Greco, then stripped off his damp clothing and went to take a shower. If he hurried, he'd have time to visit his mother at the home before picking up Janine for the fights.

chapter 19

Ray and Earl Boone stopped at the red light on Michigan and North Capitol. Ray dragged on his cigarette and Earl sipped from a can of Busch beer. On the corner, a neon-colored poster was stapled to a telephone pole, announcing some kind of boxing event that was scheduled for that night.

"Feel like goin' to the fights tonight, Daddy?" said Ray, knowing full well that his father didn't even like to step outside the car in D.C. "They got some good ones over at that convention center. Looks like Don King's gonna be there, too."

"Don King?" said Earl. "I'd sooner have a dog lick peanut butter out the crack of my ass."

"That a no?"

"You got a green light, Critter. And stop bein' so silly, too."

Ray made a call to Cherokee Coleman's office, told one of Coleman's people that he and his father were coming in. They drove into the old warehouse district off Florida Avenue.

Ray saw an MPD cruiser idling on the street near

Coleman's office. He recognized the small numbers on the bumper of the Crown Vic and the same numbers, printed larger, on its side. Coasting past the driver's-side window, Ray caught a quick glimpse of the uniform behind the wheel, a big, ugly spade who was staring straight ahead. Coleman had once told him the name of their pocket cop, funny kind of name for a man, funnier still for such a big one, but Ray could not exactly remember what the name was. Sounded like Madonna, some bullshit like that.

They dropped the kilo off at the garage. The usual types were waiting, with a couple of new, young faces in the bunch, skullcap stockings worn over the tops of their heads, dead eyes, kill-you-while-I-laugh smiles. There was a north side–south side argument going on as Ray and Earl stepped out of the car, one kid playfully feinting and jabbing another as the rest moved their heads to some jungle-jump coming from a box. Ray could give a good fuck about any of them. And as he and his father smoked and watched them scale out the heroin, he could only think, Everything goes right, this'll be the last time I ever set foot in this shit hole of a city again.

Tonio Morris came out of the dark room on the first floor of the Junkyard, where he lived with the other last-stage junkies and the bugs and the rats, lying on a moldy mattress in his own filth. When he was not here he was out on the street, stealing or begging, or collecting cigarette butts gathered along the curbs, or rummaging through the garbage cans in the alleys behind the houses in Trinidad and LeDroit Park.

Here in the Junkyard, he experienced mainly boredom,

relieved by the threat of drama, the occasional quick act of physical violence, or the odd joke that struck him funny and made him laugh deep in his wheezy chest. He slept fitfully and ate little, except for the small bites of chocolate he cadged from the others. Mostly his life was blocks of time between getting high, and mostly he waited, sometimes knowing but not caring that he was only waiting for death.

Tonio crossed the big room, his feet crunching pigeon droppings, puddles dampening his brown socks, water entering where the soles had split from the uppers of his shoes. He stood by the brick wall, in a place that had been hammered out, and watched the Ford Taurus pass, driving by the cop car that idled on the street. They were here, on schedule, and he turned and headed for the stairs.

He passed one of Coleman's and went up to the second floor, to the open-stalled bathroom area where those who were still strong and those who had something to trade had staked out their spots. The once-beautiful girl named Sondra was in the last stall, leaning against the steel wall, rubbing her arm with her hand as if she were trying to erase a stain.

Tonio went into the stall and stood very close to her so that he could make out her face. He was beginning to go blind, the final laughing insult of the plague.

"Hello, Tonio."

"Hello, baby. Your boys are here."

Sondra smiled and showed filmy teeth; zero nutrition had grayed them. Her lips were chapped and bleeding in spots, raw from the cold. She wore a heavy jacket over her usual outfit, the white shirt and black slacks. An old woman back near Gallaudet College had seen her on the street a week ago and handed the jacket to Sondra out the front door of her row house.

"You better get fresh for your man," said Tonio.

"I got some water here," she said. She had found an empty plastic Fruitopia container in a Dumpster and filled it with water from a neighborhood spigot.

"Use this to clean your face," said Tonio. He handed her a filthy shop rag from his back pocket. "Go on, girl." She took it, examined it, and poured freezing water from the bottle onto the rag. She dabbed it on her cheeks. The oily dirt from the rag smudged her face.

"You're good to me," said Sondra.

"And don't you forget to be good to Tonio, hear?"

"I won't forget you, T. I always get a little bit for you."

He eyed her in a hungry but completely asexual way. He wanted things from her but not that. Tonio could no longer make it with a woman even if he wanted to. He no longer wanted to or thought of it at all.

"I better be goin' back down," he said.

"See you later," she said, watching him walk away, hitching his pants up where they had slipped down his behind.

Sondra was fond of Tonio. He never tried to do her like the others did. Tonio was her friend.

"What's wrong, Cherokee?" said Ray. "Thought you'd be happy. Way you were talking last time, thought you wanted to get out from under the pressure the Rodriguez brothers were puttin' on you."

"Didn't ask you to doom 'em, Ray," said Coleman.

"They asked for it their own selves."

"Committed suicide, huh?"

"Damn near like it. Anyway, I can't wake neither of them up now, so we're wasting time frettin' on it, right? Besides, I handled it, you can believe that."

Cherokee Coleman sat behind his desk, his hands tented on the blotter, staring at Ray. His lieutenant, Big-Ass Angelo, stood behind him, his face a fleshy, impassive mask. Earl Boone got a kick out of Angelo's sunglasses, the Hollywood-looking kind with the thick gold stems. Dark as it was already in here, with that green banker's lamp the only light in the room, Earl wondered how fat boy could even see.

"You want to go ahead and tell us how you handled it?" said Cherokee.

"The day after their visit," said Ray, "I called Lizardo's wife, asked her where in the hell he and Nestor was. Said that they was due but hadn't showed up or called. 'Bout a New York minute later I get a call on my cell from one of the Vargas people down in Florida. I told him the same thing I told the wife. He mumbled somethin' in Spanish and hung up the phone. Next thing we did was, me and Daddy made two trips with those Contours they was drivin', drove those cars down to Virginia and dumped 'em near Richmond, off Ninety-five south. Dripped some of Nestor's and Lizardo's blood on the seats of those cars. Pulled some hairs from their heads and scattered them in the cars, too. When the cops break into those cars and trace the owners, gonna look like the brothers got killed down there on their way up north."

"What about the bodies?"

"The bodies I got stashed on my property, until this weather turns. I'm gonna take care of that, too."

"What happens," said Cherokee, "when I get the call from the Vargas family?"

"Hell, Cherokee, you're just gonna have to tell 'em the same. That you heard from me and that Nestor and Lizardo never showed."

"Why would I do that?"

"'Cause partners gotta stick together," said Ray.

"We're partners now. You hear that, Angie?"

"Look here." Ray leaned forward in his chair. "I got nine keys of pure brown I'm sittin' on right now."

"Got it with you?" said Coleman.

"Nah, man," said Ray. "I ain't stupid!"

Ray laughed. Coleman and Angelo laughed, and kept laughing long after Ray was done. Ray frowned, watching them. Were they fuckin' with him now? He couldn't tell.

Coleman drew a handkerchief from the breast pocket of his pretty suit and wiped his eyes.

"Anyhow," said Ray. "Me and Daddy, we been wantin' to get out of this business for a while now. What I was thinkin' is, we unload the rest of that brown to you directly, at a price you're really gonna like, and we are gone."

"Oh, yeah? What kind of price is that?"

"You were payin' a hundred a key, right?"

"Including your bounce. It's *all* bounce now, so you don't have to add that back in, seein' as how there wasn't any, what do you call that, *cost of goods* involved."

"That's right. So I was gonna say sixty a key you take the load. Nine keys time sixty —"

"Five hundred and forty grand."

"Five forty, right. But, 'cause I like you, Cherokee —"

"You like me, Ray?"

"I do. And 'cause of that, I'm gonna sweeten the pie even more."

"How you gonna sweeten it?"

"Say an even five hundred grand to you, Cherokee, for the whole shebang."

"Generous of you, Ray."

"I think so."

"So when you gonna bring it in?"

Ray looked over at Earl, back at Coleman. "We were kind of thinkin', Daddy and me, I mean, that we wouldn't have to come into the city again for this last deal."

"Got somethin' against D.C.?"

"We prefer the country, you want the truth."

"For real?"

Coleman and Angelo laughed again. Ray and Earl, expressionless as stones, waited until they were done.

"Tell you what," said Coleman. "We'll split the difference, hear? You bring in the first half of the load straight away, and for the last half, I'll send someone out your way to pick it up."

"What's this half stuff?"

"You don't think I can get my hands on five hundred grand all at once, do you? Think I can walk on over to NationsBank and take out a loan?"

"No, but —"

"Got to turn that inventory first, man, get some cash flow goin' in this motherfucker. Only way we can do this deal, Ray."

"I don't know," said Ray.

"Fuck it," said Earl, surprising Coleman with his voice. It was the first time Earl had spoken since he and his son had walked through the office door.

"You got somethin' on your mind, *Daddy?*" said Coleman.

"We'll bring the next load down," said Earl, "that's what you want. But I want somethin', too."

"Let me guess," said Coleman. "This somethin' got light skin and green eyes?"

"That's right," said Earl. "I want to take that pretty girl home with me, the one you got livin' over there across the street. I'm gonna take her with me today."

"Shit, Daddy."

"Hold up, Critter. I'm talkin' now."

"Aw, you're sweet on her," said Coleman. "That's real nice."

"Got no problem with me takin' her, do ya?"

"No problem at all. I ain't got no kind of claim on it. Course, some of the fellas over at the Junkyard, they might want to up and flex on you, you try to take her away. 'Cause most of them been kickin' it, one behind the other, the last month or so."

"Kickin' it?"

"Fallin' in love with her, Ray."

Big-Ass Angelo went *"ssh, ssh, ssh,"* his shoulders jiggling hard.

Earl ignored him and said, "That'll do it, then. We'll be on our way."

Ray stood. "I'll call you. We'll be back with that first load in a couple of days. Then you can come on out and get the rest."

"Oh, I don't think I'll be makin' the trip personally, Ray. I'm gonna send out a po-lice escort, make it nice and official."

"You're gonna send that guy Madonna?"

Coleman chuckled. "Sure, Ray. I'll send Madonna."

"All right, then. See you fellas later."

"Ray," said Coleman. "Earl."

Coleman and Angelo watched them go out the door.

Coleman said, "Call all our dealers, Angie. Tell 'em we got a lot of good product comin' in. And don't forget to call that white boy, too. He can move it on the other side of town, and we need it moved out quick. Get that first load out on the street so we can do the same with the second. This a big opportunity we got right here. We gonna make some large bank on this motherfucker, Angie."

"Yeah, but we got to go all the way the fuck on out to Hooterville to pick it up."

"That's all right. Got to throw dirt on the Boones sooner or later, might as well do it while we're out there. Make a nice pile of bodies, them and the Rodriguez brothers. Get it lookin' like Jonestown out there and shit. Make it right for those Colombians. 'Cause you know I don't want to see the Vargas family in town, lookin' to start a war."

"*I* ain't goin'."

"Don't worry, big dawg. I'm gonna send Adonis and his shadow."

Angelo grinned. "You mean *Madonna,* don't you?"

"Ray Boone," said Coleman. "That's a real genius, right there."

"I ain't *stupid!*" said Big-Ass Angelo.

Coleman cracked up and held out his palm. Angelo gave him skin.

Earl Boone walked along the doorless stalls, stopping at the very last one in the row. Sondra Wilson stood there, the flame from a single candle throwing light upon her face. Her white blouse was filthy, and dirt streaked her cheeks. She seemed unsteady on her feet.

"Hey, honey girl," said Earl.

"Earl."

He stepped in close and looked into her eyes. One was brown and one was green.

"What happened to your eyes, young lady?"

"I lost a contact, I guess." She tried to curl her lip seductively. "You got somethin' for me, Earl?"

"I got it. But not here. I'm takin' you out of this place."

"Where we goin'?" she said.

"You're coming to live with me for a while. You're gonna have a shower and new clothes and clean sheets to sleep on every night."

"What about the other thing?" she said, because that was all she cared about now.

"You're gonna have plenty of that, too."

Sondra turned to the wall and untaped the magazine photo of the model. She folded it and picked up the paper-weight off the toilet-paper dispenser and looked around for her other possessions. She picked up a wet, half-used book of matches from the tiles and realized that there was nothing else.

"Come on, baby doll. Ray's waiting on us out in the hall."

"Can I get a little somethin' for my friend Tonio before we go?"

"Forget about him. We want to get out quiet and quick. I understand some of the other fellas in here might have fallen in love with you, and we wouldn't want them getting jealous."

"Love?" said Sondra. She rubbed her nose and laughed.

They took her down the stairs and went through a large hole in the brick wall. From deep in the darkness of the side room, Tonio Morris watched Sondra leave with the old white man and his son. He wondered why Sondra would go without saying good-bye. He was sad for a moment, then felt a shudder of panic, realizing that maybe his source was gone for good.

In the street, the cop behind the wheel of the idling cruiser watched the Boones emerge from the Junkyard with the pretty junkie from the second floor. The three of them were headed for the garage where the others were holding their car. The cop snapped the cigar that he was holding between his fingers and tossed it to the floor.

"SHARMBA Mitchell," said Strange. "That's a beautiful fighter right there."

"Look at that left," said Quinn.

"I had a left like that one, I'd never throw a right."

Strange and Quinn sat in the bleachers of the Washington Convention Center, drinking a couple of four-dollar drafts. In the crowd of four thousand, Quinn was among a small number of whites, the others being the parents of a light heavyweight Texan, four frightened-looking fraternity boys, and several white women accompanied by black men. The convention center was a grim, outdated white elephant that had underserved the city from day one. But the sport almost lent itself to unattractive, spartan arenas; as boxing venues went, this wasn't a bad place to see a fight.

The white, light heavyweight Texan, who fought under the name of Joe Bill "Rocky" Jakes, was walking along the edge of the stands, having changed into street clothes after his disastrous defeat. His face was marked and puffy, and one eye was swollen shut.

"Hey, Rocky!" shouted a guy from the stands.

"Yo, Adrian!" shouted another.

"You'll get 'em next time, Rock," shouted a third, with a Burgess Meredith growl, to much laughter from the spectators in the surrounding seats.

"They're usin' the hell out of that guy," said Quinn.

"You ever notice," said Strange, "how many white fighters call themselves Rocky?"

"I think there's been one or two."

"There's that hook again," said Strange, pointing to the ring.

Takoma Park's Sharmba Mitchell was defending his WBA super lightweight title against Pedro Saiz, out of Brooklyn. Saiz, a late replacement for a scratched William Joppy, had not been expected to show too much, but he was proving himself tonight. Mitchell wore trunks cut in strips of red, white, and blue. Saiz wore white.

The fourth round ended. As the fighters went to their corners, a blonde showing a whole lot of leg climbed into the ring and walked around the edge of the ropes, a round-card held up in her hands.

"You see the ladies?" said Strange.

"I liked Round Two, myself," said Quinn.

"Shame about the face."

"Hey, I bet she's got a big heart."

"A big *inverted* heart, you mean."

"Her ass *was* pretty big. But I thought you guys liked that."

"You thought. Anyway, I'm not talkin' about the ring girls, Terry, I'm talkin' about *our* ladies. Our dates."

"They went to get a couple of beers."

"Fifteen minutes ago."

"They're okay. Probably down there with their faces together, having a firefight. Talking about us."

"I hope they are. It's when they stop talkin' about us, then we're in trouble." Strange sipped his beer and looked at Quinn out of the corners of his eyes. "You didn't tell me about Juana, man."

"That she was fine?"

"That she was a sister."

"She's half Puerto Rican."

"Half nothin'. You got a drop of black in you, you are *black*."

"Got a problem with it?" said Quinn.

"Uh-uh. I mean, I'm not gonna lie to you, it took me back at first, 'cause I didn't expect it."

"It's the way we're programmed, is all it is."

"Now you're gonna tell me what it is."

"I was up in Wheaton Plaza a couple of weeks back, the mall? Half the young couples, some of 'em had babies in strollers, were interracial. Fifteen years ago, when I was hanging out up at the Plaza, you wouldn't have seen it. It's just natural for these kids now. And it made me think, the way my generation is, and especially the way your generation is, it's *our* hang-up, man. It's something *we've* got to get over, 'cause the world's changing whether we like it or not."

"Case you didn't notice, you been getting a lot of looks here tonight. From people in all sorts of generations."

"She's been drawing the looks, and I don't blame the guys who been lookin'."

"You're gonna have to at least face this, Terry: There's a whole lot of people, black and white, they just don't believe in mixin', man. That doesn't make them racists or anything like that. It's just their opinion, straight up."

"Long as they stay out of my business, they can have any kind of opinion they want."

The fifth round began. A fight broke out by the men's room to their right, and security guards swarmed the guilty parties, carrying one man out as he kicked his legs and yelled obscenities over his shoulder. There had been a few fights in the crowd that night, and they had occurred with more frequency as more beer and liquor had been served.

"You been seein' Juana long?"

Quinn rolled his eyes. "Shit, man, you still on that?"

"I got to admit, when we came up on the two of you, first thing I thought was, Terry got himself a one-time date with a black woman for my benefit. Trying to make an impression on old Strange, like, Here I am, Terry Quinn, lovin' all the people, can't you see I just want us *all* to get along?"

Quinn laughed. "I'm through trying to impress you, Derek. You ought to know that by now. I've told you everything I know. I mean, can we just hang out and not deal with it for one night?"

"So how long you been seein' her?"

"Not too long, I guess. I'm crazy about her, too, you want to know the truth."

"I got eyes."

"How about you and Janine?"

"Shoot. We been seein' each other now, I don't know, about ten years. Not exclusive, nothin' like that."

"She's in love with you."

"Go ahead, man."

"Look, I got eyes, too."

"My mother always tells me that old parable about the guy, went all around the world lookin' for diamonds, when all the time he never did think to look in his own backyard."

"Diamonds in your backyard. I've heard that one plenty of times."

"Yeah, she didn't make it up. But when it's your mom tellin' you, you tend to listen. Anyhow, I guess me and Janine, we're good for each other in a lot of ways."

Strange knew it was deeper than that between him and Janine. But he was a private man, and that was all he could bring himself to say.

Saiz issued a flagrant low blow to Mitchell, sending him to his knees. The increasingly raucous crowd booed loudly as the ref directed Saiz to his corner and deducted a point. At Mitchell's nod, the ref restarted the fight. Mitchell came out with fury, throwing a flurry of punches in a blur of speed and power.

"You're gonna see somethin' now," said Quinn.

"Yeah," said Strange. "Sharmba's gonna fuck him up."

Mitchell decisioned Saiz unanimously. Janine and Juana walked up the stands carrying two beers each. An elderly couple on the end got up to let them pass.

"Damn, where y'all been?" said Strange, as they took their seats. He sounded mildly cross, but it was plain from the relieved look on his face that he had been worried about Janine.

"Juana wanted to see Sugar Ray," said Janine. "He's down at ringside."

"You see him?"

"Mm-huh," said Juana, and she and Janine laughed.

"Saw Don King, too," said Janine.

"Must have made you hungry for some cotton candy," said Strange.

"Wondered why my stomach was growling," said Janine, "looking at that hair of his."

"How you doin'?" said Quinn, touching Juana's hand.

"Janine's really nice," she whispered.

"Havin' fun?"

"Uh-huh."

He kissed her lips.

A tuxedoed man came into the ring, pulled down the hanging microphone, and began to describe, with flourish, the participants in the main event.

"Who's that guy?" said Quinn.

"Discombobulating Jones," said Strange with affection. "Best ring announcer in D.C."

"Here we go," said Quinn. "Bernard Hopkins."

"Hopkins took out Simon Brown," said Strange. "You know that?"

The main event had Hopkins in a rematch with Robert Allen for the IBF middleweight crown. Their first pairing, in Vegas, had been marred by Allen's shoves and holds, and ended as a no contest when Hopkins fell through the ropes and sprained an ankle.

"Allen's doin' it again," said Strange, well into the first round. "He's headlockin' him, man; he doesn't want to fight."

Allen seemed to fake an injury, claiming himself the victim of a low blow. The spectators became angry, calling Allen a punk and a bitch. As they grew more boisterous, they moved en masse toward the ring. The fight continued, with round after round the same. The crowd's taunts became louder and more threatening.

"These people want blood," said Strange.

"Let's get out of here," said Quinn. "This fight stinks anyway, and you know Hopkins is gonna win."

The four of them moved through the dense crowd. The

young women in the crowd were mostly attractive, with shoulder-length, relaxed hairstyles that Juana called Brandy cuts. The oversized look was out for the young men. Many wore baseball jackets with leather sleeves and colorful sayings embroidered on the back. Someone bumped Quinn and he kept on, not knowing and trying not to care if it was intentional or not. But he felt his face flush as he walked away.

Out in the auditorium, as they walked down the carpeted lobby, a young man in a group of three made a comment directed at Juana, saying how he'd like to "kick that shit deep." Quinn felt his face grow hot and the tug of Juana's hand on his leather. He kept walking, and the movement calmed him.

Once outside, they walked down 10th. Strange and Quinn followed Janine and Juana, who were stepping quickly, talking to one another up ahead. A young black man was standing on the median, yelling at passing cars. "I hate cracker motherfuckers!" he screamed. "I swear to God, I'm gonna kill the next white motherfucker I see!"

"Sounds like the man's got some kind of *hang-up,*" said Strange, a playful light in his eyes. "Doesn't he know, Terry, that the world is *changing?*"

"Think I ought to go tell him?" said Quinn.

"Go ahead," said Strange, with a small grin. "I'll make sure your lady gets home safe."

Juana and Quinn followed Strange and Janine over to Stan's, where they had a round, and then another, before last call. By now they were all a little bit drunk, and Juana and Janine didn't seem to want the evening to end, so they agreed to meet up at Strange's row house for "one more."

Strange bought a twelve-pack at a market and drove up Georgia. Janine sat beside him on the bench, her thigh touching his, while Strange messed with the stereo, popping in *War Live* and fast-forwarding the tape to a song he liked.

"What you lookin' for?" asked Janine.

"'Get Down.' Here it is." Strange turned the bass dial and put more bottom into the mix. "What's Ron doin' on Monday, you know?"

"He's workin' a couple of jumpers, I think."

"I could use his help."

"We need the money he's gonna bring into the business, Derek. Don't tell me this Wilson thing is going to result in a big payday, 'cause I know you're not gonna end up charging his mother enough. Let Ron do his thing and go on and do yours."

"Yeah, you're right." Strange turned up the volume and sang, "'The po-lice . . . We're talkin' 'bout the po-lice.'"

Janine laughed. "You're in rare form tonight, honey."

"Havin' a good time, I guess."

"Me, too. I like Juana. That's a together young lady right there. Going to law school down at GW, you know that? Might have her talk to Lionel about it, let him know in a backdoor kind of way that anybody can do anything, they set their mind to it. You know she didn't come from any kind of privilege or nothin' like that."

"What about Terry? You think he's good for her?"

"They stay together, they're gonna have problems they don't even know about yet. Not to mention, all you've got to do is look in his eyes and see, that's an intense young

man. He's got a lot of things to work out his own self
before he can take on the responsibilities of a real relationship. But I do like him."

Strange nodded, looking in the rearview mirror at the
black VW following his car. "So do I."

In the Bug, Quinn shifted the stick while Juana worked
the clutch and steered with her left hand. Her right hand
was going through a box of tapes that sat in her lap.

"How about Lucinda Williams?" said Juana.

"The chick on *Laverne and Shirley?*"

"You're thinkin' of *Cindy* Williams."

"I'm fuckin' with you, girl."

"Here, put this in, you'll like it."

Quinn slipped the tape into the deck. "Metal Fire-
cracker" came through the system, filling the interior of
the car.

"This rocks," said Quinn.

"Yeah, Lucinda is bad."

Quinn chuckled, looking through the windshield.
"Derek's got that Caddy all waxed up. I bet he really loves
that car."

"What's wrong with that?"

"Nothin'. I'm sayin' he's proud of it, is all. His age
group, the symbol of success is a Cadillac. You know
what I mean."

"I guess I do."

When Juana was a kid, she heard a white boy in her
elementary school class call a Cadillac a 'nigger boat.'
She had told herself from the start that Terry wasn't 'like
that' in any kind of way. But how could you know what
was really in a person's heart? He had downed more than
a few beers tonight, and maybe this was him for real,

loose and talking truly for the first time. Maybe what he believed was out of his control, that everything he had learned had been taught to him, and had been ingrained in him irreversibly, long ago. And maybe she was just being too sensitive. Once you started going in that direction, you could drive yourself crazy over something that was probably nothing at all.

"What's wrong?" said Quinn, looking at her face.

"Nothing, Tuh-ree," said Juana, finding his hand and giving it a gentle squeeze. "I was just thinking of you, that's all."

chapter **21**

STRANGE was doing something he called the chicken leg, Janine dancing beside him, as "Night Train" blared through his living room stereo. Quinn was nearby, shouting out encouragement between hits from a can of beer. Juana sat on the couch, twisting up a number from some herb and papers she had found in her purse. Greco lay on the floor with his head between his paws, his tail slowly thumping the carpet.

"Sonny Liston used to train to that one," said Strange, as the song ended.

"Like you were doin' right there?" asked Quinn.

"Naw, man, that was a dance we used to do. Check this out." Strange held up a CD with a photograph of a sixties-looking white girl on its cover. "Mr. Otis Redding. *Otis Blue*."

"You already played that Solomon Burke. What, are we working our way up to modern times here?"

"This is the man right here," Strange said, as Steve Cropper's bluesy guitar kicked it off on "Ole Man Trouble," the horns and then Otis's vocal coming behind it.

"Got any Motown?"

"Shoot, Terry, Motown ain't nothin' but soul music for white people, man."

"How do I know? I wasn't even alive when this shit was playin' on the radio."

"And I was still gettin' press-and-curls," added Janine. "Barely a child."

"I was there," said Strange. "And it was right."

Juana walked over with a joint in her hand. "You guys want some of this?"

"I do," said Quinn.

"Been a while for me," said Strange.

"Come on," said Juana.

"You all aren't gonna start acting funny now, are you?" asked Janine.

"What's this 'you all' stuff?" said Strange.

The four of them stood in the middle of the living room floor and smoked the joint. Strange took Quinn's shotgun, but Juana refused it. Janine just waved her hand and laughed. By the time the joint was a roach, they were all alternately giggling and arguing over the next piece of music to be played.

Strange put *Motor Booty Affair* on the CD player and turned up the volume. "The power of Parliament. Now we're gonna roll with it, y'all."

The four of them danced, tentatively at first, to the complex, dense songs. The bass line was snaky and insistent, and the melodies bubbled up in the mix, and as the rhythms insinuated themselves into their bodies they let go and found the groove. They had broken a sweat by the fifth cut.

Strange dimmed the lights and put on Al Green's *The Belle Album*.

"Reminds me of those blue-light parties we used to have," said Strange.

"That was before my time, too," said Janine, kissing him on the mouth.

They slow-dragged to the title tune. Janine had her cheek resting on Strange's chest, moving in her stocking feet. Quinn and Juana made out like high schoolers as they danced. As the cut ended, Janine checked her watch and told Strange that it was time to go.

"Lionel ought to be getting back to my house by now," she said. "I want to be there for him when he arrives."

"Yeah, we need to clear out of here," said Strange.

"Where's the head?" asked Quinn.

"Up the stairs," said Strange.

Quinn went up to the second floor. He saw the bathroom, an open door that led to a bedroom and sleeper porch, and two more bedrooms, one of which had been set up as an office. Quinn looked over his shoulder at the empty flight of stairs and walked into the office.

The office appeared to be well used. Strange's desk was a countertop set on two columns of file cabinets. Atop the desk was a monitor, speakers, a keyboard, and a mouse pad, and scattered papers and general clutter. Quinn went around the desk.

Beside the desk, Strange had mounted a wooden CD rack to the wall. In the rack were western movie sound tracks: the Leone *Dollars* Trilogy, *Once Upon a Time in the West*, *The Magnificent Seven*, *Return of the Magnificent Seven*, *My Name Is Nobody*, *Navajo Joe*, *The War Wagon*, *Two Mules for Sister Sara*, *The Professionals*, *Dual at Diablo*, *The Big Country*, *The Big Gundown*, and others. There was no evidence in this room of the funk and soul music from the sixties and seventies that Strange loved so much. Quinn wondered if Strange was hiding this collection here, if he was embarrassed to have his taste for western sound tracks on display for his friends.

Quinn looked at the papers on the desk. Stock-related documents, mostly, along with report forms with the Strange Investigations logo printed across the top. A heap of matchbooks and a faded photograph of a pretty young woman. He picked the photograph up, recognizing the image as that of Chris Wilson's striking sister. Quinn remembered her from the newspaper stories and television reports that had been broadcast the day of the funeral.

"You see a toilet in here?" said Strange from the doorway.

Quinn looked up. "Sorry, man. I'm naturally nosy, I guess."

Strange's eyes were pink and lazy. He folded his arms and leaned on the door frame.

"Why have a photo of Wilson's sister?" said Quinn.

"For the simple reason that I'm beginning to think Sondra Wilson's the key to this whole thing."

"You talk to her?"

Strange shook his head. "Gonna have to find her first. Her own mother doesn't know where she is. Sondra's a junkie, man, got a deep heroin jones. Been away from the house a long while now. Wilson was looking to hook up with her, maybe bring her back home, is what I think. And another thing I think is, on the night he was killed, Chris got a phone call had something to do with Sondra."

Quinn dropped the photograph to the desktop. "You think Ricky Kane had something to do with that?"

"I like your instincts, Terry."

"Well, do you?"

"It crossed my mind."

"You need to talk to Kane."

"If he's involved, it won't do any good to talk to him. It would shut him up for real, and I got no kind of leverage. It might even hurt my chances of finding Sondra."

"That's what you're looking to do now?"

"Yeah," said Strange. "Finish what Chris Wilson started. Bring her home."

"Because you know you got nothing else for Leona Wilson, right? You know there was nothing deeper than what got put on the record about my involvement in the death of her son."

"You tellin' me?"

"I'm *asking* you, Derek."

"Look here, man." Strange rubbed his cheeks and exhaled slowly. "God *damn,* I am fucked up. Haven't smoked herb in years, you want the truth. Don't know why I did tonight. But I got to blame it on something, I guess."

"Blame what?"

"The crazy thing I'm gettin' ready to ask you to do. See, my associate, Ron, he's gonna be busy next week. And I could use your help."

"Name it."

"A tail and surveillance on Ricky Kane, for starters. I was thinkin' Monday morning."

"Tell me what time."

"You don't even have a car."

"I plan to go out this weekend and buy one."

"Just like that."

"Gettin' tired of Juana chauffeuring me around."

"Okay, then. I'll call you Sunday evening, let you know where we can meet."

"Derek?"

"What?"

"This mean I'm off the hook?"

"Aw, shit," said Strange, chuckling from deep in his gut. "You're somethin', man."

"I'm serious, Derek."

"Okay." Strange unfolded his arms. "That hook you're talkin' about, you put yourself on it. You got to admit to yourself the reality of the situation. You got to free your *own* self, man."

"You just said —"

"I said that I suspect there was something with Chris Wilson and his sister. That her lifestyle is what drove him to D Street that night. But you yourself admitted that Wilson was tryin' to tell you and your partner that he was a cop. He was screaming his badge number out to you, man, but you wouldn't listen."

"Look —"

"You wouldn't *listen*. You saw a black man with a gun and you saw a criminal, and you *made up your mind*. Yeah, there was noise and confusion and lights, I know about all that. But would you have listened to him if he had been white? Would you have pulled that trigger if Wilson had been white? I don't think so, Terry. Cut through all the extra bullshit, and you're gonna have to just go ahead and admit it, man: You killed a man because he was black."

Quinn stared into Strange's eyes. Quinn wanted to say more in his defense, but the words wouldn't come. He was certain that any words he could choose would be insufficient. How could a white man ever tell a black man that he wasn't that way without sounding self-serving or duplicitous?

They heard Janine's voice, calling them from the bottom of the stairs. Strange lowered his gaze to the floor.

"C'mon, Terry," he said, his voice nearly a whisper. "We better go."

Quinn and Juana drove east to her row house on 10th. They went straight to her bedroom, where he stripped naked and undressed Juana from behind. He ran both hands up her inner thighs and slipped two fingers inside her. She arched her back and moaned as he pinched her swollen nipples. Then, very quickly, they were fucking on the bed, Juana on the edge of it with her calves resting on his shoulders, and Quinn thrusting with his feet still on the floor. It was fast and nearly violent; Juana came with a groaning howl. Quinn was right behind her, veins standing out on his forehead and neck. The bed had slid across the room, stopping when it hit the wall.

Quinn pulled out and slid Juana up to the center of the bed, putting a pillow under her head. They got beneath the blankets, holding a tight embrace, and what was left from them wet each other and the sheets. She stared up at him, not saying a word, her eyes saying everything. Soon she was breathing evenly. Her eyes fluttered, then closed completely, and she fell asleep.

Lionel Baker came home at one forty-five in the morning, nearly two hours past his curfew. Janine had been waiting in the living room, parting the curtains of the front window every few minutes to check for her son, as Strange sat patiently beside her. A Lexus finally pulled up on Quintana in front of her house, and when she saw her son emerge from the car, Janine said, "Thank the Lord."

Strange knew Lionel had been smoking herb, or doing something other than just drinking, as soon as he walked through the front door. Lionel's pupils were dilated, his movements awkward and slow. He didn't look his mother in the eye as he greeted them with a "Hey" and tried to get past them and up the stairs without another word.

"Hold on a minute, Lionel," said Janine.

"What is it?" he said, looking at her directly for the first time. He glanced at Strange, then back at his mother, and an impudent smile threatened to break on his face.

"Where you been, son?"

"Out with Ricky, just rollin', listenin' to music. . . . Can't you just let me go up to my room for a change? You always be *stressin'* and shit."

Janine rose up from her seat. "Don't you be takin' a tone with me, young man. Me and Mr. Derek been sitting up, worried that you were in some kind of trouble, or worse. And now you come walking in here late, lookin' all red-eyed —"

"How about y'all?"

"*What?*"

"Forget it, Mama," said Lionel, with a wave of his hand. He turned and went up the stairs.

Janine froze for moment, then moved to follow her son. Strange took hold of her arm.

"Hold up, baby. I'll talk to him, all right?"

On the second floor of the house, Strange knocked on

Lionel's closed door. Lionel did not respond. Strange turned the knob and walked inside the bedroom. Lionel was standing, looking through his window, which gave to a view of the street. Strange crossed the room and stood beside him. Lionel turned to face him.

"Lionel?"

"What?"

"You know your mother loves you, right?"

"Sure."

"When she asks you where you been all night, it's just her way of lettin' off a little steam. She's been sittin' down in that living room, worried sick about you, for the last two hours, and you come through that door, she's got to give you a taste of what you been puttin' *her* through all night."

"I know it. It's just . . . I'm nearly a man, Mr. Derek. I don't need all these questions all the time, see what I'm sayin'?"

"While you're livin' under her roof, and she's payin' for that roof, it's something you're just gonna have to deal with."

"And there goes Mama, tellin' *me* my eyes are lookin' red, when y'all look like you been smokin' cheeva your own selves."

"We drank a few bottles of beer, tonight, that's all," lied Strange. "I don't know, maybe we had one too many, but we did have fun. I'm not gonna go and apologize for that, 'cause your mama deserves it, hard as she works. But I never did claim I was perfect, even when I was trying to warn you about all the ways you can mess your life up before you even get out of the gate. Now, I told you what I thought about you drivin' around in that fancy car, gettin' high. I still think you're setting yourself up for something that could affect you your whole life. And your life ain't even started, son."

"You're not my father," said Lionel softly, and at once his eyes filled with tears. "Don't call me son."

Strange put his hand on Lionel's shoulder. "You're right. I never did have the kind of courage it takes to be a father to a boy for real. But there's some times when I look at you, when you're making one of your jokes at the dining room table, or when I see you dressed up, lookin' all handsome and ready to go out and meet a girl, and I get a sense of pride. . . . There's some times when I *look* at you, Lionel, and I get the kind of feeling that I know a father must have for his own."

Strange pulled Lionel to him. He felt Lionel's heart beating hard against his chest. He held Lionel for a little while and let him break away.

"Mr. Derek?"

"Yes?"

"The way it is with you and my mother . . . What I'm tryin' to say is, I know what time it is, see? I know you're tryin' to not disrespect her by staying in her room while I'm here, but I was thinkin' . . . I was thinkin', see, that you disrespect her even more in some way by not waking up in her bed."

"Huh?"

"What I'm sayin' is, I'd like it if you just went ahead and stayed the night."

"I'll, uh, talk to your mother," stammered Strange. "See if that's all right."

Strange went down the hall to Janine's room. Inside, Janine was sitting on her bed, the toes of her stocking feet touching the floor. Ronald Isley was singing "Voyage to Atlantis" from the clock radio set on her nightstand, and she had turned the light down low.

"Everything okay?" she said.

"Fine," said Strange. "He wants me to spend the night."

"Do you want to?"

"Yes."

"You feed Greco?"

"I opened a can of Alpo for him before we left my house."

"Come here," said Janine. She smiled and patted the empty space beside her on the bed.

Quinn got out of bed, covering Juana to the neck with her own blanket and sheets. He had been watching the numbers change on the LED display on Juana's clock for the last two hours, and he knew that he would not fall asleep.

He was sober now. He stretched and walked naked to her window, turning the rod of the miniblinds to open an angle of sight. He looked out the window to the sidewalk on 10th, illuminated by street lamps. A young black man was walking down the sidewalk in an oversize hooded jacket, glancing in the windows of the parked cars he passed.

Quinn made some immediate presumptions about the young man, all of them negative. Then he tried to think of other explanations for why the kid would be out at this hour on the street. Maybe the young man had been unable to sleep, like Quinn, and was simply taking a walk. Maybe he was just leaving his girlfriend's place, was feeling bold and proud, and was checking out his reflection in the windows of the cars. These were logical scenarios, but they were not the *first* scenarios he had thought of when he had seen the young black man.

Quinn thought of the first time he had seen Juana, when she had walked into the bookstore on Bonifant.

Strange had been right about something, whether Quinn had been fully conscious of it at first or not: He had approached Juana initially to make some kind of point, to himself and the world around him.

"God damn you, Terry," whispered Quinn. He closed his eyes tightly and pinched the bridge of his nose.

chapter 22

ON Sunday morning, Strange ate breakfast with Janine and Lionel at the Three Star Diner, on Kennedy Street in Northwest. The Three Star was owned and operated by Billy Georgelakos, the son of the original owner, Mike Georgelakos. Strange's father, Darius Strange, had worked for Mike as a grill man at the diner for twenty-five years.

Billy Georgelakos and Strange were roughly the same age. On Saturdays, when Mike and Darius both had their sons with them, Billy and Strange had played together on these streets while their fathers worked. Strange had taught Billy how to box and make a tackle, and Billy had introduced young Derek to comic books and cap pistols. Billy was Strange's weekend playmate, and his first white friend.

When Mike Georgelakos died of a heart attack in the late sixties, Billy had dropped out of junior college and stepped in to take over the business, as there was no insurance or safety net of any kind for the family. He had not intended to stay, but he did. The neighborhood had gone through some changes, and the menu had moved closer to soul food, but Billy ran the place the same way his old man had, breakfast and lunch only, open seven days a week.

Strange knew that Mike Georgelakos had bought the property long ago — the Greeks from that generation were typically smart enough to secure the real estate — and consequently the nut at the Three Star was very low. The diner had sent Billy's two sons to college and had also managed to support his mother as well. The other thing Billy did like his old man was to cut the register tape off two hours before closing time. With a cash business like this, you could hide a whole lot of money from the IRS.

"Pass me that hot sauce, Lionel," said Strange.

Lionel slid the bottle of Texas Pete down the counter, past his mother to Strange. Strange shook some out onto his feta cheese-and-onion omelet, and a little onto the half-smoke that lay beside it.

"Good breakfast, right?" said Strange.

"Mm-huh," said Janine.

"The breakfast is tight," said Lionel, "but they could play some better music in this place."

"The music is fine," said Strange. Billy played gospel in the diner on Sunday mornings, as many of the patrons were coming straight from church. His father had done that, too.

"Why you name your dog Greco?" said Lionel. "'Cause of this Greek joint right here?"

"Nah. I knew this other Greek kid back when I was a boy, kid named Logan Deoudes. His father had a place like this, John's Lunch, over on Georgia, near Fort Stevens. Anyway, Logan had this dog, a boxer mix, called him Greco. Bad-ass dog, too — *excuse* me, Janine — and I always liked the name. Decided back then, when I got a dog of my own, I was gonna name him Greco myself."

Billy Georgelakos walked down the rubber mat behind

the counter, carrying a pot of coffee he had drawn from the urn. He wore a white shirt rolled up to the elbows and had a Bic pen wedged behind his right ear. Billy was big boned, with large facial features, most prominently his great eagle nose. With the exception of two patches of gray on either side of his dome, he had lost most of his hair.

"Want me to warm that up for you, Janine?" said Billy, chin-gesturing in the direction of Janine's coffee cup.

"A little bit more, thanks," said Janine. Billy poured her some coffee and filled Strange's cup to the lip without asking.

"How's your mom doin', Derek?"

Strange made a so-so, flip-flop movement of his hand. *"Etsi-ke-etsi,"* he said.

"Yeah," said Billy, "mine, too. Tough old women, though, right?"

He walked down to the grill area to talk with his long-time employee Ella Lockheart, who had come up in the neighborhood as well.

"You speak Greek, Mr. Derek?"

"Little bit," said Strange mysteriously. Billy had taught him one or two useful expressions and a whole lot of curse words.

"Dag," said Lionel.

"You got somethin' planned today?" said Strange to Janine.

"What'd you have in mind?"

"Want to stretch my legs. I'll be gettin' real busy tomorrow, and I might stay that way. It's cold, but with all this sunshine I was thinkin' I'd take Greco for a walk down in Rock Creek. Maybe go by the home and visit my mother after that."

"I'm up for it," said Janine.

"Lionel?"

"I got plans," said Lionel. "That Wilderness Family trip sounds good and all that. But if you don't mind, I'd just as soon spend my day lookin' at the women up at the mall."

Billy rang them up at the register. On the way out, Strange stopped, as he always did, at the wall by the front door, where several faded photographs were framed and hung. In one, Strange's father stood tall, with his chef's hat cocked rakishly, a spatula in one hand, a smile on his chiseled, handsome face. Mike Georgelakos, short and rotund, stood beside him.

"That's him right there," said Strange, and neither Lionel nor Janine said a thing, because they knew that Strange was just having a moment to himself.

"*Yasou,* Derek," said Billy Georgelakos from behind the counter.

"*Yasou, Vasili,*" said Strange, turning to wave at his friend. Strange winked at Lionel, who was obviously impressed, as they headed for the door.

Quinn walked south on Georgia Avenue, through Silver Spring and down over the District line, sometime after noon on Sunday. He passed tattoo parlors and car washes, auto detailers, African American–owned barber shops and clothing stores, beer markets and fried-chicken shacks, and stores selling cell phones and pagers. He walked for an hour without stopping. The day was cold, but the sun and his movement kept him warm.

He stopped at a small used-car lot on the west side of

Georgia. Multicolored plastic propellers had been strung around the perimeter, and they spun in the wind. There was a trailer on the edge of the lot where salesmen went for the close, and above the trailer door a large sign had been mounted and encircled with marquee-style lights. The sign read, "Eddie Rider's, Where Everyone Rides!" Quinn walked onto the lot.

Quinn wasn't a car freak, but his stint as a police officer had put him in the habit of mentally recording models and model years. The trouble he'd had the last few years of his job, and the trouble he was having now, standing in the lot and looking at the rows of cars, was distinguishing one manufacturer from another. Most of the cars from the early nineties on looked the same. The Japanese had built the rounded prototypes, and the Americans and the Koreans and even some of the Germans had followed suit. So the back end of a late-model Hyundai was, at a glance, indistinguishable from that of a Lexus or a Mercedes. A fifteen-thousand-dollar Ford looked identical to a forty-thousand-dollar Infiniti. And all the Toyotas — especially the ultra-vanilla Camry, the nineties equivalent of the eighties Honda Accord — were as exciting as the prospect of a house in the suburbs and an early death. Quinn had done without a car for so long because nothing he saw turned him on.

"How ya doing today, sir?" said a startlingly nasal voice behind Quinn.

Quinn turned to find a short, thin, middle-aged black man standing before him. The man wore thick glasses with black frames and a knockoff designer sport jacket over a white shirt and balloon-print tie. He gave Quinn a toothy, capped grin.

"Doin' fine," said Quinn.

"The name's Tony Tibbs. They call me *Mr.* Tibbs. Ha-ha! Just kiddin', man. Actually, they call me Tony the Pony round here, *'cause I give good ride,* y'know what I'm sayin'? I didn't catch your name, did I?"

"It's Terry Quinn."

"Irish, right?"

"Uh-huh."

"I never miss. Pride myself on that, too. Hey, you hear about the two Irish gay guys?" Tibbs frowned with theatrical concern. "You're not gay, are you?"

"Listen —"

"I'm playin' with you, buddy; I can see you're all man. So let me ask you again: You hear about the two Irish gay guys?"

"No."

"Patrick Fitzgerald and Gerald Fitzpatrick. Ha-ha!" Tibbs cocked his hip. "You lookin' for somethin' special today, Terry?"

"I need to buy a car."

"I don't think I can help you, man. Just kiddin'! Ha-ha!"

Quinn looked Tony Tibbs over: pathetic and heroic, both at once. The privileged, who had never had to work, really work, to pay their bills, could ridicule guys like Tibbs all they wanted. Quinn liked him, and he even liked his lousy jokes. But in the interest of time, he thought he needed to set him straight.

"Listen, Tony," said Quinn. "Here's the program. I see something I like here and the price seems fair, I'm not gonna haggle with you over it, I'm just gonna pull out my checkbook and write you out a check, today, for the full amount. I don't want to finance anything, hear, I just want to pay you cash money and drive the car off the lot."

Tibbs looked a little hurt and somewhat confused. Places like this were selling financing, not cars, and they were selling it at a rate of over 20 percent. The no-haggle bit seemed to knock Tibbs down a notch, too.

"I understand," said Tibbs.

"Also, we go in that trailer there, I don't want to buy a service contract. You even mention it, I'm gonna walk away."

"Okay."

"Good," said Quinn. "Now sell me a car."

Nothing stoked Quinn as they walked around the lot. Then they came to a small row of cars beside the trailer, where three old Chevys sat waxed and gleaming in the sunlight.

"What are these?" said Quinn.

"Eddie Rider's pets," said Tibbs. "He loves Chevelles, man."

"They for sale?"

"Sure. He turns them over all the time." Tibbs saw something in Quinn's eyes. He smelled blood and straightened his posture. "That's a high-performance sixty-seven right there. Three-fifty twelve bolt."

Tibbs pointed to a red model with black stripes. "There goes a seventy-two. Got a cowl induction hood and Hooker headers, man."

"What about that one?" said Quinn, chin-nodding to the last car in the row, a blue-over-black fastback beauty with Cregar mags.

"That's a pretty SS right there. Three ninety-six, three

hundred and fifty horses. Four-on-the-floor Hurst shifter, got those Flowmaster mufflers on it, too."

"What year is that?"

"Nineteen sixty-nine."

"The year I was born."

"You ain't nothin' but a baby, then."

"Pop the hood on it, will you?"

Quinn got under the hood. The hoses were new, and the belts were tight. You could pour a holsterful of french fries out onto the block and eat off the engine. He pulled the dipstick and smelled its tip.

"Clean, right?" said Tibbs. "You don't smell nothin' burnt on there, do you?"

"It's clean. Can I take it for a ride?"

"I got the keys inside."

"How much, by the way?"

"I'm gonna go right to the bottom," said Tibbs, "seein' as how you don't like to *haggle*."

"How much?"

"Sixty-five hundred. That's grand theft auto right there. Boss finds out I sold it for that, I might have to just go ahead and clean out my desk."

"Sixty-five hundred is right for this car?"

"Sixty-five?" said Tibbs, pursing his lips and bugging his eyes. "It's right as rain."

Quinn chuckled.

"What's so funny?"

"Nothin'," said Quinn. "This car rides as good as it looks, you got yourself a deal."

chapter **23**

QUINN met Strange for breakfast on Monday morning at Sweet Daddy's All Souls Paradise House of Prayer, occupying much of M Street between 6th and 7th in Northwest. The church was a modern, well-funded facility serving the community through religious and outreach programs, with a staff of motivated individuals who kept an eye on the grounds in what was a marginal neighborhood at best. Quinn parked his Chevelle in the church-owned, protected lot, and went to the cafeteria on the ground level of the complex.

Uniformed and plainclothes police, community activists, businessmen, parishioners, and local residents ate here every morning. The portions were generous and the prices dirt cheap. The staff's cheer and pleasant manner were fueled by religion.

Quinn built a tray of scrambled eggs, bacon, toast, and grits, and had a seat across from Strange at a long table where several other chairs were occupied by people of various colors and economic backgrounds. Strange was working on a plate of scrapple, eggs, and grits.

A white guy with a friendly smile named Chris O'Shea

came over to the table and had a brief conversation with Strange.

"You take it easy now, Derek," said O'Shea.

"All right then, Chris," said Strange. "You do the same."

Quinn noticed that everywhere they went in D.C., people knew Strange.

"You ready to go to work?" said Strange, pushing his empty tray aside.

"What've you got lined up?"

"We'll hang out near Ricky Kane's house this morning. He lives with his mother out in Wheaton. If he leaves, we'll follow him, see how he fills up his day. Here." Strange slipped a cell phone out of his jacket along with a slip of paper. "Use this, it's Ron's. My number is on there and so is yours."

"No two-way radios?"

"This is easier, man. And unlike a two-way, no one double-takes you these days if you're walking down the street talking on a phone."

"Like all the other dickheads, you mean."

"Uh-huh. You got yourself a car, right?"

Quinn nodded. "Think you're gonna like it, too."

Out in the lot, Strange laughed when he saw the Super Sport Chevelle with the racing wheels.

"Somethin' wrong?" said Quinn.

"It is pretty."

"What, then?"

"You youngbloods, always got to be drivin' something says, Look at me. Ron Lattimer's the same way."

"That Caprice you got looks exactly like a police vehicle. We got less chance of gettin' burned in mine than in yours."

"Maybe you're right. Anyway, we'll take both of 'em, see how things shake out."

Ricky Kane's mother owned a small house, brick based with siding, off Viers Mill Road on a street of houses just like it. The builder who'd done the community in the 1960s had showed little ambition and less imagination. From the activity he'd observed in the last hour or so, Strange could see that the residents here were what was left of the original middle-class whites and America's new working-class immigrants: Spanish, Ethiopian, Pakistani, and Korean.

Strange phoned Quinn, who was parked down the street at the next corner.

"You still awake?"

"I got coffee in a thermos," said Quinn.

"Bet you gotta pee, too."

"Now that you mention it."

"You see our boy when he came out?"

"I saw him."

"Another little punk with a big dog."

Kane had walked his tan pit bull halfway down the block an hour earlier while Strange took photographs with his long-lensed AE-1. Kane, medium height, blond, and thin, was wearing a thermal vest under a parka, a knit watch cap, and oversized jeans worn low on his hips. He had a hint of a modified goatee on his bony face.

"Tryin' to be an honorary black man," said Strange.

"He looks like every other white kid I see in the suburbs these days."

"Yeah, till they figure out what it means to be a black man in America for real."

"But this guy's got to be close to my age."

"Uh-huh. He sure doesn't look like the same guy was on the TV interviews, does he?"

"Check out that car of his, too. Kane got rid of that shit-wagon Toyota." There was a new red Prelude with shiny rims and a high spoiler sitting in the driveway of Kane's house.

"I see it. He did get a settlement."

"Yeah. That could be it."

Quinn took a sip of coffee from the thermos. "I tell you how much we enjoyed meeting Janine the other night?"

"She's cool. Hell of an office manager, too. You got yourself a fine young lady there as well."

"I know it," said Quinn.

"All right, here comes our boy."

Kane was coming out of the house with a gym bag in his hand. He opened the trunk of the Prelude and dropped the gym bag in, closing the lid and locking it.

"Goin' to work out," said Quinn. "You think?"

"Maybe."

"I'll go first," said Quinn.

"Yeah," said Strange. "Wouldn't want him to burn me or nothin' like that."

Strange and Quinn circled the block while Kane went into a 7-Eleven for coffee and smokes, then picked him up again as he headed south into D.C. They hung back several car lengths, as Kane's red car was easy to track. He took 13th Street all the way downtown, cutting over to 14th and pulling into a Carr Park garage down past F.

"Should I follow him into the garage?" asked Quinn.

"Park on the street," said Strange into the phone. "Park illegal if you have to; I'll pay the ticket."

Quinn curbed the Chevelle. Strange did the same to the Caprice, a half block south.

"What now?" said Quinn.

"Elevators in that garage go up into that building to the left of it. Unless he's got business in that building — and I don't think he does — he'll be coming out those double glass doors right there in about three or four minutes."

"Why don't you think he's going up into the building?"

"'Cause he's goin' to that restaurant, the Purple Cactus, across the street."

"Want me to follow him?"

"He knows what you look like, but not since you grew that lion's head of hair you got. So go ahead. You got shades?"

"Sure."

"Wear 'em. Only kind of disguise you'll ever need without overdoin' it. And when you're following a man, use the city, Terry."

"Explain."

"Keep the subject's image in your mind all the time, but indirectly. Watch where he's goin' in the reflection of the plate glass windows, in the car windows, in the metal of the cars themselves. Lose yourself in the crowd."

"There he is."

"Go on."

Quinn got out of the car and loitered near the building. Kane emerged from the building's glass doors. Strange watched Quinn follow, staying back in the moderate, late-morning throng moving along the sidewalk. With his shades and the hair, Quinn looked more like a rocker with shoulders than he did a cop. Kane crossed the street and entered the Purple Cactus.

Strange phoned Quinn. "Go on in. They'll be settin' up for lunch; just tell 'em you're thinking of bringing a date there or somethin' and you're checking the place out. Try and see what he's doin' in there."

"Don't let Kane recognize me, right?"

"Funny."

Quinn came out of the Purple Cactus five minutes later and crossed the street. He got into the Chevelle and phoned Strange.

"He was talking to a couple of the waiters and a bartender downstairs. Old home week, I guess. He's coming out now."

When Kane pulled the Prelude out of the garage and onto 14th Street, Strange said, "Let's roll."

Kane parked four blocks north in another garage. Strange followed him on foot this time, making a bet to himself that he knew where Kane was headed.

Kane walked into Sea D.C., the fancy seafood dining room and bar at the corner of 14th and K. The restaurant was fronted in glass, so Strange didn't need to risk going inside. Kane was talking to a man behind the bar, which was elevated on a kind of platform above the rest of the dining room.

Back in the car, Strange said into the phone, "He's making the rounds."

"What is he, a food broker?"

"He sellin' *something;* that's a bet. Usually, you see a guy hangin' around with restaurant employees like that, it means he's making book."

"Or taking orders for something else."

"I heard *that.* Here he comes, man. Get ready to move." Strange pushed the "end" button on the cell phone. He didn't tell Quinn that Sea D.C. was the last place Sondra Wilson had worked before she disappeared.

Kane drove to a velvet-rope, exclusive club over at 18th and Jefferson, where people were often refused entry for having the wrong haircut or the wrong label on their trousers. He next hit a Eurodisco on 9th, across from the old 9:30, a notorious nightspot for beret wearers and Middle Eastern trust-fund kids with coke habits. He drove to U Street and parked in front of a buppie nightclub. The pattern was the same: five minutes, in and out.

Kane drove east on Florida Avenue. Quinn and Strange followed.

Cherokee Coleman took the gold pen off his desk and tapped it on the blotter before him. "You lookin' large, Adonis."

Adonis Delgado, seated in front of the desk, glanced down at his crossed arms, defined beneath the blue of his uniform. He flexed a little, and the folds and wrinkles in his sleeves disappeared. "I been workin' on it."

"Looks like you have been. Think he looks bigger, Angie?"

Big-Ass Angelo stood behind Coleman, who was in

his leather chair. Angelo shrugged, his face impassive behind his designer shades.

"You ain't been using them steroids, have you?" asked Coleman with mock concern.

"You know I don't use that shit," said Adonis. He had shot himself up that very morning, after a two-hour session at the gym.

"'Cause you know those drugs fuck up your privates. Make you tiny as a Chinaman and shit."

"My privates are fine," said Adonis with a scary smile, his mouth a riot of widely spaced, crooked teeth.

Adonis Delgado was an ugly, light-skinned man. His forehead was high and very wide, and he had a stove-in nose with nostrils that flared upward in a porcine manner. His eyes were dead black and Asian in shape. Big-Ass Angelo said that Delgado looked like one of those mongoloid retards, like the one on that television show he used to watch on Sunday nights when he wasn't much more than a kid. Angelo called Delgado "Corky," but never when he was in the room.

"So what do we owe this honor to today, Adonis?" said Coleman. "Ain't many times you like to face-to-face it with us. Mostly you just drive around the perimeter, makin' the streets safe for our citizens. Me and Angie, we were getting the idea you didn't like associatin' with us types anymore."

"I came in to make sure we're clear on that Boone thing. Time comes, I want to make the last run out there myself."

"You and Bucky, you mean."

"Sure."

"He gonna be down with it?"

"He does what I tell him to do."

"Okay." Coleman cocked an eyebrow. "You seem kind of tense. You're not mad at me, are you, Adonis? Wouldn't be because I let Earl Boone take away your girl-friend, is it?"

"Shit. You talkin' about that skeeze over in the Yard?"

"So you're not *mad*."

Coleman and Delgado stared each other down for a moment.

Delgado sniffed and rubbed his nose. "Like I said, she's just a fiend attached to a set of lips. I let her suck my dick once or twice is all it was. I'm through with Ray and Earl, I'll just go ahead and add her to the pile."

"You want my advice, you're gonna kick it with her one last time, I'd wear two or three safes, man."

"I always double up," said Delgado. "Four-X Mag-nums, too."

"No doubt," said Coleman.

The cell phone rang on Coleman's desk. Coleman answered it, said, "Okay," and killed the connection.

"What is it, Cherokee?" said Angelo.

"Our little Caucasian brother is on his way in."

"I'll wait right here," said Adonis, "you don't mind."

"You got personal business with him?"

"He owes me money."

"Hittin' him up, too. Nice to see you expandin' your client base, *Officer* Delgado."

"I did plenty for that white boy. And I don't do a got-damn thing for free." Delgado pulled a cigar from his blue jacket hung on the back of his chair.

"Prefer you didn't smoke that in here," said Coleman. "Me and Angie, we can't take the smell."

* * *

Quinn and Strange followed Kane to a side street just east of Florida and North Capitol. As Strange saw the drug setup and the boys on the street, he said into the phone, "Hold up, Terry; I'm gonna take off and go up ahead. Tail me until I pull over and pick me up."

"Right."

Kane pulled up to an open garage door and drove through it into a bay. Strange watched him, then made a right turn. Quinn followed. Strange got back on Florida and went east to the Korean food market complex, parking his car in the lot. He grabbed his AE-1, jumped out of his car, and got into Quinn's Chevelle.

"Punch it," said Strange.

Quinn drove quickly back to the street off Florida where all of the drug activity was in plain sight. He parked far away, three blocks back from the action, and let the engine idle. Up ahead, young men stood lazy as cats against brick walls, on corners, and around a decaying warehouselike structure encircled with broken yellow police tape. Along with Japanese and German sedans, and several SUVs, an MPD cruiser was curbed on the street in front of a short strip of row houses, many of their windows boarded.

"You see that Crown Vic?" said Quinn.

"I see it," said Strange, his voice little more than a whisper.

"You need me to get closer?"

Strange leaned out his open window and snapped off several photographs. "I'm all right. Five-hundred-millimeter lens, it's like having a nice set of binos."

"There's our boy."

They watched Ricky Kane come out of the garage and cross the street like he owned it. He met a couple of the young men on the corner of the strip of houses and was escorted into the row house nearest the cop car parked beside the curb.

"What the *fuck* we got goin' on here?" said Strange.

"You tell me," said Quinn.

"Ever hear of Cherokee Coleman?"

"Yeah, I've heard of him. Like every cop and most of the citizens in D.C. What do you know about him?"

"Coleman played guard for the Green Wave over at Spingarn. He came out in eighty-nine. He could go to the hole, but he didn't have the height and his game wasn't complete, so college wasn't in the picture. Rose up in the ranks down here real quick after committing a couple of brazen murders they couldn't manage to pin on him. So the high school that gave the world Elgin Baylor and Dave Bing also gave us one of the most murderous drug dealers this town's ever seen."

"I read this interview the *Post* did with some of the kids over in LeDroit Park. They talk about Coleman like he's some kind of hero."

"He employs more of their older brothers and cousins than McDonald's does in this city, man."

"Cherokee," said Quinn, side-glancing Strange. "Why do so many light-skinned black guys claim they got Indian blood in 'em, Derek? I always wondered that."

"'Cause they don't want to admit they're carrying white blood, I expect." Strange lowered the camera. "Coleman works out of this area right here."

"Everybody knows it, and it keeps goin' on."

"Because he's smart. Drugs don't ever touch his hands, so how they gonna bust him, man? You see those boys out there on that street? All of 'em got a separate function. You got the steerers leading the customers to the pitchers, making the hand-to-hand transactions. And then there's the lookouts, and the moneymen, who handle the cash. The ones just gettin' into the business, always the youngest, they're the ones who touch the heroin and the rock and the cocaine. And even they don't carry it on 'em. You look real close, you see they're always nearby a place where you can hide a crack vial or a dime in a magnetic key case or in a space cut in a wall. And they're always close to an escape route where they can get out quick on foot: an alley or a hole in a fence.

"Once in a while the MPD will come through here and run a big bust. And it doesn't do a *god*damn thing. You can bust these kids, see, and you can bust the users, but so what? The kids serve no time on the first couple of arrests, especially if there's no quantity to speak of. The users get a night in jail, if that much, and do community service. And the kingpins go untouched."

"You sayin' that Coleman'll never do hard time?"

"He'll do it. The Feds'll get him on tax evasion, the way they get most of 'em in the end. Or one of his own will turn him for an old murder beef on a plea. Either way, eventually he'll go down. But not until he's fucked up a whole lot of lives."

Quinn nodded toward the warehouse, where addicts were walking slowly in and out of large holes hammered out of brick walls. A rat scurried over a hill of dirt, unafraid of the daylight or the humans shuffling by.

"There's where they go to slam it," said Quinn.

"Uh-huh. I bet a whole lot of junkies be livin' in there, too."

Quinn said, "What about Kane?"

"Yeah, what about our boy Ricky Kane, huh? You ask me right now, I'd say he's makin' a pickup. I'd say he was takin' orders back there from the staffs of those restaurants and bars. What do you think?"

"I was thinkin' the same way."

Kane came out of the row house. He crossed the street quickly and headed in the direction of the warehouse structure.

"Fuck's he doin' now?" said Strange, looking through the lens of the camera and snapping off two more shots.

"Derek," said Quinn.

Kane ducked inside one of the large holes that had been opened in the warehouse walls.

"We can't be hangin' out here too long, Derek. We can't wait for Kane to come back out."

"I know it. One of Coleman's boys is gonna burn us soon for sure, and that cop, wherever he is, he's gotta be getting back to his car."

"Let's take off. We've got enough for today."

"Get me to within a block of that cruiser, man, then book right."

Quinn pushed the Hurst shifter into first gear, worked the clutch, and caught rubber coming off the curb. He slammed the shifter into second. A couple of the boys on the corner turned their heads, and one of them began to yell in the direction of the car. Strange got himself halfway out the window and sat on the lip, his elbows on the roof of the car. He took several photographs of the police cruiser, shooting over the roof, and got back into the car just as Quinn cut a sharp right at the next side street. In the rearview, Quinn saw one of the boys chasing them on foot.

"God damn, Terry. I tell you to make all that noise? You must have left an inch of tread on the asphalt."

"I'm not used to the car yet."

"Yeah, well, we can't bring it down here again."

"Why, we comin' back?"

"*I* am," said Strange, sitting back in the seat and letting the cold wind blow against his face. "There's more to learn, back there on that street."

chapter **24**

QUINN woke up on Tuesday morning in the bedroom of his apartment and sat up on the edge of his mattress, which lay directly on the floor. There was a footlocker in his room and a nightstand he had bought at a consignment shop, with a lamp and an alarm clock on the nightstand and four or five paperback westerns stacked beside the clock. There were no pictures or posters of any kind on the bedroom walls.

Quinn rubbed his temples. He had downed a couple of beers at the Quarry House the night before, then walked by Rosita's, but Juana was not on shift. He went down to his apartment on Sligo Avenue, phoned her and left a message on her machine, and waited a while for her to call him back. But she did not call him back, and he left the apartment and walked down the street to the Tradesmen's Tavern, where he shot a game of pool and drank two more bottles of Budweiser, then returned to his place. Juana had not phoned.

Quinn made coffee and toast in his narrow kitchen, then changed into sweats and went down to the basement of the apartment building, where he had set up a weight bench and a mirror and mats, and had hung a jump rope on a nail driven into the cinder-block wall. The resident manager had allowed him this space if he agreed to share the exercise equipment with the other tenants. A handful of black kids and a Spanish or two from nearby apartment buildings found out about the basement and occasionally worked out with Quinn. He often helped them, if they were not the kind of boys with smart mouths and attitudes, and sometimes he even learned their names. Mostly, though, he worked out down here alone.

After his shower, Quinn went to the bottom drawer of his dresser and retrieved the nine-millimeter Glock he had purchased several months earlier after a conversation with a man at the bar of a local tavern off Georgia. He took the gun apart and used his Alsa kit to clean it, then reassembled the weapon. He had no logical reason to own the Glock, he knew. But he had felt naked and incomplete since he'd turned in his service weapon when he left the force. Cops got used to having guns, and he felt good knowing there was one within reach now. He replaced the Glock in its case, which sat alongside a gun belt he had purchased at a supply house in Springfield, over the river.

He watched a little television but quickly turned it off. Quinn phoned Strange at the office and got Janine.

"He's out, Terry."

"Can you beep him?"

"Sure, I'll try. But he might be into something, you know, where he can't get back to me right away."

Quinn heard something false and a bit of regret in Janine's voice.

"Let him know I'm looking for him, Janine. Thanks a lot."

Quinn got off the phone. Juana had been avoiding him. Now it seemed like Strange was ducking him, too.

Strange stood before Janine's desk.

"Ron call in?" he said.

"He's out there working a couple of skips. They should bring some money into the till this week."

"Good. You go to the bank for me?"

"Here," said Janine, handing Strange a small envelope. "Two hundred in twenties, like you asked."

"Thanks. I'm gonna be out all day. It's an emergency, you know how to get ahold of me. Otherwise, just take messages here, and I'll check in from time to time."

"You're puttin' all your focus into this Wilson case."

"I'm almost there. Pick up those photographs I put in yesterday, will you? And phone Lydell Blue for me, tell him I might be callin' him for another favor."

"You keeping track of your hours, Derek? Your expenses?"

"Yeah, I'm doin' all that."

Janine crossed her arms, sat back in her chair. "I didn't like lying to Terry like that."

"You're just doin' what I told you to do. The next couple of days, I got to work this thing by myself. It's too tricky for two. Time comes, I'll bring him back in."

Strange went for the door.

"Derek?"

Strange turned. "Yeah."

"This weekend was nice. It was nice waking up next to you, I mean. Good for Lionel, too. The three of us going out for breakfast on Sunday morning, it was like a family —"

"All right, Janine. I'll see you later, hear?"

Out on 9th, Strange buttoned his leather against the chill and walked toward his Caprice, passing Hawk's barber shop, and Marshall's funeral parlor, and the lunch counter that had the "Meat" sign out front. He thought of Janine and what she'd said. She was right, the weekend had been pretty nice. Knowing she was right scared him some, too.

Strange decided that he ought to call that woman named Helen, the one he'd met in a club over Christmas, see if she wanted to hook up for a drink. He'd been meaning to get up with her, but lately, busy as he was, the girl had just slipped his mind.

Strange parked the Caprice on North Capitol, near the Florida Avenue intersection, and walked east. He walked for a while, and as he approached Coleman's street he picked up a handful of dirt and rubbed it on his face, then bent over and rubbed some on his oilskin workboots. He had upcombed his hair back in the car. He wore an old corduroy jacket he kept folded in the trunk.

On the street he began to pass some of Coleman's young men. He put a kind of shuffle in his step, and he didn't look at them, he looked straight ahead. He passed a crackhead who asked him for money, and he kept walking, toward the warehouse surrounded by the broken yellow tape. Today, the cop cruiser was not on the street. He walked over a large mound of dirt, stumbling deliberately as he came down off the other side, and he headed for a hole in the warehouse wall. He stepped through the hole.

The room was large, its space broken by I beams, bird

shit, and puddled water on the concrete floor. Pigeons nested on the tops of the I beams, and some flew overhead. Strange liked birds, but not when they were flying around indoors. He kept the dead look in his eyes, staring ahead, as he heard the flap of their wings.

From the shadows of his room, Tonio Morris watched the broad-shouldered brother come into the main room of the first floor, mumbling what Tonio recognized as an early rap off a Gil Scott-Heron LP he'd owned once and sold. The man, square in his middle age, was moving slow and had a zero kind of look on his face like he had the sickness, and he was dirty and wearin' fucked-up clothes, but he wasn't who he was tryin' to appear to be. Tonio had lived it and lived around it for too long. He *knew*.

Tonio watched the brother cross the room, mumbling to himself, sloshing through the deep puddles without bothering to pick up his feet, heading for the stairs. He wasn't no cop. No cop would come in this motherfucker right here alone. The man wanted somethin', thought Tonio. Had to want it bad to come into a place like this, too.

" 'Kent State,' " said Strange, " 'Jackson State . . .' "

Strange neared a young man at the bottom of the stairs who was holding an automatic pistol at his side. The young man looked him over as he passed, and Strange slowly went up the exposed steps. He mumbled the spoken verse to "H2Ogate Blues" under his breath; he knew the entire piece by heart, and reciting it allowed him to ramble on without having to think about what he would say, and it calmed his nerves.

"'The chaining and gagging of Bobby Seale,'" said Strange. "'Someone tell these Maryland governors to be for real!'"

He was upstairs in a hall and followed the sounds of muted chatter and activity to a bathroom facility with open stalls. A man yelled something in his direction, and he kept walking, taking measured breaths through his mouth, steeling himself against the stench. Candles illuminated the stalls. The floor was slick with excrement and vomit. He came to the last stall, which was occupied by a man in a sweater, the cuffs of which completely covered his hands. The man, a skeleton covered in skin, was smiling at Strange, and Strange turned around and headed back the way he'd come. There was nothing here, no one to talk to or see, nothing at all.

The brother was back in the main room, heading toward the hole he'd come through, pigeons fluttering above his head. Walking slow but not as slow as before, Tonio Morris thinking, he didn't find nothin', and now he's fixin' to get out quick.

"Psst," said Tonio, his face half out of the shadows of his room. "Got what you're lookin' for, brother."

The man slowed his pace but he didn't stop or turn his head.

"Got information for you, man." Tonio wiggled his index finger, keeping his voice low. "Come on over here and get it, brother. Ain't gonna hurt you none to find out. Come on."

Strange turned and regarded a sick little man standing in the open doorway of a black room. The man wore a filthy gray sweatshirt, and his trousers were held up loosely with a length of rope. His shoes were split completely, separated from the uppers at the soles.

Strange walked toward the man, stopping beside a large puddle by an I beam six feet from the doorway. The I beam blocked the sight line of the young man standing by the stairs. Strange stared at the skinny man's face; his eyes were milky and glaucomic. Over the years he'd seen this death mask many times on the faces of those who were ready to pass, when he visited his mother at the home.

"What do you want?" said Strange, keeping his voice low.

"What I want? To get high. Higher than a motherfucker, man, but I need money for that. You got any money?"

Strange didn't answer.

"Suck your dick for ten dollars," said Morris. "Shit, I'll suck that motherfucker good for five."

Strange turned his head and looked back toward the hole in the wall.

"Hold up, man," said Morris. "The name is Tonio."

"I ask you your name?"

"You lookin' for somethin', right? Something or someone, ain't that *right*. Any fool can see you ain't one of us. You tryin', but you ain't. You can dirty yourself all you want, but you still got your body and you still got your eyes. So what you lookin' for, brother? Huh?"

Strange shifted his posture. Water dripped from an opening in the ceiling and dimpled the puddle pooled beside his right foot.

"White boy come in here yesterday afternoon," said Strange. "Don't imagine you get too many of those."

"Not too many."

"Skinny white boy with a knit cap, tryin' to be down."

"I know him. I seen him, man; I see *every*thing. You got money for Tonio, man?"

"This white boy, what's he doin' in here? Is he slammin' it upstairs?"

"The white boy ain't no fiend."

"What, then? What kind of business he got with Coleman?"

"Do I look crazy to you? I ain't know a *mother*fuckin' thing about no Coleman, and if I did, I still don't know a thing."

Strange pulled folded twenties from his wallet. He peeled one off, crumpled it in a ball, and tossed it to the floor at Morris's feet. Morris picked the bill up quickly and jammed it in the pocket of his trousers.

"What was the white boy doin' in here?" said Strange.

"Lookin' for a girl," said Morris. "A friend of mine. Old friend to him, too."

Strange's blood ticked. "A girl?"

"Girl named Sondra," said Morris.

"This girl got a last name?" said Strange, his voice hoarse and odd to his own ears.

"She got one. I don't know it."

"This her right here?"

Strange pulled the photograph of Sondra Wilson from his corduroy jacket, held it up for Morris to see. Morris nodded, his mouth twitching involuntarily. Strange slipped the picture back into his pocket.

"He find her?" asked Strange.

"Huh?"

"Is she *here?*"

Morris licked his dry lips and pointed his chin at the bankroll in Strange's hand. Strange crumpled another twenty and dropped it on the floor.

Morris smiled. His teeth were black stubs, raisins stuck loosely in rotted gums. "What'sa matter, brother? You don't want to touch my hands?"

"Where is she?"

"Sondra *gone,* man."

"Where is she?" repeated Strange.

"Two white men took her out of here, not too long ago. Little cross-eyed motherfucker and an old man. I don't know 'em. I don't know their names. And I don't know where they went."

Strange didn't speak. He balled and unballed one fist.

"They're comin' back," said Morris playfully.

"How you know that?"

"Word gets out in here. . . . The ones across the street, that one by the stairs . . . they know when we be gettin' too hungry. They tell us when we're about to be fed. And we are about to be fed. Those white men are bringin' it in."

"When?"

"Tomorrow. Leastways, that's what I hear."

Strange reached into his breast pocket and withdrew one more folded twenty. Morris held his hand out, but Strange did not fill it.

"What do you know about the girl?"

"The white boy, he used to bring her with him when he made his visits. He'd take her with him to that place across the street. One day he left her in there. She was across the street for a few weeks, comin' and goin' in those pretty-ass cars. A month, maybe, like that. Then she made her way over here. She kept her own stall up there on the second floor. But she never did make it back across the street."

"You know what time those two white men are coming back tomorrow?"

"No," said Morris, looking sadly at the twenty, still in Strange's possession.

Strange placed the bill in Morris's outstretched hand. "You see me around here again, you don't know me, 'less I tell you that you know me. Understand?"

"Know who?"

Strange nodded. Most likely he'd just given that junkie more money than he'd seen at one time in the last few years.

Strange turned and shuffled off toward the hole from which he'd entered. There was a racing in his veins, and he could feel the beat of his own heart. It was difficult for him to move so slowly. But he managed, and soon he was out in the light.

chapter **25**

STRANGE woke from a nap in the early evening. His bedroom was dark, and he flicked on a light. Greco, lying on a throw rug at the foot of the bed, lifted his head from his paws and slowly wagged his tail.

"Hungry, buddy?" said Strange. "All right, then. Let this old man get on up out of this bed."

After Strange fed Greco, he listened to the sound track of *A Pistol for Ringo* as he sat at his desk and went through the matchbooks spilled across it: Sea D.C., the Purple Cactus, the Jefferson Street Lounge, the Bank Vault on 9th, the Shaw Lounge on U, Kinnison's on Pennsylvania Avenue, Robert Farrelly's in Georgetown, and many others. These were Chris Wilson's matchbooks; Wilson *knew*.

Strange reached for the phone on the desk and called the Purple Cactus. He got the information he needed and racked the receiver. Strange rubbed his face and then his eyes.

He stripped himself out of his clothes. He took a shower and changed into a black turtleneck and slacks, then phoned the woman named Helen. Helen was busy that night and on the upcoming weekend. He called another woman he knew, but this woman did not pick up her phone.

Strange got into his black leather, slipped a few items into its pockets, patted Greco on the head, and left his house. He drove his Cadillac downtown, listening to *Live It Up* all the way, repeating "Hello It's Me," because he really liked the Isleys' arrangement of that song. He parked on 14th at H, walked to the K Street intersection, and entered Sea D.C.

The dining room and the dining balcony were full, and the patrons were three deep at the elevated bar. Many were smoking cigarettes and cigars. A narrow-shouldered manager with a tiny mustache was trying to get a group of men, all of them smoking, to step closer in toward the bar. His emotional, exasperated, high-pitched voice was making the men laugh. A television mounted above the call racks was set on the stock market report, and some of the fellows at the bar were staring up at the ticker symbols and figures traveling right to left across the screen as they sipped their drinks.

Strange politely muscled his way into a position at the end of the stick. White people, in a setting like this one, generally let a black man do whatever he wanted to do.

Strange waited for a while and finally caught the bartender's eye. The bartender was trim, clean shaven, and of medium height. He had a false smile, and he flashed it at Strange as he leaned on the bar and placed one hand palm down on the mahogany.

"What can I get ya, friend?" said the bartender.

"Ricky Kane," said Strange, giving the bartender the same kind of smile.

"What, is that a drink?"

Strange placed his hand over the back of the bartender's hand. He ground his thumb into the nerve located in the fleshy triangle between the bartender's thumb and forefinger. The color drained from the bartender's face.

"Saw you talkin' to Ricky Kane yesterday," said Strange, still smiling, keeping his voice even and light. "I'm an investigator, *friend*. You want me to, I'll pull my ID and show it to you right here. Show it to your manager, too."

The bartender's Adam's apple bobbed, and he issued a short shake of his head.

"I don't want you," said Strange, "but I don't give a *fuck* about you, understand? What I want to know is, was Ricky Kane hooked up with Sondra Wilson?"

"Sondra?"

"Sondra Wilson. She worked here, case you've forgotten."

"I don't know . . . maybe he was. He picked her up once at closing time when she was working here, but she didn't work here all that long. She lasted, like, a week."

"She get fired?"

"She had attendance problems," said the bartender, his eyes going down to the stick. "My hand."

"Barkeep!" yelled a guy wearing suspenders, from the other end of the bar.

Strange said, "Kane and Sondra Wilson."

"He met her over at Kinnison's, that seafood restaurant over near George Washington. She was working at Kinnison's before she came here. He was a waiter over there before he took the gig at the Cactus."

"Bartender!"

Strange leaned forward. "You tell Kane or anyone else I came by, I'm gonna send my people in here and shut this motherfucker down. Put you in the D.C. jail in one of those orange jumpsuits they got, in a cell with some real men. You understand what I'm tellin' you, friend?"

The bartender nodded. Strange released him. He bumped a woman as he turned and he said, "Excuse me." He unglued the smile that was on his face, shifting his shoulders under his leather jacket as he went out the door.

Strange went over to Stan's on Vermont Avenue and ordered a Johnnie Walker Red with a side of soda. The tender was playing Johnnie Taylor's "Disco Lady" on the house system, the one that had Bootsy Collins on session bass. Strange liked the flow of that song. A man took a seat next to him at the bar.

"Strange, how you doin'?"

"Doin' good, Junie, how *you* been?"

"All right. You look a little worn down, man, you don't mind my sayin' so. You all right?'

Strange looked at his reflection in the bar mirror. He took a cocktail napkin from a stack and wiped sweat from his face.

"I'm fine," said Strange. "Little hot in this joint, is all it is."

Strange sat at the downstairs bar of the Purple Cactus. There were several empty tables in the dining area of the restaurant, and Strange was alone at the bar. The smiles and relaxation on the faces of the waitstaff told him that the evening rush had ended.

Strange ordered a bottle of beer and drank it slowly. The brunette named Lenna, the sensible girl with the intelligent eyes he'd seen on his earlier visit, was working tonight. He knew she'd be here; he'd phoned earlier to confirm it. Strange caught her eye as she dressed a cocktail with fruit and a swizzle stick down at the service end of the bar. The woman smiled at him before placing the drink on a round tray with several others. Strange smiled back.

The next time she passed behind him he swiveled on his stool and said, "Pardon me."

She stopped and said, "Yes?"

"Your name is Lenna, right?"

She brushed a strand of hair off her face. "That's right."

Strange handed her a cocktail napkin with the words "one hundred dollars" printed in ink across it.

"I don't understand," she said.

"It's yours for real if you give me fifteen minutes of your time."

"Now wait a minute," she said, making the "stop" sign with her palm, but he could see from her crooked smile that she was more curious than annoyed.

"I'm an investigator," said Strange, and he flipped open his wallet to show her his license. "Private, not police."

"What's this about?"

"Ricky Kane."

"Forget it."

"I'm not lookin' to get you or anyone you work with in any trouble. This isn't about him or what he does here. You've got my word."

Lenna crossed her arms and looked around the room.

"Meet me at the upstairs bar," said Strange. "I'm gonna double your take tonight for fifteen minutes of conversation. And I'll buy the drinks."

"I've got to close out my last table," said Lenna, not meeting his eyes.

"Half hour," said Strange.

Strange watched her drift. Prostitutes and junkies were the best informants on the street. Waitresses, bartenders, UPS drivers, and laborers were pretty good, too. They cost a little more, but whatever the cost, Strange had learned that most people, the ones who knew the value of a dollar, had a price.

"How long did Ricky work here?" said Strange.

"Not too long," said Lenna. "The incident with the police officer happened about a month after he came. The settlement came pretty quickly after that, and then he was gone."

Strange hit his beer, and Lenna took a sip of hers. Her eyes were a pale shade of brown, her lips thick and lush. She had changed into her street clothes and combed out her shoulder-length, shiny brown hair. Strange noticed she had sprayed some kind of perfume on as well.

"What'd you think when it went down? Given that you knew Kane was dealing drugs, did you have any doubts about what you read in the papers? Did you think that maybe there was something else going on that night that they had missed?"

"Sure, it crossed my mind." Lenna looked around her. The nearest couple was seated four stools down the bar, and the tender was working under a dim light by the register. "A few of us talked about it between ourselves. Look, I put myself through undergrad waiting tables, and this place has financed half of my grad school tuition so far. Over the years I've worked at some of the most popular restaurants in this city. You got any kind of late-night bar business, you're gonna have someone on the payroll, whether you're aware of it or not, who's a drug source for the staff and the customers. A restaurant has a natural client base, and a bar's about the safest place you can cop. I mean, it's not unusual or anything like that, given the environment.

"And then there's the perception most of the people in this city have of the police. What I'm saying is, you're talking about two different issues here. Ricky Kane was a dealer, but nobody really believed he had been stopped that night for selling drugs. He probably got stopped and hassled for urinating in the street, just like they said. The feeling was, it could have been any of us out there. At one time or another, we've all had some kind of negative experience with the police."

"All right. How you feel about him now, then?"

"What do you mean?"

"Old Ricky is still comin' in here, doin' business. He was in here yesterday, taking orders, right?"

"I told you I wasn't going to talk about my coworkers and friends. They want to get involved with Ricky, it's their business, not mine."

"You must have an opinion about what he's doing, though, right?"

Lenna nodded, looking at the glass of beer in her hand. "I don't like Ricky. I don't like what he does. I'm no user now, but I walked through that door when I was younger. For me it was coke. Now it's heroin for the younger ones and the after-hours crowd. That's the low ride down. The ones who are using it don't know it or won't admit it, but there it is. Anyway, like I say, it's none of my business. Anything else?"

"One more thing." Strange slipped the photograph of Sondra Wilson from his leather. "You recognize this woman? Ever see her with Kane?"

"No," said Lenna, after examining it closely. "Not exactly."

"What's that mean, not *exactly?*"

Lenna shrugged. "Ricky liked light-skinned black women, exclusively. She fits the bill. None of them had grass growing under their feet, I can tell you that. I don't recall ever seeing him with the same one twice."

Strange took a long pull off his beer. He set the bottle on the bar and slipped five folded twenties into Lenna's palm. "I guess that's it. Sorry if I insulted you earlier. I didn't mean to imply that I was offering you money for something else."

Lenna shook hair off her shoulder and smiled, the light from the bar candle reflecting in her eyes. "You're a handsome man. I noticed you when you were in the other night, as a matter of fact. I was kind of hoping it *was* something else."

"I'm flattered," said Strange. "To be honest with you, though, I'm spoken for."

"I understand." Lenna got off her stool and drained her beer standing. "Nice to meet you."

"And you."

He watched her leave the restaurant and walk north on

14th. Strange finished his beer, realizing that he was hungry, and maybe a little drunk. Lenna was a good-looking young woman, and he was feeling the need. And it always was nice to get hit on by a woman twenty-five years his junior. These days, it happened less and less. But this Lenna girl didn't interest him. The truth of it was, white women had never been to his taste.

chapter **26**

TERRY Quinn sat at the bar at Rosita's, on Georgia Avenue in downtown Silver Spring, waiting for Juana Burkett to finish her shift. While he waited, Quinn read a British paperback edition of *Woe to Live On* and drank from a bottle of Heineken beer. Juana had smiled at him when he came through the door, but he had lived long enough to know that it was a smile with something sad behind it, and that maybe things between them were coming to an end.

As the last of the diners left the restaurant, Juana came out of the women's room, still dressed in her wait outfit but washed and combed, with a fresh coat of lipstick on her mouth.

"I tipped the busboy out extra to finish my side work. You ready?"

"Yeah," said Quinn, slipping the paperback into the back pocket of his jeans. "Let's go."

Raphael, sitting at a deuce and putting dinner tickets in numerical order, waved them good-bye as they were going out the door.

"Got something in today you'd like," said Quinn. "An old George Duke — from the Dukey Stick days."

"'Talk to me quick,'" said Raphael. "Hold it for me, will you? I'll be in to pick it up."

Quinn walked with Juana down Georgia to where the Chevelle sat parked under a street lamp. It shone beautifully in the light.

"This is me," said Quinn. "What do you think?"

"For real?"

"C'mon. Let's go for a ride."

Quinn headed into Rock Creek Park, driving south on the winding road that was Beach Drive, Springsteen coming from the deck. The night was not so cold, and Quinn rolled his window down a quarter turn. Juana did the same. The wind fanned her hair off her shoulders and bit pleasantly at her face.

"Now I know what you like to listen to," said Juana.

"It speaks to the world I came up in," said Quinn. "Anyway, you buy a new ride, you got to christen it with *Darkness on the Edge of Town*. There is no better car tape than that."

"I like this car," said Juana.

Juana's hands were in her lap, and she was rubbing one thumb against the knuckle of the other. Quinn reached over and separated her hands. He took hold of one and laced his fingers through hers.

"I'm gonna make this easy on you," said Quinn.

"Thanks."

"I got all this baggage, Juana. I'm aware of it, but I don't know what to do about it. If I didn't care about you I'd say, I'm gonna stick around and let *her* work it out. Because I'd stay with you as long as you let me, you know?"

Juana nodded. "I thought when we met that it could work. But then, out in the world, when other guys were staring at us, making comments when we were walking down the street, I could see that you couldn't handle it. And it's not like it was going to go away. In this wonderful society we got here, no one is ever going to let us forget. There were times, I swear to God, it seemed like you wanted the conflict. Like the promise of that was what got you interested in me in the first place. I never wanted to be your black girlfriend, Tuh-ree. I only wanted to be your girlfriend. In the end, I wasn't sure what was really in your heart."

"I'll tell you," said Quinn. "Maybe, in the beginning, you were some kind of symbol to me, a way to tell everyone that, inside, I was right. But I forgot about that, like, ten minutes after we were together. After that, in my heart, there was only you."

"It's too intense with you," said Juana. "It's too intense *all the time*. Even sometimes when we're making love. The other night —"

"I know."

"I'm young, Tuh-ree. I got my whole life to deal with the kinds of relationship problems that everyone has to face eventually. Money problems, infidelity, the death of love . . . but I don't want to deal with those things yet. I'm not ready, understand?"

"I know it," said Quinn, squeezing her hand. "It's all right."

Quinn turned left on Sherrill Drive and headed up the steep, serpentine hill toward 16th. He downshifted and gave the Chevy gas.

"Nice night," said Quinn. "Right?"

Quinn drove back into Silver Spring and parked on Selim. He said to Juana, "You up for a little walk?"

They crossed the pedestrian bridge over Georgia and came to the chain-link fence.

"I'll give you a leg up," said Quinn.

"You said a walk, not a climb."

"C'mon, it's easy."

On the other side of the fence, they walked by the train station and along the tracks. A Metro train approached from the south. Quinn stopped and embraced Juana, holding her tight to his chest. He looked over to the traffic lights, street lamps, and neon of Georgia Avenue.

"It's beautiful, isn't it?"

Her fingers touched his face.

"Don't forget me," said Quinn.

He kissed her on the mouth as the train went by, and held the kiss in the storm of dust and wind.

Strange was starving, and he decided he could handle another beer. He left the Purple Cactus and drove over to Chinatown. He parked in an alley, behind a strip on I Street, between 5th and 6th. There was a hustler in the alley, and Strange gave him five dollars to watch his car, promising another five when he returned.

Strange entered the back door of an establishment that fronted I. He went by a kitchen and down a hall, passing several closed doors, and on through a beaded curtain into a small dining room that was sparsely decorated and held a half dozen tables. Several young Chinese women and an older one were working the room. A single white guy sat at a four-top, looking about as much like a tourist as a man could look, drinking a glass of beer.

"Gonna have some dinner, mama," said Strange to the

older woman. She rattled off something to one of the young ones, who led him to a table.

"You like drink?" said the girl.

"Tsingtao," said Strange.

She brought him a beer and a menu while the other young women tried to catch his eye. There was a slim one with a little bit of back on her that he had already picked out; he had noticed her when he'd walked in.

One of the girls was talking to the tourist sitting at the table, who had set one of those booklet maps next to his beer.

"Whassa matter," said the young woman to the tourist. "You neeby be ray?" The other girls laughed.

Strange ate a dish of sesame chicken and white rice, with crispy wontons and a cup of hot-and-sour soup. He drank another beer, listening to the relaxing string music they were playing in the place. When he was done he broke open a fortune cookie and read the message: "Stop searching forever, happiness is right next to you."

Strange dropped the message on his plate. He signaled the older woman and told her what he wanted and who he wanted it from.

"Whassa matter," said the young woman to the tourist, who now looked somewhere between confused and frightened. "You neeby be ray?"

Strange left money on the table and got up from his chair. The tourist said, "Excuse me," and Strange went over to his table.

"Yeah?"

"Do you know what they're trying to ask me?" said the tourist.

"I think she's sayin', ain't you never been *laid*."

Strange went through the beaded curtain, muttering "stupid" under his breath. He opened one of the closed doors in the hall and entered a series of rooms.

Strange undressed and took a hot shower in a tiled stall. Then he went to a clean white room, dropped the towel he had wrapped around his waist, and lay down nude on a padded table. The young woman he had chosen came into the room and began to give him a full massage. He felt her bare breasts brush his back as she straddled his hips, and he became aroused. She asked him to turn over. It was a relief to lie on his back, as he had a full erection now.

The young woman pumped her fist a couple of times and smiled. Strange said, "Yes, baby," and squeezed one of her nipples between his thumb and forefinger. She rubbed lotion on her hands and jacked him off. Afterward, she cleaned him with a warm wet towel.

Strange dressed and dropped forty dollars into a porcelain bowl set by the door. The young woman gave him a look of disappointment and made a clucking sound with her tongue. But Strange was unmoved; he knew that forty was the price.

Out in the alley, he handed the hustler another five on the way to his car.

"All right," said the hustler.

Strange said, "All *right*."

Strange drove north and parked his Caddy on 9th, directly in front of his business. He turned the key in the front door, went inside, and flicked on the lights. He walked toward his office, glancing at the neatness of Janine's desk. The woman just didn't go home until she had taken care of all the details of her day. He kept on walking to the back room.

In his office, he had a seat at his desk. Janine had picked up the packet of photographs he'd taken down off Florida Avenue. He went through the pictures: Ricky Kane had come out clearly, as had the numbers on the bumper and side of the police cruiser parked out on the street.

Strange reached for the phone. He called his old friend Lydell Blue and left a message on his machine. He didn't want to leave the cruiser's identifying number on Lydell's tape. He phoned Quinn, got his machine, told him they had work to do the next day, told him where and when he'd pick him up.

It was going to be an early day. I shouldn't have drunk so much tonight, thought Strange. I shouldn't have . . .

"Ah, shit."

Strange saw a PayDay bar sitting on a piece of paper on the corner of his blotter. He lifted the bar and looked at the paper. Janine had drawn a little red heart on the paper, nothing else. Strange looked away and saw the Redskins figure, the one Lionel had painted for him, staring at him from the back of the desk.

"You all right, Derek," said Strange. But his voice was unconvincing, and the words sounded like a goddamn lie.

chapter **27**

EDNA Loomis was straddling Ray Boone atop their bed, sliding up and down on his thick, short cock, moving her hips in awkward rhythm to the Alan Jackson tune that was blasting in the room. Her head was bent forward as she whipped her orange-blond, feather-cut hair across his pale chest, shaking her head in time to the music.

"'She's gone country,'" sang Edna. "'Look at them boots!'"

Ray chuckled and grabbed one of her tits real good and hard. Edna kind of grunted. He couldn't tell if it was from pleasure or pain.

Ray shot off inside her, and right after that she faked like she was coming, too. He almost laughed, watching her shiver and howl, making a sound like a dog did when you went and stepped down on its paw. She must have seen some actress do that on one of her TV shows. Ray didn't know why she felt the need to fake it; he didn't care if she came or not.

Edna got off him and walked across the room. She turned the music down, then lit a Virginia Slims cigarette from that leather pouch of hers. The hand holding the lighter shook some from the speed that was still racing through her body.

"Turn that music off all the way," said Ray. "I'm tired of listenin' to it."

Edna clicked off the compact stereo. Ray watched her, and when she caught him looking at her she sucked in her stomach. Aside from those dimples she had all over the tops of her legs, the girl was gettin' a belly on her, too.

"Me and Daddy gotta get goin'," said Ray, sitting up on the edge of the bed. He squeezed the rest of his jiz out and wiped it off on the sheets.

"You gonna leave me a little somethin', so I'll have somethin' to do while you're gone?"

"You just smoked up a mess of that crystal before we fucked, girl."

"Bet your daddy's gonna leave *his* girlfriend a little somethin'."

"Aw, shut up about that," said Ray.

Edna stuck her tongue out playfully at Ray, then dragged hard on her cigarette. She wasn't going to make a fuss over it or nothin' like that. She still had that key to the room where he kept his stash, out there in the barn.

Earl Boone zipped up his trousers and looked at the girl stretched out there on his bed. She drew the sheets up to her birdlike shoulders and gazed at him with those funny, sexy, different-colored eyes. He didn't have no, what did you call that, *delusions* about her or anything like that. Sure, once he had got her out here in the country and cleaned her up, and kept her showered and smelling nice, she almost looked like any other good-looking young lady you'd see out there on the street. She was just a junkie, he knew, and if she kept up that pace of hers, she wasn't gonna live too much longer. But damn if she wasn't the prettiest junkie he'd ever seen.

"You gonna be all right, honey girl? 'Cause me and my boy, we got to make a trip into the city."

"You'll leave me somethin', Earl?"

"Course I will. You know I wouldn't let you have any pain."

Earl finished dressing. He heard that godawful music Edna was playing in Ray's bedroom down the hall. He hated that new stuff sung by those pretty boys with the department store–bought hats and the tight jeans, wondered why anyone would want to listen to that shit when they could be listenin' to Cash, Jones, Haggard, or Hank. Just when he thought he couldn't stand to listen to it any longer, the music ended. He figured his boy was getting himself ready for their last run.

Earl took a small wax packet of brown heroin from his coat pocket and dropped it on the dresser.

"Be back in a few hours," he said.

Sondra Wilson watched him leave, closing the bedroom door behind him. She tried not to look at the packet on the dresser. She didn't want to do it up now; she wanted it to last. But then she began to shake a little, thinking of it sitting up there all alone. She thought of her mother and her brother, and began to cry. She wasn't sure why she was so sad. Everything she wanted was here, ten feet away from where she was lying now.

She wiped the tears off her face and got out of the bed. She walked naked across the room.

* * *

From the bedroom window, Edna Loomis watched Ray and Earl out in the yard, arguing over something, Earl pointing to a row of stumps at the edge of the woods, where Ray had set up empty beer cans. Ray had his gun in his hand, and Edna figured he was getting ready to shoot the cans off the stumps. Ray liked to do that before their runs, said it got him "mentally prepared" to deal with those coloreds down in D.C. Earl didn't like Ray shooting off that pistol; he didn't care for all that noise.

He must have talked Ray out of it, because Ray left, then came out of the barn with his gym bag and loaded the heroin into the space behind the bumper of the car. Edna drained her third Jack and Coke of the afternoon, watching him complete his task.

She felt kind of funny, clammylike, and her heart was racing really fast.

You can always be higher, though. Ain't no question about that.

She rattled ice in the glass and sucked out the last few drips of mash as Ray and Earl got in the Taurus and drove away.

Edna got dressed, slipped the barn key into her jeans, and went down the hall, knocking on the door to Earl's room, where that half-colored junkie, Sondra, spent all her time. She opened the door and went through it when the girl didn't respond.

Sondra was naked, sitting on the edge of the bed, using a razor blade to cut out lines of heroin on a glass paperweight. Edna didn't think she'd ever seen a girl that skinny, not even those New York models she'd seen on

TV. She didn't know what Earl saw in her, but it wasn't any of her business, and anyway she didn't care.

"I'm goin' for a walk," said Edna.

"Okay," said Sondra, not even raising her head.

"I feel like takin' a long one in the woods."

"Okay."

"Fine."

Edna didn't know why she bothered covering her tracks with this one. She left the room.

Sondra bent forward and snorted up a thick line of heroin. She snorted the one beside it at once.

The warmth came almost immediately to the back of her neck. It spread behind her eyes and to the top of her skull. Then it was in her legs and buttocks and traveling like hot, beautiful liquid up her spine and racing through her veins. The edges of the room bled off, and Sondra lay back on the warm bed.

Sondra remembered that she had been crying moments earlier, but she couldn't remember why.

Edna patted her pockets as she walked into the barn and strode briskly through the saloon area toward the back room. She had her little brass pipe in one front pocket, the key in the other. She had wedged her leather pouch holding her pack of Slims and Bic lighter in the ass pocket of her jeans.

Edna used her key in the lock of the steel-fortified door, opened the door, and flicked on the lights. She closed the door behind her. She went quickly to the shelf mounted over Ray's homemade lab. She snatched a vial off the shelf and opened its lid. The vial was filled to the top with crystal rocks.

Edna shoved the entire vial into the pocket of her jeans. Ray wouldn't be back for some time. She was going to mix a tall drink and take a walk out in those woods for real. Smoke up those rocks and have a party her *own* self. She deserved a little treat, the way Ray always left her hangin' like that, when she was doing her best to service him good.

Edna heard a door open from the front of the barn. She turned her head and stumbled back, her own reflection in the weight-lifting mirror giving her an awful startle. Looking down at the floor, she saw the carpet remnant beside the weight bench, not completely covering the trapdoor.

Edna heard boot steps clomping on the barroom floor. She had always been a quick thinker, her friend Johanna told her that all the time. She thought fast and decided. There wasn't but one thing to do.

Ray and Earl had only gotten a mile down the interstate when Ray told Earl they had to turn around and go back to the property.

"I forgot somethin'," said Ray.

"What, that speckled powder?" said Earl.

"It gives me an edge when I'm dealin' with those rugheads."

"Go on back if you need it," said Earl, lifting a Busch from the six-pack cooler at his feet. "Me, everything I need, it comes from a bottle or a can."

Ray U-turned the Taurus and headed back for the property.

Earl cracked his window, then rolled it down halfway. "Weather turned yesterday."

"It'll get cold again."

"It stays like this, them greasers are gonna get ripe. You best put 'em deep, first chance you get."

"Ground's still too hard, Daddy."

"You better get to it, Critter."

"I'll take *care* of it, Daddy."

Ray took a deep breath, wondering if his father would ever stop tellin' him what to do.

Ray walked hard across the saloon floor, his fists balled tight. He needed to calm down, but how could he, havin' to take care of all these people, and his business, and on top of it all having to take a boatload of shit from his old man. He pulled his keys off his belt loop and fitted one to the lock on the back door.

The lock had already been turned. He reached for the knob. God damn, the door was already open.

"Edna," said Ray, shaking his head, because he knew it had to be her had been back here; somehow she'd gotten hold of his key. There wasn't anyone else stupid enough to test him like that.

Ray went to the shelf and took down the spansules of crystal meth. He shoved the vial into a pocket of his jeans. He scanned the shelf: That other vial, the one held the ice, was gone. Edna was probably out in the woods, smokin' it all up at once, greedy bitch that she was. He knew she hadn't driven anywhere, as the F-150 was still parked in the yard.

Ray turned at the sound of the car horn. That would be his daddy, just landin' on it, tellin' him it was time to go.

Ray looked around the room. Somethin' wasn't right. . . . Damn, there it was, too, the carpet remnant had been moved off the trapdoor. Must have been moved with

all that activity they'd had back here with the Colombians, what with them all floppin' around and shit. Even
so, thought Ray as he moved the carpet aside and lifted
the trapdoor, holding his breath against a familiar smell, it
doesn't hurt to check.

He looked down the wooden ladder that led into the
tunnel. The lights were on down there, but that didn't
mean nothin', they worked off the master switch.

Earl landed on that horn again.

"All right!" yelled Ray, though he knew his daddy
couldn't hear him.

Ray closed the trapdoor, placed the carpet remnant
over it, and dragged the weight bench over a few feet.
Now the weight bench sat atop the trapdoor.

Ray shut down the lights before he locked the door from
the outside. He took no pleasure in hurting Edna. But he
sure was gonna give her some when he came back home.

Edna wasn't scared, not really. Even when Ray had shut
the lights down, because she never had been frightened of
the dark. She sat on the cold dirt patiently, waiting to
make sure Ray had gone away for good, and when she
was satisfied, she kind of crawled around some until she
found the ladder, and climbed up it to the trapdoor.

The door wouldn't budge. Ray had put somethin' over
it. She wasn't surprised. She went back down the ladder
and sat, gave herself some time to think.

She'd seen enough of the tunnel, when the lights had
been on, to know that it went straight back fifty yards or
so, then went off hard to the right. It was a narrow open
shaft, and she'd have to go through it like a dog, on her

hands and knees, but there wasn't nothin' tricky about it; *it went back and cut right.*

Edna had no doubt that Ray and Earl had rigged some kind of opening at the end of the tunnel, a way for them to escape into the woods from all those imaginary FBI and ATF boys they were always goin' on about. Even Ray, he wasn't dumb enough to go through all that trouble of diggin' a tunnel without providing for a back door.

There was the smell of expired animal down here. Ray said there was snakes in this tunnel, but she wasn't afraid of no snakes, either. She'd lost count of all the black snakes she'd killed with a hoe, growin' up out this way. Maybe there was rats. But rats weren't nothin' but overgrown mice. *Somethin'* had cacked down here, that was for certain, maybe one of those barn cats that were always hanging around. She knew that smell.

Anyway, if she lost her bearings or something, crawling around down here, she could use the disposable lighter she had in her pocket. She was glad she had brought it with her. And the drugs.

Edna had an awful headache. It seemed to be getting worse. She found the vial of ice and the lighter and the pipe, and she hit the lighter so that she could fill the pipe. A little pickup would motor her out of this place quick and just right.

She smoked the rocks, coughing furiously on the last hit, and let the flame go out. The buzz started to build. It was a pleasant buzz at first. Then it was violent and it left her shaking. She realized that maybe she had smoked too much. The space felt very close, and for the first time she was frightened, though she wasn't sure of what. She wanted to get out.

Edna put everything but the lighter back in her pockets. Her hands were trembling, and she couldn't do it fast enough. She thumbed the wheel of the lighter, looked ahead, and began to crawl.

She could hear her own breath as she crawled. She started to hum, thinking it would calm her, but it only scared her, and she stopped and crawled on. Her head pounded and it hurt something fierce. She crawled with sudden velocity and found good purchase on the hard earth.

"Shit!" she said, as her head hit a wall of dirt.

I am at the end of the straight shot now, she thought, and she scrabbled, turning right and finding more space. The smell had grown awful, and she gagged, but she crawled on. She was dizzy and she panicked at the thought that she might be running out of air.

She gagged again at the lousy stench, heard a kind of crunching sound, struggled to draw in breath as she kept on and touched something soft, and crawled over another thing that was cold and hard.

Edna raised the lighter in front of her and got flame. Two corpses covered in writhing maggots lay before her.

"Aaah!" screamed Edna. "Oh, God, Ray, God, Ray, *God!*"

She turned, the lighter flipping out of her hand.

Edna fell forward onto her belly. She clawed at the cold earth. But she was too dizzy to move, and it seemed as if a hatchet had cleaved her skull. She vomited into the darkness of the tunnel and lowered her head to the ground, feeling the warmth of her own puke on her face. Her eyes were fixed and glassy, and her tongue slid from her open mouth.

chapter 28

"THEY'RE comin' out," said Strange looking through the 500-millimeter lens of his AE-1.

"They weren't in there long," said Quinn.

"Droppin' off the goods, I expect. Now they're goin' to get their money. Couple of *Mayberry R.F.D.*-lookin' motherfuckers, too."

"The short one's got high heels on. You see that?"

"Like I told you, it's the little ones got somethin' to prove. Those the ones you got to keep your eye on."

Strange and Quinn sat in a rented Chevy Lumina two blocks west of the Junkyard. They had been there for several hours, and Strange had filled Quinn in on everything he'd learned the day before.

They watched Ray and Earl Boone leave the garage, cross the street, and head toward the row house where Cherokee Coleman kept his office. Ray and Earl spoke briefly to a couple of unsmiling young men, who led them up the stoop and through a door.

"Gettin' the royal escort," said Quinn. "Wonder how many guns we got out here on this street."

"They ain't nothin' but kids."

"Just as deadly as anyone else. Anyone can pull the trigger of a gun."

"They don't have to be out here, though. They think they do, but they don't. They watch television, they see what everyone else has, what they're supposed to have, they want some, too. But how they gonna get it, Terry?"

"Work for it?"

"C'mon, man, you're smarter than that. 'Cause of some accident of birth these kids came into the world in a certain kind of place. Where they were born, and learnin' from the older kids around them — the only examples they got, most of the time — a lot of these kids, their fate was decided a long time ago."

"I'll give you that. But what would you do about it now?"

"Two things I would do," said Strange. "First thing, I'd legalize drugs. Take away what they're all fightin' over, 'cause in itself it's got no meaning anyway. It's like those MacGuffins they're always talkin' about in those Alfred Hitchcock movies — just somethin' to move the drama along. Legalization, it works in some of those European countries, right? You don't see this kind of crime over there. The repeal of prohibition, it stopped a lot of this same kind of thing we got goin' on right here, didn't it?"

"Okay. What's the other thing?"

"Make handguns illegal, nationwide. After a moratorium and a grace period, mandatory sentences for anyone caught in possession of a handgun. A pistol ain't good for nothin' but killing other human beings, man."

"You're not the first person who's thought of those things. So why isn't anyone talking about it for real?"

"'Cause you put all those politicians down on the Hill

in one room and you can't find one set of nuts swingin' between the legs of any of 'em. Even the ones who know what's got to be done, they realize that comin' out in favor of drug legalization and handgun illegalization will kill their careers. And the rest of them are in the pockets of the gun lobby. Meantime, nearly half the black men in this city have either been incarcerated or are in jail now."

"You tellin' me it's a black thing?"

"I'm tellin' you it's a *money* thing. We got two separate societies in this country, and the gap between the haves and the have-nots is gettin' wider every day. And the really frustrating thing is —"

"No one cares," said Quinn.

"Not exactly. You got mentors, community activists, church groups out here, they're tryin', man, believe me. But it's not enough. More to the point, some people care, but most people care about the wrong things.

"Look, why does a dumb-ass, racist disc jockey make the front page and the leadoff on the TV news for weeks, when the murder of teenage black *children* gets buried in the back of the Metro section every day? Why do my own people write columns year after year in the *Washington Post*, complainin' that black actors don't get nominated for any Academy Awards, when they should be writin' every goddamn day about the fucked-up schools in this city, got no supplies, leaking roofs, and fifteen-year-old textbooks. You got kids walkin' to school in this city afraid for their lives, and once they get there they got one security guard lookin' after five hundred children. How many bodyguards you think the mayor's got, huh?"

"I don't know, Derek. You askin' me?"

"I'm makin' a point."

"You gotta relax," said Quinn. "Guy your age, you could stroke out. . . ."

"Aw, *fuck* you, man."

A block ahead, a Crown Vic cruiser rounded the corner and headed east, driving slowly by the junkyard.

"That our friend?"

"I'd bet it," said Strange, narrowing his eyes. "Ain't nothin' I hate worse than a sold-out cop."

"What did you find out?"

"Just got the pictures back last night." Strange thought of the packet of photographs Janine had left on his desk and something stirred in his head.

"You gonna run the number?"

"Got a friend working on it now."

"We better get out of here," said Quinn. "He'll be turning around, I expect."

"I was thinkin' the same thing. Those rednecks, when they leave, most likely they'll be drivin' out of here the same way they came."

"I'd go back over to North Capitol and park it there."

Strange ignitioned the Chevy and said, "Right."

Quinn sipped coffee from the cup of a thermos and stared out the windshield. Strange uncapped a bottle of spring water and drank deeply from the neck.

"Me and Juana," said Quinn. "We broke up."

"What's that?" said Strange. He had been thinking of Janine and Lionel.

"I said, me and Juana are through."

"That's too bad, man."

"She told me I was too intense."

"Imagine her thinkin' that." Strange shifted his position behind the wheel. "That's a wrong move, lettin' a together young lady like that get away from you. It have anything to do with your color difference?"

"It did." Quinn tried to smile. "Anyway, like my old man used to say, women are like streetcars; you miss one and another comes along sooner or later. Right?"

"It sounds good. You're puttin' on a good face, but you don't see too many streetcars rollin' down the street lookin' like Juana. And you don't find too many with her heart, either."

"I know it." Quinn looked across the bench at Strange. "Since you're givin' me the benefit of a lifetime of wisdom —"

"Go ahead."

"When are you gonna marry Janine?"

"Marry her? Shit, Terry, I'm long past thinkin' about marrying anybody." Strange capped his bottle and looked down at his lap. "Anyway, she deserves better than me. But thanks for the advice, hear?"

"Just tryin' to help."

"So you got a father. You know, that's one of the first personal things you've told me in the time I've known you. He alive?"

"My parents are both dead," said Quinn. "I got a brother out in the Bay Area who I almost never hear from. What about you?"

"It's just my mom now."

"No brothers or sisters?"

"I had a brother. He's been gone thirty-one years."

"That was about the time you left the force, right?"

"That's right," said Strange, and he didn't say anything after that.

"Here they come," said Quinn, as the Ford Taurus approached from the east.

"Pa and Son of Pa Kettle."

"You got a full tank?"

"Yeah."

"They don't exactly look like they're from around here," said Quinn. "I got a feeling we're in for a long ride."

They drove out of the city to the Beltway, then hit 270 north. The Taurus, a nondescript vehicle to begin with, had the same basic body style as half the other cars on the road. The driver of the Taurus did the speed limit, and Strange stayed ten car lengths back, unconcerned that they would be burned. The heavy traffic was their cover.

"Don't you have one of those homing devices in this thing?" said Quinn.

"Yeah," said Strange. "Let me just go ahead and bring up their vehicle on the Batscreen."

"I figured, you know, that you got everything else. All those things you hang on your belt line, and those night-vision goggles you got in that bag back there. You get those out of a cereal box or somethin'?"

"Don't go makin' fun of my NVDs, man."

"What're we gonna do when we get there?"

"Wherever they're goin', that's where we're gonna find Chris Wilson's sister."

"Because some junkie snitch told you?"

"You go with what you got."

The traffic lessened as cars got off the highway at the exurban exits of Gaithersburg, Germantown, and Darnestown, the innermost fringes of the new megalopolis that was Washington, D.C. Strange eased off the gas and kept the Lumina farther back than it had been. Ten miles later, he saw the right-turn signal flare on the Ford up ahead. Strange took the off-ramp, keeping the Taurus in sight.

"We lose 'em?" said Quinn.

"I don't think so," said Strange. They were on a long curve that ran along open country and then dense forest. When they came out of the curve and hit a straightaway, the Taurus was up ahead. The driver had parked it at a gate of some kind on a gravel path cutting a break in the woods.

"Drive past 'em," said Quinn. "Don't even slow down."

"I look like Danny Glover to you? Do I look like white America's pet African American sidekick, man? I'm in *charge* of this investigation, Terry, case you've forgotten."

"Drive past 'em," said Quinn. "Punch it, man."

"What the fuck did you think I was *gonna* do?"

They blew past the Taurus. The short one, standing at the wooden gate and putting a key to a padlock, glanced up as they passed, giving them a brief and unfocused hard look.

"Boy is cross-eyed," said Quinn. "You see that?"

"Uh-huh. Noticed when I was looking at 'em through the lens. The older one has the same look, too. Got to be his daddy, right?"

They went into another long curve running beside more woods. Strange pulled over on the shoulder, cut the engine, and grabbed his day pack off the backseat.

"Let's go," he said.

They walked into the woods, dense with oak and pine, past a No Trespassing sign affixed to a tree and peppered with buckshot.

Quinn said, "This way," and pointed northeast. There seemed to be a trail of sorts, and they followed it.

"Looks like there's a break in the woods up ahead," said Strange.

"I see it. But we can't get too close to 'em, if that's where they are. This time of year there's no foliage on these trees. We got no cover."

"Right."

"And watch where you walk. Don't go snapping too many branches, 'cause the sound travels in the open country. This isn't the city, Danny. I mean *Derek*."

"Funny," said Strange.

Quinn looked over his shoulder and made a halting sign with his palm. Both of them stopped walking. Quinn looked around and motioned with his chin to a deer blind that had been built in the low branches of an oak. He pointed to the blind, and Strange nodded his head.

Quinn went up first, using the ladder of wooden blocks that had been nailed to the trunk of the tree. Strange tossed his bag up to Quinn and followed. The platform was narrow and shifted a little under their weight.

"This gonna hold us?" said Strange, keeping his voice low.

"I guess we'll find out."

They looked through the trees to a clearing about one

hundred and fifty yards away. They could see the father and son getting out of the Ford, parked between a pickup and a motorcycle in a cluttered yard. Past the vehicles was a large barn with a ramshackle house beside it. Strange looked through the lens of the AE-1, snapping photographs of the son as he took a gym bag from out of the trunk.

"I can't see anything," said Quinn. "My eyes are going on me, man."

"Got a set of ten-by-fifty binos in the bag. Help yourself."

Quinn dug the binoculars out and adjusted them for his nose and eyes.

The two men headed for the house, the son carrying the gym bag, looking back once into the woods before both of them stepped onto the leaning porch and went through the front door.

Strange squinted. "She's in there, I expect."

They waited, listening to the call of crows, twigs snapping, the wind moving the tops of the tall trees. Squirrels chased each other in the high branches of the oaks. They waited some more and neither of them spoke. A doe crashed through brush and went by them, disappearing down a rise that dropped west of the blind.

"Here they come," said Strange.

The two men came out of the house. Sondra Wilson was beside the father.

"That's her," said Strange.

The father took her arm as they descended the porch steps. Even at this distance, Strange could see that she was near death. Beneath the coat she wore, her shoulders were like garden shears, and her eyes were hollowed ou above sunken cheeks.

Now they were all standing in the yard, and the son was gesturing wildly toward the woods, the anger in his voice carrying through the trees, reaching Quinn and Strange. The older man was talking to his son in a quiet way, trying to calm him down. Then the son grabbed hold of Sondra Wilson's arm and shook her violently. Her head kind of flopped around on her shoulders, and that was when the father took three steps forward and shoved the son in the chest, sending him down to the gravel and dirt.

The son got up slowly, not saying a word, not looking at his father anymore or at Sondra. The father took hold of Sondra gently and walked her back into the house.

The son waited until they were inside. He pulled a gun from beneath his jacket and began firing in the direction of the tree line. His face was twisted into something between a grimace and a smile. Strange blinked with each shot, the rounds ricocheting metallically into the woods.

"What the fuck did we just see?" said Quinn.

Strange was thinking about the photograph packet on his desk, once again. He pictured himself in Chris Wilson's room, the items on his dresser and in his cigar box. He saw himself talking to Wilson's mother, the pictures hung on his wall, *one picture* . . .

"Derek?"

"Sorry, man. Was thinkin' of something."

"What?"

"Wilson had a stub from a grocery store, a Safeway, I think, in the cigar box on his dresser. There was a camera on that dresser, too."

"So there are some pictures he never got around to pickin' up."

"Uh-huh. Also, if he was trying to find his sister . . . if

we been covering the same tracks he was makin', I mean, then he probably has some kind of documentation related to what he was doin'. I'm thinkin' that maybe I know where that is."

"What are we waitin' on, then?"

"It's just that I hate to leave her," said Strange. "You got a look at her, man; she doesn't have much time."

"We can't do anything today. Not unless you want to pull that Buck knife off your hip and wave it at that guy with the automatic."

"You're right," said Strange. "But I'm coming back."

chapter 29

STRANGE lifted the framed photograph of Larry Brown and a young Chris Wilson, and placed the photograph on Wilson's bed. As Strange had suspected, the frame covered a hole of sorts in the wall. A tablet-sized notebook was wedged inside the hole among chips of particleboard, covered with a thick coat of dust. The hole was just large enough to accommodate the notebook; it looked as if Wilson himself had punched it through.

Leona Wilson had said that Chris had become visibly upset when she'd gone to straighten the picture. From everything Strange knew, Chris Wilson seemed to be the type of young man who would need an awful good reason to rise up at his own mom. Whatever Wilson had found — and Strange was certain that what he'd found was reflected in the notebook — he had kept it from his mother, his girlfriend, and the department as well.

Strange stashed the notebook in his day pack, along with the ticket stub from Safeway. The stub was redeemable at the Piney Branch Road location in Takoma, D.C., near his church.

In the living room, Leona Wilson peered out from

behind her parted curtains at the Lumina parked on the street. She released the curtain and turned as Strange walked into the room.

"Did you find what you were looking for?"

"I did."

"Then you're making progress."

"Yes, I am." Strange slung the day pack over his shoulder. "Mrs. Wilson?"

"Yes."

"I believe I've located your daughter."

Leona Wilson's lip trembled up into a smile. "Thank you. Thank the good Lord." She rubbed her hands together in front of her waist. "Is she . . . what is her health?"

"She's gonna need help, Mrs. Wilson. Professional help to get her off the kind of trouble she's found. You best . . . you *need* to start lookin' into it right away. There's programs and clinics; you can get a list through the church. You need to set that up *now,* understand? Do it today."

"Why?"

"'Cause I plan on bringin' Sondra home."

Strange headed for the door.

Leona Wilson said, "Who is that white man in the car out front? I'm afraid I can't make anything out but his color without my glasses."

"An independent I been using."

"Is he helping you with this?"

"Uh-huh." Strange opened the door.

"Mr. Strange —"

"I know. Just doin' what you're paying me for, Mrs. Wilson. Don't forget, you *will* be gettin' a bill."

"I'll say a prayer for you this Sunday, Mr. Strange."

"Yes, ma'am."

He stepped outside and stood for a moment on the concrete porch. He'd gone and promised this woman something, and now he'd have to see it through.

"I saw the Wilson woman looking at me through the curtains," said Quinn. "She recognize me?"

"She wouldn't recognize her own face in the mirror without her glasses on," said Strange. He blew a late yellow on Georgia, catching the red halfway through the intersection.

"I went to Chris Wilson's funeral. I tell you that?"

"No."

"Word must have gotten around with the relatives that I was there. There weren't many white faces to begin with, except for a few cops. Anyway, Mrs. Wilson found my eyes through the crowd — she was wearing her glasses *that* day — and I nodded to her. She gave me the coldest look —"

"What'd you expect?"

"It wasn't that I was expecting anything, exactly. I was hoping for something, that's all. I guess I was wrong to even hope for that."

Strange didn't feel the need to respond. He passed Buchanan and continued north.

"Hey," said Quinn, "you missed your house."

"I'm droppin' you off at your place, Terry. When I get close like this I need to think everything out my own self."

"You're not gonna cut me out of this now, are you?"

Strange said, "I'll phone you later tonight."

After he dropped off Quinn, Strange stopped at the Safeway on Piney Branch. When the woman behind the glass handed him the packet of photographs, she said, "These been in here a long time, Mr. Wilson," and Strange said, "Thanks for keepin' 'em safe."

He drove back to the car rental on Georgia, dropped off the Lumina, and picked up his Caprice, which he had left on the lot. Back at his row house, he fed Greco, showered, changed into sweats, went into his office, and had a seat at his desk. There was a message from Lydell Blue on his machine: The numbers on the cruiser matched up with a Crown Vic driven by a street cop named Adonis Delgado. Strange wrote down Delgado's name.

Strange angled his desk lamp down and studied the photographs he had picked up at Safeway. Halfway through them, his blood jumped. He said, "I'll be goddamned," and said it again as he went through the rest. He opened the notebook and read the ten log-style pages of text, detailing by date, time, and location the progress of Chris Wilson's own investigation. Strange reached for the phone, lifted the receiver, then replaced the receiver in its cradle. In an envelope in his file cabinet, he found the taped conversations he had recorded. He listened to them through. He rewound the tape to the sections that interested him and listened to those sections two more times.

Strange sat back in his chair. He reached down and patted Greco's head. He folded his arms and stared at the ceiling. He ran his finger through the dust that had settled on his desk. He exhaled slowly, sat forward, and pulled the telephone toward him. He dialed a number, and on the third ring a voice came on the other end of the line.

"Hello."

"Derek here. You remember which house is mine?"

"Sure."

"Better get on over here, man."

"I'll be right there," said Quinn.

Cherokee Coleman pressed "end" on his cell and laid the phone on the green blotter of his desk. "They're here."

Big-Ass Angelo adjusted his shades so that they sat low on his nose. "We ready for them to finish this thing?"

"Tomorrow night. We been sellin' this shit faster than I thought we would. We'll send our boys out there to Shitkickersville and let them bring back the last load. Bring back our money, too. Doom all those motherfuckers out there, so I can tell my Colombian brothers I went and avenged the deaths of their own. Stay in their good graces so we can keep on makin' that bank. Like to see those cracker cops out in Fredneck County when they find all those bodies, scratchin' their fat heads and shit, tryin' to figure out who and what and how come."

"Let God sort 'em out."

Coleman looked up. "That's a good name for this next batch, Angie."

"We used it, man."

"Fucked in D.C.?"

"That ain't bad, right there."

Coleman got up from his chair and walked to the office window. Two men got out of a black Maxima and were met by several younger men.

"Delgado got himself a brand new short," said Coleman. "Got some nice rims on it, too."

"He just wants what we got," said Angelo.

"Let him keep wantin' it. The want is what makes this world go round, black."

"How his partner look?"

"Boy has *got* some teeth."

"Wil-bur," said Angelo, whinnying like a horse and using his foot, dragging it front to back on the floor, to count to three.

Coleman and Angelo were still laughing as the two men entered the office.

"Somethin' funny?" said Delgado.

"Angelo here was just tellin' me a joke," said Coleman.

"How you doin', Bucky?" said Big-Ass Angelo to the second man.

"I told you not to call me that," said the man. "The name's Eugene Franklin, understand?"

chapter 30

QUINN sat on a hard-back chair in Strange's living room, the tablet-sized notebook and an empty bottle of beer on the floor at his feet, the package of photographs clenched in his hand. There were two photographs of Eugene Franklin and Adonis Delgado in the bunch, wearing street clothes and walking from Eugene's civilian car to the row house of Cherokee Coleman. Quinn had yet to read the contents of the notebook, but Strange had filled him in on the pertinent details.

"You want another beer, man?" said Strange, who sat on a slightly worn living room sofa.

"No," said Quinn. "I better not."

Quinn's eyes were blown out in his pale face, and jaw muscles bunched beneath his tight skin.

"Play me the tape again. The part where Eugene was talking in Erika's."

Strange played the tape. Eugene's voice filled the silence of the room: *"I saw where Wilson's gun was headed. I saw in his eyes what he planned to do. There's no doubt in my mind, if Terry hadn't shot Wilson, Wilson would have shot me."*

Strange hit the stop button on the micro recorder.

"Wilson would have shot *me*," said Strange. "Franklin slipped right there."

Quinn nodded obtusely at the recorder. "Play the tape of me. The first conversation we had, down at the scene, on D Street."

"We already did this once."

"Play it," said Quinn.

Strange popped in another tape. He cued up the spot that he knew Quinn wanted to hear.

Strange: *"You do what next?"*

Quinn: *"I've got my gun on the aggressor. I yell for him to drop his weapon and lie facedown on the street. He yells something back. I can't really hear what he's saying, 'cause Eugene's yelling over him —"*

Strange stopped the tape. "Your partner was *yelling over him* 'cause he didn't want you to hear what Wilson was sayin'. He was adding to the confusion, and he didn't want you to know that Wilson was a cop."

"Play the other part," said Quinn.

Strange: *"What happened when he looked at you, Quinn?"*

Quinn: *"It was only for a moment. He looked at me and then at Gene, and something bad crossed his face. I'll never forget it. He was angry at us, at me and Gene. He was more than angry; his face changed to the face of a killer. He swung his gun in our direction then —"*

Strange: *"He pointed his gun at you?"*

Quinn: *"Not directly. He was swinging it, like I say. The muzzle of it swept across me, and he had that look on his face. . . . There wasn't any doubt in my mind. . . . I knew. . . . I knew* he was going to pull the trigger. Eugene *screamed my name, and I fired my weapon."*

"That's enough," said Quinn.

Strange stopped the recorder.

"Here's the way I see it," said Strange, speaking softly. "Your partner was driving the cruiser that night. Y'all comin' up on Chris Wilson like that, it wasn't an accident. Franklin turned down D Street because it was a setup. He knew Kane was going to lure Chris Wilson there. He knew it wouldn't take much for Kane to get Wilson to draw his gun."

"Or for me to fire mine," said Quinn.

"Maybe. The fact remains, your partner was involved. We got the photographs and Chris Wilson's notebook. That young man did some really fine police work, putting it all together. The tapes I got corroborate —"

"I just don't want to believe it, Derek."

"Believe your own words," said Strange. " 'He looked at me *and then at Gene,* and something bad crossed his face.' 'His face changed to the face of a killer' when he saw Eugene. Your own words were, 'The muzzle of the gun swept *across* me.' Chris Wilson wasn't lookin' to hurt *you,* Terry. He was pointing his gun at a sold-out cop. A dirty cop who was in the pocket of the drug dealer who had put his sister in a junkhouse. You understand what I'm tellin' you, man?"

"Yes," said Quinn, staring at the floor.

"All right, then. Now, who's Adonis Delgado?"

"Big, bad-ass cop. He was sitting at the bar of Erika's the day we spoke to Eugene."

"Muscle-bound and ugly, with a stove-in nose?"

"Yeah."

"That's the one tried to step to me in the bathroom. Wanted to send me some kind of message, I guess."

"Eugene," muttered Quinn.

"You're goddamn right, *Eugene*."

Quinn stood out of his chair. He lifted his leather off the back where he'd hung it and put it on.

"Where *you* goin'?"

"To get the rest of it."

"You need my help?"

"This one's me," said Quinn. He turned as he reached the front door. "Don't go to sleep."

"I'm gonna see you again tonight?"

"Yeah. Gonna bring somethin' back for you, too."

Eugene Franklin had a one-bedroom apartment in a high-rise across the road from the Maine Avenue waterfront in Southwest. Franklin, like many single cops, considered his apartment little more than a place to eat, sleep, and watch TV. The living area was sparsely decorated and furnished, with a couch and chair facing a television, a coffee table, and a telephone set on a bare end table beside the couch. Franklin answered the ringing phone.

"Yeah."

"Gene, it's Terry, man. I'm at the front door in the lobby."

"Terry —"

"Buzz me in, buddy. I got somethin' I need to talk to you about."

Franklin pressed a button on the phone. He stood from the couch and ran his finger slowly over his protruding upper lip. It was a habit of his to do this when he was troubled or confused.

Franklin went to the door of his apartment, opened it, and stood in the frame. Quinn was walking toward him, down the long, orange-carpeted hall.

"Hey," said Quinn, a smile on his face.

Quinn's long hair bounced as he walked. He was moving very quickly down the hall, his head pushed forward. Franklin was thinking, He's like one of those cartoon characters, determined, walking with purpose . . . and now he could see that Quinn's smile was not really a smile but more of a grimace, a forced smile that had pain in it and something worse than pain.

"Hey, Eugene," said Quinn as he reached him, not slowing down, and Franklin saw the automatic come up from beneath the waistband of Quinn's jeans.

Franklin stepped back from the doorway as Quinn swung the barrel of the gun viciously, its shape a blur cutting through the fluorescent glare of the hall. The gun connected at Franklin's temple, and the room spun instantly as he stumbled back.

Franklin's feet were gone beneath him. He began to fall, and as he fell through the dimming light the gun streaked toward him, and this time he barely felt the blow. At the end, he saw his partner's face, ugly and angry and afraid, and Franklin loved him then. Falling into a soft bed of night, Franklin felt only relief.

Quinn stood in the center of Eugene Franklin's living room, the automatic held loosely in his hand.

Franklin sat on the couch, his head tilted back, holding a damp towel tight to his temple. The towel was pink where the blood of a deep gash had seeped through.

Quinn had placed a yellow legal pad on the coffee table before him and set a pen on top of the pad.

"How'd you turn, Gene?"

"How?" repeated Franklin.

"Delgado drew you in."

"Yeah. Used to see him down at Erika's all the time. In there every night, drinkin', talkin' mad shit, then goin' home alone. Delgado, he was like me. Neither one of us had many friends or was gettin' any play. So we got to talkin', Adonis and me. I knew he was all bad; everyone knew. But I talked to him anyway."

"What'd you talk about?"

"This and that, you know. Went from one thing to the other, until it came to this other thing. Delgado was tellin' me how a man with some money in his pocket didn't have to worry about finding women, they'd find *him*. How you could kick it with anyone out there if the woman had the idea you were holdin' bank. I knew his mouth was overloadin' his asshole, man, but with the alcohol runnin' through me and shit —"

"How'd it go to the next level?"

"He started talkin' about Cherokee Coleman's operation, down off Florida. How Cherokee wasn't never gonna see no time, how no one could touch his ass 'cause he was too smart. That the operation would keep goin' on as long as there was a market for drugs, and fuck all those junkies, anyway, they weren't nothin' but the low end of Darwin's theory. And then he told me how he was making a little extra on the side, how he figured out that if Cherokee was gonna be all that and no one was gonna do a goddamn thing about it, why didn't he, Adonis, deserve to get some, too.

"It wasn't no big deal, he said. A load came in twice a month to Coleman's, and twice a month Delgado cruised the perimeter of the area during drop-off day and made sure there wasn't anything goin' on out there in the way of interference, local or federal law. Never even got out of his car. He said it wasn't any more complicated than that."

"Why tell you? Why did he need to cut you in?"

"'Cause he couldn't always be there. And because they had a problem that Delgado couldn't or didn't want to handle on his own. Course, I didn't know what that problem was when I got in."

"Chris Wilson."

Franklin's eyes moved to the floor. "That's right. His sister had got hooked up with Ricky Kane. He followed Kane's trail the same way y'all did, and it took him to Coleman's. On one of those trips, Kane went into the office with Sondra Wilson, and when he came out, he was alone. Sondra was Coleman's woman, just like that, and it pushed Wilson way over the edge."

"You were in at this point?"

"Right about then, yeah. It was easy, just like Delgado said; wasn't nothin' but drivin' around the block a couple of times, twice a month. I didn't see anything all that wrong with it at the time."

"Bullshit."

"Just trying to explain it to you, how it was."

"Bullshit," said Quinn, a catch in his voice. "What happened next?"

"Wilson was surveilling now in his street clothes, by the Junkyard and on the corners. I guess that's when he got those pictures of me. He knew he couldn't go up against Coleman's army himself, and he didn't know who to trust anymore inside the department. But by now he was all fucked up over his sister, and he was gettin' out of control. He threatened Delgado outside of Erika's one night. He threatened me."

"You and Delgado went to Coleman."

"Delgado did. They decided to get rid of Chris Wilson. For Delgado, it was easy. By then I'd found out he'd killed before for Coleman. It didn't matter what I knew at that point; I was damn near one of them. They wanted me all the way in, locked in for real."

"They wanted you to kill Wilson."

"That's right." Franklin dropped the towel at his feet. A drop of blood burst from his cut and trickled down his cheek.

"They had Kane call Wilson out?"

Franklin nodded. "Kane told Wilson he'd gotten his sister back. To meet him on D Street at a certain time. They knew Wilson would lose it when he got there and found Kane alone. I drove us up on the scene. You know what happened next."

"You tell me, Eugene. You tell me what happened next."

"I never shot a man. Never even shot at one, Terry. I had my gun out and I had it pointed at him, but —"

"Why *didn't* you shoot him, Eugene?"

"Because you shot him first."

Quinn looked down at the gun in his hand. "You knew I would."

"No, I didn't know. But I knew you were more capable of it than I was. And I knew . . ."

"What?"

"I knew *you*. I knew what you'd see when you saw Chris Wilson holding a gun on Ricky Kane."

Quinn raised the gun to his hip, pointing it at Franklin on the couch. Franklin's lip trembled, and his eyes filled with tears.

"You won't do it, Terry. There's a part of me that wishes you would. But you won't."

"You're right," said Quinn, and he moved the muzzle of the Glock, pointing it at the pad on the table. "Write it out. All of it, Gene. Go ahead. I'm going to disgrace you to your family, and your fellow cops, and to all the folks you came up with over in Northeast. They're all gonna know what a lowlife you are. And I'm gonna make good and goddamn sure your fellow inmates know you used to wear the uniform when they haul your ass to jail."

"I'm sorry, man."

"Fuck you, Eugene. Fuck your apologies, too. Write it down."

Franklin wrote a full confession out on the yellow pad, signed and dated the bottom of the last page, and dropped the pen when he was done.

"I'd like to talk to my father before this makes the news," said Franklin. "When are you going to turn this in?"

"After we get the girl home."

"She's not in D.C."

"I know it," said Quinn. "Me and Strange, we were out there today. We followed those rednecks out to their property, where they're keeping her."

Franklin dabbed at the cut on his temple. The bleeding had stopped, and he lowered the towel. "I'm going to be there with Delgado tomorrow night."

"Why?"

"We're dropping off money and bringing back a load of drugs."

"Thought you never had to do anything but drive around the block."

"We met with Coleman earlier," said Franklin. "Those rednecks you followed, the Boones: the short one's named Ray, and his father's name is Earl. They killed a couple of Colombian mules, out at that property. Coleman wants us to kill the Boones, to make himself right with the Colombians."

"What about the girl?"

"They didn't mention the girl, maybe because they knew I wouldn't like what they had to say. Delgado used to hit it himself, and he still has her on his mind. He starts killin', though, I don't see him stopping until everyone's put to sleep."

"And you'll do what?"

"I can't shoot anybody, Terry. I already told you —"

"This is going down tomorrow night?"

"I'm meeting Delgado at eight. . . . That would put us out there near nine o'clock. They're going to pick us up somewhere else, then drive us back to the place."

"There's a barn and a house there."

"Yeah. Coleman says the Boones like to do business in the barn. They got a full bar in there; it's set up like one of those old-time casinos or some shit like that."

"Sondra stays in the house?"

"Far as I know."

Quinn holstered the Glock in the waistband of his jeans. "Tomorrow night, you keep them all in the barn, hear? Give me and Strange the chance to get Sondra Wilson out of that house."

"What am I gonna do when Delgado starts all that killin'?"

"I don't care what you do. It makes no difference to me." Quinn picked up the legal pad off the coffee table and slipped his pen into the breast pocket of his shirt. "Whatever you decide to do tomorrow night, I want you to know it won't change what I'm going to do with this."

"I didn't think it would."

"So long, Gene."

Quinn walked away. The door clicked closed behind him.

Strange was sleeping on the couch when the doorbell buzzed. Greco's barking woke him up. Strange opened the front door after checking the peephole. Quinn stood on the porch, his breath visible in the night.

"I got it," said Quinn, holding up Franklin's confession for Strange to see.

"Fill me in on what I don't know," said Strange.

Quinn told him everything, standing there.

When Quinn was done, Strange said, "Tomorrow night, then."

And Quinn said, "Right."

chapter 31

S T R A N G E hit the intercom-system buzzer on his desk and spoke into its mic: "Janine?"

"Yes, Derek," came the crackly reply.

"Come on in here a minute, will you?"

Strange leaned over, picked up a package, a padded, legal-sized envelope, off the floor, and placed it on his desk. In the package, addressed to Lydell Blue at the Fourth District Station, was the full evidence file Strange had collected on the Wilson case.

Strange had come in early that morning, made Xerox copies of the evidence, and dropped the duplicate package in the mail, addressed to himself. Next he'd called his attorney and confirmed that his will was up to date. He had filled his attorney in on the whereabouts of his modest life insurance policy, for which he had named Janine and Lionel joint beneficiaries.

Janine Baker came into the room.

"Hi," said Strange.

"Hi."

"I'm gonna be gone for the rest of the day, maybe a little bit into tomorrow."

"Okay," said Janine.

"You need me, you can get me on my beeper."

"Just like always. Nothing unusual about that."

"That's right. Nothin' unusual at all." Strange rubbed an itch on his nose. "How's Lionel doin'?"

"He's doing well."

"Listenin' to you, gettin' all his homework done, all that?"

"He's got his moments. But he's fine."

"All right then." Strange leaned forward and tapped the padded envelope on his desk. "You don't hear any different from me, say by noon tomorrow, I want you to take this package here and drop it in the mailbox, understand?"

"Sure."

"Keep it in the safe until then. There's another package like it, will be coming *here*, in the mail, a couple days from now. When it arrives, I want you to put *that* one in the safe."

"Okay."

"You got the billing done for Leona Wilson?"

"Soon as you tell me you've concluded the case, it'll be done."

"It's done. Bill her for eight more hours, and don't forget to add in all those receipts I collected in the way of expenses, too."

"I'll do it."

"Good. I guess we're all set." Strange got up from his chair, took his leather off the coat tree, and shook himself into the jacket. He walked up close to Janine and glanced at the open office door. "Ron out there?"

"He's off on an insurance fraud thing."

Strange slipped his arms around Janine's waist and pulled her to him. He kissed her on the lips, and held the kiss. She looked up into his eyes.

"First time you ever did that in here, Derek."

"I'm not all that good at putting things I got in my head into words," said Strange. "Listen, I'm tryin' to say —"

"You did say it, Derek."

Still in his arms, Janine wiped her thumb across his mouth, clearing the lipstick she had left there.

"I need to be gettin' out of here."

"It's early yet."

"I know it. But I wanted to spend the day with my mom."

Janine watched him walk away, through the outer office and out the front door. She picked up the package off his desk and headed for the safe.

Quinn put in an early shift at the bookstore, then came back to his apartment, worked out in the basement, showered, and dressed in thermal underwear, a flannel shirt, Levi's jeans, and hiking boots. He microwaved a frozen dinner, ate it, made a pot of coffee, and drank the first of three cups. He put *London Calling* on the stereo. He listened to "Death or Glory" while he sat on the edge of his bed. He put on *Born to Run* and turned "Backstreets" up loud. He paced his bedroom and found his gun and belt in the bottom drawer of his dresser.

Quinn stood in front of his full-length mirror. He wrapped his gun belt around his waist and buckled it in front, the holster riding low and tight on the right side of his hip. He had taken the Mace holder, bullet dump, pen holder, and key chain off the belt, leaving only his set of handcuffs, in their case and positioned at the small of his back. He holstered the Glock, cleared it from its holster, holstered it and cleared it again.

Quinn released the magazine and checked the load. He picked up the Glock, closed one eye, sighted down the barrel to the white dot on the blade, and dry-fired at the wall. The black polymer grip was secure in his palm. He slapped the magazine back into the butt of the gun and slid the Glock down into its holster.

The phone rang, and Quinn picked it up.

"Hello." Quinn could hear symphonic music on the other end of the line.

"Derek here. I'm ready to go."

"I'm ready, too," said Quinn. "Come on by."

Strange hung up the phone. He was sitting at his desk at home, the Morricone sound track to *Once Upon a Time in the West* filling the room. The main title theme was playing, and Strange briefly closed his eyes. This was the most beautiful piece of music he owned, and he wanted nothing more than to sit here and listen to it, into the night. But the sky had darkened outside his rain-streaked window, and Strange knew that it was time to go.

Adonis Delgado's black Maxima cruised north on 270, its segmented wipers clearing the windshield of the rain that had lightly begun to fall. The rush hour traffic had thinned out an hour earlier, and the road ahead was clear.

"They like to do their business in the barn," said Delgado, sitting low under the wheel. Delgado wore a black nylon jogging suit, his arms filling the sleeves, with a gold rope chain around his horse-thick neck.

"I know it," said Eugene Franklin, beside him in the passenger bucket.

"Back when the Colombians were still breathin', they used to laugh about it with Coleman, tell 'em how it went down. We call 'em after we get off Two-seventy, and they meet us in the parking lot of a strip mall. They drive us back —"

"I know all this."

"They drive us back, *Eugene*. They like to pour a few cocktails out in the barn before the business gets transacted."

"I don't drink."

"Have one or two to be polite, but don't go gettin' drunk. What I'm gonna do is, I'm gonna excuse myself, pay a visit to that little junkie. I'll take care of her, then come back to the barn."

"You think that's a good idea?"

"Fuck you mean by *that?*"

"Maybe you better take care of the girl after. I mean, the sound of a gunshot in that house is gonna travel back to the barn."

"I'll take care of the sound."

"You got a suppressor or somethin'?"

"You got a suppressor or somethin'?" said Delgado, imitating Franklin's shaky voice and issuing a short laugh. "Shit, Eugene, I don't know who in the fuck was ever stupid enough to give you a badge. I don't need no goddamn suppressor, man. I'll put a pillow over her face and shoot her through that."

Delgado kicked up the wiper speed. The intensity of the rain had increased.

"Now," said Delgado. "When I come back in the barn,

and I mean as soon as I come back in, I'm gonna walk
straight up to Ray and do him quick. You do his father the
same way, hear? I don't want to have to worry about you
backin' me up."

"You don't have to worry," said Franklin.

"There's our exit," said Delgado, pushing up on the
turn signal bar. "Grab my cell phone out the glove box,
man. Call that little cross-eyed white boy, tell him we're
on our way in."

Ray Boone broke open a spansule of meth and dumped its
contents onto a Budweiser mirror he had pulled off the
wall. He used a razor blade to cut out two lines and
snorted up the blue-speckled, coarse powder. He threw
his head back and felt the familiar numbness back in his
throat. He swigged from a can of beer until it was empty
and tossed the can into the trash, wiping blood off his lip
that had dripped down from his nose.

"Phone's ringin', Daddy."

"I hear it," said Earl. He had a cigarette in one hand and
was playing electronic poker with the other.

"That's them."

"Then answer it, Critter."

Ray lifted his cell phone off the green felt table where
he sat. He spoke to one of Coleman's men briefly, then
pushed the "end" button on the phone.

"They're down the road," said Ray.

Earl nodded but did not reply.

Ray had everything he needed on his person. His
Beretta 92F was loaded and holstered on his back, in
the waistband of his jeans. He had a vial of crystal meth

spansules in one of his coat pockets and a hardpack of
Marlboro Reds in the other. As for the heroin, he had
brought the rest of it out earlier and placed the bags
behind the bar.

Ray had brought the heroin out because he didn't want
to go back in that room more than one time tonight; it was
beginning to smell somethin' awful back there. His daddy
had been right, and knowing that made Ray even more
disturbed than he already had been since Edna up and left
him. The weather had warmed un expectedly, and those
dead greasers down in the tunnel were gettin' ripe.

Earl picked up his six-pack cooler full of Busch, patting his coat pockets to check that he had brought his cigarettes and his .38. He and Ray left the barn. Out in the
yard, Earl flicked his cigarette toward the woods and said,
"I'll be back. Need to check on the girl."

Ray knew that his father was going in the house to give
that colored junkie a bag of love, but he couldn't bring
himself to care. He wasn't even mad at his father for
pushing him down the day before. He had problems of his
own that were weighing on his mind.

Ray went to the edge of the woods and looked into its
darkness, letting the rain hit his face. Where the fuck was
Edna? All right, so she'd gone into his stash and smoked it
up, and now she was scared. But a day had passed, and
he'd heard not one thing from her. He'd called that big-
haired, smart-as-a-stump girlfriend of hers, Jo-hanna, and
she claimed to not know where Edna was either. Lyin'-ass
bitch, she *had* to know where Edna was, the two of them
was asshole buddies goin' way back to grade school. That
Jo-hanna, she'd even acted suspicious when he called,
like he'd done somethin' to Edna his own self. Shit, he'd

never hurt Edna. Course, he'd have to slap her around a little when she did come back, but that was something else.

"You're gettin' wet, Critter," said Earl, standing behind Ray. "Gonna mess up the leather on them boots of yours, standing out in this rain."

"Just thinkin' on something, Daddy," said Ray.

"I know what you're thinkin' on. We get through tonight, you can buy a whole bunch of heifers, you want to, take your mind off that girl."

"I guess you're right. C'mon, let's go pick up those boys."

They walked to the car. Earl said, "Startin' to smell back in the barn."

"I'll bury 'em tomorrow," said Ray.

"Told you that warm weather was comin' in."

What with Edna, and his daddy always tellin' him what to do, and the speed rushing through his blood, Ray had a mind to bite clear through his own tongue.

"You all set?" said Strange, standing in Quinn's bedroom, nodding at the day pack in Quinn's hand.

"Yeah," said Quinn. "How about you?"

"Spent the day with my mother. Doctors say she's shuttin' herself down. She's just kinda layin' in her bed, looking out her window. Wanted to be with her, just the same."

"I worked at the bookstore myself. Kept me busy, so I didn't have to think about things too much."

"How's Lewis doin'? He keepin' his hand away from it?"

Strange and Quinn chuckled, then stared at each other without speaking. Strange handed Quinn a pair of thin black gloves.

"Wear these when we get out there. They'll warm you some, and they're thin enough, you can pick up a dime with 'em on."

"Thanks." Quinn dropped the gloves into his pack.

Strange looked toward Quinn's bedroom window. "Rainin' like a motherfucker out there. Gonna be messy, but the rain'll cover a lot of noise."

"And the clouds will cover our sight lines, goin' through those woods."

"My NVDs will get us through those woods."

"You and your gadgets," said Quinn. He looked at Strange's belt line, where his beeper, the Leatherman, the Buck knife, and the case holding his cell were hung.

"Speaking of which," said Strange, "put this on." He took his beeper off his hip and handed it to Quinn. "We'll take two cars in case we don't leave at the same time."

Quinn nodded. "Otherwise I'll meet you at that No Trespassing sign on the second curve."

"Okay, but if we get separated or somethin —"

"I'll see you," said Quinn, "back in D.C."

RAY Boone went behind the bar and found the bottle of Jack where he'd left it, by the stainless steel sink next to the ice chest. His daddy's Colt was where it always was, hung on two nails, the barrel resting on one and the trigger guard on the other, driven into the wood over the sink. Ray put the bottle of Jack on the bar, took a glass down from the rack behind him, and filled the glass near to its lip.

"You boys want a taste?" he said, shouting over the George Jones coming from the Wurlitzer.

Ray watched the funny-lookin' coon with the buck teeth, sitting glumly with a beer can in his hand at the felt-covered card table, shake his head. The other rughead, the big ugly one with the fancy running suit, didn't even acknowledge the question. He was standing in the middle of the room, rolling his head on his stack of shoulders like he was trying to work something out of his fat neck. A cigar was clenched between his teeth.

"How about you, Daddy?" said Ray.

"I'll have a little," said Earl. He was at the jukebox, punching in numbers and drinking from a can of Busch beer.

Ray poured one for his father. He almost laughed, thinking of him and his daddy and their guests, all of them still wearing their coats in the heated barn. Ray knew, and each and every one of them knew, that they all were carrying guns. It was part of the game. Ray and Earl wanted out, and with all this money they were makin', they really didn't need to be doing this anymore. But when Ray thought about it, he had to admit he would miss this part, the drinking with the customers, the tension, the guns . . . the game.

Coleman's pocket cops had put the bag of money up on the bar, near the end. Ray had put the bags of heroin right next to it. Neither of them had made a move to weigh or even have a look at the drugs. Ray had said it would be rude for them not to have a drink first, and they had complied.

Ray broke open a spansule of meth and poured it out onto the bar. He didn't bother to track it out with his blade. He leaned over the bar and snorted it all up his nose. Fuck it, he didn't care what his daddy or the rughead cops thought, he was gonna celebrate the end of this thing tonight.

"Whoo!" said Ray. He lit up a smoke.

"Tonight, the bottle let me down," came the vocal from the juke.

Country-ass, cracker trash, thought Adonis Delgado, killing the rest of the cheap, piss-tastin' beer they'd given him. First they make him lie down in the backseat of that Ford with his head in Eugene Franklin's ass, making his neck all stiff, and now he had to listen to this backwoods bullshit on the record machine. Delgado had a throwdown automatic, a Browning 9, in his clip-on holster. He was gonna enjoy pulling it, the time came.

Eugene Franklin watched Earl Boone walk by him and take a seat on a stool set in front of a video game that had playing cards on its screen. Franklin reached into his coat pocket and touched the Glock 17, his service weapon, sitting loosely there. He checked his wristwatch, thinking of Quinn and Strange.

"Got someplace you need to be?" said Ray, coming around the bar with a glass of whiskey in his hand, a cigarette dangling from his lips. "Huh, Eugene? It's Eugene, ain't that right?"

"I'm comfortable," said Franklin, not looking into the fucked-up eyes of Ray Boone. "I'm fine."

"*I'm* not fine," said Delgado. "I need to use the bathroom."

"Piss outside," said Ray, "like we been doin' all night."

"I gotta take a shit," said Delgado. "Ain't you got a toilet in this place?"

"Got one in the back, but it's broke," said Earl.

"Use the one in the house," said Ray. "It's open."

Delgado saw the father turn his head and give the son a look.

"Don't worry, I won't touch nothin'," said Delgado. "Where's it at?"

"Top of the stairs," said Ray.

"Be right back," said Delgado to Franklin. Delgado snapped his cigar in half and tossed it in the card table ashtray.

Franklin watched Delgado leave by the barn door. He raised the beer can to his mouth and was thankful for the loud music and the sound of the rain hitting the roof. He could feel his teeth chattering lightly against the can.

* * *

Quinn and Strange hiked through the woods. Strange had his goggles on, and Quinn stayed close behind him. The wind and water whipped against their faces. They wore layers of clothing under their coats and the thin black gloves on their hands, but it wasn't enough. Strange slipped once on a muddy rise, and Quinn grabbed his elbow, keeping him on his feet.

They made it to the area at the edge of the woods and dropped their day packs on wet brown needles in a dense stand of pine. A spot lamp mounted above the barn door illuminated the yard, and the heavy rain slashed through its wide triangle of light. In the house, a dim light shone beyond the darkness of a bedroom window.

Strange dropped his goggles in his bag and withdrew a short crow bar. Quinn reached into his bag and pulled the gun belt. He stood and buckled it, unsnapping its holster.

"Look at you," said Strange. "Gettin' all Lee Van Cleef."

"Somebody's got to."

"Yeah, I know. I always take the light work, when I can."

Strange looked up at the second floor of the house. He looked back at Quinn, dripping wet, his long hair slick and stuck to the sides of his face. "I guess she's in there. And I guess the rest of them are in the barn."

"Lotta guessin'."

"Anyway, we're gonna find out." Strange took a couple of deep, even breaths. "Put that beeper on that gun belt, man."

Quinn clipped it to his left hip. "Okay, it's on."

"If I get back out here and I don't see you, I'm gonna keep right on goin' with Sondra, you understand? I don't like leavin' you, man, but we accomplish one thing here tonight, it's to get that girl back to her mother, Terry —"

"I hear you."

"So I'm not gonna stop and wait for you, man. I get Sondra back to my vehicle, I'm gonna phone you from my cell. That beeper goes off, it's your signal that I got her out safe, hear? You get out then, but only then. Till you hear from me, you hold them in that barn."

"I'll hold 'em till hell freezes over or you say different."

"God damn, you are somethin', man."

"Get goin', Derek."

"Listen, Terry . . ."

"Go on," said Quinn. "I'll see you out front of Leona Wilson's house, hear?"

Strange went into the yard, zigzagging combat style through the light. He got up onto the leaning porch of the house, ready to use the crowbar in the jamb of the door. But the knob turned in his hand, and Strange opened the door and walked inside.

Quinn removed his coat. He dropped it on his day pack, lying on the pine needles at his feet.

Adonis Delgado stripped off his shirt and pants, and left them in a heap on the floor. He got out of his briefs and dropped them atop the rest of his clothing, walking naked across the bedroom to where the girl sat, backed up against the headboard atop the sheets. He thought he heard a creak on the stairs outside the closed door but then became distracted as he caught a glimpse of himself in the dresser mirror; he looked good, hard in the stomach and pumped in the arms, shoulders, and chest. His erection was fully engorged as he reached the foot of the bed.

"C'mere, girl," he said to the Wilson junkie, depleted to bones and drawn skin, a mile away from the way she'd looked when he'd had her the first time, over in the junkyard. That was all right. Her irises were pinpoints. He knew she'd just gotten high, and that was all right, too.

"Please," said Sondra Wilson, her voice little more than an exhaled whimper.

Delgado grabbed hold of one of her thin wrists. "Trick-ass bitch."

Outside the bedroom, past the landing, Strange ascended the stairs.

"Where's your shadow?" said Ray. "He's been gone twenty minutes."

"He'll be back," said Franklin.

"I'll *get* him back," said Earl, standing from the seat in front of the electronic poker game.

"I will, Daddy," said Ray. "I gotta drain my lily, anyhow."

Earl watched his son go out the barn door. He went behind the bar to mix himself a drink, keeping an eye on the one with the horse teeth. The bottle of Jack was sitting on the sink. While his hands were down there, Earl took the Colt off the nails and racked the slide, placing the gun on its side on the stainless steel.

Earl had his .38 in his coat pocket, but he thought he'd keep another weapon live and within reach. You never could have too many guns around when you were dealing with common trash.

"This is a good one right here," said Earl, motioning with his chin to the jukebox. "Orange Blossom Special." But the colored cop sitting at the card table didn't respond. "What'sa matter, fella? Don't you like Johnny Cash?"

Quinn rolled out into the yard as he saw the barn door begin to open. He got up on his haunches and pinned himself against the Ford pickup that was parked beside the Taurus. He drew his Glock and jacked a round into the chamber, keeping the barrel pointed up beside his face. He rose slowly, watching the son, the one named Ray, go by and head for the house.

For a moment, Quinn studied the rhythm in Ray's stride. Quinn silently counted to three and stepped out into the yard, walking behind Ray, closing in quickly on Ray, and then shouting, "Hold it right there!" as Ray put one foot up on the porch steps.

Ray stopped walking. Quinn said, "Put your arms up and lace your fingers behind your head. Do it and spread your legs!"

Ray put his arms up, turning his head slightly. He was slow to spread his legs, and Quinn moved in and kicked one of Ray's legs out at the calf.

"Who the *fuck* are you?" said Ray.

"Shut up," said Quinn, pressing the barrel of the Glock to the soft spot behind Ray's right ear. Quinn frisked Ray quickly, found an automatic holstered at the small of his back, pulled it, nimbly released the magazine, let it drop

to the muddy earth, and tossed the body of the gun far
aside. Quinn nearly grinned; he hadn't lost a step or forgotten a goddamn thing.

"Walk back into the barn," said Quinn.

"Easy," said Ray.

"I said walk."

Ray turned, and Quinn turned with him. They moved
together, the gun still at Ray's ear, and made it to the barn
door. Then they were through the barn door, Quinn blink-
ing water from his eyes. Then they were inside.

Quinn speed-scanned the scene: The father was behind
the bar, his eyes lazy and unfazed, his hands not visible.
Eugene was sitting at some kind of card table, drinking a
beer. Delgado was not in sight.

"Get your hands up, both of you!" shouted Quinn.
"Don't come up with anything, or I swear to God I'll blow
his shit out across the room."

"Take it easy, fella," said Earl, as he slowly raised his
hands.

Quinn could barely hear him. The music coming from
the jukebox echoed loudly in the big room.

"You at the table," said Quinn. "Lay your hands out flat
in front of you!"

Franklin did as he was told.

"Move over to that bar," said Quinn, giving Ray a
shove. "Put your back up against it, hear?"

Ray walked to the bar, stopping about six feet down
from where his father stood on the other side. He turned
and leaned his back against the bar and placed the heel of
one Dingo boot over the brass rail. His forearms rested on
the mahogany, and his hands dangled limply in the air.
Blood trickled from one nostril and ran down his lip.

Quinn moved the gun from father to son. He moved it to Franklin and then quickly back to the Boones.

"You," he said, his eyes darting in the direction of Franklin. "Get up and pull the plug on that jukebox. Do it and get back in your seat."

Eugene Franklin got out of his chair, walked to the jukebox, got down on one knee, and yanked the plug out of the receptacle. The music died instantly. Franklin walked back to his chair, sat down, and placed his hands flat on the green felt of the table.

Now there was only the sound of the rain. It beat against the wood of the barn and clicked steadily on the tin roof.

"What're you?" said Ray. "FBI? DEA?"

"Whatever he is," said Earl, "he's all alone."

"Must be one of those agents likes to do it solo," said Ray. "A cowboy. That what you are?"

That's what I am, thought Quinn.

They heard the muffled scream of a woman. Then the rain alone, then the woman's steady, muffled scream.

"You hear that, Critter?"

"I hear it."

"Just shut your mouths," said Quinn.

Delgado wrapped a meaty hand through Sondra Wilson's hair and dragged her toward him across the sheets.

The door burst open. Delgado turned, naked. A man was rushing toward him with a crowbar raised in his hands. Delgado took the blow on his forearm and used his fist to clip the man on the ear as the man body-slammed him into the dresser. Delgado threw the man off of him, the crowbar flipping from his grasp. The man stumbled, gained his footing, and took a stance, his feet planted firmly, the fingers of his hands spread wide.

"Strange," said Delgado, and he laughed.

Strange saw Delgado glance at his clothing heaped on the floor. Strange kicked the clothing to the side. Delgado balled his fists, touched one thumb and then the other to his chin, and came in, Strange backpedaling to the wall.

Delgado was on him then. He led with a left jab that stung Strange's ribs, then hooked a right. Strange tucked his elbows in tight, his left bicep absorbing the blow down to the bone. Strange grunted, exploded with an uppercut, connected to Delgado's jaw. It moved Delgado back a step and brought rage to his eyes. He crossed the room in two strides. The right came furiously. The right was a blur, and it caught Strange on his cheek and knocked him off his feet.

Strange rolled, came up standing, and shook the dizziness from his head. His hand found the sheath on his hip. He unsnapped it and freed the Buck knife. He pulled the blade from the handle and hefted the knife in his hand. Delgado smiled from across the room. His gums were red with blood.

"I am gonna take that motherfucker *from* you, old man."

"Take it," said Strange.

Delgado bobbed, moved in, feigned a left and threw a right, putting everything into the right and aiming three feet behind Strange's head. Strange slipped the punch. The momentum carried Delgado through, and he stumbled, slipping so that he was on one knee before Strange and looking up at him, his eyes wide and white. Strange came down violently with the knife, burying the blade to the handle in Delgado's thick neck. The blade severed his carotid artery and pierced his windpipe. A crimson fountain erupted into the room. Sondra screamed.

Delgado pawed weakly for the handle as he crashed to the floor. He coughed out a mist of red and fought for air. Delgado's brain died, and he kicked like an animal as his head dropped into a spreading pool of blood.

Strange put the sole of his boot to the side of Delgado's face and withdrew the knife. He wiped the blade off on his jeans, pushed down on the brass safety, and folded the blade back into its handle. Sheathing it, he turned to the girl. She had balled herself up against the headboard, and her screams were shrill in the room. Strange picked up the crowbar and slipped it into the back pocket of his jeans.

Strange crossed the room and slapped Sondra hard across the face. He slapped her again. She stopped screaming and began to sob and shake. She was afraid of him, and that was good. He ripped the wool blanket off the bed and wrapped it around her shoulders.

Strange picked Sondra up and carried her from the room, out onto the landing, and down the stairs. He managed the front door and walked out to the porch, down the steps, and out into the rain. He didn't look at the barn. He stopped at the stand of pine, laid Sondra down, slung his day pack over his shoulder, and picked her up again. He saw Quinn's pack and coat and left them there. He moved quickly into the dark shelter of the trees and did not look back.

*   *   *

"Screamin' stopped," said Ray.

"I know it," said Earl, looking over at Franklin.

"I told you to shut your mouths," said Quinn, side-glancing Franklin, seeing Eugene's right hand slip off the green of the table.

"I'm just gonna go ahead and keep talkin'," said Ray, "it's all the same to you."

"Keep talkin', Critter."

"Makes me feel better. Don't it make you feel better, Daddy, to talk all this out?"

"Yep," said Earl, who scratched his nose.

"Keep your hands on the bar," said Quinn.

"Yessir," said Earl, and Ray laughed.

"What is it you want, exactly?" said Ray. "Money? Drugs? Hell, boy, it's right up there on top of the bar. Get it and get gone, that's what you're here for."

Quinn said nothing.

"Your gun arm must be gettin' tired," said Earl.

The rain sheeted the walls of the barn.

"You gonna stand there like that all night?" said Ray. "Shit, boy, you gotta do *somethin'*. I mean, shoot us or rob us or walk away. What's it gonna be?"

The beeper sounded on Quinn's hip. No one said anything, listening to it. Then the beeping ended.

Quinn began to walk backward, still covering the men with his gun.

Ray laughed, and Quinn felt the blood rise to his face.

"Look at that, Daddy. He's gonna back on out of here now."

"I see him," said Earl, the lines of his cheeks deepening from his thick smile.

"That what you gonna do, pussy-boy? Just walk away?"

Quinn stopped. He stood straight and holstered his weapon. He glanced at Eugene Franklin, turned, and gave them his back. Quinn headed for the barn door.

Earl picked up the Colt and slid it down the bar to his son. Ray's boot heel caught momentarily on the brass rail as he swiveled his hips. He lost a second of time, reached out for the Colt's grip, got his hand around it, and swung the muzzle toward Quinn as Earl found the .38 and drew it from his coat pocket.

"Hey, Terry," said Franklin in a quiet, even way.

Quinn cleared his Glock from his holster. He crouched and spun and fired from the hip. The bar splintered around Ray. Quinn fired again, and the slug tore open Ray's shirt in the center of his chest. Ray dropped his gun and fell to the slatted wood floor.

A gunshot exploded into the room. Earl's pistol jumped, and Quinn felt air and fire burn at the side of his scalp.

Franklin kicked the card table over as he stood. He squeezed the trigger on his Glock four times, the gun jumping in his hand. Earl was thrown back into the bar mirror. The bottles on the call rack exploded around him in a shower of glass and blood. Earl spun, dropped, and disappeared.

A bell tone rang steadily in Quinn's ears. He heard someone moan. Then a short cough and only the ringing sound and the rain.

Quinn walked through the roiling gun smoke. He kicked the .38 away from Ray's corpse. He went around the bar with his gun arm locked and looked down at the father. Quinn holstered his gun.

"The girl," said Franklin.

"Strange got her," said Quinn.

"Delgado?"

"If Strange got the girl, he got Delgado, too. Let's go."

Quinn picked up his coat and pack in the stand of pine. He and Franklin entered the woods and headed for the row of lights on the interstate, glowing faintly up ahead.

An hour later, Quinn parked the Chevelle in the lot of Franklin's apartment house and let the motor run.

Franklin said, "What now, Terry?"

"You've got a little bit of time," said Quinn. "Strange sent a package off today to someone he trusts in the department. Chris Wilson's notebook and the photographs."

"What about my confession?"

"Strange made a copy of that." Quinn reached across Franklin and opened the glove box door. "I've got the original right here."

Franklin took the yellow piece of paper from Quinn's hand. Quinn nodded, and Franklin slipped the paper into the pocket of his coat.

"Thank you, Terry."

Quinn stared through the windshield and pushed hair behind his ear, careful not to touch the tender spot where Earl Boone's bullet had grazed his scalp.

"You're not off the hook. The evidence Strange mailed in is enough to convict you. However you want to plead your defense, that's up to you. As far as what happened tonight, and the girl —"

"Ain't no one ever gonna know about what happened tonight, or about the girl. Not from me." Franklin swallowed. "Terry —"

"Go on."

Franklin offered his hand. Quinn kept his grip tight on the steering wheel.

"All right, then," said Franklin. He stepped out of the car and crossed the parking lot, his head lowered against the rain.

Later, and for the rest of his life, Quinn would not forget Eugene Franklin's sad, odd face, or the hang of his outstretched hand.

Near dawn, Derek Strange exited the house of Leona Wilson, closing the front door softly behind him. The rain had ended. He stood on the concrete stoop and breathed the cold morning air, turning his collar up against the chill.

Down on the street, parked behind his Caprice, was a pretty blue Chevelle. A long-haired young white man sat behind the wheel.

"Thank you, Lord," said Strange.

He locked eyes with Quinn and smiled.

chapter **33**

THAT evening, the suicide of Eugene Franklin made the six o'clock news.

A resident in the apartment next door had heard a gunshot around noon and phoned the police. They found Franklin upright on the couch. His eyes were bugged from the gas jolt, and his nose was blackened and scorched. Blood and bone and brain matter had been sprayed on the walls and the fabric of the couch. His service weapon lay in his lap. A letter written in longhand had been neatly placed on the coffee table before him.

On the eleven o'clock news, Franklin's suicide was eclipsed by the discovery of a mass homicide on a wooded property at the east-central edge of Montgomery County. Six bodies had been found in various stages of decomposition. The police had been alerted by a friend of one of the victims, a woman named Edna Loomis. The friend, Johanna Dodgson, had not heard from Loomis for days and had called the local cops when her concern became great. After two bodies were discovered in the barn, and another in the house, police found three additional bodies, including the corpse of Edna Loomis, in a tunnel underneath the property. Johanna Dodgson had mentioned the existence of the tunnel in her initial call to the police.

The Out-County Massacre, as it was immediately dubbed by the press, dominated the news for the next three days. A rumor surfaced that one of the victims was a D.C. cop, and then the rumor was publicly confirmed. Drugs and large amounts of money were said to have been found at the scene. Another rumor surfaced, alleging that the suicide of Officer Eugene Franklin was somehow related to the Out-County Massacre, but this rumor remained unconfirmed. Police spokesmen promised a speedy resolution to the case, claiming that an announcement regarding the findings was "imminent."

Strange went to work daily and kept to his general routine. He followed the news reports closely but did not discuss them, except with Ron and Janine, and only then in passing. He phoned Quinn and spoke to him twice, and on both occasions he found him to be uncommunicative, remote, and possibly in the grip of depression. He visited Leona and Sondra Wilson briefly and was pleased with what he found.

It was a tentative time for Strange, and though he picked up a couple of easy jobs, mostly he waited. By the end of the next week, he welcomed the phone call that he knew with certainty would come. The call came on Saturday morning, when he was returning from a long walk with Greco, as he stepped into the foyer of his Buchanan Street row house.

"Hello," said Strange, picking up the phone.

"Lydell here. You ready to talk, Derek?"

"Name the place," said Strange.

Oregon Avenue, south of Military Road, led into a section of Rock Creek Park that contained a nature center, horse stables, and miles of hilly trails. A huge parking lot sat to the right of the entrance, where people met to train and run their dogs on the adjacent field. The parking lot was a popular rendezvous spot for adulterous couples as well.

Strange and Lydell Blue sat in Strange's Caprice, parked beside Blue's Park Avenue in the lot and facing the field. Blue's hair had thinned and it was all gray, as was his thick mustache, which he had worn for thirty years on his wide, strong-featured face. His belly sagged over the waistband of his slacks. He held a sixteen-ounce paper cup of coffee in his hand, steam rising from a hole he had torn in its lid.

Over a dozen large-breed dogs ran and played in the field, all of their owners white, well-off, and dressed in casual, expensive clothes. At the far end of the lot, near the tree line, a middle-aged man and a younger woman necked in the front seat of a late-model Pontiac.

"You shoulda brought Greco," said Blue, looking through the windshield at an Irish wolfhound and a white Samoyed sitting side by side on a rise, a woman in a Banana Republic jacket telling them to hold from fifteen feet away.

"Greco's not a dog lover," said Strange. "Right about now, he'd be barin' his teeth at those two."

"Wouldn't want to bust on all these folks' perfect day."

Strange looked over at Blue. "Tell me what you got, Lydell."

"You gonna be up front with me if I do?"

"How long we been knowin' each other, man?"

"Okay, then. Okay." Blue ran his thumb along his mustache. "The cops who found Eugene Franklin found a suicide note at the scene. More like a confession, really."

"You see the note?"

"Got a copy of it from a friend over in Homicide. Written with an ink pen on a plain white sheet of paper. Handwriting was clean and precise, like he was under no kind of duress when he wrote it. Signature on it matched the signature of Franklin we had on file."

"What'd the note say?"

"Franklin admitted that he and Adonis Delgado were on the payroll of that drug lord, Cherokee Coleman. He detailed his role in the Chris Wilson shooting. How Wilson had gotten onto him and Delgado, and how Coleman had ordered a hit on Wilson. They used Ricky Kane, who was a drug dealer to the restaurant trade, not the clean-cut suburban boy the papers had made him out to be, to get Wilson out there in street clothes and make him look wrong. Franklin was supposed to shoot Wilson. But his partner, Quinn, who Franklin claimed was clean, shot Wilson first."

Strange digested what Blue had told him. "The news people been talkin' about these rumors, that Franklin is somehow connected to the Out-County thing. If he was hooked up with Delgado —"

"Franklin put it all in the note. Him and Delgado were sent by Coleman out to that property to make a drug transaction, and also to kill the two wholesalers, Earl and Ray

Boone. Somethin' about makin' it right for Coleman over two Colombians the Boones had murdered out there. That part checks out; two men were found in a tunnel on the property, their death date much earlier than the date of death on the Boones. They've ID'd the corpses as two Colombian brothers, Nestor and Lizardo Rodriguez, who were recently reported missing down around Richmond."

"What about the Boones and Delgado? Who killed them?"

"Franklin claimed that he did. Claimed he had a crisis of conscience and had to end the whole thing the only way he saw fit. He and Delgado fought over it in the house, they went at it, and he killed Delgado. Then Franklin went down to the barn and shot the father and son. He left the drugs and the money sitting in the barn and drove back to D.C. Ate his own gun the next day."

"There was a girl found in that tunnel, too."

"Edna Loomis. Died of natural causes. That is, if you call a woman having a stroke at thirty years old 'natural.' Methamphetamine will do that to you, you ingest enough."

"Hell of a story," said Strange.

"Yeah. Trouble is, it doesn't check out."

"What's wrong with it?"

"Plenty of things. Start with the crime scene, out at the barn and the house. Okay, so Franklin says he had a change of heart, and he and Delgado got down to it. Why was Delgado naked, then? And Delgado was stabbed. Why wouldn't Franklin just go ahead and shoot him like he did the others?"

"I don't know."

"They found a boot print tracking out of Delgado's

blood, too. Size twelve, I believe it was. Franklin wore a ten."

"What else?" said Strange.

"The Boones were killed by the same type of gun, a Glock Seventeen. But it was two *different* Glock Seventeens that killed 'em. The markings on the slug found in the body of the son and another bullet found in the wood of the bar were inconsistent with the markings of those found in the father and those found around the father. The trajectory angles were inconsistent, too. There were two shooters that night, Derek. *Had* to be."

"No fingerprints, nothin' like that?"

"No prints other than those of the deceased, Franklin, and another, unidentified woman."

"A woman, huh?"

"They found vaginal fluid and pubic hairs in the same bedroom where they found Delgado."

"The Loomis girl?"

"Didn't match. But if there was some kind of phantom woman there, it explains why Delgado died in his birthday suit."

"Sounds like y'all got a genuine head-scratcher."

"Uh-huh."

Blue turned his head and stared at Strange.

"Why'd you call me here, Lydell?"

"Well, Derek, I'll tell you. I got an anonymous package in the mail, no return address, mailing label out of a printer just like any of a thousand printers in this city. Had Chris Wilson's investigation detailed in a notebook, and photographs of Franklin and Delgado headin' into Coleman's compound." Blue took a sip of coffee. "That was you sent me that, right?"

"It was," said Strange.

"Didn't take a genius to figure it. You had called me and asked me to run the numbers of Delgado's cruiser, remember?"

"I do."

"So tell me how you came to get all that information."

Strange shrugged. "I was hired by Leona Wilson to try and clear her son's reputation. Among other things, she wanted his name etched onto that police memorial they got downtown. I started by interviewing Quinn, and then Franklin, and the natural progression was to follow Ricky Kane and see what he was all about."

"Okay. What'd you find?"

"Same thing Wilson did. Kane led me to Coleman, and that was when I noticed the same Crown Vic cruiser patroling the perimeter of the operation on two separate days. I called you and got Delgado's name. I found Wilson's notebook and the photographs and mailed them off to you. See, I saw that this thing was bigger than me, Lydell. I thought if y'all could connect the dots, Wilson's story would naturally get told. I didn't give a goddamn about no conspiracy thing, man, I was only trying to do what Leona Wilson had hired me to do."

"A couple of cops came forward, said they saw you and Quinn talking to Franklin down at Erika's."

"That's right."

"They're gonna bring you in for questioning, man. They're gonna bring Quinn in, too."

"You tell them I mailed you the information?"

Blue drank the rest of the coffee in one long gulp. He dropped the empty cup at his feet.

"They don't even know I got it," said Blue. "The notebook and photographs, they're in the trunk of my Buick, man. Gonna give it all back to you before you leave."

"You can't use it?"

"How could I explain the fact that it was sent to me in the first place?"

"You couldn't, I guess."

"Either I'd have to lie or I'd have to implicate you. And those are two things I'm not gonna do. Anyway, the department doesn't need the notebook or the photographs to make the case. Kane's been picked up. What I hear, he's already rolled over, and he's confirmed the background information that was in Franklin's note. They're gonna get him to turn Cherokee Coleman in exchange for some kind of country club jolt. Whether it sticks to Coleman or not, we'll see. Nothin' has so far."

"Kane say how he got Wilson out in the street that night?"

"Kane said he heard that Wilson had a sister was hooked on junk. He told Wilson he'd found her and to meet him on D."

Kane *heard* that Wilson had a sister. . . . Lyin' motherfucker, thought Strange, tryin' to make himself look good.

"You knew about the sister?" said Blue.

"She lives with her mother," said Strange, with a casual nod. "Everything that family's been through, I'd hate to see that junkie sister rumor get thrown out to the press."

"We know what that family's been through. How Kane got Wilson out to the street that night is immaterial. Far as anybody's ever gonna know, the sister's clean."

"And Chris? What about him?"

"Yeah, Chris Wilson. It's delicate, how the department's gonna handle that. For obvious reasons, they don't want too much play on this bad-cop thing, and they don't want the public to think that what Wilson did — being some kind of rogue enforcer out there — is something they condone, exactly. In the end, I don't know how this will be spun for the general public. But I do know what they're saying about Wilson down at headquarters. He's gonna get some kind of posthumous, low-key commendation from Chief Ramsey."

"Good," said Strange. "That's real good."

"You stirred the pot, Derek."

"I guess I did."

"Funny about that other cop. Quinn, I mean."

"Yeah. He's not gonna come out of this smellin' any better than he did to begin with."

"You think he should?" said Blue.

"He made a mistake," said Strange. "I've gotten to know Quinn a little, and I can tell you, he's still payin' for what he did. I think he's always gonna pay."

"Ending a fine young man's life the way he did, that's not just a mistake. And you can't tell me that if Chris Wilson had been white —"

"I know it, Lydell. You don't have to tell me, 'cause I know."

Strange cracked his window. The afternoon sun had warmed the interior of the car.

"All the good people in this city," said Blue. "And all you ever hear about is the bad in D.C. Now you're gonna hear about bad cops, too, when most of 'em are good. And most of the people I come across every day, they come from good families. I'm talkin' about the people in the church, people who go to work every day to take care of their own, good teachers, good, hard workers . . . and here

we are, all these years we been out here, fuckin' with the
bad ones. Why'd we choose this, Derek?"

"I don't know. I guess it chose us."

"If we'd only known, when we were young men." Blue
chuckled, looking over at his friend. "Lord, I been knowin'
you now for nearly fifty years. I even remember the way
you used to run when you were a little boy, with your fists
balled up near your chest, back in grade school. And I can
remember the way you looked in your uniform, as a
young man, back in sixty-eight."

"Sixty-eight," said Strange. "That was some kind of
year, Lydell, wasn't it?"

"Yes it was."

A look passed between Strange and Blue.

"Thank you, Lydell."

"*You* know how we do."

Strange shook Blue's hand. "So the department's
gonna be callin' me in."

"Any day," said Blue. "The way you just explained
it —"

"What, somethin' about it you didn't like?"

"It was just a little rough, is all. I'd work on it a little, I
was you."

Strange returned to his row house and phoned Terry
Quinn. He relayed the conversation he'd had with Lydell
Blue.

"I hated to lie to my friend," said Strange. "But I didn't
know what else to do."

"I guess Eugene destroyed the original confession,"
said Quinn.

"Looks like he did. The one the police found was written on plain white paper. I'm fixin' to destroy some things, too. Gonna lose the clothing I wore that night, my boots, my knife . . . you need to do the same. Get rid of your day pack and that Glock."

"It's already done."

"I don't like the way you sound, Terry," said Strange. "Don't do anything stupid, hear?"

"Don't worry," said Quinn. "I'm not as brave as Eugene."

The phone clicked dead in Strange's ear.

chapter **34**

On a Sunday morning in early April, when the cherry blossoms along the tidal basin were full and brilliant, and magnolias and dogwoods had erupted pink and white on lawns across the city, Strange, Janine, and Lionel met at church.

Strange had not been to services for some time. He decided to go this day, the weekend after Easter, to pray for his mother, and though he did pray in the privacy of his home from time to time, he thought it might be wise to be in the Lord's home for this, considering his mother's dire condition. He knew that attending church for personal favors was wrong and, on some level he didn't fully understand, hypocritical, but he went just the same.

The pews inside the New Bethel Church of God in Christ, on Georgia and Piney Branch Road, were nearly full. Strange paid some attention to the sermon, prayed intently for his mother while Janine rested her hand atop his, and enjoyed the gospel singing from the choir, his favorite part of the service.

Outside, as the congregation exited, Strange recognized many. In the faces of some of the children he saw their parents, whom he'd known since they were kids themselves. And he saw several former clients, whom he greeted and who greeted him with firm handshakes and claps on the arm. Though he had often given these people less-than-happy news, he was glad he'd never padded his hours with them or done a second-rate job. They knew who he was and what he was about, and he was proud that they knew.

"We goin' to that Greek joint for breakfast?" said Lionel.

"Billy's closed today," said Strange. "It's his Easter Sunday."

"I was gonna make a nice turkey," said Janine. "Will you come over for dinner?"

"Was thinkin' I'd take Greco for a long walk down in Rock Creek," said Strange. "But yeah, I'd love to come over for dinner, long as it's early. Need to spend the evening with my mom."

"We'll have it early, then," said Janine. "See you around five?"

"Lookin' forward to it, Janine."

He kissed her there, in a cluster of azalea bushes planted beside the church.

"Look at y'all," said Lionel. "In front of God, too."

Strange walked to his Caddy, parked on Tuckerman. Along the curb, on the other side of the street, sat a gray Plymouth K-car. Leona Wilson had opened the passenger door for her daughter, Sondra, who was ducking her head to get inside. Strange caught a quick look at Sondra, still thin and shapeless in her dress, her hair salon done and shoulder length, her eyes bright and a bit unfocused. Not there, but *getting* there, Strange could see.

As Strange crossed the street to greet Leona Wilson,

Terry Quinn's face flashed in his mind. He hadn't seen Quinn or spoken to him for quite some time.

Leona Wilson walked around the K-car to the driver's-side door, stopping as she saw Strange approach. For a moment she didn't seem to recognize him, dressed as he was, but then she smiled at the broad-shouldered, handsome man in the pinstriped suit. She reached out with a white-gloved hand and cocked her head.

"Mrs. Wilson," said Strange.

"Mr. Strange."

Strange sat behind the wheel of his Cadillac Brougham, parked on Bonifant Street in Silver Spring. Greco was snoring, lying on his red pillow on the backseat. Strange and the dog both had a bellyful of Janine's cooking inside them, and Greco had taken the opportunity to nap.

Across the street, Terry Quinn locked the front door of the bookstore, checked it, and turned to go up the sidewalk.

Strange leaned his head out the window. "Hey, Terry!"

Quinn found the source of the voice and smiled. He crossed the street and walked toward the car. Strange thought that Quinn had lost weight but realized that it was the hair that had given him that mistaken impression; Quinn had cut it short.

"Get in for a minute, man," said Strange.

Quinn went around the Caddy and dropped into the passenger seat. Greco woke, sat up, and smelled the back of Quinn's neck as Quinn and Strange shook hands.

"Derek."

"Terry."

"What brings you out this way?"

"Was thinking of you, is all," said Strange. "And look at you, all clean-cut."

"Yeah. Went down to this barbershop on Georgia, Elegant and Proud?"

"I know that joint."

"They didn't look too happy to see me in there. But all I wanted was a close cut, and they gave it to me. Anyway, it feels good to get rid of all that hair."

"You look like a cop again."

"I know." Quinn thumbed his lip. "You said you were thinkin' of me. Why?"

"Well, we're friends, for one."

"We're friends now, huh?"

"Sure."

"What else?"

"I saw Leona and Sondra Wilson today, at church."

Quinn nodded. "How's the girl doin'?"

"You know what that road's like. Once you're in, you're in forever. Always gonna be a struggle. But her mother got her into one of the city's best programs. She'll make it, I expect."

"You did good."

"So did you." Strange looked over at Quinn. "Chris Wilson got a commendation. They did a quiet kind of ceremony, but he got it. And they put his name up on that wall."

"I heard about it," said Quinn. "The department didn't get the press involved in it, but word reached me from inside."

"Yeah, the department's played the press pretty good on this whole thing. But what else they gonna do? They don't have all the answers their *own* selves. They've got Franklin's confession, and the conflicting forensic evidence from the scene, and Kane's self-serving testimony. They know there's more, but they can't seem to get to it."

"They didn't get anything out of you and me."

"No." Strange studied Quinn. "You're lookin' better."

"I'm doin' all right."

"You out of that funk you were in?"

"I guess I am," said Quinn. "You said that someday I'd learn to walk away from a fight. Maybe I'm getting to that place."

"I guess, workin' in that bookstore over there, with Lewis and all them, you have plenty of time for meditation."

"Yeah, Derek, I've got nothin' but time."

"I was thinkin', you know, there are special instances when I could use another operative. You did some pretty good work with me, man. I was wonderin', would you ever consider taking on a case for me, now and again?"

"While you do the light work?"

"Funny."

"What about Ron Lattimer?"

"This time of year, Ron's busy pickin' out his spring wardrobe and shit. Haven't seen him much the last week or so."

"I don't have an investigator's license."

"Easy enough to get one."

"I'll think about it, okay?"

"Sure, do *that*. With all that time you got . . . to think."

Greco licked Quinn's neck. Quinn turned in his seat and scratched the boxer behind his ears.

"You seein' a woman?" said Strange.

"Nobody special. How's Janine?"

"She's good. Just left her and Lionel."

"Spending a lot of time with her, huh?"

Strange nodded. "Finally woke up. Was always lookin' for someone else . . . chasing after women who didn't care nothin' for me, even goin' after that anonymous kind of sex —"

"Hookers, you mean."

"Yeah. Always lookin' for somethin' else, when the best thing was right next to me, staring me right in the face. Just like my mother always said. Not that I'm thinkin' of getting married or anything like that. But I do plan to be there, for her and the boy."

"Tell her I said hey."

"I will."

Quinn looked at his watch. "I better be goin'."

"Me too. Where's your car at?"

"I didn't bring it."

"You need a lift back to your place?"

"No, thanks. I think I'll walk."

Quinn reached for the door handle. Strange put a hand on Quinn's arm.

"Terry."

"What?"

"I just want you to know, in light of how all this ended up, I mean . . . I wanted you to know that I was wrong about you, man."

Quinn smiled sadly. "You were wrong about some things, Derek. But not everything."

Quinn stepped out of the car. Strange watched him cross the street in the gathering darkness.

Terry Quinn walked up Bonifant and cut left on Georgia Avenue. The street lamps and window lights glowed faintly in the cool dusk. As Quinn went down Georgia, a group of four young black men in baggy clothing approached on the sidewalk from the opposite direction. They split apart, seeing that Quinn was not going to step aside. One of the young men bumped him lightly on the arm, and Quinn gave him an elbow as he went by.

I lied to Strange, thought Quinn. I'm lying to myself. I am never going to change. I am never going to walk away.

Quinn heard laughter from the group and he kept walking, past Rosita's without looking through its window, then left into the breezeway, where he patted the head of the bronze Norman Lane bust as he went on into the alley. He took the alley south.

Quinn crossed Silver Spring Avenue and continued through the alley to Sligo Avenue, then across to Selim and along the Napa auto parts shop and the My-Le *pho* house and foreign-car garages that faced the railroad and Metro tracks. Then he was on the pedestrian bridge spanning Georgia Avenue, and on the other side of it he jumped the chain-link fence and went past the commuter station and down the steps into the lighted foot tunnel beneath the tracks.

Quinn walked the wooden platform beside the fence that bordered the Canada Dry bottling plant. He turned, his hands dug in the pockets of his jeans, and watched the close approach of a northbound train.

This place had always been his. But now he shared it with a woman he'd kissed here on a clear and biting winter night.

Quinn closed his eyes and listened to the sounds of the train, felt the rush of the cars raising wind and dust.

He didn't come here for answers. There were no answers. There was only sensation.

No answers, and there would be no closure. Chris Wilson had been exonerated, but for Quinn nothing had changed. Because Strange had been right all along: Quinn had killed a man because of the color of his skin.

Strange walked down the drab, third-floor hall of the District Convalescent Home, passing a couple of female attendants who were laughing loudly at something one of them had said, ignoring a man in a nearby wheelchair who was repeating the word "nurse" over and over again. A television played at full volume from one of the rooms. The hall was warm and smelled of pureed food and, beneath the mask of disinfectant, urine and excrement.

Strange entered his mother's room. She was lying on her side, under the sheets of her bed, awake and staring out the window. He walked around to the side of the bed.

"Momma," said Strange, kissing her clammy forehead. "Here I am."

His mother made a small wave of her hand and smiled weakly, showing him the gray of her gums. Her body was tiny as a child's beneath the sheets.

Strange found a comb in the nightstand and ran it through her sparse white hair, pushing what was left of it back on her moley scalp. When he was finished, she pointed past Strange's shoulder. He went to the window and looked to the corner of the ledge.

A house wren had built a nest there and was sitting on her eggs. The small bird flew away at the sight of Strange.

Strange knew what his mother wanted. He tore off several paper towels from the bathroom roll, found some Scotch tape on a supply cart out in the hall, and taped the squares of paper to the window. His mother had done this every spring in the kitchen window of the house in which he'd been raised. She had explained to him that a mother bird was like any mother, that she deserved to tend to her children privately and in peace.

From her bed, Alethea Strange blinked her eyes with approval at her son, examining the job he'd done.

Strange brought a cushioned chair over to the side of her bed and had a seat. He sat there for a while, telling her about his day.

"Janine," she said, very softly.

"She's good, Momma. She sends her love."

"Diamonds . . ."

"In my backyard. Yes, ma'am."

Sitting in the chair, Strange fell asleep. He woke in the middle of the night. His mother was still awake, her beautiful brown eyes staring into his.

Strange began to talk about his childhood in D.C. He talked about his father, and the mention of her husband brought a smile to Alethea's lips. He talked about his brother, the trouble he'd had, and how even with the trouble his brother's heart had been good.

"I love you, Momma," said Strange. "I'm so proud to be your son."

As he talked, he held her hand and looked into her eyes. He was still holding her hand at dawn, and the birds were singing outside her bedroom window as she passed.

More
George P. Pelecanos!

Please turn this page
for a
bonus excerpt
from

Hell to Pay

a new Little, Brown
hardcover available
wherever books are sold.

Derek Strange was coming out of a massage parlor when he felt his beeper vibrate against his hip. He checked the number printed out across the horizontal screen and walked through Chinatown, over to the MLK library on Ninth, where a bank of pay phones were set outside the facility. Strange owned a cell, but he still used street phones whenever he could.

"Janine," said Strange.

"Derek."

"You rang?"

"Those women been calling you again. The two investigators from out in Montgomery County?"

"I called them back, didn't I?"

"You mean *I* did. They been trying to get an appointment with you for a week now."

"So they're still trying."

"They're being a little bit more aggressive than that. They're heading into town right now, want to meet you for lunch. Said they'd pick up the tab."

Strange tugged his jeans away from his crotch where they had stuck.

"It's a money job, Derek."

"Hold up, Janine." Strange put his hand over the receiver as a man who was passing by stopped to shake his hand.

"Tommy, how you been?"

"Doin' real good, Derek," said Tommy. "Say, you got any spare love you can lay on me till I see you next time?"

Strange looked at the black baggage beneath Tommy's eyes, the way his pants rode low on his bony hips. Strange had come up with Tommy's older brother, Scott, who was gone ten years now from the cancer that took his shell. Scott wouldn't want Strange to give his baby brother any money, not for what Tommy had in mind.

"Not today," said Strange.

"All right, then," said Tommy, shamed, but not enough. He slowly walked away.

Strange removed his palm from the receiver. "Janine, where they want to meet?"

"Frosso's."

"Call 'em up and tell 'em I'll be there. 'Bout twenty minutes."

"Am I going to see you tonight?"

"Maybe after practice."

"I marinated a chuck roast, gonna grill it on the Weber. Lionel will be at practice, won't he? You're going to drop him off at our house anyway, aren't you?"

"Yeah."

"We can talk about it when you come back by the office. You got a two o'clock with George Hastings."

"I remember. Okay, we'll talk about it then."

"I love you, Derek."

Strange lowered his voice. "I love you, too, baby."

Strange hung up the phone. He did love her. And her voice, more than her words, had brought him some guilt for what he'd just done. But there was Love and Sex on one side and just Sex on the other. To Strange, the two were entirely different things.

Strange drove east in his white-over-black, '89 Caprice, singing along softly to "Wake Up Everybody" coming from the deck. That first verse, where Teddy's purring those call-to-arms words against the Gamble and Huff production, telling the listener to open his eyes, look around, get involved and into the uplift side of things, there wasn't a whole lot of American music more beautiful than this.

His Rand McNally street atlas lay on the seat beside him. He had a Leatherman tool-in-one looped through his belt, touching a Buck knife, sheathed and attached the same way on his right hip. His beeper he wore on his left. The rest of his equipment was in a double-locked glove box and in the trunk. It was true that most modern investigative work was done in an office and on the Internet. Strange thought of himself as having two offices, though, his base office in Petworth and the one in his car, right here. His preference was to work the street.

It was early September. The city was still hot during the day, though the nights had cooled some. It would be that way in the District for another month or so.

"The world won't get no better," sang Strange, "if we just let it be . . ."

Soon the colors would change in Rock Creek Park. And then would come those weeks near Thanksgiving, when the weather turned for real and the leaves were still coming down off the trees. Strange had his own name for it: Deep Fall. It was his favorite time of year in D.C.

Frosso's, a stand-alone structure with a green thatched roof, sat on a westside corner of Thirteenth and L, Northwest, like a pimple on the ass of a beautiful girl. The Mediterranean who owned the business owned the real estate, and had refused to sell, even as the offers came in, even as new office buildings went in around him. Frosso's was a burger and lunch counter, also a happy-hour bar and hangout for those remaining workers who still drank and smoked or didn't mind the smell of smoke on their clothes. Beer gardens in this part of downtown were few and far between.

Strange made his way through a noisy dining area to a four-top back by the pay phone and head, where two women sat. He recognized the investigators, a salt-and-pepper team, from an article he'd read on them in *City Paper* a few months back. They worked cases retrieving young runaways gone to hooking. The two of them were aligned with some do-goodnik, pro-prosti organization that operated on grants inside D.C.

"Derek Strange," he said, shaking the black woman's hand and then the white woman's before he took a seat.

"I'm Karen Bagley. This is Sue Tracy."

Strange slid his business card across the table. Bagley gave him one in turn, Strange scanning it for the name of their business: Bagley and Tracy Investigative Services, and below the name, in smaller letters, "Specializing in Locating and Retrieving Minors." A plain card, without any artwork, Strange thinking, They could use a logo, give their card a signature, something to make the customers remember them by.

Bagley was medium-skinned and wide of nose. Her eyes were large and deep brown, the lashes accentuated by makeup. Freckles like coarse pepper buckshotted her face. Sue Tracy was a shag-cut blonde, green-eyed, still tanned from the last of summer, with smaller shoulders than Bagley's. They were serious-faced, handsome, youngish women, hard-boned, and, Strange guessed—he couldn't see the business end of their bodies, seated at the table—strong of thigh. They looked like the ex-cops that the newspaper article had described them to be. Better-looking, in fact, than most of the female officers Strange had known.

Tracy pointed a finger at the mug in front of her. Bagley's hand was wrapped around a mug as well. "You want a beer?"

"Too early for me. I'll get a burger, though. Medium, with some blue cheese crumpled on top. And a ginger ale from the bottle, not the gun."

Tracy called the waitress over, addressed her by name, got a burger working for Strange. The waitress said, "Got it, Sue," tearing a top sheet off a green-lined pad before turning back toward the lunch counter.

"You're a hard man to get ahold of," said Bagley.

"I been busy out here," said Strange.

"A big caseload, huh?"

"Always somethin'." A glass was placed before Strange. He examined a smudge on the lip of the glass. "This place clean?"

"Like a dog's tongue," said Tracy.

"Some say that about a dog's hindparts, too," said Strange. "But I wouldn't put my mouth to one."

"Maybe they ought to put that on the sign out front," said Tracy, without a trace of a smile. "Good food, and clean, too, like the asshole on a dog."

"Might bring in some new customers," said Strange. "You never know."

"They don't need any new customers," said Bagley. "The regulars float this place."

"I take it you two are numbered with the regulars."

"We used to come here plenty for information," said Tracy. "Here and the all-night CVS below Logan Circle."

"Information," said Strange. "From prostitutes, you mean."

Bagley nodded. "The girls would be in the CVS at all hours, buying stockings, tampons, you name it."

"Them and the heroin lovers," said Strange. "They do crave their chocolate in the middle of the night. I remember seein' them in there, grabbing the Hershey bars off the racks with their eyelids lowered to half-mast."

"You hung out there, too?" said Bagley.

"Back when it was People's Drug, which must be over ten years back now, huh? Used to stop in for my own essentials when everything else was closed. I was a bit of nightbird then myself."

"The demographics have shifted some the last couple of years," said Tracy. "A lot of the action's moved east, into the hotel cluster of the new downtown."

"But this here tavern was a known hangout for prostis, wasn't it?"

"More like a safe haven," said Bagley. "Nobody bothered them in here. It was a place to have a beer and a smoke. A moment of quiet."

"No more, huh?"

Bagley shrugged. "There's been an initiative to get the girls out of public establishments."

Tracy moved her mug in a small circle on the table. "The

powers that be would rather have them shivering in some doorway in December than warm in a place like this."

"I guess y'all think they ought to just go ahead and legalize prostitution, right? Since it's one of those victimless crimes, I mean."

"Wrong," said Tracy. "In fact, it's the only crime I know of where the perp *is* the victim."

Strange didn't know what to say to that one, so he let it ride.

"What about you?" asked Bagley. "What do *you* think about it?"

Strange's eyes darted from Bagley's and went to nowhere past her shoulders. "I haven't thought on it all that much, tell you the truth."

Bagley and Tracy stared at Strange. Strange turned his head, looked toward the grill area. Where was that burger? All right, thought Strange, I'll have my lunch, listen to these Earnest Ernestines say their piece, and get on out of here.

"You come recommended," said Bagley, forcing Strange to return his attention to them. "A couple of the lawyers we've worked with down at Superior Court say they've used you, and they've been pleased."

"Most likely they used my operative, Ron Lattimer. He's been doing casework for the CJA attorneys. Ron's a smart young man, but let's just say he doesn't like to break too much of a sweat. So he likes those jobs, 'cause when you're working with the courts you automatically got that Federal Power of Subpoena. You can subpoena the phone company, the housing authority, anything. It makes your job a whole lot easier."

"You've done some of that," said Bagley.

"Sure, but I prefer working in the fresh air to working behind a computer, understand what I'm saying? I just like to be out there. And my business is a neighborhood business. Over twenty-five years now in the same spot. So it's good for me to have a presence out there, the way—"

"Cops do," said Tracy.

"Yeah. I'm an ex-cop, like you two. Been thirty some odd years since I wore the uniform, though."

"No such thing as an ex-cop," said Bagley.

"Like there's no such thing as a former alcoholic," said Tracy, "or an ex-Marine."

"You got that right," said Strange. He liked these two women a touch more now than when he'd walked in.

Strange turned the glass of ginger ale so that the smudge was away from him, and took a sip. He replaced the glass on the table and leaned forward. "All right, then, now we had our first kiss and got that over with. What do you young ladies have on your minds?"

Bagley glanced briefly over at Tracy, who was in the process of putting fire to a cigarette.

"We've been working with a group called APIP," said Bagley. "Do you know it?"

"I read about it in that article they did on you two. Something about helping out prostitutes, right?"

"Aiding Prostitutes in Peril," said Tracy, blowing a jet of smoke across the table at Strange.

"Some punk rock kids started it, right?"

"The people behind it were a part of the local punk movement twenty years ago," said Tracy, "as I was. They're not kids anymore. They're older than me and Karen."

"What do they do, exactly?"

"A number of things, from simply providing condoms to

reporting violent johns. Also, they serve as an information clearinghouse. They have an eight hundred number, and a website that takes in e-mails from parents and prostitutes alike."

"That's where you two come in. You find runaways who're hookin'. Right?"

"That's a part of what we do," said Bagley. "And we're getting too busy to handle all the work ourselves. The county business alone keeps us up to our ears in it. We could use a little help in the District."

"You need me to find a girl."

"Not exactly," said Bagley. "We thought we'd test the waters with you on something simpler, see if you're interested."

"Keep talking."

"There's a girl who works the street between L and Mass, on Seventh," said Tracy.

"Down there by the site for the new Convention Center," said Strange.

"Right," said Tracy. "The last couple of nights a guy's been hassling her. Pulling up in his car, trying to get her to date him."

"Ain't that the object of the game?"

"Sure," said Bagley. "But there's something off about this guy. He's been asking her, Do you like it rough? Telling her she's gonna dig it, he can *tell* she's gonna dig it, right?"

Strange shifted in his seat. "So? Girl doesn't have to be a working girl to come up against that kind of creep. She can hear it in a bar."

"These working women get a sense for this kind of thing," said Bagley. "She says there's something not right, we got to believe her. And he doesn't want to pay. Says he doesn't *have* to pay, understand? She's scared. Can't go to the cops, right? And her pimp would beat her ass blue if he knew she was turning down a trick."

"Even a no-money trick?"

Strange stared hard at Tracy. Her eyes did not move away from his.

Tracy said, "This is the information we have. Either you're interested or you're not."

"I hear you," said Strange, "but I'm not sure what you want me to do. You're lookin' for me to shake some cat down, you got the wrong guy."

"You own a camera, right?" said Tracy.

"Still and video alike," said Strange.

"Get some shots for us," said Bagley, "or a tape. We'll run the plates and contact this gentleman ourselves. Trust me, we can be pretty convincing. This guy's probably got a wife. Even better, he has kids. We'll make sure he never hassles this girl again."

"Damn," said Strange, with a low chuckle, "you ladies are *serious.*"

The waitress came to the table and set Strange's burger down before him. He thanked her, cut into it, and inspected the center. He took a large bite and closed his eyes as he chewed.

"They cooked it the way I asked," said Strange, after he had swallowed. "I'll say that for them."

"The burgers here are tight," said Bagley, smiling just a little for the first time.

Strange wiped some juice off his lips. "I get thirty-five an hour, by the way."

Tracy dragged on her smoke, this time blowing the exhale away from Strange. "According to our attorney friend, he remembers paying you thirty."

"He remembers, huh?" said Strange. "Well, I can remember when movies were fifty cents, too."

"You can?" said Tracy.

"I'm old," said Strange, with a shrug.

"Not too old," said Bagley.

"Thank you," said Strange.

"You'll do it, then," said Tracy.

"I assume she works nights."

"Every night this week," said Tracy.

"I coach a kid's football team early in the evenings."

"She'll be out there, like, ten or twelve," said Tracy. "Black, mid-twenties, with a face on the worn side. She'll be wearing a red-leather skirt tonight."

"She says what kind of car this guy drives?"

"Black sedan," said Bagley. "Late-model Chevy."

"Caprice, somethin like that?"

"Late-model Chevy is what she said." Tracy stubbed out her cigarette. "Here's something else for you to look at." She reached into the leather case on the floor at her feet and pulled out a yellow-gold sheet of paper. She pushed it across the table to Strange.

The headline across the top of the flyer read, IN PERIL. Below the head was a photo of a young white girl, unclear from generations of copying. The girl's arms were skinny and her hands were folded in front of her, a yearbook-style photo. She was smiling, showing braces on her teeth. He read her name and her statistics, printed below the photograph, noticing from the DOB that she was fourteen years old.

"We'll talk about that some other time," said Bagley, "you want to. Just wanted you to get an idea of what we do."

Strange nodded, folded the flyer neatly, and put it in the back pocket of his jeans. Then he focused on finishing his lunch. Bagley and Tracy drank their beers and let him do it.

When he was done, he signaled the waitress. "I see on the specials board you got a steak today."

"You're still hungry?"

"Uh-uh, baby, I'm satisfied. But I was wondering, you guys got any bones back there in the kitchen?"

"I suppose we do."

"Wrap up a few for me, will you?"

"I'll see what I can do."

The waitress drifted. Strange said to the women, "I got a dog at home, a boxer, goes by the name of Greco. Got to take care of him, too."

Later, Bagley and Tracy watched Strange exit the dining room, his paper bag of steak bones in hand. Bagley studied his squared-up walk, the way his muscled shoulders filled out the back of his shirt, the gray salted nicely into his close-cropped hair.

"How old you figure he is?" said Bagley.

"Early fifties," said Tracy. "I liked him."

"I liked him, too."

"I noticed," said Tracy.

"Like to see a man who enjoys his food, is all it is," said Bagley. "Think we should've told him more?"

"He knew there was more. He wanted to find out what it was for himself."

"The curious type."

"Exactly," said Tracy, draining her beer and placing the mug flat on the table. "I got a feeling he's gonna work out fine."

VISIT US ONLINE @
WWW.TWBOOKMARK.COM

AT THE TIME WARNER BOOKMARK WEB SITE YOU'LL FIND:

- CHAPTER EXCERPTS FROM SELECTED NEW RELEASES

- ORIGINAL AUTHOR AND EDITOR ARTICLES

- AUDIO EXCERPTS

- BESTSELLER NEWS

- ELECTRONIC NEWSLETTERS

- AUTHOR TOUR INFORMATION

- CONTESTS, QUIZZES, AND POLLS

- FUN, QUIRKY RECOMMENDATION CENTER

- PLUS MUCH MORE!

Bookmark Time Warner Trade Publishing
@ www.twbookmark.com